Night
Beat

Dave Rasdal

Sarah —
thanks for everything.

Dave Rasdal

For my mother, Helen Kathleen Johnson Rasdal, who has been gone 30 years. She always encouraged me to follow my heart, to write and write until I can no longer write.

1

An early October wind whistled through the dark alleys of Cedar City, whirling dust and debris and dirty newspapers into chaos, as Mike Rockwell, warm inside the Fox and Hounds Lounge, weathered yet another verbal attack from Dan Goldberg. The two cop-beat reporters, as had happened more frequently of late, were the last remnants of the regular Friday after-work gathering of *Cedar City Argus* news staffers in the dimly lit tavern where alcohol tended to drive sane conversations into the gutter.

At a table for twelve – the shiny red tablecloth cluttered with foam-coated beer glasses and empty pitchers, black plastic ashtrays overflowing with cigarette butts, and wadded-up napkins fingerprint stained with sauce from devoured chicken wings – Mike fidgeted on a chrome-legged chair while Dan, on the opposite side, picked at a cold wing on a paper plate.

"Everybody hates us," Dan Goldberg said, beginning to slur his words as he dropped his fork on the plate. He tossed a handful of beer nuts into his mouth and chased them with half a mug of beer. "Everybody. It's just a fact of life."

"Not true," Mike Rockwell replied, his voice not any steadier. He polished off the backwash in his beer mug. "That's the lament of journalists everywhere. When we're good, we're good, but when we're bad, we're sooooo bad."

"We are," Dan said. "We're nasty. They hate you. They hate me. They hate us all."

Mike held up an empty pitcher. "Another?"

"Did you hear me? They hate you. Laugh, you jerk."

"I need more beer." Mike held the pitcher high above his head for Nicole, the familiar and congenial young waitress, who retrieved it for a refill.

"Maybe people don't like what we do, but they don't hate us," Mike said. "Not as people, anyway. Just as journalists."

"That's what I'm saying," Dan said. "They only see us as journalists, though, so they hate us."

"That's like you saying you hate all Germans because you're Jewish."

"I do," Dan laughed.

"Right," Mike said sarcastically. "You can't generalize, not in this business and last very long."

"Ha," Dan said. "The next thing you're going to tell me is that I'm wrong when I say all editors are right all the time. Just ask them."

"Now, you make me laugh," Mike said, not realizing his mug of beer was empty until he put it to his mouth again.

The year was 1986, when Ronald Reagan sat in the Oval Office, and the press hounded his administration about the failure in his Star Wars program, even though the Russians were still a nuclear threat. It was when the eyes of the world watched as the Challenger Space Shuttle exploded after takeoff and when terrorism reigned as more than three-hundred lives were threatened with the hijacking of Pan Am Flight 73 in Pakistan.

These were the days before security cameras on every corner and in every convenience store, before smart phones and instant video, before the explosion of the internet and social media.

This was the era when the task of keeping a finger on any city's pulse belonged to newspaper beat reporters, the men and woman who covered the city's government, the schools, the courts, and law enforcement.

In Cedar City, Iowa, population nearly 200,000, "The Cop Shop" beat for the seven-morning-a-week *Cedar City Argus* belonged to Dan Goldberg by day, to Mike Rockwell by night. Dan had joined *The Argus* five months earlier after a stint at weekly newspapers based in Chicago's Lake Forest suburb where the pay was such a pittance he couldn't afford to live where he worked. He'd thought bringing his talents to Cedar City could bolster not only his bank account, but also his ego. Mike had spent short stints at two small Iowa dailies before taking the day cop beat at *The Argus* nearly five years ago, then switching to the night beat for the adrenaline rush of writing breaking news on deadline.

On the surface, Dan Goldberg and Mike Rockwell were opposites. Dan Goldberg, twenty-eight, since he worked the day-cop beat, slept at night. He was born in Chicago to Jewish parents, was dark-haired, brown-eyed, and often easily excited and uptight. Mike Rockwell, thirty-one, on the night beat, slept during the day. He grew up Protestant in a small Iowa town not far from Cedar City and was blond-haired, blue-eyed, laid-back and even-keeled.

The problem for both, though, was that crime in Cedar City consisted mostly of insignificant burglaries, car crashes, house fires and false alarms. Occasionally a woman's body was found in a near east-side apartment or a drug dealer from Chicago gunned down a rival gang member who'd also moved to Cedar City. But, for the most part, these eager young men suffered through mundane reporting, the listing of drunken driving arrests, assault charges, forgeries and major property-damage accidents. Boring stuff. Dan had made it clear he hoped to return to Chicago while Mike had aspirations of moving on to a larger newspaper in Minneapolis, Kansas City or St. Louis.

On this Friday, though, the dreamers remained stuck in Cedar City. Dan had just polished off his work week, Monday through Friday days, while Mike would not report for duty until Sunday evening, his shift running nights through Thursday. Thus, Friday night was the perfect occasion for Mike to join his co-workers, which always included Dan, for a couple of beers and a few philosophical discussions.

As Nicole filled their mugs with cold beer from the full pitcher she'd brought over, the two chuckled, Dan the loudest.

"We were discussing our images as reporters, not editor's opinions of themselves," Dan said. "Everybody hates us because we write the truth."

"The truth?" Mike said. "Or the truth people tell us?"

"That is the truth." Dan held his right hand up as if taking a courtroom oath. "So help me, God."

The public often criticized *The Argus* for sensationalism. As the only newspaper competing against three television stations and two news radio outlets, *The Argus* weathered cycles of public judgment two or three times a year. While broadcast reports were here one minute and gone the next, the morning newspaper had at least an all-day shelf life. To present an image of fairness, *The Argus* printed every letter it received that lambasted the newspaper.

"Insensitive cowards who hide behind a computer screen," wrote one high school teacher. "You should all have your press credentials yanked."

"Unsympathetic machines out to ruin people's lives," wrote a Catholic priest.

"One day, you'll get yours," wrote a widow who labeled *The Argus* "The National Enquirer of Cedar City." She added, "This crass sensationalism is your way of selling more papers."

Dan laughed at the accusations. "You're buying it, aren't you?" he wanted to tell each and every one of them.

"They're all hypocrites," Mike shouted, the beer doing more of the talking as he glanced around the Fox and Hounds and swung his beer mug around for emphasis. "Look at this place, the red carpet and tablecloths, the scarlet wallpaper, the crimson vinyl chairs. You'd think we slaughtered their values right here and splashed their blood and guts all over the walls and furniture."

"You'd think we put a gun to their heads," Dan yelled a little louder than Mike. "Forced them to walk the sidewalk to a vending machine to buy a bloody *Argus*."

"They read all about it," Mike shouted as if he were a midnight courier. "They talk it up at their coffee shops and taverns and symphony concert intermissions and sometimes even embellish the stories in the retelling. Even if they get angry enough to cancel their subscriptions, they're back in a month because they don't want to miss anything the neighbors might know."

Nicole returned to their table, even though they hadn't requested her presence.

"Hey, guys," she said, waving her hand up and down for emphasis, "can you keep it down? You're infringing on everybody else's right to have a quiet conversation."

The reporters reluctantly allowed silence to return to their corner of the tavern. Dan pulled a Kool cigarette from the pack in his shirt pocket and lit it. "You're right, Mike," he whispered hoarsely as he blew a cloud of white smoke over his compatriot's head. "Hypocrites. Everybody's a hypocrite, and they don't even know it."

* * * * *

Mike Rockwell had been waiting a long time for the drug bust to come down and Monday night it happened.

He sat slumped in the soft end of the brown vinyl couch in *The Argus'* interview/conference room, nestled into the indentation where he'd sat millions of times to monitor the six o'clock news for anything new. He crossed his legs, balanced a can of Coke on his thigh and nibbled at a dry bologna sandwich as the Action 10 News Team rehashed stories from the morning newspaper. He sipped the Coke often, swishing it around in his mouth to wash dry bread from his teeth. When he'd made the sandwich that afternoon and trimmed specks of mold from the bread crust, he realized it had been more than a week since his last trip to the grocery store.

Linda Marie Reynolds, he thought. She'd laugh at him for eating dry bread. Linda Marie Rockwell. He often considered how her initials wouldn't change if they married. He'd once joked that she could keep Reynolds if she preferred, to which she'd testily replied, "That's mighty big of you." He hadn't meant to sound overbearing, he just wanted her to know he was open to it, that she could keep her individual identity. "Let's take it one step at a time, buster," she had said. "I haven't even decided if I want to get married yet, let alone if I want to marry you."

That likelihood seemed more remote every day. She'd become upset when he didn't return to the day shift after Jennifer Drake's resignation, so they could work the same hours. Linda said she needed adult conversation in the evenings after spending five class periods a day with struggling sixth- and seventh-grade math students.

Until a couple of months ago, she'd welcomed him with open arms and a half-conscious smile after midnight whenever he used the key she'd given him to slip into her apartment and her bed after his last rounds. They'd fall asleep tangled in the sheets and each other. Then, the evening he decided to remain on the night beat, she accused him of wanting nothing more than a warm body. The more he tried to dispel that notion, the more she seemed convinced she was right.

Then there was last night. When he turned the key in her lock and opened the door, the living room was ablaze in light as she sat on the couch wrapped in her white terry cloth robe, running a brush through her long auburn hair. She had returned that evening after visiting her parents for the weekend in St. Louis.

"It might be better if we don't see each other until next weekend, when we're both more rested," she said. Instead of offering him a drink and conversation, she forced a hollow smile, kissed him lightly on the lips and said she was going to bed.

After a couple of minutes, Mike followed her into the bedroom where he found her curled up under the covers clutching a pillow instead of him. Stunned into silence, he drove home and couldn't sleep. So often they'd talked about love, commitment, goals, family, friends, desires, all of the abstract values that cement relationships or complicate them. Seeing her after work was one ritual Mike could count on, so he wasn't sure he could take a step back. He sensed the beginning of the end.

In the interview room, as Mike watched the weather forecast, he knew Linda was home, probably watching the same program. He considered calling her but didn't know if it would be interpreted as a welcome gesture or an annoying one. He speculated that she might be interested in someone else as Bill Jackson, the night editor, poked his head through the door.

"Mike, telephone."

He set his Coke on the floor, dropped the remainder of his sandwich on top of it. He entertained hope, however slight, that Linda had been reading his mind, that she had called at the office, something she hadn't done in weeks.

Mike stood beside his desk to pick up the phone. "Hello," he said tentatively. "This is Mike Rockwell."

"Rockwell?" The voice was deep and not immediately recognizable.

"Yeah."

"It's going down in half an hour. Get your butt over here if you want to tag along."

Lieutenant Sanders, head of drug enforcement for the Cedar City Police Department. Months ago, he had promised Mike he could participate in a drug bust for a story when the time was right. This was it.

"Be right there, lieutenant," Mike said.

The only reply was a click in the receiver.

Grinning, Mike stuffed his notebook into his back pocket and sprinted to the coat closet. This was it, the break he'd been waiting for, a story that could end his drought, a story that could pull him out of his funky "she loves me, she loves me not" doldrums, a story that would entice prospective employers into hiring him after it became the first entry in his news-clips file.

Mike checked his shirt pocket to make sure he had a backup pen and raced back to the interview room for his sandwich and Coke. He chugged the pop, tossed the dried sandwich and empty can into the metal wastebasket with a gong that made him wonder if there would be any gunplay, any rough stuff to write about. As much as anything, he hoped the story would make a front-page banner headline in the morning paper. He'd point to it for Linda, show her exactly why he had to work the night beat. Why he, Mike Rockwell, couldn't settle for anything less than top billing.

"Hey, Jackson," Mike shouted, back-pedaling between desks toward the rear stairway. "I'm off to a drug bust. Don't count on much else from me tonight."

Jackson casually looked up from his computer and pushed the bridge of his wire-rimmed glasses to the top of his nose, as if Mike ran out for a story like this every night. His glasses shimmered with reflections from the fluorescent overhead lights, hiding his eyes. "You'll have it for tomorrow's paper?" Jackson asked.

"Who knows?" Mike said. "It might be the story of the year, and it might be nothing. I'll keep you posted."

Mike let the door slam behind him as he ran down the steps two at a time. He followed a zigzag route through the hallways of *The Argus* building to the parking garage. His heart pumped adrenalin through his veins and into his brain as he jogged through the press room where the large blue Goss Metro press sat idle, waiting for the aluminum printing plates of the next morning's edition. The silent press, two stories of gears and rollers and computerized electronic controllers, gave Mike Rockwell a sense of immense power. The presses couldn't run until the plates were in place, the plates couldn't be burned until the negatives were processed, the negatives couldn't be shot until the pages were built, the pages couldn't be laid out until typesetting was completed, the typesetting couldn't begin until the copy was written. Like plankton in the food chain, his copy was the first step of the cycle. The entire process depended on him.

* * * * *

The drive to the cop shop was cold and quick. In ten blocks, the heater of the newspaper's beat-up Ford Escort didn't blow anything but cool air. Mike hit all but one of the five stoplights while they were green and pulled up directly in front of the gothic-style Cedar City Police Department building. He rubbed his ungloved hands briskly together to warm his fingers before climbing out of the car. No doubt about it, this might be the story to send him on his way.

Mike Rockwell chuckled to himself as another thought crossed his mind. He had always wanted to write a story at deadline that was so big the editor in charge had to push the red emergency button in the newsroom to stop the presses while he put the finishing touches to it. In his nine-year career at three newspapers, that had never happened. Then he remembered his conversation Friday, how Dan Goldberg had gotten the best of him, and he knew that this story would prove that Mike Rockwell was the better reporter, the better man.

A glorious sunset painted the sky red, yellow and orange as Mike skipped up the wide, shallow front steps toward the massive, intimidating three-story cop shop. He understood why so many people hated the police. To file a report, they had to come face-to-face with such a cold building – its huge gray columns, cold reflective glass with crisscrossed wire reinforcement, blinding spotlights shining down from above and two dozen steps up to the large steel front doors. A welcome mat wouldn't be noticed.

Inside the small, tiled lobby, the clock on the wall above the front desk read 6:43 p.m. as the red second hand swept past the nine. Mike wrote 6:44 in his notebook and the notation: "Arrived – cop shop." He wasn't certain how he'd write the story, but to keep each event in order, he'd take notes in diary form. Dan Goldberg sarcastically referred to it as "Dragnet" style, even though he admitted cop reporters probably took notes that way long before Friday and Gannon appeared on television.

The uniformed desk officer glanced up from sorting a pile of paperwork and hitched a rubber-coated thumb in the air, pointing over his shoulder toward the rear of the station. "Lieutenant's waiting for you back in the interrogation room."

After five years on the beat, Mike was known by every office cop, even if he didn't know them all by name. Anyone who showed up on such a regular basis either had to be a nut, a drunk, a criminal or a reporter. The first three were behind bars; the Fourth Estate was allowed only slightly more freedom.

The battleship gray walls of the long hallway led past a large plate glass window sealing off the darkened radio room from the distracting noises of the world. In the soundproof silence, three officers glided around on caster-equipped chairs. They flipped through papers wedged onto clipboards and fiddled with knobs, toggle switches and dials that glowed orange and blue on the banks of electronic equipment. From outside you could see lips move, but they were unaccompanied by voices.

Marcia Fuller spun around in her chair as Mike breezed past the window. They exchanged brief smiles as she waved. If Mike hadn't been in such a hurry, he would have rapped on the window, so she would come out to talk. Radio personnel were the most valuable sources a cop reporter could develop. When Marcia transferred from the dayside to the nightside radio shift a year ago, she quickly became Mike's favorite and most trusted source.

Of course, as head of night communications, Marcia possessed the authority to hold back information as well as feed it to Mike. But, lately, she was also a central character in his emotional consternation. There was something about women cops, the guts, the fortitude and the mind-set needed to become the physical equal of men that intrigued Mike.

Marcia Fuller exuded that toughness while maintaining her femininity. In her blue uniform, with the brass buttons and broad shoulders and black equipment belt, she seemed like one of the guys, only with curves in the right places. Mike ran into her on the street once, sans dangling handcuffs, leather holster, two-way radio and hard leather sap, and he was smitten by the transformation. The lavender knit dress had fit like a glove and subtle make-up around her sparkling brown eyes made them appear larger and more liquid than they ever seemed at the cop shop. But the change that nearly knocked him over, that prevented him from noticing her at first that day, was the fullness of her long auburn hair instead of the thin wisps that escaped from beneath her on-duty hat and headphones.

Mike had thought about Marcia more in the past couple of months than he'd thought about her since they'd met. He told himself Linda's attitude change contributed to his wandering mind as much as Marcia herself, but he still felt a twinge of guilt.

Walking down the hallway, Mike wondered what it would be like to have either woman along on the drug bust. Would Marcia be as calm under pressure as he guessed? Would Linda gain a better understanding of why he needed to be a night crime reporter, or would she just freak out?

Speculating on the answers sent a shiver from his lower back up between his shoulder blades. He couldn't be any more certain about their reactions than he could be about his own, especially if a confrontation with the drug dealers became tense.

The door to the interrogation room was ajar, so Mike let himself in and slid along the back wall.

"Make yourself comfortable," Lieutenant Sanders said. "This is Rockwell. From *The Argus*."

The men in the room turned toward Mike all at once, then refocused their attention on the white board behind Sanders. With six men packed into the room, the confined quarters smelled of perspiration and a pungent mixture of cologne. Mike unzipped his lined jacket, pulled out his notebook and took notes.

Two uniformed officers sat thigh to thigh on red plastic chairs in the center of the room, their broad shoulders filling the gap between metal shelves on the left and gray file cabinets on the right. A short, stocky man in a rumpled charcoal business suit leaned on one shelf, resting his rough, shadowed chin in the crotch of thumb and forefinger. Front and center, at Sanders' feet, sat a thin wiry man with curly black hair wearing white sneakers, faded blue jeans and a bulky ski sweater with red, white and blue horizontal stripes.

Lieutenant Sanders, in uniform, stood tall with thinning hair and a square jaw. He drew the rectangle of a city block on the white board and jotted down information beside it. He tapped his marker sharply against the board as he made each point. He had talked to Mike about this drug dealer, Morgan, for weeks.

Mike leaned against a file cabinet, copying the diagram and each of the notations carefully in his notebook: Central Avenue. Small house – slight elevation. Faces west. Driveway south. Tall fence around back yard. Warrant: Ronald Michael Morgan. Cocaine dealer. 33. 6' 2", 230. Beard. Long sandy hair. Tailing for seven months.

"We want this scumbag bad, and we want him now," Sanders said.

The interrogation room heated up by the minute as the contempt in Sanders' voice made his desire more obvious by the second. Mike wasn't the only one taking slow, deep breaths to keep a clear head. Perspiration glued the back of his shirt to his skin. His knees felt rubbery. The scribbles in his notebook became nearly illegible as he found himself concentrating more on the lieutenant's words than on his handwriting.

"Rockwell," Sanders said. "You'll ride with me. Let's go."

A new wave of heat flushed across Mike's face as each cop filed out of the room and gave him a grim smile that said, "You don't belong here."

"We're going to get this bastard," Sanders said as he held the door open for Mike.

"You bet," Mike said. "We're going to get him."

* * * * *

Mike Rockwell and Lieutenant Sanders strolled down the corridor and out the officers' rear entrance in brisk silence. The chilly night air stung Mike's face and crept inside his open coat, freezing the perspiration on his back. At first, he had thought participating in a drug bust would simply be an adventure, a fascinating story to write. But Sanders made the danger of this little escapade perfectly clear. Everyone, Mike included, was to assume that Morgan and anyone else in the house would be armed.

The youthful passion of invincibility had faded from Mike's psyche year by year as he developed new values for life. Taking risks was perfectly fine as long as every possible consequence was clear in advance. That's why he had never harbored a desire to become a news correspondent in South Africa or the Middle East where war was unpredictable, and guns were a threat in even the most stable hands.

As Mike climbed into the patrol car, he stared at the shotgun mounted on the dash.

"Eighteen years on the force, and I've never had to use that," Sanders said. "I don't plan to use it tonight if that's what you're thinking."

The police radio cackled as Lieutenant Sanders started the car. This was the chance of a lifetime, Mike thought. No Geraldo Rivera, no exaggerated dramatizations, no gathering information second-hand from witnesses. This was the real thing.

As Sanders pulled out of the parking lot, Mike realized he was looking forward to the drug bust not so he could participate in it, but so he could say he had. His byline would be proof that he was as good as any reporter, that he should be working for a large newspaper in a major market.

Fall's early darkness fell about the patrol car. The halogen streetlights glowed like flying saucers from above as Sanders cruised through the central business district toward the northeast quadrant of Cedar City. Cars lining the streets belonged to moviegoers and restaurant patrons and after-work social drinkers. A few pedestrians on the sidewalks glanced at the patrol car but didn't give it a second look since the lights and siren weren't on. The fact these spectators had no idea where the cop car was going gave Mike a sense that he knew a secret they'd all be dying to know, a secret that would be revealed in the morning paper.

"Collins will make the buy," Sanders said. "He's the guy in the sweater and jeans."

Mike nodded. He'd assumed as much, then couldn't contain a chuckle as Sanders gunned the car through an intersection as the stoplight changed from green to yellow.

"Something funny?" Sanders asked.

"Yeah. Cop's privilege. I was just thinking how I hate it when the light changes on me like that. I always glance in the rear-view mirror to see if a cop's behind me."

"Me, too." Sanders said, winking.

Mike had ridden in a patrol car before and knew officers were human, too. But this was the first time he'd been with Lieutenant Sanders outside the police station. Mike wasn't uncomfortable with the officer, but he wasn't at ease either. He was pleased they could joke with each other. The exchange must have put the lieutenant at ease, too, because he began to divulge information Mike wasn't used to receiving.

"Collins, that's his real name," Sander said. "I'd appreciate it, and he would, too, if you don't use it in your story. We still need to keep him undercover. Make up a name. Or use the one Morgan knows him by. Bill Mills."

Mike jotted both names in his notebook, but the undulations of the car as it bounced over railroad tracks sent his pen skating across the page. The sporadic waves of darkness and light from the street made it nearly impossible to see what he'd written, anyway, so he closed his notebook and decided to add information after they arrived at the scene.

"Morgan. Is he really as dangerous as you say?" Mike asked.

"Anybody who deals in drugs is as dangerous as a weasel in a hen house. You ever see a weasel?"

"Just pictures."

"Cute little critter, isn't he?" Sanders grinned. "Innocent face, button nose, long skinny body with that soft fur for making coats. Minks, ferrets, sables, even skunks. They're all weasels when you get right down to it. They all stink when you get them cornered.

"Animal lovers will tell you it isn't fair to turn them into winter coats," the lieutenant continued, "but I'd wager a month's salary against the price of one of those coats they've never seen those damn beady little eyes from under a pile of straw and chicken feathers. When weasels are hungry, they're relentless, but when they're cornered, they're just plain vicious." He turned to face Mike. "Imagine what they'd be like if they carried a loaded gun."

Mike's forehead felt warm. He was nervous again. He hated his mood shifts as much as he hated the approach of winter, as he stared out the windshield and didn't reply.

"Never been on a real bust, have you?" Sanders said.

Mike swallowed hard and wished he'd brought a Coke to sip. "Nope," he said, clearing his throat. "It should be fun."

"You don't have a thing to worry about," Sanders said. He guided the car down a quiet, dark and narrow residential street with small one- and two-bedroom houses. "We'll sit in the car and watch until everything's under control. Morgan won't even see you until the arrest is made."

Mike resisted the urge to protest. He'd pictured himself right there in the house with the cops as they drew their guns and slammed the drug dealers against a wall. Not only had his television-warped imagination excited him, it had diluted his common sense. He should have known better. He was simply along for the ride.

"Pochobradsky, the guy in the suit, is backing Collins up," Sanders said. "The uniforms, Grady and Jones, will move in when they get the word. It should be a routine bust, but Collins is playing the part for you."

"Playing the part?"

"Yeah. He gets a little excited sometimes, especially if he's got an audience."

Oh, God, Mike thought. What a fool. All the pieces fit. This was nothing but a demonstration for the media. He tried to remember if he'd suggested going along on a drug bust or if it had been Sanders' idea. The more he thought about it, the more it added up to be a PR ploy by the PD.

"Sometimes Collins thinks he's Baretta," Sanders said. "Remember that show? Robert Blake played Baretta."

"I was in college," Mike snapped, then wondered if Lieutenant Sanders detected his frustration. He wasn't so much angry at Sanders as he was pissed at himself. He should have known better. "Tony Baretta, I think," he added, trying to sound calm. "The show was about drugs every week. A couple of friends said they watched it to pick up tips on how cops worked so they wouldn't get busted."

"Your friends do a lot of drugs?" Sanders asked. He sounded annoyed.

"Uh, no, not anymore," Mike said, even though he wasn't sure about Pat and Chris. He hadn't seen them in a decade. "I don't have friends like that anymore. It was innocent college stuff. Experiment while you can, then move on."

Mike glanced at Sanders who stared straight ahead as they rounded the corner onto Central Avenue.

"All we did was a little grass," Mike said, unsure why he felt a need to explain. "A joint now and then. In college you're always looking for a cheap thrill." He chuckled. "Those guys would get paranoid every time they were high, you know, like looking in the rear-view mirror to see if a cop's behind you."

Mike wasn't sure why he continued, but he talked on as if he was somehow high, as if he couldn't stop babbling. "We were hopeless, really. You know, giggling and talking." He lowered his voice. "Whispering like it was a clandestine operation and a big deal, like every cop in the world was out to bust us."

Finally, Mike caught his breath. "Hey, looking back on it now, it was, like, you know, hilarious, but stupid kids doing stupid stunts."

Lieutenant Sanders parked the car without reply. He cut the lights and the engine, folded his hands atop the steering wheel and stared into the darkness. An occasional voice on the police radio broke the silence.

Stars, like distant pinholes in the clear black sky, were joined by the full moon that shone like a polished hubcap. Even in the dim light, the white bungalow on the hill across the street obviously needed paint. It appeared dark and deserted. The windows reflected wavering light from the overhead streetlights. The sidewalk in front and the concrete stairs leading to the front door were cracked in numerous places where decades of frost and large, water-seeking tree roots had done their damage.

Rhythmic shadows stirred on the ground below the low-hanging branches of several large trees, probably planted about the time the house was built. The grass appeared as if it hadn't been mowed in a month and a few of autumn's first fallen leaves huddled in the corners of the steps. A network movie-of-the-week director couldn't have designed a better set. Describing the scene in his story was precisely what Mike needed to do to establish tension and credibility.

"Doesn't look like anybody's home," Mike said.

"Oh, they're there," Sanders said. "The windows are blackened."

"Of course," Mike said. He could he be so naïve? He recalled how paranoid college friends had once taped the drapes together in a dorm room and walked outside to make sure no one could see inside, all just to smoke a crinkled, hand-rolled joint.

"Hey, ummm, lieutenant, I just want you to know I haven't touched marijuana since college. You know," Mike laughed, feeling nervous again. "It made me thirsty, and I'd drink beer and get drunk. A bad combination, you know. Sometimes my body would tingle all over, and I'd get sick. But, you know, most of the time I'd just fall asleep."

Sanders didn't respond.

"Hell," Mike said. "We just thought we were having a good time."

"You were, until you grew up." Sanders turned toward Mike, his eyes as large and shiny as a cat's. "Problem is, some kids never do."

As the lieutenant stared through him, Mike braced for a lecture. He was on board with first lady Nancy Reagan's "Just Say No" campaign and wanted to say so, except he didn't want to interrupt.

"My kid was busted at sixteen," Sanders said, gaze toward the house. "When Eric told me he'd been using the stuff for two years, I grabbed him by the collar and slammed his thick skull against the wall, tried to knock some sense into him. He slumped to the floor and stared at me with big glassy eyes as if I'd never even spanked him as a child. In hindsight, he was probably so doped up he didn't realize what had happened. But I was wrong. I haven't seen him since."

Mike was speechless.

"Four years," Sanders said, his voice distant with his thoughts. "That's how long it's been. Sometimes I don't give a damn that he's gone. Sometimes I miss the hell out of him. But I'd do it again, in a heartbeat."

Mike didn't know Sanders had a kid. But he'd known kids like that, running away from domineering parents. He'd wondered for a while if he might not have turned out that way, if his parents hadn't kept their noses out of his life, if they hadn't trusted him to make up his own mind. He sympathized with Sanders, but mostly he felt sorry for the kid. With a cop for a father, what would you expect but rebellion? Like the proverbial promiscuous preacher's daughter, when you're young you wonder what's so good about drugs or sex that your parents try to keep you away from it. As a teenager you know it all and you've got to prove to mom and dad, and to yourself, that you're an adult.

"They're here," Sanders said, glancing in the rear-view mirror.

Mike turned around. A silver Monte Carlo approached and then drove past, followed by a white Cedar City Police Department car with a badge on the door. Mike checked his watch in the dim light and opened his notebook. It was time to become an observer for the good of the police department, for the progress of his career, for the benefit of parents like Lieutenant Sanders who only wanted the best for their kids and could justify their no-tolerance actions by reading about another drug dealer busted.

The Monte Carlo swung into the driveway of the darkened house, and Collins climbed out the driver's side carrying a duffel bag. His walk was confident, if not a little cocky, as he threw his head back, arched his shoulders and swung the duffel bag. Pochobradsky's silhouette was barely visible on the passenger side.

The patrol car with Grady and Jones had disappeared down a side street. But it re-emerged on the other side of the street, pulling up one house away from Morgan's drug den.

"Won't Morgan be a little suspicious if he sees that cop car?" Mike asked.

"The shades are drawn," Sanders said. "Besides, they aren't expecting anything. This is just a smalltime buy for them."

"I forgot," Mike mumbled.

Mike and the lieutenant sat in the car, two pairs of eyes locked on Collins as he knocked on the front door. They were too far away to hear a sound but, as the door opened, a beam of light engulfed Collins and invited him into the house.

"Now we sit and wait," Sanders said, leaning back in his seat. "It shouldn't be long."

* * * * *

The lieutenant was right. Two minutes later, a muted explosion came from the enclosed house, a muffled bang that sounded more like a neighbor's loud television than a gunshot. So Mike had to ask.

"Was that a gunshot?"

Sanders didn't reply. But, as his body stiffened, Mike felt a bounce in the springs of the bench seat. For an instant the lieutenant froze like a statue, his shoulders back, his eyes forward, his hands gripping the steering wheel. When he did move, every motion appeared calculated.

Sanders pulled the bill of his hat down on his forehead. He unsnapped the holster at his side. He yanked the shotgun from its mounting on the dash.

"Stay put!" Sanders shouted as he threw open his car door.

Mike didn't plan to go anywhere, at least not toward the gunshot. If he had an inclination to run anywhere, it was in the opposite direction. His reporter's instinct told him to move as close to the action as possible; his human instinct screamed, "Get the hell out of here." He sat rigidly, watching Sanders crouch at the front fender of the patrol car, then sprint across the street. He became a shadow slithering across the street, kicking through a handful of leaves in the yard, scaling the steps to the front door.

Pochobradsky leaped from the unmarked car in the driveway and disappeared somewhere into the darkness behind the house.

For the first time since the shot, the two-way radio barked at Mike's feet. "We've got a shooting at 2318 Central Avenue. All units respond now. All units ..."

Mike knew he should jot down notes. But he didn't want to take his eyes off the house, not for a second, for fear of missing something. He stared at the front door hoping it would open. He didn't know what that might reveal, but at the moment everything was eerily quiet except for the pounding of his heart in his ears. He longed for a clue, any clue, about what had transpired inside the house. He strained his eyes to make out any movement at all.

Each second seemed like a minute, each minute like an eternity. Nothing moved. Not the trees. Not the streetlights. Not the stars. Not the shades on the windows of the house. Not the door.

The muscles in Mike's arms and legs tightened. His body was telling him to do something, anything, but his brain wouldn't give the command. For the first time in years, he wished someone would give him orders.

In the distance, police sirens broke the silence. Mike tried to relax. Everything would be all right, he told himself. All hell was breaking loose, and he was there to watch instead of arriving after the fact. He had a great story. Fantastic. He needed to let the news desk know.

Mike's watch read 7:54. He jotted the time in his notebook and added, "I'd never want to be a cop" with an exclamation point at the end. As he dotted the declamatory mark, another shot rang out, louder than the first, echoing outside between the house and the trees. The front door opened, streaming a wide band of light across the lawn, and Sanders disappeared inside the house.

"What the hell's going on?" Mike screamed. He couldn't help himself. Sanders promised there wouldn't be any gunplay. It was a routine raid.

Questions filled Mike's head. Was somebody dead? Two people? Morgan? Collins? A cop? Sanders?

God, Mike could have kicked himself. Why did he always have to think the worst? Maybe the first shot was a warning from Collins' gun. Maybe the second was a warning, too.

Damn it. Mike hated being alone in a cop car. He hated being in the dark.

How could he write about this on deadline? He was tense, anxious, uncertain. Was he a witness to murder? Had a drug bust turned into a nightmare? How could he write about witnessing a murder when, actually, he hadn't seen a thing? Some witness.

The front yard went dark again, but Mike thought he could still see the open front door. As sirens wailed closer he waited for someone to emerge from the house. He hoped it would be Sanders or at least one of the other uniformed cops.

"7:57," he wrote. "Door open. Sirens. Everything OK?"

Instantly, the dome light above Mike's head popped on, bathing the patrol car's interior in bright yellow light.

"What the hell?" a gravely male voice shouted.

Mike turned his head toward the driver's side of the car. He came face to face with the barrel of a pistol pointing at his nose. The car door slammed shut, blinding him again, this time in total darkness.

2

The day had begun as a Mundane Monday, as Mike Rockwell liked to call it, even though he relished the fact that his life as the night beat reporter for *The Cedar City Argus* was different than anyone else's. He worked "bartender's hours," so to speak, staying up late, sleeping late. He had mornings free to play golf or schedule a haircut or lounge around his apartment past noon, while most college-educated men his age had become slaves to a desk all day long. Every night he had his finger on the pulse on the city while those other poor saps sat home exhausted. At any moment, he could run into a story that would have the metropolitan area's 200,000 citizens standing in line to buy the morning paper, or so he liked to think.

Lately, Mike wondered if he lived in a fantasy world. He had decided to pursue an education and career in journalism on the heels of the Watergate investigation by Bob Woodward and Carl Bernstein, who became household names. But Mike's banner headline stories came too few and far between. More frequently he found himself doubting if the advantages of the night beat outweighed the sacrifices he made to a normal life.

Thinking. That's how he had spent most of his Monday at home.

"Contradictions," he'd said aloud as he drove to work after four on the overcast but otherwise pleasant early October day. Traffic seemed more congested than normal, or was it his imagination? Where were all these people going?

"Congestion," Mike had thought. It triggered the occasional yearning he felt for his early career in a two-stoplight town where his beat consisted of walking across the street from the newspaper office to city hall, the jail and the courthouse. He could have married, settled down, found an agreeable position as a managing editor at a small daily or, if he'd been frugal, bought a small weekly newspaper by now. He could be raising a family, covering occasional school board meetings and city council sessions if he didn't want to send an underling. He could be stopping at the corner tavern with community leaders for an after-work beer. He could be working nine-to-five like everyone else, planning for early retirement.

"Contentment," Mike had mumbled. That would be so boring, but would it be any worse than his life was now? In five years at *The Argus*, he'd become too much a part of Cedar City. It had engulfed him like an old oak tree he once saw growing around an abandoned plowshare. He kept telling himself he wanted out, that it was time to move on to a larger market, to Minneapolis or Kansas City or Denver. But no one had responded to his resumes.

Contradictions. Congestion. Contentment.

The words had floated through Mike's mind as he drove down First Avenue toward *The Argus* building in the heart of the city. Maybe he was too comfortable. There it was, another "C" word. He knew every building along the route, from the antiquated two-story brick fire-house No. 6 to the twelve-story Bowden House condo-miniums. It had become second nature to drive thirty-seven-miles-per-hour to time the sequence of the green lights, so he never had to stop. When he did pull over, it was at the Vickers convenience store to buy gas, the Hardee's fast food joint for roast beef sandwiches, Frank's Food Mart to buy groceries.

As with any community of any size, Cedar City's thor-oughfares were lined with quick-rise buildings and fake neon signs. Founded a hundred and fifty years earlier, its main street – First Avenue – ran perpendicular to the Ce-dar River. An outdoor shopping center built at the north end in the 1960s faced competition from the new en-closed mall at the south end. Mike knew more about Ce-dar City than most natives, for when crime news trickled to routine, he'd been assigned to research and write doz-ens of historical pieces about the city. Even Linda, who hadn't lived anywhere else, read his articles with a pio-neering interest.

Linda Reynolds. Her name had become synonymous with comfort. Mike met her nearly three years ago – thir-ty-four months to be precise – and fell in love soon thereafter, beginning the longest continuous relationship of his life. But he wasn't sure where it was headed. He'd missed her when she visited her parents in St. Louis over the weekend but hadn't seemed that disappointed upon her return when she didn't want him to spend the night. The relationship seemed to be crumbling, and he worried that he didn't care.

Mike's eight-year-old gold Buick, rust encroaching the rear wheel wells, approached *The Argus* building with a squeal of slipping belts beneath the hood. He slowed for the speed bumps in the alley, pushed a button on the remote clipped to his visor to open the electronic parking gate, slipped his car into the assigned parking space. He strolled across the alley past a flatbed truck backed up to a loading dock, waving casually to a familiar mountain of a man leaning against a two-thousand-pound roll of newsprint.

Mike Rockwell stood a shade under six feet tall, a height reached in his mid-teens, about the time he decided to become a writer. His youthful, clean-shaven face and the golden glow of his thick hair gave the illusion that he might still be capable of growing taller. Despite the absence of serious exercise in the last few years, his stomach remained washboard firm, his upper arms and thighs well defined as remnants of high school track workouts. Contact lenses made his blue eyes appear a little brighter and a lot friendlier. Even though his teeth had been aligned with braces, they weren't perfectly straight. But, when Mike Rockwell interviewed sources, he could flash a grin that conveyed such a trusting nature that people revealed secrets they wouldn't tell God.

Ask colleagues what made Mike Rockwell an excellent reporter, and they'd point to his ability to make anyone feel at ease. People in their forties and older embraced him as a son or grandson. Men his own age thought of him as a brother. Women in their thirties and younger often become flirtatious in his presence.

Although Mike couldn't afford to buy a lot of clothes, he was always impeccably dressed – a tie knotted firmly at the base of his throat, his shirts neatly pressed and his shoes shined.

Wearing a lined, navy-blue jacket tight around the waist to ward off the fall chill, Mike scaled the large step from the alley to the cramped side entrance to *The Argus*. He stood in the concrete-block enclosure, slipped his plastic identification card into an electronic reader and waited for the door's lock to click. Once it did, he had five seconds to pull the heavy metal door open, retrieve his ID card and step inside. The trick was to accomplish the feat in one easy motion before the door slammed against your heels.

Mike liked to think that no door could keep him out, particularly these new security doors publisher C.J. Moore installed to transform *The Argus* into its own Fort Knox. Contrary to popular opinion, security was not increased to keep people out, but to prevent valuable stacks of pre-printed coupons from "walking out of the building on their own accord." Mike considered the measure extreme, but he wasn't the type to steal anything, let alone newspaper coupons in bulk.

As the door slammed shut behind him, Mike sprinted up the long flight of stairs to the newsroom. He enjoyed hearing his hard-soled shoes tap on the bare concrete steps, the sound echoing off the unpainted walls of the narrow dimly lit stairwell. Naked light bulbs suspended from black cables hung in front of tall slits of windows covered with wire mesh. Gazing up or down the stairwell, the steel handrail produced the optical illusion of an infinite maze, although there was no danger of anyone getting lost. Only employees used this entrance.

At the upper landing, Mike inserted his ID card into another image reader, waited for the click and entered the newsroom.

The Blue Room. Everyone called it that, as if it belonged in The White House. The newsroom was filled with bright shiny blue metal desks with fake wood grain tops arranged end-to-end in miniature convoys of three on a sea of deep blue carpet. Each desk was accessorized with a blue molded plastic wastebasket and a chair covered in navy fabric. Sky blue ceiling tiles floated in the low suspended ceiling, giving the open and expansive room an air of infinity. Even the subdued white walls seemed to have a blue tint. The whole place could overwhelm any stranger into submission, a fact that Mike had been told was Mr. Moore's intent, to use the subtleties of color to create a serene atmosphere. He'd simply gone overboard.

"It's only been this way for ten years," Jennifer Drake had told Mike on his first day of work. "We don't notice it anymore."

"Why blue?" he asked

Jennifer had raised her eyes as if to pray to the Heavens. "It's the first thing everyone wants to know when they start work. Mr. Moore learned that blue has this calming effect, you know, matter over brain. Experts claim blue counteracts impulsiveness, restlessness, violence, all the detrimental elements of society. They say it lowers your blood pressure, slows your pulse rate, even reduces the number of times you blink your eyes." She paused with an over-obvious blink for Mike's benefit. "It's supposed to give us inspiration and creativity," she said, punching a small fist into the air. "Truth and wisdom. Justice and the American Way. Make us serene and loyal subjects. You know. Slaves."

Jennifer's fist had fallen open at her side. The smile that had brightened her cameo face, soured. "We've been talking about a mutiny for six years," she said, "and, you know, it's never come off. That old coot must have been right!"

On Monday, as he had done that first day, Mike glanced around the cavernous room at the fifty or so reporters and editors clicking away at their computers, flipping open notebooks, dialing telephones, engaging in intimate two- and three-person conversations. Many of the men's ties hung loose at their necks and the women's hair had lost its morning bounce. This was the shift change, the transformation of day into night, as reporters wrapped up stories to head home for supper while copy editors settled in for an evening of checking grammar, writing headlines and drawing red lines on layout paper.

Mike didn't even look for Jennifer. No need. She'd made her escape from The Blue Room six months ago, pregnant and praying for a girl so she could decorate the nursery in pink.

Mike missed Jennifer's humor and perspective on life, qualities that kept him aware that not everyone sees events the same way. Then again, she had become infatuated with the prospects of motherhood and talked incessantly about little else up to the day she cleared out her side of the desk they shared.

Five months ago – there always seemed to be a gap when *The Argus* hired replacements – Dan Goldberg moved into Jennifer's half of the desk. He came from *The Weekly Enterprise* in Chicago with an attitude. He knew all the answers and wasn't shy about telling you so.

Often, as Mike approached their desk, Dan sat with a telephone receiver glued between his left shoulder and ear, his right hand busily scratching a pen across the page of a reporter's narrow lined notebook. Whether he was busy or not was anybody's guess. Dan loved to talk and always managed to appear overworked, whether he was running across the newsroom to summon a photographer or hammering his computer keyboard with quick staccato taps or taking voluminous notes in his indecipherable handwriting. His intense demeanor seemed genuine at first but became transparent as Mike learned more about him out of the office.

When Dan joined *The Argus*, Mike took the lead in building rapport. Often cops on the night beat revealed a slice of information that Mike could pass along to Dan during the day for a follow-up story and vice versa. Like ink and paper, news and newspapers, performer and audience, the day cop reporter and the night cop reporter needed each other. Even though Mike became leery of Dan's Jekyll-and-Hyde personality, from his nail-the-bastards-to-the-wall motivation in the newsroom to his lackadaisical mindset with a beer in hand, he knew he could learn something from the guy's frank, sometimes crass, aggressiveness. A bond of sorts had developed more quickly than Mike thought possible because, even though they weren't exactly buddies, they were a team.

Although Dan was three years younger than Mike, he appeared older with his curly black hair, his cleft chin dark with stubble, his thick mustache below a wide prominent nose too big for his face. He had deep brown eyes, piercing even through the blue tint of his glasses. A silver chain circled his neck, something Mike had not worn since high school.

"Five o'clock already?" Dan said, dropping the receiver into its cradle. "My how time flies when the phone rings off the hook."

"What's up?" Mike asked.

Dan tossed his pen onto his notebook and leaned back in the chair as if he was about to prop his feet on the desk. "Oh, not much. Three fires, a twelve-car pileup on the interstate, a shootout at the OK Corral ..."

"I hope you wrote it all up, so I don't have to," Mike said.

"No sweat. And we've still got the rest of the week."

"Maybe my night will be a thrill a minute, too."

"Seriously," Dan said, "I've got one more call to make, to double check the address of this drunken driver, and it's all yours."

As Mike walked through the newsroom to hang up his coat, he hoped it would be a quiet night. He wanted an easy week, to simply check the day's story list so he wouldn't duplicate any of Dan's efforts, to read other newspapers to catch up on area events, to eat supper while watching the six o'clock news and to make his rounds to the cop shop, jail, sheriff's department and fire station. Nothing much had happened for a month. Mike wasn't in the mood for that to change.

Mike grabbed his coffee mug from the desk and walked the half dozen steps to the drinking fountain to rinse it out, pick up the glass coffee urn from the warmer and fill his cup with lukewarm coffee. He added a spoonful of sugar as he wondered why his motivation had been lacking. He hadn't chosen this career for routine. Although he'd endured his share of boredom, the night beat usually provided twinges of excitement even on the dullest evenings. If a reporter learned anything on the job it was that, as an observer of life, a bizarre occurrence could grab you by the hair at any moment and drag you through the funhouse. You learned to realize that the contrast between boredom and adventure was why you wouldn't trade your job for what anyone else did for a living.

At least Dan had that mindset, too, Mike thought. He didn't have aspirations of sitting on an editor's throne, rewriting a reporter's lead simply because he could. Like Mike, Dan would rather chase an ambulance than calculate the letter and space count for a headline.

Gazing around *The Argus* newsroom, Mike could neatly slip each staff member into a category. Anderson and Slater wanted editorial power, the opportunity to move up and call the shots. McMahon, a clock watcher who complained when she had to work overtime and complained even louder when she couldn't, was dying to find a way out of what she considered the lowest paid, least respected, most unrewarding profession on earth. Jack Crawford and Sandy Griffin had become "Lifers," with a capital "L," eating, sleeping, drinking and breathing the news. Then you had Jeff Pritchard, a history major, Jackie Shepherd, a marketing specialist, and Elizabeth Anne Dawson, an archaeologist, who all couldn't find "real" jobs anywhere else, so they settled for temporary positions as cheap labor on the copy desk. And, of course, every newsroom had an Anthony A. Aaronson, author-to-be who would someday write The Great American Novel and become filthy rich and world famous, if only in his dreams.

Yeah, Mike thought, not a lot of reporters these days got into the business to become reporters. At least Dan had. And *The Argus* was a decent, well-respected newspaper in the world of news. It had proved to be a journalistic steppingstone for several writers, editors, photographers and artists who made it to the big time, while it remained as comfortable as a La-Z-Boy recliner for those who wanted to stay.

Mike's master plan to move on after five years had expired in January without even one step in the right direction. He knew he was good enough for Kansas City, Minneapolis or St. Louis. He knew at thirty-one, though, that the clock was ticking. If he was to control his own destiny, as Dan purported to want, he had to do it soon.

As Dan hung up the phone, Mike flipped open his notebook. "Anything special I need to know about?"

"Are you kidding?" Dan reclined in his laid-back position. He locked his hands at the base of his neck, elbows protruding on either side of his face like horse blinders. "You're not going to believe the assignment I got today. An expose on shoplifting."

"Ha," Mike said. "I'm jealous."

"It's all yours."

"Ha. I've had to write that annual shoplifting story the last four years." Mike closed his notebook, tossed it on the desk and placed his coffee mug on it. "I say it's about time somebody else reaped the glory."

"Right. You probably told Margaret you wouldn't have time to do it, what with chasing down flaky broads who drive around on flat tires until the rubber burns off and starts a fire."

"It made page one," Mike said.

"Only because the driver was an idiot, not for anything you did," Dan retorted.

"I interviewed her instead of letting it pass. She didn't want to talk, but I convinced her she needed to tell her side of the story."

"Full moon," Dan said. "That's how I'd explain it. It's the only reason I'm doing this shoplifting story instead of you."

"Margaret likes you," Mike said with a grin. "You're the new kid on the block."

"Knock it off," Dan said. "You probably told her I'd love to do it."

"Me?" Mike laughed. "You think I'd actually do something like that to my dearest, kindest, most cherished colleague?"

"I'm out of here," Dan said, rising from his chair. "I need a brewski."

"Adios." Mike extended his right hand in a sweeping motion toward the door. "You can have my hangovers, too."

"Friday night a little much?" Dan asked.

Mike smiled. He could count the murderous hangovers he'd had since college on one hand. He seldom drank more than a couple of beers any more. He must have had at least a dozen Friday when he and Dan wound up as the last reporters at the Fox and Hounds Lounge. Mike knew it hadn't affected Dan nearly as much because he drank every night. He was a guy who could easily work with a hangover and often did.

3

As Dan Goldberg heard police sirens a little before eight Monday night, he increased the volume of his television. After work he had stopped at the Fox and Hounds Lounge for a couple of beers, but the place was dead, so he arrived home by seven.

After heating and eating a frozen pizza, Dan sipped another beer while watching his new videotape of "Risky Business." He'd watched the classic drive-in flick to the point he'd memorized most of the dialogue, so he was only half interested, paying attention to only the good parts like when the "U-boat" Porsche 928 sped across the screen or when Rebecca De Mornay appeared in Tom Cruise's dining room.

After nearly half a year at *The Argus*, Dan wondered if leaving Chicago had been a mistake. He missed the Els, Rush Street, P.J.'s, Grant Park, the beach along Lake Michigan. "Risky Business" made him nostalgic. Could *The Argus* really be his ticket back to Chicago, or should he have stayed with *The Weekly Enterprise* for a shot at *The Chicago Tribune*?

Then again, his story about the five-year-old kid decapitated by the train had stirred up Cedar City. Mike hated him for it, called him insensitive for using two much detail, but Dan loved the attention, the notoriety, and defended himself because Margaret had approved his story. Dozens of people called the newsroom to complain, though one guy, who talked to Dan personally, said it was the best story he'd read in the paper in decades. Dan needed more stories like that.

Most of the time it seemed Dan did nothing but check and recheck the police log to see if Mike had missed anything. Finding a Rockwell error was as rare as a page one story falling in his lap during the day. Dan hadn't been joking Friday night when he told Mike the good stuff happened at night.

Much of Dan's days were spent making the rounds. He'd sit in whatever chair was handy to pick up the latest nonsense gossip from cops, secretaries, radio operators and skeleton key carriers at the cop shop, the central fire station, the sheriff's department and the jail. By midmorning, he was usually back in the newsroom, bored from meaningless conversation and free to spend a couple of hours writing assigned puff pieces while he listened to the scanner, hoping for real news to break.

Monday morning, when he heard the single syllable of his first name carry all the way across the newsroom, he knew City Editor Margaret Myers had another "fascinating feature idea." Her voice was the most recognized in the newsroom – feared by some and respected by others.

Dan thought it a nuisance. He couldn't believe how her voice made news interns leap into action and seasoned reporters scurry to her side. That she had become the self-proclaimed godmother of the newsroom was ludicrous. No woman, no matter how much common sense she had or how intelligent she might be, should have that much authority.

Whenever anyone like Margaret yelled at him, Dan was reminded of his father, a Chicago businessman who managed the two dozen employees of his men's clothing store the same way. His loud manner, iron fist and my-way-or-the-highway attitude usually followed him home, too, where Dan learned at an early age to stay out of his way. His father always thought Dan would join him in the business, but a part-time job while in school straightening stock on the floor at the store put an end to that notion. His father criticized Dan's lackadaisical manner and said he'd never amount to anything more than a stock boy.

Whenever his father's voice filtrated through his mind, Dan thought about 1976, the year he graduated from high school, the summer he worked construction for PDM Contractors. The owner, John, told him the company specialized in painting, decorating and maintenance and that he preferred to hire young men so he could train them properly.

At PDM, Dan became handy with a hammer and nails, with a tape measure and a circular saw, even with a shovel when asked to help dig a ditch at the owner's home in Norwood Park. Dan hated the physical labor of digging, though, and, on a hot afternoon that July, told John he wouldn't do it anymore.

At first, John tried to be nice, wrapped his arm around Dan, told him he wouldn't have to dig much longer. He invited Dan into the house for lemonade. The squeeze of the hand on his shoulder was a bit too aggressive for Dan, so he refused to go inside. He dropped his shovel, asked for his last paycheck, and quit on the spot. "You Jews are all alike," John said, "cheap and distrustful, thinking everybody's out to kill you."

When his father learned about the incident, he insisted that Dan return to PDM, apologize, and pick up his last check. Dan lied to his father, claimed John refused to pay him and lounged around the rest of the summer until college started.

It wasn't until more than two years later, shortly before Christmas in 1978, that Dan learned, along with the rest of the world, that John Wayne Gacy had been raping and killing teenage boys and young men that summer, that he had been doing it before and since, that he confessed to more than thirty murders, burying his victims under his house and in ditches they had dug for themselves.

Dan wasn't sure if his father ever added it up, because they weren't speaking by then, but the news changed Dan's life forever. He became obsessed with Gacy, especially after reading that his Polish-Catholic grandparents came from an old part of Germany, meaning his relatives could have been partially to blame for the Holocaust. He changed his college major from general studies to mass communications after spending so much time in the college library reading newspapers. And resisting authority became second nature.

"What's up?" Dan had said, leaning his hip lazily against the side of Margaret's desk. If she expected him to stand at attention and salute, she'd have to give him those rules in writing. He wouldn't be surprised if they weren't already hidden somewhere in the stacks of newspapers and news releases cluttering her desk.

"We need a general story on shoplifting," she said. "Get hold of your police contacts and talk to Mike if you need to. Check with store security. Find out if there's been an increase this year and why. There's a *New York Times* story ..."

Blah, blah, blah. Dan couldn't believe his ears. He'd finished a story about spring car care for a special section and now he was assigned another puff piece. He watched

Margaret Myers' short-curly-haired head bob with her words, her thick eyeglasses reflecting her long witch-like fingers tapping at the keyboard, and knew immediately why she had never married, why, now that she had to be in her late forties, Margaret Myers would never have children except for her newsroom slaves.

"... about the national trend in the wire directory," Margaret continued. "You'll need to talk to everyone locally, Kmart, Penney's, Target, so it doesn't look like we're biased toward our advertisers." She paused to make eye contact, as if that was necessary to convey her message to Dan. "We'll plan to use it a week from Sunday, so you might as well start today."

"Is that it?" he asked, but Margaret didn't appear to catch his sarcasm.

"For now," she said, scrolling through another story on her computer terminal.

The newsroom was deathly quiet, just the sound of a couple of reporters tapping computer keys to file stories. Dan felt like screaming at the top of his lungs to see if anybody was awake. Instead, he retrieved the shoplifting story from the wire service directory and watched the dark green letters scroll up on his light green computer screen.

If he wanted a different angle, Dan thought, he could talk to convicted shoplifters and write it from their perspective. Find out how often they did it, the best times not to get caught, the hottest items to steal, how they fenced merchandise they didn't want or couldn't use.

No way, he told himself. That would go over like a lead balloon.

So, Dan thumbed through the telephone book and punched the buttons on his phone with an angry urgency because he wanted to finish the story as quickly as possible.

"Kmart West," a female voice said. "Can I help you?"

"Yeah," he said, as if he were the one being interrupted. "I'm Dan Goldberg at *The Argus*. I'm doing a story about shoplifting. Can I talk to the manager?"

"Just a minute, sir," she said.

Dan heard the phone drop rather than be put on hold. He listened to muffled voices in the background as he waited for the manager. He knew his approach would have to be routine. No one would give him the names of shoplifters, and the criminals wouldn't talk to him anyway. What was in it for them? Only publicity for being a five-finger discount artist. Not something to build fame and fortune around.

"Jeff Barnes," a man said. "Can I help you?"

"Yeah, I'm Dan Goldberg at *The Argus*," he said again. "I'm doing a story about shoplifting ..."

And that's the way Dan's day had gone all afternoon. He hated introducing himself a million times and chatting with people who five minutes later wouldn't remember if they'd talked to Dan Gimble or Don Goldberg or Dave Gibson. That wasn't the way to fame and glory.

At home watching the movie, Dan laughed as Joel pleaded with "Guido, The Killer Pimp" on the screen. He figured Mike was out chasing the police sirens he heard outside for another story that would wind up on the front page.

Dan turned his attention to Guido, who chuckled from the back of a moving van as he tossed a glass egg into the air. Joel, played by Tom Cruise, frantically dove across his parents' furniture to catch it.

A former boss once told Dan routine assignments presented opportunity, that it was up to the reporter to recognize that.

"Bullshit," he said aloud, reaching for the pack of cigarettes on the end table. He lit a cigarette as Joel's dad learned that his son had been accepted to Princeton. "Every once in a while you've just got to say, 'What the heck?' and take some chances," the old man said.

There had to be an angle, Dan thought, blowing a cloud of smoke toward the television. A different way to look at this damn job. You couldn't go around wearing a catcher's mask your whole life. You didn't get anywhere unless you were willing to take a few risks.

"Twenty dollars, Lana?" Tom Cruise asked Rebecca De Mornay. "What are we going to do about that?"

"Can I send it to you? I don't have that much on me," she said. "How about if I write a check?"

"You think I'd accept a check from you?" Tom Cruise replied. "Am I stupid?"

As Tom Cruise and Rebecca De Mornay walked into the Chicago skyline she whispered, "I've got a bond at the bank ..."

Dan laughed. "What the hell?" he said aloud. "Sometimes you've just got to say, what the hell?"

4

Mike Rockwell felt the police car shudder as the engine turned over. He tried to adjust his eyes to the darkness. He couldn't tell if the gun was still pointed in his direction, but he knew the barrel had seemed as big as a cannon. It had all happened so fast.

Mike backed into the corner of the front seat, against the door, as the car began to move. He could make out a stocking cap. Glasses. A beard. Who was this guy? Not a cop. Morgan? A murderer? Had he killed Collins? Had he killed a cop?

"Hey, I'm not a cop," Mike shouted. He held up his hands as if to surrender. "I'm not a cop!"

"Shut up and get down on the floor."

"What?"

"On the floor and shut up!"

Mike tucked his knees into his stomach, curled his feet up to his buttocks, slid onto the floor, the back of his head banging into the two-way radio. As he faced away from the driver, he smelled the heat from the blower and, on his back, felt the vibrations of the moving car as it bounced along uneven pavement. All he could see was his legs and the inside of the passenger footwell. He closed his eyes. Was the gun still pointed at his head? He expected it to go off at any moment.

Mike's ears filled with the sound of the transmission working below as the car jostled him inside his captive cocoon. This was not life; it was death. Unrelated visions flashed through his mind, and he couldn't grasp any of them. Linda in a red dress walking where the air smelled clean and fresh. A juicy steak melting in his mouth. Falling into an aqua swimming pool with the black lines along the bottom slithering like water snakes. The sting of chlorine in his nose. The stench of sweaty gym socks as locker doors slammed shut. Computer printers clacking. A story to write. Deadline.

The wailing siren wasn't going away. Mike realized it belonged to the car that held him hostage, the car that leaned to one side, bouncing his head against the hard metal radio box, grinding his chin into his collarbone.

"Ouch," Mike yelled.

"Shut up!"

Mike tried to remember what he'd seen of his abductor as the car swerved erratically again, slamming his head against the underside of the dash. Not much. Long blond hair curled over the ears. A stubble of a beard. Dark eyes behind wire-rimmed glasses. The gun. The gun. The gun.

The horn honked as the car took another abrupt turn. Tires screeched. Mike pulled his head back toward the seat to look through the passenger side window. The blackened windows of tall buildings and the flashes of bright streetlights raced past in a rhythm like the yellow dashes on a highway. Thoughts of dying in a traffic accident replaced those of being blown away by a gun. How fast were they going?

For a moment Mike considered kicking the door open, leaping to safety. Could he get the leverage? At sixty miles an hour? Seventy? Crazy. He envisioned the pain as his body bounced along the pavement. His chance of survival was better riding it out.

Mike closed his eyes again and prayed for the car to stop. It did, abruptly. How strange, he thought, to wish for something to happen and it does. He'd wanted to participate in a drug bust and now that he was in the middle of one, he wanted out. No such luck.

Before Mike could react, a hand grabbed the back of his collar and pulled him onto the seat.

"Up!" his abductor shouted. "Now!"

Mike tried to push with his legs, but they were useless as he was dragged across the seat and around the steering wheel, then tossed onto a rough blacktop surface landing on his hands and knees. The blacktop, the yellow lines, the smell of oil identified his place of rest as a parking lot, but he had no idea where. Lifting his head, a blue car door swung at his face, so he ducked as it flew above his head. He was yanked up again and tossed into the front seat of another car with such force that his face crashed against the steering wheel. The door slammed shut behind him, then another car door opened, and the car bounced on its springs twice before the second door thumped shut and the dome light went out.

"Sit up and drive," his captor's voice barked from the back seat. "The gun's pointed at your back. Don't try anything or I'll shoot."

Mike quickly gathered himself, slid his legs beneath the steering wheel, sat up. The key was in the ignition, so he turned it and the engine started on the first try. He flipped on the headlights, pulled the column shift lever to "D" and drove from the parking lot.

"Get on the interstate and go south," the voice behind his head said. "Stay five miles over the speed limit. No more, no less."

Mike oriented himself, drove west on Second Avenue, left on First Street and through a green stoplight to the on-ramp heading south. He accelerated to sixty miles per hour and eased the car into the middle lane. He was driving a blue Chevrolet Impala, a 1972 or 1973. But to where?

Mike's right cheek and his palms burned from scrapes on the blacktop. He constantly scanned the rearview mirror, trying to catch a glimpse of the man in the back seat, praying for a cop car to appear. He tried turning his head slightly to the side, but he didn't want any movement to seem obvious. He couldn't forget about the gun. This guy knew what he was doing. By slouching low in the back seat, he gave other motorists the impression that Mike was driving alone.

The AM radio played country-western music, a tune Mike didn't recognize. He hated it. Without thinking, he changed the station and John Cougar Mellencamp's "R.O.C.K. in the USA" came on, but Mike didn't feel like dancing. Immediately, he feared his captor would object to the song and shoot him in the back over rock and roll. As he leaned back in the seat, his cold, sweat-soaked shirt sending a chill up his back, he hadn't realized how much he'd perspired. And nothing happened, so he drove on beyond the city limits.

The lights above the interstate glowed an alien orange, different than the white lights of the city. Mike kept the Chevy at a steady seventy, five miles an hour over the speed limit. No other cars passed him, and he didn't pass anyone. He was out here alone, a gunman in the back seat. Who was he? Mike thought again. It had to be Morgan. How deranged was he? Was he high on cocaine? Would he pull the trigger?

"Take the airport road exit," the voice behind him said. "But we're not going there. Drive past it."

Mike nodded, as if his reaction meant anything. "Danger Zone" by Kenny Loggins came on the radio and he raised his eyes at the irony. But his head did begin to clear. All of this had been planned, he thought. It didn't make sense, otherwise. A mysterious man popping out of nowhere abducting a reporter in a cop car, a non-descript car waiting for them in a dark parking lot, specific directions to drive, a gun that might not even be loaded.

The gears in Mike's head spun out of control with the beat of the music, and then he grinned. This was a joke, he thought, a prank pulled on him by Lieutenant Sanders and the Cedar City Police Department. Sanders had schemed the whole thing to give him a scare, to make him think that he'd been kidnapped at gunpoint, that he'd have an unbelievable adventure to write about when, in reality, the cops would be waiting wherever he ended up, and they'd jump out of the bushes and yell, "Gotcha!"

All night Mike hadn't seen anyone but cops, the undercover cops, the uniforms, Sanders, all people who had been at the briefing. Nobody else. The house they'd targeted was dark, probably vacant. The gunshots were within earshot, but Mike had not personally witnessed anyone wielding a gun except Sanders. He'd looked so concerned grabbing his shotgun from the car, making sure Mike knew it was the first time he'd ever done that. It had to be a setup. Mike wanted to laugh.

"So, you a cop?" Mike said.

"Hell, no!" the back-seat voice yelled. "You're the cop. Just shut up and drive."

Mike had to rethink the situation. It was real. Sanders didn't know him well enough to try something like this. He talked about Morgan so often he couldn't have made him up. Was that Morgan in the back seat? If so, he was dangerous. But why not ask him? Just come out and say, "Are you Ronald Morgan?" That would solve it. It also might get him shot.

Mike searched the darkened horizon, the rear-view mirror, for flashing red lights. As he turned off the interstate, all he saw was the airport beacon sweeping low across the sky. At least he felt comfortable driving. He had a role and that made his life necessary. But where were the cops? Didn't someone report a stolen patrol car? Where in the hell were they?

The airport was illuminated like a miniature city. Cars turned from the entrance and came Mike's way. He considered veering into the wrong lane, scaring one of the drivers into reporting an erratic motorist. But there was no way he'd be rescued in the fraction of a second it would take a bullet to leave the gun, to slice through the seat and lodge in his heart. It was a stupid idea. He kept driving, straight and sixty miles per hour, precisely five over the speed limit.

West of the airport, the countryside darkened again. The blacktop turned to a rough pebble-grain surface causing the tires to hum. Mike felt a tug on the seat behind his back, a puff of warm air against the hair on his neck.

"Pull over at the next driveway," the voice blew in his ear.

The first driveway came up immediately and Mike missed it. He slowed the car and for the next quarter mile kept his eyes on the road until the next driveway appeared. He turned right onto the gravel, following it to a darkened, run-down farmhouse where a single light on a pole cast a circle of light about the yard. As the car rolled to a stop, Mike realized his ride was over.

Mike knew cops never bothered with places like this. He recalled grabbing a case of beer with a few buddies in his senior year of high school and drinking it at an abandoned farmhouse safe from detection. Only they always picked a farmhouse on a seldom traveled gravel road, and there'd never been a spotlight for security.

"Out," the voice shouted.

Mike opened the car door and stepped onto the crunchy gravel. A breeze from the northwest slipped beneath his collar. He shivered as a car door slammed behind him. He never prayed much, but he prayed now that another car would come along. As he turned to face his abductor, he was shoved to the ground, face first. For the second time that night, he landed on his hands, this time the gravel cutting deeper where the blacktop had already opened wounds.

"Cut it out," Mike yelled, a natural reaction. He was tired of being pushed around.

The gun exploded in Mike's ear and pain instantly shot through his left ankle. He reached for his leg and felt blood trickle through his fingers. He became light-headed when he thought about what had happened, that he'd been shot. He bit his lip hard, hoping to stay conscious, but the pain was too intense. He passed out.

* * * * *

Red and green and blue starbursts exploded in the sky like fireworks as if Mike's eyes were still closed. But the horizon glowed with the distant lights of the Cedar City airport, and he smelled the aromas of damp hay and fresh manure. He sat crumpled on the gravel, holding his ankle, his hands sticky with blood as it seeped through his sock and filled his shoe. Tears on his cheeks felt warm against the cold breeze of the October night. What kind of a wimp am I? he thought. I get shot and pass out. I'm alone at some farmhouse where God only knows. Could you see this picture in the morning *Argus?*

Mike stared away from the lights into the darkness and realized the blue Chevy was gone. He felt very small, insignificant, in a big world with a black sky filled with stars. The beam of the spotlight on the barn surrounded him, but the old family farmhouse remained dark and quiet, shuttered and left vacant to rot away while a cooperation bled the land.

Mike forced himself to stand, but his palms ached as he pressed them onto the biting gravel. His ankle hurt like hell when he tried to stand. Still, he had to move. He couldn't wait here forever to be rescued. So he pulled his pant leg tightly around his calf and twisted the excess material with his thumb and index finger to fashion a sling, a pant-leg handle to keep his injured foot off the ground.

An icy sweat broke out on Mike's forehead as he hopped down the gravel toward the road. He wished for a stocking cap to keep his head warm, yet he unzipped his jacket to let heat escape from his body. The pain in his ankle would not go away no matter how much he occupied his mind with other thoughts.

He wanted a hot shower. He wanted Linda in his arms and a back rub. He wanted to be angry at the man who shot him, who left him in the farmyard, but he knew it could have been worse. If the police radio had been right, if a cop had been shot, what was the difference if a criminal shot one man or two? If the voice in the back seat belonged to Morgan and if he killed a cop during the drug bust, why didn't he kill Mike, too? If he was never caught, what difference would it make? If he was caught, big deal. He'd be in prison for life, anyway.

Mike leaned against a mailbox to catch his breath and knew he could be dead. His right leg ached from hopping. Even as he rested the toes of his left foot on the ground, pain shot through his ankle and calf. He wondered if the bullet was still in his ankle, if it would fester up with infection and gangrene and require amputation. Would he have a plastic foot? A wooden leg? Nothing be a stub?

"Help me!" Mike yelled into the darkness as loud as he could. "Help me!"

Then, after he realized how fruitless his shouts sounded, the image of walking into a shoe store crossed his mind and he laughed. He'd only have to buy right shoes from now on. What would happened to the left ones? At least he wasn't dead.

Deadline. Mike had a story to write. He had to find a telephone, to call the newsroom. He pushed a button on his digital watch to illuminate its face. 9:43. Still two hours.

Why wasn't anybody driving along this road? Why wasn't somebody looking for him? Surely, someone in the newsroom heard the scanner traffic and called the police station to find out what happened. Who was putting a story together? Dan? Would they have called Dan in?

Dammit. This was his story. He needed to talk to the cops, to find out what went wrong. He needed to reach Sanders. He needed to get back to the office.

Mike looked at the black sky again, the stars he used to wish upon as a kid and wondered where the hell the city's police helicopter had been. The copper chopper always seemed to be shattering the silent nights when he couldn't sleep, always hovering in a circle above his house keeping him awake with the fear that he was missing a story. The chopper cost the city, the taxpayers, hundreds of thousands of dollars to fly and maintain, but assistant chief Schmidt insisted it was worth every cent if it saved just one life.

"So, chief," Mike shouted, "where's your precious chopper now?"

Mike took a deep breath. First things first. Anger wouldn't get him home. If he could find another farmhouse, one that was occupied, he could make a telephone call or hitch a ride somewhere. God forbid, that he'd have to hobble all the way to the airport.

He hopped along the road, stopped to catch his breath, hopped some more, as he put the story together in his mind. He'd call Jackson. A first-person story was out for now, but it could be a powerful follow-up. If he'd had his tape recorder, he could organize his thoughts, but it was on the corner of his desk at *The Argus*.

The left leg grew heavy. Bent over, holding it up as he hopped on his right foot, Mike remembered playing hopscotch as a kid. He laughed and thought it was the first time he smiled since leaving the police station. Then he remembered talking to Lieutenant Sanders about drugs in college and how he laughed aloud a moment ago about buying one shoe. Was he becoming delirious? Would he bleed to death?

When Mike was seven or eight, he wasn't sure, he thought he'd die after falling off a teeter-totter. He had blacked out and when he awoke, tingles snaked through his body into his fingertips. His vision had blurred, and he saw little gold stars exploding in darkness as the faces of classmates stared down at him. He heard one of them ask, "Is he dead?" and another reply, "No, he's moving." After he'd caught his breath, Mike stood up, only to have Johnny Applegate in a red plaid shirt that reminded him of blood taunt him for being a klutz. Mike had to wear a cast on his broken arm for only six weeks, but that ugly sneer on Johnny Applegate's face would stay with him for the rest of his life.

When a pair of headlights appeared on the road, Mike wondered if he was hallucinating. He stared at them as they drew closer and his heart beat faster as his mind oscillated between good and bad, between savior to the rescue and abductor returning to finish the job. Think good thoughts, he told himself, because he needed help.

Mike waved his right arm in the air as the headlights swerved to the shoulder of the road and stopped a few feet away. A bear of a man wearing a gray coveralls uniform emerged from the driver's side and broke the beams of the headlights, casting a monstrous shadow over Mike.

"Hey, man, you all right?" the bear asked.

"I'm fine," Mike said.

"Yeah, you look fine."

The man, a good head taller than Mike and twice his weight, clamped the reporter in a bear hug and guided him to the passenger side of a pickup truck. "What happened, you get hit by a car?"

"No. Shot in the leg."

"Shot? No shit?"

Mike knew immediately that his confession had been a mistake. Now he'd have to explain it all. He was too tired for that. "Just get me to a telephone," he said. "I've got to make a call."

"You need a hospital." The man dropped Mike into the wide bench seat of the pickup. "I'll take you."

"A phone, damn it. That's what I need first. A phone."

"Yes, sir."

In the face of his pain, Mike was surprised at the strength of his convictions. He closed his eyes as the rescuer turned the truck around and sprayed gravel until the tires hit the pavement and squealed with urgency. Mike was relieved to finally sit down, but his left leg felt as if it was asleep, as if it didn't have any blood. Suddenly he became nauseous.

"Can you slow down?" Mike said. "We're not going to a fire."

The pickup pilot eased up. "I work at the Shell station up the road," he said. "Just closed up for the night, but there's a drive-up pay phone outside."

Mike mumbled acknowledgement. Warm air from the air vents bathed his face in welcome heat. The motion of the truck as it floated along the pavement began to rock him to sleep.

"I know it ain't none of my business, but since I'm helping you out, I was just wondering," the man said. "What happened?"

"Please," Mike said, his eyes closed. "I'd rather not explain it twice. Listen to my phone call."

Mike didn't see the man nod. He didn't see or hear anything until the truck pulled onto the station's concrete apron and the bright overhead lights burned through his eyelids. When he opened his eyes, the lights were hazy. His mind wasn't functioning properly, and he knew it. But he could make out "Phone from your car," on a blue and white illuminated sign as the truck swung around so the drive-up pay telephone was on his side. He pulled himself erect in the truck's seat and cranked the window down.

Rather than dig in a pocket for change, Mike punched the buttons for the newspaper's toll-free number. The phone rang five times before a voice said, "*Argus* newsroom."

Mike recognized the voice of Mark Peters, assistant city desk editor. "Peters," he said. "This is Rockwell."

"Rockwell. Where are you?"

"Never mind that."

"We've been worried. We heard about the shooting on the scanner and how somebody took you for a ride in a cop car."

"Don't talk," Mike said, "just listen." He took a deep breath. "I'm at a pay phone along the airport road. I can't think straight enough to dictate a complete story, but I'll give you what I've got. The facts. You should be able to make something by deadline. I've been shot."

"Shot?" Peters sounded genuinely concerned.

"No," Mike said, "scratch that." He rubbed his temples. "I mean, yes. It wasn't at the house, and it's nothing. Just my leg." Mike felt like he'd pass out at any moment. "I've lost a ton of blood. I'm so tired. I've got to get to a hospital."

"You call an ambulance?"

"I'm getting a lift from this guy who works at the service station."

"Gary Thomas," the driver said, pointing to the embroidered name above his breast pocket. "My name's Gary Thomas."

Mike looked across the dimly lit interior of the truck. Obviously, Gary Thomas had finally realized he'd rescued an *Argus* reporter. He wanted his fifteen minutes of fame.

"Peters, I'll be all right," Mike said. "This guy, Gary Thomas, common spelling?" The man nodded. "He works at the Shell station and he picked me up. Put that in, okay? Here's what else I've got."

Mike reached into his jacket pocket for his notebook. It wasn't there.

"Oh, God," he said. "I've lost my notebook."

"You lost your notebook?"

"Yes, damn it! I lost it."

Mike felt around on the seat to see if it had fallen out of his pocket in the truck. No luck. He reached down on the floor and asked Gary to help. It could be anywhere. He was angry at himself. A reporter never loses his notebook. It was his life. But he didn't have the energy for all-out panic.

"I'll find it somewhere," he said into the phone. "Let me tell you what I remember."

"Okay, shoot," Peters said.

Mike didn't catch the pun, intended or not, until much later, after he'd spent ten minutes relaying the information to Peters as Gary Thomas sat quietly behind the wheel listening to every word.

"So, that's all I've got," Mike said. "My buddy here, Mr. Thomas, will drive me to Mercy. Do a good job."

"Good luck," Peters said. "We want you back alive"

After Mike hung up the phone, his eyes closed, Gary Thomas drove away from the lights of the service station. Mike curled up in the warmth of the cab, as safe as a cub in momma bear's arms. Peters hadn't said anything about calling in Dan Goldberg. What a relief. He'd be so jealous once the story hit print. As he fell asleep, Mike Rockwell chuckled to himself. "Eat your heart out, Danny boy."

5

Dan Goldberg sipped coffee from a Styrofoam cup as he sat on the corner of Mike Rockwell's hospital bed, Mike's head propped up on a pair of pillows, his arms crossed over his chest, his left leg wrapped in bandages with an ice pack protruding from the sheets.

"Some people have all the luck," Dan said.

"You call getting shot in the leg, luck?" Mike replied.

"You lived to tell about it."

The cop reporters laughed – Dan strong and almost sinister, Mike cautious and feeble.

Mike knew he'd been lucky. The bullet had pierced his tibia, not the delicate tarsal bones of his ankle. He'd been shot in the leg, not the ankle, so if he stayed off his feet and allowed it to heal properly, he'd be good as new in a few weeks. What he'd interpreted as intense bleeding the night before had been pure exaggeration, mind over matter, under stress.

Since awakening in the hospital sometime after sunrise, Mike realized how close he had come to death. In the darkness of sleep, his mind had played tricks on him, one bad dream after another. More than once he summoned a nurse with the handy call button.

In one nightmare, Mike was diving off a cliff, his arms spread to guide flight as he had done in childhood dreams, only this time he didn't fly. He fell helplessly to his death. In another, a police car raced at him and he was unable to move his legs to jump out of the way. But in the worst dream, the one he remembered most vividly, he stood alone in a vast grassy field while flames from the barrel of a gun flashed at his head. The gun was suspended in midair. No one pulled the trigger yet bullets, fired deliberately one at a time, tore his flesh apart. He didn't try to stop them. He couldn't. It didn't matter. After each shot, a voice called out his name. He didn't feel a thing.

Mike considered telling Dan about his nightmares. He didn't understand why the last one hadn't awakened him with the first shot, why he had stood there and took it, bullet after bullet. Maybe Dan had a clue. But Mike decided he had to figure this one out himself before mentioning it to anybody, especially Dan.

Early in their working relationship Mike had learned that Dan possessed little compassion. Once, Mike explained his dilemma with Linda, her reluctance to discuss marriage, and Dan's reply was that no woman was worth that much trouble no matter how good she was in bed. Mike said their relationship was more than sex, but Dan laughed it off as if that wasn't plausible.

The nightmares bothered Mike because he rarely remembered any dreams, good or bad. Then he recalled another one, where he'd been chased by a huge brown dog with drooling chops. Maybe he'd tell Linda about that one, about all of his nightmares, when she came to visit.

Mike didn't believe in broken mirrors or black cats or walking beneath ladders, but he was certain that dreams could foretell the future. That's why the nightmare of being shot so many times terrified him. What if his abductor was Ronald Morgan? What if Morgan decided to get rid of him? What if he simply stood there and took the bullets one by one?

When Mike had awakened with a dry throat and perspiration on his forehead, he tried to picture the face in the patrol car. He couldn't. As in the dream, there was no face, no details. All he had seen was a stocking cap, glasses, a bearded chin, dirty blond hair over the ears. It could have been a thousand guys.

"You'll be getting out in a day or two," Dan said, "if you behave yourself."

Mike stared at Dan Goldberg's tightly drawn mouth and the dark stubble surrounding the cleft in his chin. He watched Dan's lips move but didn't hear what he said. He was thinking how Dan could grow a beard in a week while it would take him a month.

"Earth to Rockwell," Dan said, leaning forward. "I said you'll be out of this place in no time."

"Yeah," Mike said. His leg ached with a phantom pain thanks to medication. "I lost more blood than was good for me. The doctor said I should have come to the hospital before I called in the story."

"Byline before lifeline," Dan said. He clenched a fist and raised it in the air. "That should be a cop reporter's creed. I'd have done the same."

Mike recalled how Jennifer Drake had made similar sarcastic motions with her fist, but Dan's intent seemed more personal, as had his comment about luck. Mike reasoned it was Dan's way of elevating his self-esteem, so he played along.

"You'd have jumped the guy and got yourself killed in the line of duty," Mike said.

"Now that would be a hell of a story," Dan said. "The only negative I can see is that I wouldn't be alive to collect another page one byline."

Mike laughed. Dan was as jealous as a monkey with an armload of bananas and no thumbs to peel them. Mike said, "You'd probably come back from the grave to haunt whoever did write the story."

"You've got that right," Dan said.

"So, when's Collins' funeral?" Mike asked. He'd read the snippet in the morning paper and watched the early television reports, but details were sketchy. The undercover officer had been shot and killed at the house, but the cops weren't about to release much else with the shooter still on the loose.

"Don't know," Dan said. "I heard he got it in the chest. One bullet right through the heart." He pounded his chest. "Boom."

"Go to hell," Mike said.

"Hey, man, what's your beef?"

"For Christ's sake, have some empathy. A cop was killed."

"Were the cops there when you got shot?"

"They were busy."

"I'm sure that's what you'd say six feet under." Dan shrugged his shoulders. "If a cop's got to die, what better way is there than in the line of duty? You get killed on the job, you're immortalized. For some cops, that's their dream."

"Or nightmare," Mike said. "Think about their families. Are you going to immortalize him in print or kill him again?"

"I didn't want the guy dead. He was just trying to earn his pay, even if he was doing a lousy job of it."

"Lousy? What makes you say that?"

"He got shot by a two-bit drug dealer."

"A two-bit drug dealer with a gun who's always liable to go off half-cocked. You ever deal with somebody like that?"

"Nah."

"Were you there when it went down?"

"Nah."

"Then what's your point?" Mike said. "Be a journalist and keep your opinions to yourself. Wait for the official report and write a fair story."

"All I'm saying is that Collins made a critical mistake and it cost him his life. A good cop wouldn't do that. And now he'll be deified."

"He was making an undercover drug buy," Mike said, thinking about Lieutenant Sanders and his son, Eric. "He was doing his part to make sure a pile of coke didn't get delivered to a bunch of kids who might die from over-doses because they don't know how to handle it. It's happening all around the country. He was one cop who thought he could make a difference."

Mike hesitated and glanced away, speaking as if to no one but himself. "You wonder why any cop puts his life on the line for something so big when, in the scheme of things, he's only one guy."

"You're getting way too philosophical here," Dan said. He removed a pen from behind his ear and opened his reporter's notebook. "Mind if I quote you?"

"My story, my quotes," Mike said. "You just talk to the cops and leave me out of it as much as you can."

"Right," Dan replied, "but maybe I can get a cop to say what you did, even if they all know one dead cop in Cedar City isn't going to put a dent in international drug traf-ficking." He hesitated for a moment. "You know Collins was going by the name of Mills."

"Yes. They wanted me to give him that alias in the story. They said they'd be using him undercover again."

"Not in this lifetime," Dan said. "No more drug busts for him, unless he's an undercover angel."

"You really are a cold bastard." Heat rose to Mike's temples. He was disgusted with Dan's relentless put-downs, his attitude that the only reason anything happened at all was so a reporter could write about it and, if the story was any good, earn a page one byline. "You really don't give a damn that a cop died. You don't."

"I never said that. You've got to expect it. Some guys would rather kill a cop than spend a night in jail. That's reality."

"You learn that in Chicago?"

"Yep. Chicago. A murder a day. Maybe two."

Mike shook his head. Friends, he thought. What kind of a friend gloats over the death of a cop trying to do his job? What kind of a friend sees that as a steppingstone to his own glory?

But, as Mike stared at Dan, he realized his co-reporter was simply trying to do his job in his way. Sometimes reporters needed to play the devil's advocate. Big cities could make you cold. You couldn't worry about everyone, couldn't let little things like friendship and trust interfere. Some jobs are easier to do if you don't have a heart. Get involved and what happens? You lose objectivity. Stay out of people's minds, out of their motives. People don't turn into criminals or become cops so some newspaper reporter can write about them. They do what they want. That's the way they are.

Mike wished he could believe all that, maybe even learn to live that way on occasion. He wanted to be tougher. He wanted to be friends with people but being nice could get in the way of objective news. When it came to crime stories, you had to put your job first and worry about making friends, or enemies, later. If you didn't, you'd screw yourself out of a good story, maybe even out of your job.

"Did they catch the guy who shot Collins?" Mike asked.

"Not yet. They figure it was the same guy who shot you. The other two guys in the house weren't even armed. They only found one gun, beneath the underwear in a dresser drawer back in the bedroom. It hadn't been fired recently, but they're checking it for prints."

"The same guy?" Emptiness echoed in Mike's voice as he shifted his gaze toward the puke green hospital wall. It was as much a question as a statement. He'd assumed all along that the same guy shot him, but he didn't want to think about it that way. A cop killer. The worst kind. Once he killed a cop, he'd kill anybody. What was to stop him from finding Mike and gunning him down, especially if he thought Mike could identity him?

"What's the matter, Mikey?" Dan chided. "You don't look so hot."

"Any leads?"

"Not that Margaret said. She called me at home and gave me details, said Collins was killed and you were shot. She told me I should get on it right away. I haven't been to the cop shop yet. I thought I'd talk to you first." He put his pen to paper. "What do you remember?"

"I told you, put your damn pen away," Mike ordered. His voice was firm. His stare would have burned a hole through Dan's head if that were possible. "I'm writing that story. It's mine."

"A follow-up is between you and Margaret." Dan remained calm. "But I've been assigned the story for tomorrow. She told me to find out what I could from you, the eyewitness report." He grinned. "You know it's hard enough finding witnesses who will go on the record. I figured this is one story where we've got that in our hip pocket. A reporter who'll tell us everything he knows and keep quiet to all the other media."

"You think so?" Mike said. As he sat up, the phantom pain returned to his leg. "Your story is about the cop getting shot during a drug bust. Me getting abducted, that's my story. No one's writing that but me. If Margaret doesn't want to wait for it, you tell her I'll have the story for her tomorrow. Bring me a portable Radio Shack computer, and I'll do it right now."

Dan laughed. "I was just pulling your leg. Margaret said you'd want to write your own story." He reached down by his feet and hoisted a small black case onto Mike's bed. "Use my Radio Shack. I'll pick up another one at the office."

Mike unzipped the case to reveal the beige portable computer, about the size of one volume of an encyclopedia, with its tiny five-line green screen and cramped keyboard. Mike knew his story wasn't going to stop the presses, but he wanted to write it as best he could.

Secretly, Mike felt he'd fallen into any reporter's fantasy, to be the victim of a violent crime and live to write about it. A once-in-a-lifetime opportunity. But, as soon as those thoughts entered his mind, Mike realized he was no better than Dan.

Well, for once, Mike didn't care. It was true. He'd write one hell of a story, and Dan would be green with envy. He already was. It was as simple as that.

"Thanks for the computer," Mike said. "Sometimes I don't get you. You can be such a pain in the ass and sometimes ..."

"Sometimes I can be a real sweetie," Dan patted Mike on the thigh of his injured leg.

"Ouch," Mike uttered. "Yeah, just the word I would have used."

"Good thing we aren't lovers," Dan teased, smiling and squeezing Mike's thigh. "We'd be at each other's throats all the time."

"Get out of here, you jerk," Mike said.

Dan laughed like a hyena in heat.

"Just get out of here." Mike swatted Dan's hand away.

Homosexuality didn't bother Mike, at least he didn't think so, but Dan's penchant for touching did. When they'd first met, Dan always seemed to make a point by touching Mike's forearm or patting his shoulder, as if that would prompt him to pay attention.

When Mike had related a personal story about walking into a gay bar by accident on a weekend in Chicago, Dan said he'd written a piece about that very place. Then he'd proceeded to defend gay rights as if he were upholding the American Constitution in Hitler's Germany. Even so, Mike figured that Dan wasn't gay, that he was being his controversial self and that he simply enjoyed touching people like Mike to watch them squirm.

"Leave me alone," Mike said, "so I can write my story. So I can win the Pulitzer."

"Whoopee," Dan replied. "And I get to write my shoplifting story. It'll win the Golden Putz."

Mike laughed. "You're just jealous."

"Jealous of a guy who couldn't get out of the way of a stray bullet? I don't think so. I can walk out of here. You can't."

Mike watched Dan stroll from the room as he booted up the computer, then shouted after him, "Hey! Anybody find my notebook?"

Dan stuck his head back through the doorway. "Your reporter's notebook? You lost your notebook?"

"Last time I saw it was in Sanders' patrol car. I thought maybe one of the cops turned it in when they recovered the car."

"Margaret didn't say anything about it to me, but I'll ask." Dan raised an index finger. "But that's sin number one. You can go to Reporter Hell for losing your notebook."

"Knock it off. You're not my boss."

"I'm not your mother either, but I'll check around," Dan said as he disappeared into the hallway. "So long, loser."

Mike couldn't say where he'd last seen his notebook, but he'd hoped it had slipped out of his grasp in Sanders' squad car.

If it wasn't there, where did it end up?

He didn't remember if it had been in his pocket when he climbed into the Chevy. It wasn't in the pickup because they'd looked.

Mike knew he could easily duplicate Sanders' quotes with a telephone call, but reconstructing the precise timeline would be difficult without the notebook. He knew most of the details, but not all of them.

What concerned Mike as much as anything about losing his notebook was that his name and telephone number were on the cover. If it fell into the wrong hands, Morgan's hands, he'd know that Mike worked for *The Argus*, that he had abducted a reporter. Morgan might wrongly assume that he could be identified.

If he shot me once, Mike thought, he could shoot me again.

"Please be in Sanders' car," he whispered. "Please, please, please."

Mike remembered his nightmares. Morgan was a faceless stranger. He shot me once, Mike thought, so what's to stop him from shooting me again? As sure as there's motive for revenge, there's the possibility of death.

"My God," Mike said aloud in his empty hospital room. "My God!"

6

"Goldberg, you can really be an asshole," Assistant Chief Charles Schmidt said. "Sometimes, a real professional asshole."

"Funny, chief," Dan said. "A friend just told me the same thing."

"I didn't think you had any friends." Schmidt laughed.

Dan sat in a straight-back chair in front of the large wooden desk occupied by the assistant chief of police in charge of detectives in Cedar City. He crossed and recrossed his legs while pressing his tongue firmly against the side of his mouth and biting down so he wouldn't say something he'd later regret. While far from wary of confrontation, he simply wasn't in the mood to fuel the fire he'd already started.

Schmidt often didn't make himself readily available to Dan, but he'd made an exception as the result of his officer's death and Mike Rockwell's abduction. He'd told Dan as much on the phone, saying he wanted to clear everything up as quickly as possible.

Schmidt sat at the desk, as usual, looking like a lost boxer dog wearing a dark blue suit and a burgundy tie decorated with gold squares. His lower chops were covered with a dense stubble as if he hadn't shaved in a few days. His dark eyes were set deep into their sockets, his forehead tanned and sloped back to a receding hairline.

What a cliché, Dan thought, that so many cops looked like dogs. It was that way in Chicago. Once he'd described a detective with droopy eyes as a bloodhound on the hot trail of a criminal, and the next week the detective threw him out of his office before Dan could explain he was just practicing good journalism.

Schmidt had come up through the ranks in Cedar City – rookie cop, traffic cop, uniformed cop on the night beat, day cop, detective, desk sergeant, assistant chief. Like every cop with an ego, he aspired to become chief. At fifty-one, his time was running short. He had maybe one more shot, when Chief Hughes retired in another four or five years. If not, then he'd take early retirement, collect his pension and, if he needed the cash, become a part-time security guard.

Schmidt had been elevated to assistant chief after Mayor Stan Rankin appointed his friend and former partner, Conrad Hughes, as chief. Everyone inside the department joked about Schmidt's promotion as being a "con" job, and many of them meant it. Even though the appointment occurred four years ago, the joke was still brought up among the rank and file often enough that Dan, as a newcomer, had heard the story more than once.

Reporters laughed at Schmidt behind his back. He certainly wasn't one of Cedar City's finest. But nobody laughed in his face. No matter how incompetent he seemed, he was the main source of cop shop information in the detective bureau and that had to be respected.

"Sometimes you reporters make me wish I didn't have to be such a sweet guy," Schmidt said, leaning forward and aiming a pen at Goldberg as if it were the barrel of a gun. "Sometimes I'd like to eliminate all of you journalists."

"That a threat?" Goldberg said. "Why don't you put your little pop gun away?"

The pen made a dull thud on the blotter calendar as Schmidt tossed it on his desk. "Not at all," he laughed. "Just wishing out loud that I didn't have to waste so much time writing stories for the media." His blotter was covered with swirls and doodles, the work of an idle mind as he chatted with reporters during frequent phone calls.

This semi-rare, in-person discussion had begun when Dan asked how Collins could have let himself get killed in a simple drug bust. It wasn't so much the question that rankled Assistant Chief Schmidt, it was the tone Dan had used, implying that Collins was set up or that he was an incompetent cop, or both. Schmidt knew enough about psychology to realize reporters wouldn't cross him if they wanted information. He also knew most of them were ego-driven and arrogant. But this new kid from *The Argus*, Dan Goldberg, was often over the top. Schmidt had told him so on more than one occasion.

Schmidt knew it was his obligation to defend Collins, and he'd done so vehemently as Dan criticized the entire undercover detective force. That's when Schmidt couldn't hold himself back any longer and had called Dan an asshole.

"Just ask your questions and get the hell out of here," Schmidt said. "We've got crimes to solve."

"So, when you gonna solve this one?" Dan asked, extending the point of his pen toward Schmidt as he held his hand palm side up. He bounced the pen up and down because he knew the rhythm of the motion, the impatience it implied, irritated Schmidt to no end. It was Dan's way of showing he wouldn't be bullied. "What kind of leads you got on this Morgan guy?"

"We're working on it," Schmidt said.

"Are you sure Morgan's the trigger man?"

"Read the news release. Only one weapon was found on the premises, and it was stashed underneath the underwear in a dresser drawer in the bedroom. Collins got shot in the living room. Morgan escaped after the shooting, took his gun with him. He was the only one who could have done it."

"Are you sure he ran off alone, that somebody else didn't escape with him?" The pen was still bouncing.

"Ask your reporter," Schmidt said. "He was there. You guys are supposed to be so damned observant. If there was more than one person, he should know. Reporters can count, can't you?"

"Yeah," Dan said. He couldn't hold his tongue any longer. "I can also count one less assistant police chief because he can't answer simple questions."

"Don't ask such stupid questions."

"Was it Morgan? That's all I want to know. Was he the shooter?"

"We're ninety-nine percent sure," Schmidt said. "Rockwell's description was pretty sketchy. He said he was forced down on the floor in the squad car, so he didn't get a good look. But, yeah, it's got to be Morgan. He's the guy we were trying to bust. He wasn't in the house when our officers entered. It's the same M.O. he's used before."

"Stealing a cop car?"

"No. Taking a hostage and shooting him in the leg."

"Shooting a hostage in the leg? You never said anything about that in the news release."

"A couple of years ago. In Kansas City," Schmidt said.

"You know who the victim was?" Dan asked. "I'd like to talk to him."

"Hell, no. We just got that information from his rap sheet. Call K.C."

"How dangerous is Morgan, anyhow?"

"He hasn't killed anyone that we know of."

"You mean, until Collins."

"Until Collins."

"So, you've got a description of Morgan, and it matches this guy they're also looking for in Kansas City. So, what's he look like?"

"It's in the release," Schmidt said. He grabbed a copy from his out box. "Can't you read? Six-two, two-twenty, shoulders like a bodybuilder. I don't understand how these asshole criminals get their muscles. They certainly don't spend their spare time working out."

"You might be surprised," Dan said. "When you don't work for a living you've got all the time in the world to hang out at a gym. Besides, you've got to be ready for competition. In their world, only the strong survive."

"And you would know this, how?" Schmidt said

"Forget it," Dan said. "You got any more on him?"

"Blond hair, blue eyes, a tiny scar on his left check that you can't see unless you get close enough to kiss him."

"Is that how you know?"

"I know because it's on the goddamned description I gave you in the press release."

"Right," Dan said. He smiled.

"Are we done? I've got to get on with this investigation."

"I was just wondering," Dan said. "If this guy was so dangerous, why didn't you have more cops on the bust?"

"We had five cops there. What do you want, an army to get one guy?"

"Might not have been such a bad idea," Dan said.

"You do your job, and we'll do ours."

Dan nearly responded that he could perform both jobs with his eyes shut better than Schmidt could do either, but he held his tongue. He had pulled Schmidt's chain enough for now. Like any good reporter, it was time to ask his final question, the one saved for last in case it resulted in ejection from the interview.

"So, one more thing," Dan said, waving his pen in the air for emphasis again. "Why did your Lieutenant Richard Sanders leave our reporter alone in the cop car? Isn't that against police procedure?"

Schmidt scowled. He knew Sanders had been wrong to leave his patrol car from an observation point. There would be a reprimand. But Schmidt knew he would've done the same if he thought a fellow officer had been shot. You protect your own. And Sanders was as much an advocate of that as anyone on the force.

Goldberg waited, his pen pressed onto a page of his notebook.

Schmidt knew that how he answered this question would be important, not only for Sanders, but for himself. He knew what he said would appear in the morning paper, verbatim. He chose his words carefully and spoke slowly.

"Our policy is to come to the aid of officers in trouble, especially in a situation that involves a shooting," he said. "Lieutenant Sanders had two choices. He decided to help the police officer if he could. He had no way of knowing that your reporter would be abducted."

"Don't you, as cops, have a responsibility to protect the public? Aren't reporters citizens?"

"Most definitely, reporters are citizens," Schmidt said. "But they know there's a certain risk when they go out on an assignment, just like a police officer knows that, and the risk is heightened when they're out on assignment with a police officer. That's why Rockwell signed the waiver, that if anything went wrong, it wasn't our liability."

"Reporters don't expect to get shot at," Dan said.

"Don't make me laugh," Schmidt said. "I may not like you, but I know you're not stupid. When you're a cop, you understand there are no rules in the criminal world. Nothing tells thugs like Morgan they can't shoot a reporter who gets in the way."

"So, you're saying, 'Tough shit.'"

"Not at all." Schmidt was so calm he surprised himself. "I'm saying that circumstances beyond our control can happen at any time. No matter how much we anticipate what some lunatic will do, we can never do it with one-hundred percent accuracy."

Schmidt had obviously been prepared, Dan thought, as he watched the assistant chief lean back in his chair, cross his arms over his barrel chest and let the corners of his mouth turn slightly upward.

Dan was not pleased. He skimmed his notes. If the public read that quote, nobody would quarrel with Sanders' actions. In fact, Dan wondered how much sympathy there would be for a reporter shot in the leg when a cop had been killed. No matter how the story might make the police department look incompetent, the public would undoubtedly canonize a police officer shot in the line of duty. Oh, well, it had been worth a shot. He was done with Schmidt, for now. But he would be back.

"That's it," Dan said. "I'm done with my probing questions about the shooting. Now I've got to ask you about shoplifting for a story I'm writing for next week."

"Don't look at me," Schmidt said. "Talk to Billings. He's in charge of statistics."

"I just want to know if it's getting worse."

"Billings has those figures. Your time's up here. I've got more important things to worry about."

Me, too, Dan thought, as he left the assistant chief's office. He also knew the response was typical of Schmidt. He'd make a good politician, talking out of both sides of his mouth at the same time, especially when he didn't know what was going on.

* * * * *

A little red Toyota Corolla buzzed between two lanes of traffic like a hungry mosquito with a juicy human arm in sight. As always, Dan Goldberg, behind the wheel, was in a hurry. It was in his blood as a native Chicagoan. It was in his nose as a police reporter. Hurry, hurry, hurry. He'd never been able to slow down. Occasionally, he'd given it a halfhearted attempt, but as with anything that's done half-ass, it was always in vain.

The Corolla's engine sputtered as Dan depressed the clutch, then pinged as he downshifted and hit the accelerator. He peered through the smoke-tinged windshield as he guided the car into the large parking lot, veered across several rows of yellow lines painted on the blacktop and turned between two rows of parked cars. After the engine quit, he heard the rattle in the passenger door as the silenced Toyota glided into an empty space. He should have had his car tuned before he left Chicago. He knew that was his father's penny-pincher blood in him – the procrastinator who was always in a hurry.

Dan engaged the hand brake and momentarily sat among discarded cigarette wrappers, fast-food bags and empty Pepsi cans in his car. He lit a cigarette and watched a family emerge from a blue Buick across the parking lane. Two little boys slammed the rear doors shut with a maximum amount of effort. Their mother, obviously pregnant beneath her lime green parka, took their hands. Her husband and probably their father hoisted a little girl in a pink jacket onto his shoulders. They walked abreast, taking up the full width of the driving lane. The wind blew the little girl's hood down over her face and her father pulled it up while sidestepping a fast-moving Dodge.

The Target store was always packed in the afternoon. Shoppers read the supplements in *The Argus* and flocked to the store for bargains. It was a perfect day, Dan thought, looking up at the red and white target above the entryway. It seemed a rather prophetic sign. He chuckled to himself.

Despite the coolness of the October day, Dan felt warm. Sunlight streamed through the windshield, heating the interior of the car. He cracked the window open before snubbing his cigarette out in the full ashtray. He unzipped his tan ski jacket and tucked his hand into the inside pouch. Removing a book of matches, he chucked it onto the dash where a pile of papers lay. The pouch had to be empty.

After climbing from the car, Dan slammed the door shut and locked it. He didn't care about the car, he just didn't want anybody ripping off his sunglasses or cassette tapes.

Out of habit, Dan jingled the keys in his hand as he crossed the parking lot. His heart was already pumping harder. Thoughts drifted through his mind. Should he go through with it? Of course. That's why he was here. He didn't need to buy anything.

Inside, the store seemed overpopulated with clerks in red vests. To the right of the front door, behind a red counter, three women with badges pinned to their chests, as if anyone was really interested in their names, handled return merchandise. Customers extracted numbers from a red plastic dispenser shaped like a snail. The sign above the counter showed that number "53" was next.

To the left, larger numbers illuminated in individual square lights on thin steel poles indicated open checkout lanes. Less than half of the numbers were lit as young girls beneath them methodically punched cash register buttons, stapled receipts to the outside of plastic sacks, picked up intercom phones to beckon "gofers" to check prices or bag purchases. Customers lined the junk food counter to buy buttered popcorn, mustard-coated pretzels and diet pop from the fountain.

Dan browsed the record section, flipping through the "Bs" to see if the store carried any Beatles' albums. He owned them all, but he checked the racks every so often to make sure they were still available in the event he ever wanted a duplicate. His *Sergeant Peppers' Lonely Hearts Club Band* album had a scratch through the "Fixing a Hole" cut. His *Rubber Soul* was in mono rather than stereo. Someday, he'd replace them, maybe with new CDs if that format ever became popular.

He glanced at the 45-rpm list of top forty hits and saw that women held the first three spots – Janet Jackson, Tina Turner and Cyndi Lauper – which made him cringe. Genesis, Loverboy and Boston were more his speed and, further down the list, there were plenty of songs he wouldn't recognize unless he heard them on the air, because radio-station DJs seldom felt the need any more to announce songs. It was another one of life's betrayals. No one took the time to care.

Dan wandered around the store, not sure what he hoped to find, but left his options open. The merchandise in one aisle was of two varieties, either packed on clear-plastic-wrapped cardboard backing that hung on metal hooks or small appliances chained to carpeted display shelves. Everything had to be tied down. Regulations.

He remembered his last day at *The Weekly Enterprise* when he'd been fired, how Jack Newport extracted his last paycheck from a chrome spindle with its sharp tip bent over so it couldn't stab anyone. Jack was lucky that OSHA inspected his office. Dan had sworn he'd get back at the world and a straight spindle would have been mighty handy.

In his nearly half-year in Cedar City, Dan had familiarized himself with the layout of the town. When he received the shoplifting story assignment, he knew it had two Kmarts, two Target stores, two indoor shopping malls, half a dozen outdoor malls, and a grocery store in every neighborhood. There were 7-Eleven, QuickTrip and KwikShop convenience stores at every major intersection. The east-side Target appeared to be the easiest mark.

The jewelry section was packed with women and children. He couldn't understand why so many people wasted their money on costume junk. He hated wearing a ring because other people always thought it meant something. If he ever wore a ring, it would be one he bought for himself. He'd once worn a cheap gold watch, but the band turned his wrist green. He decided he didn't need one because he could always ask somebody else for the time or he could locate a clock. Or, like today, time didn't matter. His only jewelry was a silver chain around his neck with a small swastika medallion, a reminder that, as a Jew, he always had to keep an eye on his back.

Dan recalled a story he'd recently read as he strolled past the televisions and stereos. A discount store had hired "shoplifters" to test employees. One fake customer actually ripped off a twenty-five-inch television by pretending he'd paid for it and, somehow, convincing a clerk to haul it out to his car. The clerk was fired for incompetence.

A smile emerged on Dan's face. Ingenious. He'd love to get away with something that outrageous.

Absent-mindedly, as Dan wandered around the store, he wound up in the women's lingerie department. He didn't realize it until he bumped into a chubby arm holding up a lacy pair of pink panties.

"Sorry," he said.

The woman, heavyset and wearing a wild yellow Hawaiian print "tent" dress, appeared startled. Dan eyed her curiously, her basketball-sized face and sagging bulldog jowls, as she sorted through the underwear. "They won't fit," he mumbled, walking away before she could reply.

Dan cruised the toy aisles past a boy making internal combustion roars with his mouth while he ran a bright orange car along the tile floor. A small white toy computer on an eye-level shelf caught Dan's attention. He punched its blue buttons. As the computer's synthesized voice spoke a command, the little boy silenced his motor and sidled up beside Dan.

"Go ahead, try it," Dan said.

The kid turned his sucker-stained face toward Dan and grinned. He couldn't see the buttons, but he could reach up to hammer them like Liberace at the piano. Dan patted the kid on the head and left him to figure out the computer on his own. To be a kid again, Dan thought. You don't give a damn about anything because you don't know any better.

Over by a red ring-for-service phone on a pillar, Dan made his decision. A hand-sized Sony Walkman, sitting loosely on top of a box, was waiting with its little headphones to be shoved into his inside coat pocket. He picked it up, and the box, too, and strolled around the store as if he was still shopping. Suddenly, he began to feel paranoid, thinking everyone he passed in an aisle could read his mind, that they all knew he didn't plan to pay for the Walkman. He became hot under the collar carrying the hot merchandise. The veins in his neck throbbed with each beat of his heart. Perspiration trickled from his armpits and over the bumps of his ribs.

Still, Dan picked up a large mixing bowl from the housewares department and a box with a toaster in it from the appliances. Decoys. He appeared to be a serious shopper with his arms full as he made a beeline to the hardware section. As he'd scouted out the store earlier, he'd chosen this spot in the far rear corner to complete the act. With his back to the wall, he could go undetected by surveillance mirrors and clerks roaming the store, a perfect place to slip the Walkman inside his coat.

As Dan began his approach, his heels clicked on the tile floor, and the sound seemed to follow him as if it belonged to a security detective on his tail. He turned around and the aisle was void of human life. The anxiety was all in his head.

Shoplifting took more guts than Dan remembered. It hadn't seemed so difficult as a kid, placing a paperback onto a stack of schoolbooks and walking out the store. But that was fifteen years ago when he had no fear.

Dan eased his mind by reminding himself he had an excuse if he got caught. It was research for a story, he'd say, a way to comprehend how a shoplifter really would feel pilfering merchandise from an unsuspecting store.

He'd simply show security his press card, laugh and tell them they'd better keep their eyes open a little wider.

The coast was clear by the display of hinges, locks and other hardware. Dan slipped the Walkman inside his jacket and dropped it into the hidden pocket. He scratched his side, as if an itch had prompted that maneuver. Nobody in sight. He jerked his head skyward for a moment to double check that there were no two-way mirrors in the ceiling, then inhaled deeply. Relief and success. But he couldn't breathe easy yet, not until he'd made his exit.

Dan acted nonchalant, even whistling softly, as he returned to the appliance section. He replaced the toaster on a stack of boxes and spoke more to himself than to the woman who was inspecting the nearby display of blenders when he said, "I really didn't want that." Her quizzical expression popped back into his mind as he returned the mixing bowl, then shoved the empty Sony box onto its shelf.

The whole wandering-shopper routine might have been carried out better if he walked around the store a while longer, but he was desperate to get it over with. Somebody might start following him if he stuck around too long.

His body temperature was rising again. He had second thoughts about leaving the store, wondering if the portable cassette player had been secured with a magnetic device to set off an alarm at the door. But, he reasoned, this wasn't an expensive clothing store with anti-theft tags. Even if Target used a security label for the Walkman, it would be on the box, not the item itself.

Dan quickly flipped through the record albums again, but this time didn't pay attention to the titles or care if radio disc jockeys lived or died. He let the albums fan back into their original positions and sauntered past the return counter, keeping his pace as casual as possible even though he felt as if he was running with every step.

Seconds seemed like minutes when, finally, the automatic front door whooshed open and Dan stepped outside the store into sunshine.

The cold autumn air tickled the hair inside his nostrils and slipped unhindered inside his open jacket, transforming the back of his sweat-dampened shirt into an ice cube. Dan didn't turn around but stared straight ahead as he crossed the parking lot and unlocked his car door. Only after he slid behind the wheel did he glance back.

Dan Goldberg sighed and smiled. He lit a cigarette before starting his car. A calm swept through him as he wiped perspiration from his forehead with the sleeve of his jacket. The Target symbol appeared larger than life. He had hit it.

7

When Linda Reynolds entered Mike Rockwell's hospital room Tuesday afternoon, her smile reminded him of a breath of fresh air.

Trite? So, what? Love made you silly. It made you think in stupid, outrageous, senseless clichés. In words and phrases you'd never dedicate to print. So, what was wrong with that? Mike loved being in love.

"I never get tired of your smile," he said as Linda leaned over the bed to kiss him on the lips.

"Don't do anything to make me not want to smile and you won't have a thing to worry about," she said, hugging him lightly about the shoulders as if being too aggressive would cause him pain. "I've been worried about you all day."

Mike grinned as his girlfriend released him and sat on the edge of the hospital bed. She was referring to their short, stilted conversation that morning when he'd irritated her by insisting that she didn't need to come to the hospital right away, that she should go to work, call him later in the day, stop by when her day was done.

What Linda didn't realize was that Mike had been under the influence of drugs, nightmares and the shock of being shot. He apologized when she called during her lunch hour. She had seemed relieved that he was more like himself when he said he couldn't talk long because he was writing his story for Wednesday's paper, but there'd still been that hint of tension in her voice.

Now, in the hospital room, the late afternoon sun illuminated the right side of Linda's face. Her long auburn hair appeared redder than usual, a glow that only made Mike want her even more. He'd once tried talking her into lightening her hair just a shade, so it wouldn't be so red all the time, but she'd refused, saying that if he loved her, he wouldn't try to change her. For good measure, she also told him the summer sun lightened her hair enough.

"How about another kiss?" Mike said. "I really could use another kiss."

"You just had your dose of Linda medicine for the day," she teased. "No more."

"Come on," he pleaded. "I'm a sick man."

"Sick, yes," she said. "A man?"

Mike laughed. "That's not what you said a week ago."

"We were in bed together then," she said. "Now you're there by yourself."

"But I get out in a couple of days."

"And you'll want to climb right back into it." It was her turn to smile.

"You think that's all I think about?" he said.

"Well, isn't it?" Linda rose from the bed, placed a hand on each of his cheeks and kissed him on the mouth. "Men are all alike."

Mike grabbed her around the waist and pulled her on top of him. She wriggled as if to get loose, but she wasn't very aggressive, and her warmth only aroused him more. He locked his fingers around the small of her back.

"You aren't getting away this time," he said.

"Who said I wanted to," she whispered into his ear.

It had been five days since they'd slept together, a week since they had sex. Mike felt himself growing hard against her as she repositioned her body in his grasp. He wanted her, but he knew she wouldn't take the risk with nurses and doctors running the hallway.

To distract his body from its natural impulse, Mike needed to occupy his mind with other thoughts. He returned to the anxiety he'd experienced less than 24 hours earlier, the pain in his leg, the fear that he might not live to hold Linda like this again, but it didn't work.

"Feels to me like you're ready to go home now," Linda said, easing away. She still wore that magic and elusive smile.

"I need a cold shower," he laughed. "But I'd love to go home, if only you'd go with me." He kissed her again. "It's nice just laying here, getting paid for nothing."

"You lay in bed and do nothing? That would be impossible."

Mike was pleased that Linda could have a light conversation with him about his work and that she hadn't made a bigger deal out of him being shot. On the phone, in the morning, she'd scolded him, saying it was no one's fault but his own that he was in a position to get shot. Even though she had warned him she wasn't about to go through a scare like this again, she'd also urged him to get well fast and to write the best damn story ever written by a reporter shot in the line of duty.

While Mike's wound required stitches and a cast, the doctors were holding him in the hospital simply to keep him off his feet for a couple of days. Linda agreed with them and for that reason, Mike didn't object.

"I like feeling safe," he said. "The hospital isn't so bad."

"You didn't think so this morning when they gave you those hypodermic shots to kill the pain," Linda said.

"I hate shots."

"You're a big baby." She stood over him like a mother. "You're worse than a baby."

"I know. I need you to take care of me. Stay here and take care of me."

Linda scrunched her lips into a half smile, half frown. She squinted as if she knew what he was going to say next. For nearly a year Mike had been after her to marry him, but he wouldn't actually propose. He asked her to promise that if he asked, she'd say "yes" right away, so he wouldn't be disappointed. But she had said "no" to that proposal, explaining how she couldn't see the difference between making that promise and saying "yes" to the actual question. She'd kept him at bay, once again, by saying she wasn't ready to make any promises, any commitments.

"I don't need a husband who goes around getting shot at," Linda said. "If I wanted that, I'd marry a cop."

"But you're not in love with a cop. You love me."

"Oh, we're pretty confident, are we?"

Mike had been joking, but he knew that when Linda the analytical mathematics teacher used her editorial "we," she was serious. Maybe she hadn't accepted this incident as fully as she'd made him think she had.

"I'm not trying to be a smart ass," Mike said. "I'm just stating the facts." He paused for a moment as she turned her back to him. "I don't know why you can't face that. We've known each other for almost three years, and if we don't know each other by now, we never will."

"It doesn't have anything to do with knowing each other," she said.

"It has to do with you wondering if I'm the right guy for you. Of course, maybe you want to see if somebody else better comes along." Mike was being intentionally flippant. "Maybe a cop. But how long are you going to wait? All your life?"

"Michael," she shouted. "That's ridiculous. You're not being fair."

"Fair? I'm trying to be fair to both of us."

"Then don't push me."

"Then tell me you'll say yes."

Linda shook her head in frustration, then turned to stare at Mike. Her green eyes begged him for more time. He was getting tired of it. Twenty-six wasn't that young to make a commitment, and this wasn't the same situation she'd been in four years ago. She'd told him about Craig asking her to marry him the day they graduated from college and how she rebelled against the pressure by flatly turning him down. He had found someone else within a year and married her.

At the time, Linda thought it had been the right decision to let Craig go, but she admitted later to having second thoughts. There had been her career as a teacher to think about. Now, with four years of experience and teachers being in demand, she realized she could find a great job anywhere. She liked the freedom of options.

Mike had felt the same way when they met. After about a year, Linda confessed to him that her earlier decision had been right because, if she'd said "yes" to Craig, she wouldn't have met Mike.

Mike said he understood, that her new outlook was only natural since she'd become more settled in her desires and goals. But when she'd told Mike she loved him more than she'd ever loved anyone else, he bristled and replied that he didn't like comparisons. When Linda said that wasn't what she meant, he replied that he didn't like clichés either, but that one was appropriate in this case. "Love the one you're with," he'd said, "and if that works, get married."

As Mike gazed across the hospital room at Linda, he wondered what was going through her mind. If she remembered those conversations. How unsettled she really felt about him being shot. If he was pressuring her too much. But Mike didn't know what to say. He waited for her to speak.

After the long pause, Linda took several small steps to the other side of the room and turned to face him. "I don't make deals," she said. "I've told you that before. So that's why I can't promise to say 'yes.' If you really want to marry me, ask."

Mike closed his eyes. This was ridiculous, he thought, and not the time for this discussion. Here he was, laid up in bed, a cast covering his left leg, the entire room separating them. Besides, the ring he'd bought was in his apartment, nestled in its little white box, hidden in his sock drawer. He couldn't just climb out of bed, get down on one knee, propose like he'd pictured it.

"What if you say 'no?'" he asked.

"That doesn't mean I'm rejecting you, Michael, that I don't love you. It just means I'm not ready yet."

"I am," he said. "I'm thirty-one. I'm ready for a wife and kids."

Linda burst out laughing, a loud, long, exaggerated laugh. A cackle that some people might use instead of crying.

"Ha," she said, after she'd settled down. "I'm talking about not marrying you, and you're talking about having a family. Boy, you sure move fast, buster." Linda laughed again. "It's too bad you couldn't move that fast when the bullet was coming at you."

"I didn't have ... oh, never mind," Mike said.

He was flabbergasted. As he sat up and propped his pillow higher beneath his head, he felt the blood drain from his face. He gazed silently at Linda, unable to speak.

Linda stared back just as quietly. For an instant she appeared ready to say something, but she didn't.

Were they supposed to read each other's minds? Mike wondered.

After the impasse, what seemed to Mike an infinite silence, he finally spoke.

"I tell you what," Mike said. "When you're ready, you ask me to marry you. I've always wanted to wear a big diamond engagement ring."

Linda grinned.

"There we go," he said. "I knew I could get that smile back on your face." He held out his hand. "If you asked me to marry you, you know I'll say yes."

Linda crossed the room with an exaggerated sway to her hips, a smile that made her eyes crinkle, and her hand outstretched to take his hand. "You're crazy," she said. "But you're honest."

"I know. That's why you love me."

"That's why I love you." She nodded. "And that's why I'm going to take you up on your offer. I'll pop the question. If, and when, I'm ready."

"Will you marry me?" Mike said.

Linda emphatically shook her head. "Not on your life, buster!"

"I just had to try. One last time."

"That is the last time," she said. "The decision is mine now. You can't say anything about marriage unless I bring it up. Deal?"

"Deal?" Mike said. "You don't make deals."

"This is an exception," Linda said. "Every rule has its exceptions, except when it comes to math."

8

Click, click, click. The hollow tapping of computer keyboards was as close as *The Argus* newsroom got to the not-too-distant, once familiar and distracting, clacking of teletypes and electric typewriters. Even the subtler white noise was irritating to some reporters too young to remember those days, including Dan Goldberg, as he watched his story scroll to the top of the green computer screen and disappear into the memory bank.

Wednesday morning. He had wrapped up his shoplifting story. Now it would sit around for days until an editor even looked at it. Was there any justice? You beat your brains out to write a nothing story, and it proved to be exactly that. It had bored him to tears.

Well, not exactly tears because Dan rarely cried. But if he did, this story would have opened the floodgates. He was so tired of calling people and identifying himself and receiving exactly the same response from everyone: "Yes, shoplifting is a problem," "No, we haven't beefed up security," "Yes, we do prosecute," "No, I can't tell you what our success rate is."

He felt his lead had merit, though. He knew it was realistic.

As Joe Shoplifter strolled across the Target parking lot, he reached into the inside pocket of his coat to make sure it was empty. When he found a matchbook, he tossed it to the ground. An empty inside pocket was a critical element for the task at hand.

Joe Shoplifter weaved his way between the parked cars toward the department store, always crowded on Sunday afternoons. He was primed for action because, for him, this was the ideal time for five-finger discounts.

The congestion in the store's aisles would distract store security, allowing Joe Shoplifter to blend in with the crowd. No one would suspect him of stuffing a paperback book or a portable cassette player or a pair of pliers inside his coat before he walked out the door.

Joe was an amateur, out to save a few bucks on merchandise he wanted for himself. But, these days, for professionals who often work in teams, shoplifting has become big business. For the victimized stores, it can add up to astronomical financial loss.

Dan's story explained that shoplifting was a simple matter if only one or two small items were taken. But, it added, most people got caught because they try to take too much at one time or they steal objects that are too large to conceal properly. "The pregnant woman syndrome," he called it, where a woman with a hidden storage pouch over her belly goes through her first eight months of pregnancy in an afternoon of shoplifting at a store.

Dan had made the one o'clock deadline to finish his story, to get it out of the way. But early afternoon was the worst time of the day because nothing happened, and he couldn't go anywhere. The story could sit around for hours, as if editors had something better to do than read it. But, once they called the story up on their computers and began asking questions, the reporter better be there to answer questions or there would be hell to pay.

The exaggerated rush to deadline frustrated Dan, but he'd run into it everywhere he'd worked. That's why he preferred writing spot news stories. They broke at deadline, so editors had to work quickly and usually didn't have enough time to ask a lot of senseless questions and screw up the style of the story.

In *The Argus* lunchroom, Dan straightened out the corners of a one-dollar bill and slipped it into the change machine. Quarters chinked into the metal cup below like a Las Vegas slot machine. Iowa officials had discussed sanctioning casinos to go along with the Powerball and scratch-off ticket gambling program recently put in place, but when anything new would happen was anybody's guess. At least the payoff in the change machine was probably better than in a slot machine, Dan thought. At least here you received four quarters for a dollar.

In the adjacent microwave oven, someone was heating a bowl of spaghetti or lasagna and they'd left the room. The smell of warm tomato sauce and spices tantalized Dan's taste buds. He thought about stealing the pasta for lunch, but there was no way he could eat it without getting caught. It wasn't as easy as shoplifting. Even a blind bloodhound with a stuffed nose could track down that smell.

He fed two more dollars through the change machine and spent all but two quarters for a cold roast beef and Swiss cheese sandwich, two small bags of potato chips, a can of Diet Pepsi and a Snickers candy bar. What a lunch, he thought, gathering the packages and heading to his desk. At least it was cheap.

Dan tossed the processed food packets on his desk and walked to a stack of newspapers on a shelf at the back of the newsroom. He picked up copies of *The Des Moines Times* and *The Iowa City Register*, rival newspapers in Iowa, if there was such a thing as a rival any more. Very few two-newspaper towns existed, which rendered direct competition extinct. Managing Editor Dick Anderson constantly complained that television beat *The Argus* on big breaking stories, but the editors and reporters always retorted that the newspaper followed with a more comprehensive report and kept at it until all the facts were told.

Dan read other newspapers because it was an easy way to kill time and appear busy, a technique he learned early in his career. He also could pilfer story ideas. If he didn't follow this routine several times a week, Margaret Myers would find something else for him to do. The last thing he wanted was another shoplifting assignment.

Dan dropped a stack of papers on his desk and sat down. As he removed the cellophane from his sandwich, he thought about his shoplifting expedition. He'd thought about it all night, considered trying it again in another store. But he couldn't justify that as a challenge anymore. Also, even though *The Argus* didn't publish the names of shoplifters, he knew that getting caught, if somebody found out, would lead to sure discipline if not dismissal from his job.

Dan had second thoughts about why he'd shoplifted in the first place. He could have simply gone through the motions. The Walkman would have set him back fifty bucks or so. His three-hundred-fifty-dollar-a-week salary wasn't making him rich by any means, but he certainly could have afforded the device if he really wanted it. In fact, when he was restless Tuesday night and felt like driving around, he'd stopped at Kmart to buy batteries he'd forgotten to pick up at Target.

He laughed. Here he'd used the "five-finger discount" to steal the cassette player and then paid a couple of bucks for stupid batteries to power it.

Dan ripped open a bag of chips and folded a newspaper in half as the police scanner on his desk came alive with an anxious voice. "We've heard from the neighbors that the shooting is over a four-year-old boy being held hostage in the house. Send a negotiator."

Dan phoned the cop shop dispatcher. "This is Dan Goldberg at *The Argus*. Where's this kid being held hostage?"

From across the newsroom Margaret Myers yelled, "Dan, we've got a hostage situation. Get on it."

Dan waved his hand in the air, pointing angrily to the telephone to let her know he was a step ahead of her. He resented the fact she felt he couldn't do his job without explicit instructions.

"E Avenue Northwest," the dispatcher said. "An apartment in the nine-hundred block."

"Thanks, Cathy," Dan said. He hung up the phone and took another bite of his sandwich, grabbed his notebook and took a swig of Pepsi before running to the closet for his coat. On his way past his desk, he picked up the Snickers bar. Just like in the commercial, he thought, chuckling to himself.

Dan was nearly out the door when Margaret yelled again. "Take a photographer with you."

"Dammit," Dan muttered under his breath. The whole thing could be over before he found a photographer. If they weren't up to their elbows in developing chemicals, they were cruising the city for feature shots that wasted valuable newspaper space and forced editors to trim some of the best sentences from his stories.

"Where's Pete?" Dan snapped back at Margaret.

As photo editor, Pete Johnson not only chose and cropped each day's photographs, he monitored each photographers' every move. Or at least he was supposed to. That philosophy didn't work if you couldn't find him.

If *The Argus* was supposed to be so damn good in the communications business, why were there so many internal failures, Dan thought. Where the hell was communication in the newsroom?

"He was here just a minute ago," said Susan Clark, the day receptionist. She was supposed to keep track of everyone but left a lot to be desired. In due respect, it usually wasn't her fault, because most people didn't keep Susan informed. At *The Argus*, reporters and photographers came and went as they pleased as if in their own worlds, and photographers were the worst offenders. With deadlines almost twelve hours away, they were probably hiding out at long lunch breaks, Dan thought.

"Do me a favor," Dan told Susan. "When you get hold of Pete, tell him to send someone to the nine hundred block of E Avenue Northwest. I can't wait all day."

Susan was already punching the darkroom number into her phone and nodded.

"If a photographer doesn't show up, take your own pictures," Margaret shouted. "That's what that camera in the newsroom car is for. It's better than nothing."

"Got you," Dan shouted, exiting quickly through the side door.

Reporters taking their own pictures was the dumbest idea Dan had ever heard. Photographers weren't sent out to write stories, thank God. Half of them couldn't spell, and half of them didn't care. In Chicago he'd never had to use a camera. But at *The Argus*, photographers had complained about spending two hours with a reporter to snap nothing more than a mug shot, so Pete convinced Dick Anderson to buy a few cameras for the reporters. So far, Dan had managed to avoid taking even one picture for the newspaper. It was against his principles. It wasn't in his job description.

Dan climbed into *The Argus'* police-beat car, "The Beater" he called it, a 1981 Ford Escort wagon with a crumpled fender. Finally, the third time he turned the key, it started. "A brick house could burn to the ground before you'd get to the fire in this pile of shit," he said aloud, sliding the manual transmission into gear.

Even the stoplights were against Dan. They all seemed to be red, forcing him to sit impatiently through a one-minute cycle until they turned green. He cussed out the city traffic engineer, whoever he was. He'd have to find out and give him a piece of his mind. He tried a shortcut through a service station to avoid a light, but an old geezer in a Cadillac cut him off by wheeling his "boat" up to the full-service island.

Dan leaned on the horn. "You son of a bitch," he shouted from his enclosed car. "Can't you see *The Argus* logo on the side of my car? Don't you know who I am?"

The Cadillac driver acted as if he couldn't hear a word and motioned with his hand for Dan to go around to the other side of the island.

"Damn you," Dan yelled.

He slammed the Escort into reverse and floored the accelerator. He was shocked when the tires squealed. He didn't know the beater had that much power as he wound the whining engine up to what had to be the red line. There was no way to know, since there was no tachometer, but at that moment Dan didn't care if the engine exploded. He ran a couple of red lights out of spite.

It seemed as if hours had passed by the time Dan pulled up behind a squad car with flashing red and blue lights in the middle of E Avenue. Two cops held a small crowd back with a yellow plastic rope. Across the street, half a dozen spectators stood in front of the E Avenue Tap, leaning against the tinted front glass window, drinking from bottles of beer. A real spectator show, Dan thought. All right.

He shut the car's engine off, grabbed his notebook and the camera from the back seat, pulled the billfold from his back pocket as he ran across the yard. He worked his way through the crowd to show the cop his press pass.

"That don't mean a thing," the big burly cop said. "No one goes past this line when there's a hostage situation."

"This card lets me go wherever I want," Dan insisted. He lifted his leg up to climb over the rope.

The cop grabbed Dan by the arm as if he was a rag doll, clamped a vicegrip on him that froze him in his tracks. "I wouldn't move another inch," the cop said.

Dan stared at the cop as if he'd rather shoot him than obey. He stood with his legs straddling the yellow tape and caught sight of another cop's uniform in the corner of his eye. The second cop was leaving the pale green apartment building carrying a small, crying child.

"My baby," a woman in the crowd yelled. She ducked beneath the security tape and ran toward the hero cop, her arms stretched out as if she expected her child to fall from the sky.

"He'll be all right," the cop said, trying to assure both mother and child that the situation was under control. "He isn't hurt, he's just scared. He'll be fine."

The cop placed the bawling boy in the woman's out-stretched arms and watched as she gathered him to her chest. "Why don't you take the little guy home right now," the cop said, "so you can calm him down. We'll talk to you later."

From the apartment building's side door emerged a man and woman, both dressed in black motorcycle-riding leathers and looking like punk rockers. Her hair was bright orange and spiked in the center. They had been cuffed, their hands behind their backs, and were being pushed toward a patrol car by a cop in uniform accompanied by a short stocky man in a dark business suit. The second man must have been the negotiator, Dan thought.

With his legs still straddling the tape, Dan felt as if he'd been caught with his pants down. He was pissed. Everything was over. He was too late.

As the rope fell to his feet, Dan realized he should have taken a picture of the bawling woman with her crying kid and now she was gone. Damn photographers. If they were on their toes, someone would have been listening to the scanner, been here in time to get a picture.

Oh, well, Dan thought, he'd make up for it with a description of the scene in his story. And, on the way back to the office, he could make up some excuse for not using the camera.

As the police dispersed the crowd, though, Dan had a job to do. He gathered eyewitness accounts from several spectators milling about. Neighbors said the punk rockers were always making a scene. The rumor circulating in the crowd was that they'd kidnapped the woman's nephew in an extortion attempt to secure cash to buy cocaine. Someone said they'd been holding the child at gunpoint when a plainclothes cop talked them out of harming the boy. Nobody knew the woman and her hostage child, though, so he'd have to ask the cops for that.

Walking back to the car, as Dan cursed the cops for being too efficient, for diffusing the situation before he could arrive, he ran into Jimmy Wilson, a longtime *Argus* photographer wearing some kind of old floppy fishing hat with a pair of black single-lens-reflex cameras and long lenses dangling from around his neck.

"Hey, bud," Jimmy said, "I got you a picture of the rescue, of that cop handing the screaming kid over to his mom. Hope it turns out like I think it will. I won't know until I get the film in the soup."

"Glad you could make it," Dan said angrily. "Too bad nobody let me know you'd be here."

"I just happened to be in the neighborhood," Jimmy said, a silly grin on his leathery old face, his unkempt graying hair sticking out from beneath his hat, fingerprints visible on the lenses of his wire-rimmed bifocals. "I've got the names of that woman and kid, too, if you want them."

"Thanks," Dan said. He was surprised at the old geezer's efficiency. "I'll get that stuff from you back at the office."

"Fine by me, bud," Jimmy said with a wave of his hand as he turned away. "See you back at the salt mine."

Frustrated again at the lack of communication, Dan watched Jimmy saunter away and hated the way the old guy called everybody "bud." It was a lazy way to talk to a co-worker he should know by now, a hint that Dan wasn't even well-known in his own newsroom. For good measure, he kicked the fender of *The Argus'* Escort, right where it was already dented.

9

Mike Rockwell awoke Wednesday morning in a cold sweat in his hospital bed. His T-shirt was so soaked with sweat a nurse had to help him change. She warm sponged his chest, his shoulders, his arms, cleaned and then dried him off before tossing him a fresh shirt. At least he'd feel better when Linda stopped to visit after work.

The nightmare that startled Mike awake had been so vivid he'd never forget it. So many dreams he'd forget a few minutes after waking, but this one replayed over and over in his mind no matter how hard he tried to think of anything else. He'd tell Linda about it. Maybe she'd have some answers.

Linda strolled into Mike's room carrying a small white vase with two red roses and a neatly folded paper grocery sack tucked beneath her arm.

"I thought some flowers would cheer you up," she said.

"I need cheering up."

Linda set the vase on the stainless-steel table that extended over Mike's bed and kissed him on the lips.

"I brought you something else," she said, laying the package on his chest. "I told my students what happened. They made you get-well cards."

Mike smiled. "Maybe that's the medicine I need."

"Is your leg still that bad?"

"More than that," he said. "My head hurts."

"Your head?"

"I had the strangest dream last night. I can't get it out of my head."

"Tell me about it." Linda sat on the edge of his bed and held his hand, her empathy radiating though her warm, soft touch.

"A warm summer day," he said. "Perfect. Blue sky, not a whisper of a breeze, green grass in a backyard, and a white picket fence. A dozen people sit around a long picnic table and all but the man at one end are laughing, drinking, eating juicy steaks fresh off a grill. I don't recognize any of them, and I'm not sitting there either. I'm racing around the yard carrying a roast beef sandwich above my head. I'm being chased by a huge brown dog, his open jaws the size of a lion's, as he jumps at the sandwich.

"I keep running from this monster, not understanding why he cares about my sandwich instead of the steaks on the table. Maybe he doesn't see them. But I can't take my eyes off him, and he stinks as if he's been rolling around in a den of skunks. His jowls drip with saliva, and he keeps jumping, but he never touches me. Not once. But that doesn't mean I'm not scared, that I quit running.

"Finally, I toss the roast beef sandwich to the dog and he devours it in two gulps. Everybody at the picnic table cheers and applauds."

Linda nods to assure Mike that she's listening.

"But that doesn't keep me from running. Or the dog from chasing me. And, no matter how hard I try, I still can't identify anyone at the table."

"You're running from me," Linda said. "I'm the big dog."

Mike laughed "Yeah, you, the big dog."

"You want me to chase you," she said. "You want me to ask you to marry me."

He tugged at her hand, brought her head closer to his, gazed into her eyes. "I wouldn't run from you."

"You would if I was a big dog after everything you owned."

"A roast beef sandwich?"

"It's symbolic, Mike. It's a dream."

"So, who were the people at the table?"

"Ghosts of your future," she said. "I don't know. Was that your entire dream?"

"No. There's that one guy at the end of the table. Finally, a woman brings out the largest, juiciest steak on a platter for him. For some reason the dog smells that steak, so he chases the woman until she drops the steak on the ground, then he wolfs that down, too. The man at the table, with his knife and fork poised to dig in, wears the same anticipatory expression on his face as if nothing has changed. Then, suddenly, he understands what happened and he goes from being angry, to being sad, to weeping loudly. The dog comes over to him and he pets it like they're best friends. Then, poof, everything is gone. My dream ends, and I'm sweating bullets."

"You're running from something," Linda said, "and you must give up part of what you want to keep the rest."

"I figured that much out," Mike said.

"It's like the other weird dreams you've been having. The floating gun, for instance. It's got to be the drugs you're taking. They're playing games with your head."

"I don't like it."

Linda leaned over Mike and whispered in his ear. "Tell me," she said, "were you naked in any of these dreams?"

Mike laughed. "Why would I be naked?"

"I don't know. But if I'm naked in a dream, then I'm concerned. If you weren't naked, don't worry about it."

Of course, Mike had thought the big dog was Ronald Morgan, that the faceless man at the table was his boss. But he couldn't tell Linda that and expect her not to worry. He could do enough of that for both of them.

"Earth to Mike," Linda said, "Are you listening?"

"Um, yeah," he said. "I know I wasn't naked."

"Good. You were simply running from something you fear while everyone around you was enjoying a pleasurable experience."

"That hardly seems fair."

"Not everything is fair, as you like to say, in love and war," Linda said.

"As I used to say," he corrected her. "I don't like that cliché anymore."

"Not since I keep putting you off about our future."

"Not since I've come to the conclusion that clichés are for weak writers. Not since I decided I don't want to fight anymore. Our future is up to you."

"Well, then, there you go," Linda said. "As I told you before, you're running from me. I'm the big dog."

Mike enveloped Linda in his arms, kissed her on the nape of the neck, inhaled the scent of her perfume and the warmth beneath her collar.

Linda was all wrong about her role in his dream, but maybe she was right about his. He'd been a diversion for the masses, bait for a big dog, a pawn in the action. But why? Who was the man at the end of the table? Who was the big dog? At least he wore clothes.

And Linda was right on another point. He had more important things to worry about than weird nightmares.

10

The Thursday morning October wind blew in gusts, lowering the wind chill factor to nearly freezing. Mike Rockwell stood with the help of crutches in the open field at the edge of Evergreen Cemetery. He wore his heavier, dark brown, waterproof, sheepskin-lined, winter coat. He pulled a tartan blue and black scarf tighter around his neck as tears welled in his eyes.

"You shouldn't cry over a dead cop you didn't even know," Dan whispered.

"The wind's in my eyes."

"Sure," Dan nodded, but Mike could tell he didn't believe that.

Mike gazed into the distance, past the crowd of people in similar winter coats and scarves flapping in the wind, past the fifty or so police officers dressed in blue who had gathered to pay their respects to a fallen comrade, past the television reporters and news cameras, to where nearly identical marble tombstones were arranged neatly in a row. Along the vacant ground where the dead of the future would be buried, the grass had begun to die, to turn brown, as bright white clouds raced across the sky and a single, wayward bird landed on a nearly invisible high wire.

He could be that bird, Mike thought. Linda had confused him before, but never like this. He'd asked her to marry him, and she wouldn't answer. She wouldn't make deals, yet she seemed satisfied that he'd given her control under the guise that he would say "yes" if she asked him to marry her. She had visited him twice each day in the hospital but had not taken the morning off to drive him home. Instead, she insisted he accept Dan's invitation to do so.

Dan had hauled Mike's suitcase of belongings to his apartment, then convinced him to come along as he covered the police officer's funeral.

The more Linda backed away, Mike thought, the more he wondered if they'd be right for each other. He cherished the security of a planned future and felt it drifting away. He was comfortable in his job, half a decade now on *The Argus* staff, and comfortable with Linda, now nearly three years in love. He wanted a family, a house, a promise to grow old together.

A loose corner of the green canvass canopy above the casket whipped lazily in the wind and wrapped itself around a steel support pole as if to warm it, much as the mourners did with their coats around their bodies. Mike's bare face, especially his nose, felt frozen in the wind and his eyes watered and stung. He jammed his bare hands into his pockets and, in the right one, found the Sony Walkman that Dan had given him as they'd left his apartment, the surprise get-well present.

Mike had accepted the portable cassette player with gratitude, even though he thought it a rather strange gift for a guy on crutches. Dan said Mike could listen to it when he walked for rehabilitation, that wearing headphones and listening to his own selection of music while in his own world would soon become the norm.

As Mike adjusted the crutches below his sore armpits, he was secretly pleased that Dan had talked him into attending the funeral, to show his respect for the dead policeman and the police department since he'd been at the scene. Dan said Mike's presence would be a solid public-relations move for *The Argus*.

Mike stared with amazement at Dan, who was taking notes as the preacher recited the eulogy. His reasonable rationalization was unexpected after he'd predicted the media would make a hero out of an incompetent cop by the time this was over. Mike knew people often change their behavior when they want something. He wondered what Dan wanted.

Dan glanced at Mike as he tried to keep his notebook pages from turning in the wind. There was little emotion in his expression. He was heartless sometimes and could be downright cruel, Mike thought. But he doesn't really mean anybody any harm. It's his way. That's what makes him a good reporter. His emotions don't interfere with the job, yet he comprehends other people's feelings well enough to capture that in his writing. An excellent observer. Sometimes Mike wished he could be more like Dan.

"Well, that's it," Dan said. "Let's watch them bury a hero."

Most of the several hundred people who had gathered at the cemetery, the mourners, the police officers, the news crews, began to leave. Without so much as a second glance, they circumnavigated Dan and Mike as if they were statues. They kept their heads down, either because the wind was in their faces or because they didn't want anyone to see tears in their eyes.

"No, let's go," Mike said. "You've got enough for the story." He was cold and tired. He wanted to rest his good leg, take the weight off his armpits.

"I've never been to a cop's funeral," Dan said. "I'm watching it to the end. Make sure they get the guy in the ground. Besides, somebody might say something I can use while they're covering him with dirt."

What a malevolent jerk, Mike thought. He'd never stayed to the bitter end of a funeral either, and he had no desire to watch workmen fill a grave. It was morbid. He had decided long ago to be cremated. And no memorial service. Death was bad enough without dwelling on it.

"Wait in the car if you don't want to come with me." Dan said. "Do what you want."

Dan walked away as Mike turned his crutches toward the car. Then, for some reason, Mike changed his mind. "Just a minute, Dan," he shouted, repositioning his crutches. "I'm coming."

"Well, then, come on, you crip," Dan said. "We don't have all day."

"I need to ask you something," Mike said as he hobbled across the flat crusty earth, avoiding flush granite headstones with the tips of his crutches. "Do you ever wish you were dead?"

"Dead? Are you kidding?" Dan stopped. "Sometimes I'm surprised I'm not, but I've never wanted to be dead. I've got too many people to piss off before that happens."

"Does it bother you to think that you're going to die sometime?"

"Nope. I never think about it," Dan said. "Nothing lasts forever. It's usually the things you want to last that never do."

"Like the good dying young."

"Like James Dean and Jimi Hendrix and Jim Morrison?" Dan laughed. "That's a stupid expression concocted by idolizing fanatics."

Like the Kennedy brothers, JFK and Robert, Mike thought. Like Christ. Mike wasn't church-going religious, but he believed in a God and the Bible and most of the Ten Commandments, like "Thou shall not kill." He always considered himself good and wondered if sometimes he was too self-conscious, if life would be easier if he'd relax and not dwell on what he couldn't control. He knew he worried too much, not only about Linda and their future, but if he was in the right job, if the risk he'd taken on the drug bust was worth it, if Ronald Morgan knew who he was and would come after him. At times he wanted to disappear, to hide from his own thoughts.

Mike cleared his throat. "Have you ever thought about suicide?"

"Hell, no," Dan nearly shouted. "What's gotten into you? I drag you to a funeral, and you talk about fifty million ways to die."

"I didn't mean me. I mean, like somebody else. If things don't go the way they want them to, what pushes them over the edge, what makes them attempt suicide?"

"You'd have to be an idiot to kill yourself, no matter how bad you think life is," Dan said. "It's a permanent solution to a temporary problem. The best thing to do is move on. Get a new job. Start over."

Mike hadn't actually considered suicide. It was one of those nightmares that played through his mind when he felt depressed. Maybe that's what the big dog in his dream represented, and he was running from it. He wondered if Linda ever thought about suicide. Or if she ever thought about starting over.

"Is that why you moved to Cedar City from Chicago?" Mike asked. "To start over?"

"Of course."

"Did it have anything to do with a woman, with wondering if you were in love with her or if she loved you back?"

Dan twisted his face in anguish, stared at Mike with one eye closed and the other one wide open. "Are you kidding? No broad would ever get me that wrapped up in her. I do what I want when I want. Nobody tells me any different."

"Tough guy, huh? Never in love."

"Damn, Mike, what's with all the questions? You'd think you were playing reporter, and I was your victim. Lay off. You're not working today, I am."

"Sure," Mike said as they arrived at the gravesite.

"Cheer up, Mikey," Dan said. "Linda will marry you. You're too much of a sap for her to say no."

* * * * * *

The heavy canvass and chrome metal frame that had surrounded the gravesite was folded and packed onto a small open-top trailer, and two men, each with a large scoop shovel, tossed dirt into the hole in the ground which was already half full. Two other men carried buckets of hot water, steam rising from the top, to pour onto the freshly turned dirt. They went about their work without conversation.

"What's the water for?" Mike asked.

More questions, Dan thought. He wished he hadn't brought Mike. He'd become a pain in the butt.

"It compresses the dirt," Dan said, "so they don't leave a huge mound for the sod."

Mike nodded.

Dan glanced away from the muddy hole to Collins' gray tombstone. Beyond it a man in a lined topcoat with the plaid collar pulled up around his neck talked with a young woman of about thirty. From twenty feet away, it was obvious she'd been crying. Her shoulders stooped, she held a wad of white tissue in gloved hands. Dan guessed the man to be the funeral director, but he didn't know the woman.

"Collins wasn't married, was he?" Dan asked.

"No, I don't think so. Maybe she's a relative."

"That's who it is," Dan said. "His sister, Susan. I talked to her on the phone. She handled the arrangements. I need to talk to her now."

"Not me. You're the one working."

"Back in a minute."

Dan folded his notebook into his coat pocket so as not to appear reporter-rude as he approached the woman with long chestnut hair pulled tightly over her ears and tucked beneath the raised collar of her black coat. He introduced himself and shook hands with her and the funeral director, who excused himself.

"I'm very sorry about your brother," Dan said. "I understand he was a great man and an even better police officer."

"The best," she said.

The woman stood a head shorter than Dan. Frozen tears glistened in the corners of her dark brown eyes. The redness in her cheeks on the brisk day matched the paleness of her mouth. She smiled ever so slightly, her lips trembling. In her sadness, Dan thought she looked not only vulnerable, but also irresistible, a wounded bird who could use his comfort.

"I mean it," Dan said. "I am sorry. I just wanted you to know that."

"I appreciate the thought." She bowed her head, clenched her right fist and tucked it into her left hand as she held them against her coat. "Everybody has been so kind."

"It's too cold," Dan said.

"It is." She turned her face upward, new tears in her eyes. Her entire body shivered. "I never understood why he had to be a cop. I tried to talk him out of it. We all did, but ..."

For some reason she wanted to talk, and Dan wasn't about to stop her. He wanted to listen to everything she said, her voice weak but not the least bit whiny. Dan resisted the temptation to pull his notebook out to write down her words because he thought that might cause her to clam up. He concentrated on every word, taking mental notes as best he could.

"... it was what he wanted to be ever since we were kids. I was able to talk my husband out of it, out of being a cop, because he wasn't as stubborn as Bill. But it didn't do any good. He gave up being a cop to drive a bulldozer on a road construction crew. It was supposed to be safe. They never tip over."

Dan was shocked, and pleased, to hear a back story this compelling. He surprised himself with his reaction, extending his arms to this young widow who had now also buried a brother, wrapping them around her shoulders, pulling her gently into his grasp.

"I guess none of us is ever really safe," she whimpered, turning her sad eyes away from him and burying her face into his coat.

Dan felt her clutched hands push against his stomach like a knot of pain and recalled their phone conversation.

She had sounded strong, obviously shielded from the double tragedy by shock. But they had discussed only her brother, then, not how her husband had been killed, too.

Dan felt rare compassion, a tug at his heart, a numbness in his brain. After a couple of minutes, even though he didn't want to, he pulled Susan gently away by the shoulders and gazed into her eyes again. Beyond the tears, he saw a woman who could be solid in the face of adversity, desirable once a little time had passed. He reached into his coat for a business card.

"You're cold and tired," he said. "Get some rest. If you need somebody to talk to, please call me. Please call me anytime."

She nodded.

* * * * *

During Mike's solo and silent walk from the gravesite to the car, one of the last cops at the cemetery approached him from behind. The officer tapped Mike on the shoulder, so he turned around.

"Lieutenant Sanders," Mike said. He wasn't sure what else to say, for this was the man who had taken him on the drug bust, who had abandoned him in the car, who had nearly cost him his life. He was the man who had lost a fellow police officer, too, a man in mourning. "I'm sorry," Mike said.

"Rockwell, I'm the one who's sorry," Lieutenant Sanders said. "I was wrong to have left you alone in the patrol car. It is my fault you're on those crutches. For that, I sincerely apologize."

Mike looked Lieutenant Sanders in the eyes, saw they were moist, too, that he had lost a true friend with the death of William Collins.

"You had an officer in danger," Mike said. "You were only doing what you thought was right."

The police officer nodded. "I couldn't be in two places at once," he said. "If there's anything I can do for you, let me know."

"Thank you," Mike said.

He watched the lieutenant walk away and knew he should be angry for being abandoned, for nearly losing his life. Then again, Mike knew that he was alive, that Sanders had only reacted from the perspective of a cop who saw a fellow officer in trouble.

Mike climbed into *The Argus* car and, as Dan slid behind the wheel, desperately wanted to know the story about Collins' sister. But Dan didn't want to be interrupted as he wrote frantically in his notebook, reconstructing his conversation with the woman.

Mike let his mind wander, and it landed on the difference between heaven and hell, the curiosity of what an afterlife would be like, if, in fact, there was life after death. He wasn't sure why thoughts about death upset him the way they did, except that maybe it was because no one close to him had died and that mourning was a foreign experience. He knew he could never have extended comfort to a total stranger as Dan had done.

Finally, as Dan started the car Mike seized his opportunity. "Why'd you hug Collins' sister?"

"Susan?" Dan said. "Susan Holcomb. Her husband had been a cop, too. But he quit to drive a bulldozer for the state highway commission and of all things, his Cat tipped over and killed him anyway. What irony."

"What irony," Mike repeated flatly as Dan began the drive back to *The Argus*.

"Susan had talked him out of being a cop, and she was trying to do the same with her brother, but he wouldn't listen. He told her, 'Look what happened to your husband, he changed jobs and he's dead, anyway.' That was it. No job's guaranteed safe."

"So, you're using that in the story?"

"It'll be the lead. Woman loses brother to dirt ball drug dealer; husband died playing in the dirt. It's great stuff."

"It's insensitive."

"I'm not that stupid. I'm not going to write it that way. I'll treat it with respect, but she did volunteer the information. Maybe she hopes the connection will help other people cope after someone they love dies in a dangerous job."

"Maybe she just wanted sympathy," Mike said.

"If that's the case, she'll get that, too. Especially after my story hits the streets."

"She'll probably want to castrate you."

"Hey, Mikey, you've got to have balls before you can lose them," Dan said.

They rode the rest of the way in silence. Once they arrived at *The Argus*, Dan opened the car door for Mike, helped him with his crutches, even assisted him up the stairway.

Something strange was happening, Mike thought. Dan still talked like the same tough guy, but his actions showed he did have a heart. First, the Walkman, and now this. Mike was still suspicious, particularly when he thought about their conversation in the car.

As Mike hobbled into the newsroom, everyone gave him a hero's welcome, patting him on the back, shaking his hand, asking him about the details of his ordeal.

Dan shook his head, raised his eyes, squeezed past Mike toward their desk.

"Lead foot," joked Sandy Griffin.

"Great first-person story," said Margaret Myers. "It's slated for page one on Sunday along with a follow-up account of Collins' murder and the manhunt for Morgan that Dan will write."

Mike was proud of his effort, but he wondered why he'd rushed to finish it in the hospital if it wouldn't be used until Sunday, so he asked Margaret.

"We wanted you to write it while it was fresh in your mind," she said. "But we decided to hold it for Sunday's bigger audience. It's completely different than the shooting of a policeman, with different issues. It'll make people realize that other lives are endangered when police officers don't take proper precautions."

"Don't you think we're dragging this whole thing out, making a bigger deal out of it than we need to?"

"No," she said. "You took a risk riding with the police, but they blew it. You were kidnapped and got hurt. They're responsible."

"So, you're holding my story until Collins is buried so we can attack the cops for being negligent without coming off sounding like we're attacking a dead cop."

"We're simply telling readers what happened," she said. "They can draw their own conclusions. Besides, holding the story until after you're out of the hospital gives you the chance to follow up on it. You can handle the telephone calls we'll receive after it hits print."

"Thanks," Mike said, emphasizing his sarcasm. "I'm back on Sunday."

"I know," she said with a wry grin.

* * * * *

Dan finished his story about Collins' funeral, stopped at the Fox and Hounds for two quick beers, picked up a couple of burgers from McDonald's and arrived at his apartment about seven.

It was after dark, but he knew his apartment so well he didn't turn on any lights until he walked into the bathroom. As he chased four aspirins with a full glass of water, the telephone rang. He figured it was the copy desk with a question about his story.

Dan flipped on the bedroom light and picked up the receiver on his night stand. "Hello."

"Hi, Dan?"

He didn't recognize the quiet female voice. After a moment the caller must have realized it.

"This is Susan Holcomb."

"Susan," he said. "I didn't expect to hear from you so soon."

"Am I interrupting anything?"

"No, I just got home."

"I know. I tried earlier."

"Is something wrong?"

"I was just thinking about our conversation earlier today, at the cemetery," she said. "I wasn't thinking straight, and I might have said some things I didn't mean to say."

Here it comes, Dan thought. She didn't want him to use anything about her dead husband being a former cop. Why did people give reporters information, then change their minds like that and want to retract it?

"I know I was talking about my husband being a former police officer, and I didn't want it to sound like I don't have respect for the profession," she said. "It's a tough job. I know you'll probably quote me, and I don't want to come off sounding like a whining spouse, like a whining sister."

"You didn't," Dan assured her. He didn't want to rewrite his story, but he didn't want to anger her, either.

"Your concerns are legitimate, Susan. Anyone who is close to a police officer killed in the line of duty would feel the same way."

"Then you didn't make me sound like I'm anti-police, like I'm a woman who can't cope with the reality that, if your brother's a policeman, he might get killed in the line of duty?"

"Of course not. You were smart trying to talk your husband out of being a cop if it bothered you. The same with your brother. More people should speak up, if that's how they feel."

"So, I'm going to sound OK in your story?"

"Definitely," he said, recalling again how she had buried her head in his shoulder when he'd put his arms around her, how he'd thought at the time that they could become friends, if not more. "Do you want to meet somewhere tonight and talk about it?"

"Not tonight," she said. "It's been a very long day."

"Tomorrow then? After work?"

"Sure." Her voice sounded hesitant but less distant. "I'll have read your story by then, and we can discuss it."

"What about Osgood's? In the IE tower. We can grab something to eat, too."

"I've been there before," she said. "It's a nice place. That would be fine."

"About six?"

"Six."

"I'll see you then," he said.

"Good night."

Dan heard the click of the disconnect, returned his phone to the cradle and reclined for a moment on the bed. I'm going out with a cop's sister, he thought. A dead cop's sister. That was even more fascinating.

11

Osgood's was Cedar City's newest, upscale "meet market" for singles. While half of its two-dozen small tables were usually occupied most every night, Fridays featured wall-to-wall people, a floor-to-ceiling haze of smoke and loud bass-dominant music that bordered on disco.

Even in small-city Iowa, singles desperate for companionship knew their chances improved with a well-fed, inebriated member of the opposite sex. Dan was as familiar with Osgood's as he was with any bar in town, which is why he'd selected it for his rendezvous with Susan Holcomb.

Dan spotted her seated on a stool at the crowded bar sipping a Coke he assumed was mixed with rum or whiskey. He edged his way through the standing-room-only crowd and tapped her on the shoulder. When she didn't respond, he tapped harder, so she'd realize it wasn't an inadvertent bump.

After Susan smiled at him, Dan ordered a beer and they tried to make small talk, but the din of the boisterous Friday night patrons and music forced them to repeat sentences two or three times. When shouting into each other's ears became annoying, Dan suggested they go for a walk. Susan was happy to oblige, leaving half her drink behind.

The cool stillness of the streetlight-illuminated sidewalk became a welcome relief, but it had an adverse reaction to conversation. Now that Dan and Susan didn't have to yell at each other, they didn't have much to say.

They walked along the sidewalk below the Iowa Electric Light and Power building, at twenty-seven stories, the tallest in Cedar City. Dan glanced up. It was the only building in Cedar City that reminded him of Chicago.

Although Cedar City didn't have the excitement of the big city, he felt safer on its downtown sidewalks at night than he ever would on any sidewalk in Chicago at any time, day or night.

Susan must have been reading his mind.

"Mmmmm, doesn't that air smell so clean?" she said, taking a deep breath. "Doesn't it make you feel that no matter what happens, you'll always be safe?"

Cedar City was well-known for its various fragrances – the well-done oatmeal cookie odor of the cereal plant, the stench of spilled blood from a pork packinghouse, the reek of dead fish in the Cedar River. But the cold fall air seemed to freeze those odors and replace them with a fresh country scent and a touch of evergreen.

"It does," Dan said. "It almost smells like a forest."

"Like Christmas." Susan tilted her head back and looked up at the stars in the clear dark sky. "It makes you wonder what's out there."

Dan gazed up for a moment, too, then focused his attention on Susan. The vast sky made him feel small, insignificant. He hated that.

Whether Dan wanted to admit it or not, he already saw Susan as a person who could give him a sense of purpose.

She had cried on his shoulder after the funeral and called him last night. Now she was leading him down a sidewalk toward the Second Avenue Bridge that spanned the river. It had been unusually cold and windy when they'd met at the cemetery and now, a night later, it was warmer and still, evidence that the Iowa weather changes as quickly as a reporter's mood.

As they approached the bridge, Dan looked at Susan's face with its cool glow. Her dark eyes shone even in the subdued light, her hair fluttered upon her back with each bouncing step. She seemed happy, truly happy, to be living in the present. If he hadn't known she'd lost her husband and a brother within the last year, he wouldn't have guessed it. He had been prepared to offer his shoulder again, but since that didn't seem necessary now, he was rendered speechless, an unusual state of affairs for Dan Goldberg.

"You seem awful quiet," Susan said.

"I'm just enjoying the night," he said. "And the company."

"Thank you." She smiled. "You know I grew up here."

"Yes, I had that in the story."

"That's right. Thirty-one years. It's a wonderful place to be a kid," she said, tightening the collar of her coat around her neck. "I wouldn't trade that part of my life for anywhere else on earth."

"What about Hawaii?"

"I've never been there," Susan said, "but I know I wouldn't like it. Too many people, too expensive and it doesn't have seasons. Not nights like this, anyway, where you can walk until your toes freeze, then go home and warm up with hot chocolate and a fire in the fireplace, if you happen to have one."

Dan would move to Hawaii in a minute, even though he'd never been there either. He'd go for the sunshine and the ocean and the thousands of miles it would take him away from Chicago. But Susan's enthusiasm for Cedar City made his reasoning sound vain so he didn't reply. Instead, he listened to her wax poetic about her hometown, asking questions only when necessary to remain a part of the conversation.

At the center of the bridge, they stopped to lean against the rail, to watch the dark river lap at the tall white concrete floodwalls along each bank. To the right, the walls protected the downtown business district from flooding; to the left, City Hall.

"Cedar City is like Paris," she said. "Its city offices are on an island."

Dan had heard that story. It seemed to be every native's favorite claim to fame. But he nodded, encouraging Susan to tell her version.

"In its early days, the island was covered with trees. It was a retreat for horse thieves. One of them is supposed to be Osgood Shepherd, whom the bar is named after."

She explained that the island had once been an amusement park. As they walked past the entrance to City Hall she told Dan about Grant Wood, world famous for painting "American Gothic," because he had designed and built the illuminated 1930s stained glass window in the building that depicts a life-size soldier from each war the United States had fought in up to that time.

"It's a priceless window," Susan said. "Uninsurable, but protected by thick bulletproof plastic, as if anybody would try anything to harm it anyway."

They crossed the bridge to the park-like shore on the far side of the river, strolling along the meandering pebble-grained sidewalk. Urban renewal in the sixties, when

Susan had been a child, resulted in the removal of old buildings that she could barely remember. It opened the riverbank to make the city more attractive, cleaner and brighter, she said.

The large double-decked bridge – with the interstate on the top level, two city streets coming together on the lower level and a hydroelectric dam below – was completed a few years ago to a lot of fanfare.

Susan sat on a bench and patted it as an invitation for Dan to sit, too. She stared across the river's glassy surface at the bright lights of the massive Quaker Oats plant that had been there forever. Every window in the ten-story fortress-like structure, and there had to be a couple hundred, glowed in the darkness and was reflected in the water, creating the illusion that the cereal plant was even larger.

To their left, a railroad bridge spanned the river from the park to the cereal plant, looming like a dark shadow in the otherwise bright night.

"It's the largest cereal mill in the world," Susan said.

"You are a wealth of information," Dan replied, chuckling as he shifted his body on the bench. He hadn't expected a guided tour and didn't mean to let his sarcasm escape, but Susan must not have noticed. It didn't slow her down.

"Anyone who's lived here all her life could tell you the same thing. We're proud of our city."

"I can tell," he said. "It's a nice town."

"City," Susan corrected. "It's the second largest city in Iowa, so we never call it a town. We export more products overseas than even Des Moines, the largest one. Quaker has a lot to do with that."

"Cedar City," Dan said. "It's in the name. I didn't mean anything by calling it a town, it's just that I'm used to Chicago."

"I know," she said. "Big city people don't see it the same way natives do, but my brother loved it as much as I do. That's why he became a cop here, to protect and serve the city he loved. He wanted it to always be safe."

Dan saw the glistening of tears in Susan's brown eyes and thought the floodgates would soon open. He knew she'd want to talk about her brother, that she'd want to cry on his shoulder, that she couldn't hold it back forever by talking about the city's history. It was about time.

He put his arm over her shoulders and pulled her toward him, so she could rest her head on his shoulder. But Susan's body remained rigid, she kept her arms to her side instead of hugging him back, and she did not lower her head.

"I don't want you to feel sorry for me." Susan pulled away from Dan, shedding the connection of his arm with her shoulder. "I didn't call you for that. I called because I wanted to get to know you. Maybe we can become friends."

"I hope so," Dan said. He was sure he wanted more than that, but if they had to start as friends, well, so be it.

"Your story today was fair," she said. "I mean, it was good, but it was fair to me. I had to read it several times before I felt that way. At first, I only saw myself as a sorry little creature who wanted public sympathy for losing two men close to her. I suppose a lot of people saw me that way."

"You've been unfortunate," Dan said.

"Yes. That's how I saw it later. Circumstances beyond my control. People need to realize that, sometimes, things happen. You didn't have me crying once in the story. I can take care of myself."

"I know."

"You seemed to show that in your writing," she said. "Have you ever lost anybody close to you?"

"No."

"The sensitive way you wrote the story, I thought you probably did." She stared at the lights of the cereal plant, yellow in their reflections on the river. "I don't know what I want, but I do know I'll go to work in that big old building that looks so cold from here but is actually warm when I think about all my friends who work there, too. I'll go to work next week and the week after that and ... I'll order new plastic toys for the cereal boxes. I'll think about my brother and my husband a lot. And tonight, when I go to bed, I'll think about how you let me talk your ears off as if you're a tourist and I'm your guide."

Susan turned toward Dan, as if to check his eyes to determine if he was still listening, then pulled her coat collar tighter around her neck and turned away.

"I'll never get over Bill's death," she said. "I haven't gotten over John's. There's some merit in that. You have to remember the people you loved, the people who loved you. But you can't obsess over it, over the things you can't control. If you do, the fear of loss can destroy your future."

"You have to live for today not yesterday," Dan said. "That's what took me a while to understand after my dad died a few years ago."

"You lost your dad? I thought you said you hadn't lost anybody close to you."

"I don't talk about it," Dan said.

"What happened?"

"I mean, please, I don't want to talk about it. OK?"

Dan looked into Susan's eyes as if to say, "End of subject." She seemed to understand.

The evening hadn't progressed as rapidly as Dan had envisioned and, here, he was telling a lie all because he'd hoped to get a weekend of sympathy sex. His father was alive and well, at least he was the last time they'd talked on the phone a couple of years ago only because his mother wasn't feeling well.

As far as Dan was concerned, though, his father might as well be dead because that's what Dan had wished every time he faced another round of criticism, every time he also thought about that summer working for John Wayne Gacy which he had sworn never to talk about to anyone. So, maybe saying his father was dead, wasn't such a horrible lie.

Susan might have been hurting inside, but she wasn't going to take any rash actions to console her sorrow. Dan realized as soon as they'd left Osgood's that she wasn't the type to sleep with a guy to get over her pain. She had her act together, more so than he'd thought at the cemetery. He wondered why he'd bother to lie, too, because the only sex he'd get from her now would be after making a commitment, and he wasn't looking for that, short-term or long.

Then again, Dan thought, that was always the challenge. Sex without commitment. He'd never forgive himself for not trying. Just not tonight.

Susan brushed her hair away from her face, looked up at the dark sky again and blinked her eyes firmly several times as if to clear away tears. "My toes are cold," she said. "It's time to go home."

Dan was already colder than he'd intended to be. "Let's go somewhere warm."

They walked quickly along the lower level of the double-decked bridge beneath the hum of the fast-moving interstate traffic above and the rush of water over the open dam gates below. Dan put his arm over Susan's shoulders again, more in a gesture of friendship than to show affection. She seemed to understand as she led the way.

The smell of oatmeal cookies from the cereal plant mixed with the fishy odor of the river. The exhaust notes from an occasional passing car echoed from beneath the top span of the bridge, as if they were in a parking garage. The walk was only two long blocks, but they were both cold enough it seemed like two miles.

"You can walk me to my front door," Susan said.

"Your front door?"

"Yes." She nodded at the Cedar River Tower, the twenty-five-story apartment building overlooking the river, the bridges, the interstate highway and Quaker Oats. "I live here, in the tallest apartment building in Iowa," she said with a laugh. "That information is part of the tour, too. Free of charge."

Dan chuckled. "What floor?"

"The twenty-second. My window faces west. I can see all the way down the river in the day, all the way to Ellis Park and the boat harbor. I like watching the sunsets. Some of them are spectacular, but my favorite view is in the middle of the night. The lights at Quaker burn all night long, and I never get tired of staring at them. They hypnotize me when I can't sleep, make me feel small and insignificant and cozy and comfortable."

Dan opened the glass door for Susan and followed her into the lobby, to the chrome-doored elevator.

"I can make it from here." She kissed him on the cheek, then pushed the button to hail the elevator. "Thanks for the company."

"I enjoyed it, too," he said, withholding final judgment until he learned where any relationship with Susan might lead. "We could get together again for dinner, my treat. Say, next week?"

"I'd like that," she said. "Call me."

Susan stepped through the open elevator door and waved at Dan by opening and closing her fingers. "Good night."

"I'll call you," Dan said, feeling foolish as he returned her wave in the exact same childish manner until the elevator door closed.

Dan heard the whir of the elevator and watched the lights above it blink in succession up to twenty-two, where it stopped.

Someday, he thought, someday soon, he'd see that view Susan had so succinctly described.

12

Dan Goldberg arrived home shortly after seven Saturday night, exhausted. He'd been to bed early Friday after saying good night to Susan Holcomb and had slept in Saturday morning.

But after Dan crawled out of bed, he found a burst of energy and spent the day cleaning his apartment and running errands, the last to the grocery store when the dinner hour meant it was the least crowded time of the weekend.

After he threw the plastic grocery sacks in the garbage can, Dan walked into his bedroom, shed his clothes except for his underwear, pulled back the covers on his king size waterbed, plumped up the pillows and climbed into the warmth of his cocoon. He knew he might not doze off for a while, but he wasn't planning to sleep until morning.

He rolled over and set the alarm clock for ten. Until he fell asleep, this was the ideal place to think.

All day Dan had considered calling Susan, to see if she was up for dinner since they hadn't eaten after their walk along the river and dinner had been their intent all along. All day he tried to convince himself that it wouldn't be worth the effort, the money, anyway. Susan wasn't his type, and he wasn't about to make a commitment to sleep with her. Yet that was the challenge. Why he wanted her. Why he considered calling.

Dan tried to erase his infatuation with Susan from his mind. He didn't need another challenge. He hadn't planned to spend the night with her, not the entire night, anyway, but ending the evening was supposed to have been his decision, not hers.

He closed his eyes and rolled over onto his left side. The water in the mattress sloshed around, bounced him up and down like he was on a soft and warm ocean wave. Hawaii. He imagined himself a beach bum, the surf crashing against rocks, the sand hot on his feet, the sun burning his back to a golden tan.

After a few minutes, Dan flopped over onto his right side, then flipped onto his back. With the pillow tucked beneath his neck, he opened his eyes to stare at the ceiling of the dark room.

Sometimes it was easier to clear your mind with open eyes, sometimes it was easier if they were closed and sometimes it was impossible to do it either way.

Dan often visualized events as he thought they would happen and replayed past events as if he could change his memory. His mind and his eyes, open and closed, drifted between the two perspectives. He tried to forget about his plans for the night, so he rehashed his shoplifting experience. He felt nervous. He wanted everything to be perfect.

* * * * *

When the incessant, annoying buzz of the alarm went off, Dan slapped it off and didn't feel as if he'd slept at all. He was groggy, and it had seemed like hours since he'd climbed into bed. Yet it seemed like no time had elapsed at all because, somehow, deep sleep had overcome his busy mind.

In the bathroom, Dan didn't stop to look at himself in the mirror but hopped into the shower. The warm water soothed his stiff neck and made him consider, momentarily, drying off and returning to the solitary warmth of his bed. He wasn't sure he could sleep all night, but he would have been willing to try if he didn't feel the need to go through with his plans. Everything was set. It would be a while until the timing was this good again.

Dan's apartment was dark except for the light in the bathroom. When he opened the door, the soft rays bathed the bedroom in a yellow glow. He preferred dressing in the semi-darkness, especially when his eyes felt tired.

His oak bookcase waterbed dominated the room like a playpen in a child's room. But he hadn't found a partner to play in it since he'd moved to Cedar City. That would have to change, which made him think of Susan again, her laugh, her brown eyes, her slim frame. She'd look great in his bed right now, waking and stretching naked beneath the velveteen quilt.

The top drawer of Dan's old highboy dresser squealed as he opened it, the sound of wood rubbing against wood. The silence in the room afterward sent a chill up his back. The drawer always made that awful sound, but for some reason he didn't think about it until it did. He would have to be more careful later.

Dan stepped into clean underwear, pulled on a pair of socks while standing and opened his closet. He didn't need light to locate his black pants. A couple of days earlier he'd hung them at the far end of the rack, next to wall, so they'd be easy to find. His navy-blue pullover sat on top of the pile of sweaters on the shelf above. It had been arranged there on purpose, too.

Dan sat on the edge of his bed and jerked his pants on, both legs at the same time. As he pulled the sweater over his head, the silver chain around his neck caught in the loose material. He reached inside the sweater to free the small swastika, to run his fingers over it for a moment, to think about who he was.

He knew he'd have to be invisible. He had already painted his white sneakers black with a permanent magic marker rather than throwing them into the washing machine with a package of black die. He'd left them beneath the kitchen sink to dry.

Dan walked back to the bathroom and removed his glasses, folding them carefully and placing them in the medicine cabinet. He pulled out the contact lens case beside them and set it on the edge of the sink. He flipped open the left side of the case, then the right, as he put his soft contacts in for the first time since he'd moved to Cedar City.

The contacts made Dan's eyes dry and tired, especially in the winter, so he had put them away. But tonight seemed the right time to wear them again. He could tolerate the contacts in his eyes for a few hours. That's all it would take. Nobody would recognize him.

With his "eyes" in place, Dan returned to the dimly lit bedroom, to the corner furthest from the full-length mirror. He gazed at his reflection, the dark shadow of a burglar.

Dan had read once about superstitious people's belief that the image on the other side of a mirror is in a different universe. Ridiculous. But he did know that his reflection was really twenty-four feet away, not twelve, because a mirror did multiply the distance by two.

He smiled at himself. Adrenalin began to flow, through his brain, his arms, his legs. He'd never be seen. The whiteness of his teeth gleamed in the mirror as he smiled. He told himself he wouldn't smile like that, show his teeth, for the rest of the night. Not until he was done.

* * * * *

The Toyota's engine died as Dan guided it next to the curb. It was as if the little car was controlled by his brain, as if it knew exactly where he wanted to go and when he wanted it to stop.

Dan sat in the silent car, listening for his heartbeat. Instead, he heard the cackling of the hot catalytic converter in the cool night air. What he'd read in mystery novels about burglars hearing their heartbeats before they pulled a job was bogus. His heart was there all right, he could feel it beating inside his chest. But it certainly didn't sound like a bass drum.

He pulled a black stocking cap over his head, not only because it was cold outside, but because it would keep him invisible. He looked at his face in the rearview mirror as he covered his ears with the edges of the cap. A streetlight shone into the car just enough so that he could see his eyes. That would do just fine. He grinned once more, for the last time he told himself. He promised.

Dan scanned the neighborhood of large colonial two-story houses on Country Club Drive. He checked his watch. It was almost eleven. Most of the houses were dark, the inhabitants either in bed or at Saturday's annual fall fling at the Cedar City Country Club. He figured to have a little more than an hour before they'd begin arriving home.

Around the corner and three houses up on the right side of the street stood Mayor Stan Rankin's home. Dan had been there once, a week after he'd started at *The Argus*. The mayor had invited the press to a cocktail party in the spring to announce the agenda for his third term. Public relations. The press saw through it, but reporters were only human. They couldn't resist free food and drink on the mayor. It was just that he didn't realize how hospitable he'd really been.

Dan reached into the back seat of the Toyota and dragged his khaki trench coat into the front seat. He slipped his arms through the sleeves and turned the collar down. He tucked his dark brown canvass duffel bag, folded into a square, inside the coat and held it under his arm, clamping it next to his body with his elbow as if he had a wounded wing.

Dan climbed out onto the street and shook his legs, so the hem of his long coat dropped around his knees. The coat really showed up under the streetlight. Dan's theory was that if anyone saw him walking the sidewalk, they wouldn't be suspicious. Why would a burglar dress in light clothes? They'd assume he lived in the neighborhood, that he was walking home from the country club party.

His dark sneakers padded silently on the sidewalk as Dan strolled toward the mayor's house. His steps seemed quick, like he was running, so he forced himself to take each step one at a time by counting to himself, one, two, three ...

Each driveway Dan approached seemed further away than the last. Finally, he reached the front of the mayor's house. The porch light was on but, as he'd anticipated, the house was dark, and the garage door was closed.

Dan sauntered up the front sidewalk as if he belonged there and rang the doorbell as if he expected someone to be home. He heard the simple muffled ding-dong inside and waited until no one came to the door. He rang it again for good measure. Still no answer.

Reaching inside his coat pocket, Dan pulled out a silver key. He had lifted it from its nail inside the garage two days earlier when he'd stopped at the mayor's house to solicit a comment before Collins' funeral. The garage door had been open and as he walked around the house, ringing doorbells and knocking on doors, no one was home.

How dumb could people be, Dan thought, leaving a house wide open like that? It had been easy to pilfer the key. It probably wouldn't even be missed. With a wife and three kids, anyone could have misplaced it.

Dan opened the screen door, slipped the key into the front door lock and turned it easily. The bolt clicked, slick as a whistle.

He pulled the sleeve of his sweater over his right hand, so he wouldn't leave any fingerprints and turned the knob. The door opened. He dropped the key into his coat pocket and walked inside.

The streetlight shot a column of light through a window by the door and across the foyer. Dan paused for a moment, wondering if he should turn on the hall light in case someone had seen him enter the house. If someone had, they'd wonder why a light hadn't been turned on.

Then he decided against it. That wasn't part of his original plan. Some chances you had to take. Turning on a light wasn't one of them. But it made him doubt the wisdom of wearing a light-colored coat. If he were caught, he'd blame it on that error in judgment. But he couldn't worry too much about that now.

Dan locked the front door bolt behind him and knelt in the hallway. Unfolding the duffel bag on the floor, he opened it and extracted a pair of dark vinyl gloves and a silver and red glasscutter. He removed his trench coat, folded it in half lengthwise, rolled it into a tight ball and stuffed it into the duffel bag. He shoved the glass cutter into his back pocket and stretched the gloves onto his hands. He rubbed his gloved fingers over the inside doorknob and lock mechanism to erase any fingerprints. Dan was invisible now, dressed in black, no trace left behind.

His eyes adjusted to the darkness inside the house as he carried the duffel bag in front of him to act as a cushion in case he ran into something he couldn't see. It was softer than a knee and wouldn't hurt like a hard shinbone against the edge of a coffee table.

The mayor's residence was classic, no doubt about it. Dan wondered if he had received any money under the table. Then he realized Stan Rankin probably didn't need money. He'd retired after twenty years as an Air Force colonel, had lived on his pension for a while, then took a job writing defense contracts for Electronics International. His forty-five-thousand-dollar mayor's salary also was nothing to sneeze at.

The living room was brighter than the hallway because the heavy curtains were open and light from the street filtered through sheer white drapes. Dan had no problem maneuvering around the rectangular coffee table.

The double doors to the den were open so he headed there. During the mayor's party, Dan finished a drink in the den and had noted it was paneled in dark mahogany without windows. He closed the doors behind him and flipped on the light switch. He was blinded by the sudden brightness.

The mayor had good taste, Dan thought, except for the award plaques nailed to the walls. The carpet was a bittersweet orange, the ceiling paneled exactly like the walls. A massive bookcase spanned the far end and two overstuffed wingback chairs sat on either side of a small white statue of a cupid trimmed in gold.

Off to one side, copies of computer magazines were neatly arranged on top of a low table. Two remote control devices sat on top of the magazines. Just inside the doors, along the adjacent wall, a television and a VCR sat on a movable stand. The bottom shelf held a sizable collection of store-bought movies. Dan was tempted to examine them, to see if there was anything he wanted, but that wasn't what he'd come for.

Doors beneath the bookshelves hid the real treasure, the box of medals. Dan was positive. They'd been displayed on a table at the party. They didn't have much monetary value, just the sentimental kind. That's why Dan figured they wouldn't be tucked away in a safe, why it was important that he steal them. The mayor would be furious.

He stooped over and opened cabinet doors one at a time. It was like a game show. Behind which door would he find the prize? Bingo. Door number two.

Dan removed the walnut box from the shelf and opened it. The three medals were all there on a bed of red velvet – a Distinguished Flying Cross in the center, its red, white and blue ribbon mounted to the velvet so the bronze cross could hang free; a Purple Heart with its outline of George Washington suspended from a purple ribbon trimmed in white; the black and silver Iron Cross of Germany with its large "W" for King Friedrich Wilhelm III engraved where the cross bars came together, a crown on top and its 1943 date on the bottom.

Dan snapped the lid shut, the sound of wood smacking wood breaking the silence like a gunshot. He didn't care. He had his genuine Iron Cross. It was as if he could choke the entire German Army in his gloved hands.

He had hated listening to the mayor's World War II stories the night of the party until he heard how Stan Rankin had "found" the Iron Cross among the wreckage of a Messerschmitt behind Allied lines. He wasn't surprised to see the medal displayed with those that Rankin had earned. The Germans were the enemy to him, as they had been to Dan's ancestors, and the Iron Cross was a trophy. It was an excuse to talk about the war, to add some credence to the mayor's stories of bravery even if it was probably obtained by other than honorable means.

Dan stuffed the box into his duffel bag and began to leave the den. Instead, he turned and brushed the computer magazines to the floor. Then he opened every bookcase door and left them that way.

Glancing at the VCR tapes, he picked up copies of "Casablanca" and "It's a Wonderful Life," tossing them into his duffel bag. He threw the other tapes onto the floor. He unplugged the television and the VCR, dragging it to the floor. No need to be too destructive, he thought. It just needed to look good.

He flipped off the light and reached to open the den's door when a noise on the other side started him.

Dan froze.

It was the type of mysterious sound he heard when he was trying to fall asleep. He'd swear he heard something, but he wasn't sure where it came from or what made it. He had been positive he was alone in the house. He waited.

Nothing.

For a long deliberate count to sixty, Dan stood motionless in the dark den, wondering how he'd escape if someone was out there. No windows and only one doorway. Then he realized it wouldn't matter. If someone were there, they'd discover him one way or another, either in the den or trying to escape. His best chance would be to run.

Dan threw open the double doors and stood quietly, waiting for his vision to adjust to the low light from the outside windows. He stared at the lamps, two along the wall near the window and one off to the right. They cast the only shadows large enough to belong to a human and they weren't moving. It had been at least two minutes and the sound didn't return. He'd come this far. Nothing he could do but carry on with his plan.

As Dan walked into the living room, he felt something brush against his right pants leg. As he looked down, he felt a tug at his shoelace. A large black cat had appeared from the darkness to attack his feet.

Not sure how to react, Dan watched the cat for a moment before kicking his leg into the air. The cat flew across the room, crashing into a floor lamp, knocking it over. The cat scooted away in the darkness, presumably from where it had come.

Dan left the lamp on the floor. A burglar wouldn't pick it up, he reasoned, slipping around the coffee table and through the living room into the dining room-kitchen area at the rear of the house. The kitchen was off to his right, the dining room to his left. He headed for the dining room.

On top of the buffet sat the cedar box full of silverware, genuine sterling silver. It had to be worth a small fortune and it wouldn't be too difficult to fence.

Dan slung the long strap of the duffel bag over his right shoulder and hefted the heavy box of silverware with both hands. He'd probably have to carry it to the car that way, but first things first. He set the silverware box on the floor by the window and lowered himself to his knees.

Unlatching the window, Dan pushed it up and open, then stood up. The absence of a screen made the process of crawling out feet first rather easy. He dragged the duffel bag out, then closed the window. Removing the glass cutter from his back pocket, Dan ran it quickly around the window's edges, first along the left side, then the right, and finally across the top and bottom.

Dan turned his back to the window and with one swift kick of his heel, like a mule, knocked the glass into the dining room. He'd thought the inside pane of the thermal window would be difficult to break, but his foot went through it cleanly.

The shattering of the glass as it crashed against a dining room chair reminded Dan of a childhood history lesson, of Kristallnacht, the night the Germans ransacked Jewish-owned businesses and the synagogues before World War II, breaking glass in the streets. He had to move quickly.

Dan zipped the glasscutter along the sides of the inside windowpane to snap off large, jagged edges. He tossed the pieces into the house and followed them by crawling back inside where he stomped on the glass and re-locked the window latch.

As more glass crackled beneath his feet, Dan shoved the box of silverware through the window and followed it out into the mayor's back yard. He hoisted the duffel bag over his shoulder and picked up the box of silverware with both hands.

Although the ground was cold and firm, Dan felt his feet sink ever so slightly under the added weight of the silverware as he ran through the back yard. He cut toward the rear property line, along a wire fence toward his car.

Glancing back toward the house, Dan didn't see any lights come on. All of the houses on the street remained dark from the back with the exception of one and its curtains were drawn. Dan was certain he wouldn't be detected in the darkness and was pleased that no more fences blocked his escape.

Approaching a white spotlight cast on the ground by a streetlight and breathing hard, Dan carefully looked both ways as if he were a child crossing the street. No cars. No people out walking their dogs. No one was anywhere.

Dan flung the silverware and duffel bag into the front seat of his car, circled it to slide behind the wheel and jammed the key into the ignition. The trusty Toyota's engine kicked over on the first turn.

Dan felt as though his lungs would burst and, for the first time, definitely felt his heart beat inside his chest, thumping like a bass drum. He slammed the shifter into gear, released the clutch smoothly and cruised slowly, so as not to raise any suspicion, the hell out of there.

13

When the telephone rang Sunday evening, Mike Rockwell slapped himself on the forehead and sighed. He'd been sitting at his desk for ten minutes and the calls continued. A dozen messages had been left for him about his kidnapping story.

So far, according to coworkers' scribbles, most callers thought Mike was noble, brave and an upfront guy to write the story. But, as a reporter, he never knew from one telephone call to the next what somebody might think. Every story seemed to anger at least one person. He answered on the third ring.

"*Argus*," he said. "Mike Rockwell. How may I help you?"

"Hey, Rockwell, you lose something?"

That voice. Mike recognized it instantly from the night in the police car. Fear raced through his mind, rekindling the pain in his left leg. Immediately, he knew the caller was referring to his lost notebook. So, it had been in Morgan's car. Now what? Mike decided to play ignorant.

"Lost something? I don't know what you mean."

"Like, a, maybe, a notebook?" the voice said. It was urgent and deprecating.

Mike's worst fear had been realized. He recalled the barrel of the gun pointed at his head. This obviously wasn't the call of a Good Samaritan or a man who wanted to chat about today's story. Mike was speechless.

"I said, asshole, did you lose a reporter's notebook?"

"Oh, sure. That notebook. I must have lost it somewhere. Do you have any idea, do you know where it is?"

Mike felt foolish for babbling, but it seemed the natural response, an interviewing technique he learned early in his career, to stall, to give himself time to think.

"No," the voice said, "I have no goddamn idea where it is. I just called the number on the cover to bullshit with you, to see if I could be of assistance, to help you find it. Of course, I've got it, you imbecile. I figured you'd want it back after the hatchet job you did on me today."

Mike's first inclination was to dispute Morgan's opinion about his story, but he held all the cards. And Mike's notebook. Still, the telephone line provided plenty of distance between them. Mike was safely inside *The Argus* building and the cops were just another phone call away.

"I don't need any help writing my stories, thank you," Mike said firmly.

How many times had Mike Rockwell heard similar criticism? Everybody was an expert. If they could do the job, why weren't they reporters? He had to show this guy he wasn't scared.

"I thought my story was damn good," Mike continued. "I told it just the way it happened."

"You weren't even supposed to be there, and you made yourself out to be some kind of a fucking hero. Hell, you were my accomplice, ever think of that? You helped me escape, drove the getaway car. But you didn't even get a look at me. You couldn't even describe what I look like. Some fantastic reporter you are. Hell, I should have shot you in both legs."

"Who are you?" A rhetorical question. Mike knew he was talking to Ronald Morgan, the man the police had pegged as the cop shooter and his abductor. The police were looking all over for Morgan but considered him dangerous enough to keep his name from the public for at least a few days. Mike felt his voice waver as he repeated the question. "Who are you?"

"You know who I am as well as I know who you are."

"Ronald Morgan?"

"Bingo! You're a pretty smart asshole, Rockwell."

"Thank you." Mike couldn't help but fight sarcasm with sarcasm. "I wasn't sure it was you."

"Well, it is. On the phone and in the car." Morgan paused, cleared his throat, inhaled as if he was smoking a cigarette on the other end of the line. "So, you want your damn notebook back?"

"Sure, I want it back. Why don't you drop it in the mail?"

Morgan laughed, a condescending laugh.

Suddenly, Mike had the urge to call the police, to tell them Morgan was still in town, that he had him on the line. It wasn't until that moment that he considered trying to trace the call. He waved his hand in the air to get Bill Jackson's attention.

"I make my deliveries in person," Morgan said. "You know, make sure it gets to its destination safe and sound. I don't put much faith in the U.S. government."

Jackson was copy editing, staring so intently at his computer screen that only a system failure would have distracted him.

"What? You want to see me, so you can shoot me again?"

Mike had no intention of ever meeting Morgan face to face a second time. He needed to buy time. He knew a lot of criminals get off on scaring people, so he had to show Morgan he wasn't afraid. He had to convince him to mail the notebook, leave him alone, yet he had to keep him talking.

Sweat broke out on Mike's forehead as his mind churned a million miles a minute. He had to get Morgan captured. It was the only way he'd feel safe.

Mike picked up his telephone book and heaved it at Jackson. The book fluttered open as it tumbled like a wounded duck across the aisle. A direct hit, smashing into Jackson's head.

"Hey, what's the big idea?" Jackson yelled He glared at Mike.

Mike bounced his hand up and down for Jackson to keep his voice down, then motioned for him to come over to his desk.

"If I wanted to kill you, I'd have done it on the airport road," Morgan said. "I just want to have a nice little chat with you. In person. I think we can help each other out."

"How can I help you?" Mike said. "Why would I want to?"

Jackson stood at the front of Mike's desk, watching his hand skate across a blank piece of typing paper. "Trace this call," it read. "My abductor."

Jackson's eyes widened. He may have been a copy editor, Mike thought, but he did know a story when it hit him on the head.

"Sure thing," Jackson whispered. He tiptoed back to his desk, as if being quiet mattered, picked up the phone and called the police.

"You can get me off the hook on this goddamn murder rap," Morgan said. "I didn't shoot that cop. And I'll give you the fucking exclusive."

"Right," Mike said. "Why should I believe you?"

"If I already killed a cop, doesn't it make sense I wouldn't worry about killing someone else? What's one more dead body? It would have been you."

A shiver snaked up Mike's spine as he realized Morgan made a valid point. He knew Mike's identity, where he worked, where he was at that exact moment. He probably knew where Mike lived.

But Mike did his best to remain calm. Soon, if he could keep Morgan on the phone, the police would pinpoint his location.

"Your fingerprints were all over the gun they found in the bedroom," Mike said. "The cops have you nailed."

Morgan laughed again. "They're idiots. That wasn't even the gun that killed that cop friend of yours. The gun in the bedroom hadn't even been fired. Ask your cop friends about that."

Mike planned to ask them. If the gun the cops found wasn't the one that killed Collins, then why had they made it sound that way? Either the cops were playing a hunch or Morgan was lying. That was the most logical. A man who would kill a cop and deal in cocaine had to be an expert liar.

"Hey, look, pal," Mike said, figuring an aggressive tact would keep Morgan on the line. "Even if that part of your story checks out, it's a little hard for me to believe anything you say. All I know about you is that you're a drug pusher and you don't hesitate to pull the trigger. If you want me to believe you, if you want my help, you've got to give me a better reason than what I've heard so far."

"That's why I want to talk to you, in person." Morgan's voice had changed, soft-spoken, cautious, pleading.

Mike smiled. As soon as he'd become tough, Morgan backed down. But meeting in person could still be a ploy to lure Mike into a trap, to get violent with him for the allegedly negative newspaper story. Maybe Morgan wasn't lying. He hadn't been identified by name in the story because nobody alive had actually seen him.

"I need to see you in person, and I don't want anybody else there." Morgan became aggressive again. "Just you and me, Rockwell. No cops. And I'll make sure that's the way it is. I ain't out to get you, you got my word on that. I want my name cleared. It'll be a hell of a story for you. But if you bring anybody else, you don't get it. You don't get your goddamn notebook. You'll never see me again."

"I don't really need that notebook," Mike said. "I've written my stories. I don't have any reason to see you."

Mike glanced over at Jackson, who was holding the telephone receiver to his ear.

"What you've got to say to me," Mike continued, "you can say over the phone. You shot me, and you're a wanted man. I'd just as soon see you behind bars than meet you in a dark alley. I've got more important things to worry about than an old notebook and some thug who wants the newspaper to pronounce him innocent."

Jackson looked at Mike with a blank expression.

"You can be a smart ass, Rockwell, you know that?" Morgan said. "For your own good, do what I say. Look, I know where you work, when you go into the office, when you leave. I know where you live, it's in the phone book. If I wanted to get you, I could have done it by now and nobody would have been the wiser. Just meet me. You damn hotshot reporters are always desperate for a good story. I've got one for you and now you're willing to blow it."

Across the aisle, Jackson hung up his phone, shrugged his shoulders, returned to the front of Mike's desk. He slid Mike's note across the desk with his own notation. "Can't do."

"Damn," Mike said.

"What'd you say?" Morgan asked.

"Nothing. Nothing. I just don't like this whole idea. I don't want to have anything to do with you."

"Suit yourself," Morgan said. "It'd be a hell of a story. I can tell you who killed that cop. If I'm guilty, you get the confession. If I'm not, you get the real story, the name of the real killer. If you don't meet me, you don't get shit. Good luck sleeping at night, knowing you let a cop killer get away."

"Why should I think you know anything about a good story? You call and criticize me for the one I wrote today and tell me you could do a better job. I hear that all the time from 'experts' like you. Putting me down isn't the way to get on my good side."

"Who said I wanted to get on your good side? I just want to save my ass. And I could end up saving yours, too."

"What's that supposed to mean?"

"Take it any way you want, kid. It's like I said. I can find you any time I want, day or night. Just don't lose any sleep over it.'

The power of suggestion. Mike had tried using that on Morgan and now he wondered if he'd ever sleep again. Thoughts of the shooting already kept him awake at night and it had been six days. Now Morgan was filling his head with more negative ideas. He wouldn't get a full night's sleep until Morgan was behind bars. And how would he accomplish that? He needed help. But Morgan said cops were out.

"Tell you what," Mike said. "You don't want to do this, but why don't you send me the notebook in the mail? If you tell me you'll do that, and you do, then maybe I can trust you, at least a little bit. And I'll check out your story about the gun."

"What should make me think I can trust you? You'll probably take the notebook and run."

"You think I'd quit my job over a threat from you and a lost notebook?"

Mike had considered doing exactly that. Linda's reasons for working days had begun to make sense. Being a reporter inside a story like this was too dangerous, too nerve-wracking. But quitting wouldn't accomplish anything. It wouldn't get him out of this mess. As long as Morgan was free, Mike wouldn't feel safe.

"It's like you said," Mike added. "You know where I am."

Morgan's end of the line was quiet for what seemed like enough time to send the notebook from New York to Los Angeles. Mike could hear him breathing steadily. He could almost hear sensory impulses exploding in his brain.

Mike picked up a pencil, but he couldn't hold it still in his hand. In nine years as a reporter at three newspapers nothing like this had ever happened. He'd never been involved in a crime. He'd never been in a position to help apprehend a criminal. His life had never been threatened.

Finally, Morgan's voice shattered the silence like a cannon. "All right! I'll send the notebook. And I'll call you back."

The line went dead.

Mike clutched the telephone in his hand as if it was attached with Super Glue. He looked at the clock on the wall, the red second hand sweeping past the six, circling slowly to the top again. Even if Morgan mailed the notebook tonight it would be at least Tuesday until he'd receive it. That would give him time to decide a course of action. Should he tell the cops? Should he tell Margaret? Linda?

No, he couldn't breathe a word of this to Linda. She'd get hysterical. He couldn't tell anyone. Not yet.

As Mike replaced the receiver, Jackson appeared at his desk. "So, what happened?" he asked. "What did he want? What are you going to do? Did you call the cops back?"

"Nothing," Mike said, shaking his head. "It was nothing, a caller playing a trick on me. False alarm."

But Mike knew the concern on his face was obvious. His neck muscles had tensed up. He was a poor liar.

"Sure." Jackson smiled. "Sure. A cop killer calls to give a reporter a measly notebook before he blows town, and the reporter pretends like it never happened. That makes about as much sense as kissing your sister."

"It was just a guy who said he liked my story."

"Sure," Jackson said, returning to his computer. "And he carries a gun and killed a cop and shot you in the leg."

Mike ignored Jackson's comments and went about his business. Only, he couldn't concentrate on anything but Morgan's telephone call. He walked to the restroom, weighing his alternatives.

If he cooperated with Morgan, he'd get another good story no matter how it turned out. Either Morgan would give him a great tip, or he'd have another confrontation with the cop killer to write about. Unless he was dead.

If Mike could set up Morgan for capture, it would be a fantastic finish to this morning's story. But he'd have to talk to the cops, work with them, and Morgan had said no cops. But he'd be safe. That would be the best part about it. But what would Morgan do if he spotted a cop? Run? Or would he shoot again?

If Mike didn't tell the police, would he be obstructing justice? Would his secret eventually be discovered? Would he wind up in jail?

That might not be such a bad idea, he thought. At the moment, jail was probably the safest place in the world for Mike Rockwell.

14

After Mike Rockwell finished work Sunday, after midnight as usual, he didn't feel much like going home. He wondered if Ronald Morgan would be lurking in the dark alley along *The Argus* building. It was a fact that Morgan could find him anywhere, at any time, if he desired. Morgan had called him at work. He could probably outline his schedule. He'd made that threat.

Mike busied himself around the office, picking up newspapers from his desk and clipping articles from them for his files. Usually it was an early evening chore to get him in the reporting mood. But he figured now was as good a time as any. There were chances he had to take and there were chances he shouldn't consider, like walking into a death trap. Would his life be like this from now on? Why should somebody like Morgan have so much power that he controls another man's every move?

Mike timed the "completion" of his filing project perfectly. Jackson had put the last pages for Monday's final edition to bed and was slipping on his coat. Mike closed his desk drawer, grabbed his crutches and made a bee line to the closet.

"Hanging around kind of late, aren't you?" Jackson said as he helped Mike put on his coat.

"I just needed to get some stuff done so I don't have to worry about it tomorrow," Mike said as he hobbled alongside Jackson toward the side exit.

"It's Morgan, isn't it?" Jackson said.

"No."

"Come on, you know it is. Tell me about it."

"There's nothing to tell."

"Hell, then, don't worry about it. You'll get your notebook back, the guy will leave town, and your cares will be over." Jackson patted Mike on the shoulder and chuckled. "Besides, he liked your story."

"Right. He loved it." Mike wished everything was that easy.

They walked down the back stairway to the alley. As they emerged into the dark night, the heavy security door thumped shut behind them. *The Argus* building, with its heavy concrete block walls, would make an excellent prison, Mike thought. Again, he wondered if he'd be safer outside or somewhere behind bars.

"Good night," Jackson said, turning in the opposite direction of Mike's car.

"Good night."

Mike felt secure walking past the active loading dock where men talked among themselves as they scrambled around the platform, loading first edition newspapers into large blue delivery vans. Long shadows darting here and there across the parking lot accentuated the bustle. But as Mike climbed into his big gold Buick, he didn't want to go home. He felt like driving around with no destination in mind, to simply listen to music on the radio, to drive where his eyes led. At times like this, he could burn half a tank of gas going nowhere.

Mike cruised the business district, along one-way streets, and found himself on Second Avenue, the precise route he'd driven with Morgan in the back seat holding a gun to his back. Unconsciously, he glanced in the rear-view mirror as he had done that night.

The old Buick had rambled more than a hundred thousand miles and sported rust trim around each fender. The soft shock absorbers made the car float as if on water. A comfortable cruiser. A boat. A tank. If Morgan wanted to, he couldn't find a big enough car to run Mike off the road unless it was a tank.

Not until nearly three in the morning did Mike decide that he wouldn't go home at all. He didn't want to be alone. He needed to talk to somebody. After a second straight weekend spent mostly apart, he needed to be with Linda.

Maneuvering his crutches to the outside steps to Linda's apartment, Mike thought he heard the crackling of twigs in the distance. Or was the noise around the corner?

Mike hesitated momentarily, but there was only silence. He hobbled inside the lobby and up the carpeted stairway to her second-floor apartment. He decided not to use his key to let himself in since she'd been so cool toward him lately. Perspiring and out of breath, he knocked softly on the door. He didn't want to wake everyone in the building.

No answer. He knocked harder and put his ear to the door. He heard footsteps on the other side.

"Who is it?" Linda's voice. She sounded drowsy, as if he'd awakened her, and he felt guilty. He knew she'd been asleep for hours.

"Mike," he whispered. "I need to see you."

He heard the security chain slide out of its latch, then followed the slowly opening door into her apartment. He barely caught a glimpse of Linda, her rumpled auburn hair, as she disappeared into the darkness. He knew she was unhappy about being awakened in the middle of the night. He left the light off, so he wouldn't wake her any more than he already had. But he couldn't tell if she'd gone to the right, toward the kitchen, or to the left toward the bedroom.

"Where are you?" Mike whispered.

"In here." Her sleepy voice came diagonally across the living room. She'd gone back to bed.

In the dark, Mike navigated his way around the coffee table in the center of the room and the ottoman that partially blocked the bedroom entrance. Beside her bed, he stopped and stood above her.

"I'm sorry I woke you," he said. His eyes had adjusted to the low light. She was lying on her back, her arm crossed over her face. He kept his voice low, almost to a whisper, as if talking any louder would make her angrier. "I really need to talk to you."

"Mmmm, mmmm." She pulled the sheet up over her face as if she expected him to turn on the light. "At three in the morning?"

"I know it's late."

"Very," she said. "I need my sleep."

She wasn't paying attention and that frustrated Mike. He knew she was thinking how he'd done this before, shown up in the middle of the night and interrupted her nine hours of sleep. Usually, it was for sex. Sometimes she was in the mood and sometimes she wasn't. If she wasn't, it turned into a bad night, and Mike inevitably regretted stopping. Since she usually blamed him for her bad mood in the morning, it would bother him all day. Even though she would accept his apology a day later,

Mike was left with the feeling that she knew it would happen again.

This was different. He understood she couldn't read his mind. He was thankful for that. But he wished she would be more sensitive, would at least comprehend the pleading tone in his voice. He didn't know what to do. If he told her the real reason he'd come, she'd be sympathetic but also worry and lose sleep. Already, he regretted stopping. But now that he had, it was too late to turn back.

Mike sat lightly on the edge of Linda's bed. As the springs gave under his weight, he saw her silhouette roll away from him. She was lying on her side next to the wall, her back to him. He reached out and stroked her shoulder. She did not respond.

He had to choose his words carefully. He didn't want to scare her. He just wanted her to know how frightened he was. He remembered when he'd told her he got shot. She said he should quit the night beat immediately. He had defended his decision, saying reporting on crime was the only work that made him happy.

"Linda," he began. The tone in his voice sounded as much like a question as a statement. He still wasn't sure exactly what he'd say. He paused.

"I'm here," she said loudly. "Get it over with."

This wasn't going as planned. Mike had imagined them standing face to face, so she could see the concern in his expression. He had imagined her wrapping her arms around him and telling him everything would be all right.

Simultaneously, he felt disappointment and anger. Couldn't she tell he was troubled? Didn't she love him enough to pay attention when he needed her? Anger overwhelmed the disappointment.

"Oh, never mind," he said, standing abruptly. "I'm sorry I bothered you. I'll talk to you tomorrow."

As he left the bedroom on his crutches, Mike heard the bedsprings squeak as she rolled over toward him.

"Michael," Linda shouted. "What's wrong with you?"

He stopped in the middle of the living room and didn't respond. He heard the bedsprings creak under her weight. She must have sat up.

"Michael, since you woke me," she shouted, "you damn well better tell me what this is all about."

He turned to see her standing in the bedroom doorway, her hands on her hips.

"It's no big deal," he said, walking toward the front door. "We can talk about it tomorrow." He turned the knob.

"Mike," she said softly, his name hanging in the air. "Please talk to me. You come over here in the middle of the night, wake me up and then say we can talk about this tomorrow. If you've got something to say, I'm ready to listen. Now. Please."

Mike stared into her eyes and they appeared warm, lucid, understanding. Sometimes he loved her even more when she became slightly angry. She seemed so alluring in the dim light filtering through the sheer drapes in the living room. Her long red hair ruffled around her sleepy, half-opened eyes. Yellow nightgown draped loosely from her shoulders. Bare arms hanging invitingly at her side.

Mike wanted Linda to hold him. He could have called to tell her about Morgan's phone call, but he wanted to tell her in person, so he could hold her. Now he wasn't so sure he should tell her about it at all.

Mike stumbled off his crutches and wrapped an arm around Linda's waist and hugged her tightly. He could feel her soft breasts against his chest, her slow breaths, the heat of her back on the palms of his hands. She returned the hug lightly, her fingertips gently caressing the tight muscles in his shoulders. The warmth of another human body, the idea of two people becoming one, made him sigh. He had needed that for the moment, probably for the rest of his life.

"I'm scared," Mike finally confessed. He knew how insecure, how wimpy, he sounded. He didn't care. It was true. "I'm just so scared."

"Michael," she said, squeezing him tighter. "I'm sorry."

He squeezed her tightly, his chin on her shoulder.

"Just because I said I wouldn't marry you, doesn't mean I don't still love you," she said. "I do. And I'm not planning to go anywhere without you." She gently pushed him away and looked into his eyes. "OK?"

Mike nodded. He realized she didn't have a clue about what was really bothering him. She thought their relationship was foremost on his mind. Explaining that his concern was not about them as a couple would make him seem selfish now, that he was just thinking about himself.

To avoid speaking, to give him time to reorganize his thoughts, Mike hugged her again. And then he couldn't help himself. He spoke to the blank wall as they stood holding each other.

"Linda," he said, hesitantly. "I've got to be honest with you. I think I'm in trouble."

"Trouble?" Her voice showed definite concern. "What kind of trouble could you be in?"

Mike concentrated on her green eyes. They could be so many things. Sometimes they were so large and shiny and warm, like they would open up and welcome him inside. Other times they could look tiny and cold, piercing his thoughts like the sharp tip of a knife. They appeared somewhere between extremes now, wanting to comfort him, yet not wanting to draw him too close. It was impossible for him to read her mind.

"I think Morgan is going to come after me."

The name didn't register. "Morgan?"

"The guy who shot me in the leg."

"Come after you? Michael!" She shoved him away. "What are you talking about?"

"I think I'm in trouble with him. I think he's going to come after me, maybe try to kill me."

"Oh, come on," she said. "Did you have another bad dream? Every police officer in the state is looking for that guy. Probably the nation. He's long gone if he knows what's good for him."

"He called me tonight. At the office."

"He called *you*?" Her reaction was predictable and melodramatic. She stepped back, her mouth fell open and the pupils of her eyes disappeared beneath her eyelids. "*He* called *you*, and you didn't tell me until now?"

"I didn't want you to worry."

"Worry?" Linda backed away, sat on the couch, put her hands to her face, which was awash in fear. "Of course, I'd worry."

Mike knew she believed him. Finally, he had her attention.

"Did he threaten you?"

"Not exactly," Mike lied. He stuffed his hands into his pockets. "But he wants to meet me."

"You called the police."

Mike shook his head. "He told me not to call the cops, not to talk to anyone. I haven't said a word to anyone except you. I needed to think. I need to work this out."

"What's there to think about?" she said. "He's a madman with a gun. He shot you once, he'd shoot you again."

"What can I do?"

"Turn him in."

"He called on the phone. I don't know where he is."

"The police can find him."

"They haven't so far. And that doesn't mean I'd be safe. Before they do, he could still come after me."

"The police would protect you."

"I'm not so sure they could."

Linda took a deep breath, patted the couch beside her for Mike to sit down. "We've got to think," she said. "What did this Morgan say? He didn't actually come out and threaten to kill you, did he?"

"No. He claims he wants to tell me the real story, that he didn't shoot the cop but that he knows who did. When I didn't buy that, he said he knew how to find me. He said he'd had plenty of times to kill me if that's what he wanted to do."

"And you believe him?"

"Linda, I don't know what to believe about anything anymore." He sighed and immediately realized his words and the somber tone in his voice implied that he meant their relationship, too. He hadn't meant for it to come out that way.

She had interpreted his mannerisms perfectly. "Michael Rockwell," she said, "I love you, and I don't want anything bad to ever happen to you." She wrapped an arm around his head, pulled him close to her breast like a mother hugging a sick child. "We'll figure this out together."

Linda had done exactly the right thing. At times like this, Mike believed love could conquer all. He was a romantic, no doubt about it. He didn't read romance novels or believe in motion picture love stories, but he believed in dreams coming true. His parents had always been together and, when he thought about it, a relationship like that seemed like it would make a wonderful life. He had always fantasized about being that happy someday, about being the right man for the right woman. He knew he was the right man for Linda. She was right for him.

"I don't want anything to happen to us either," he said. Again, Mike knew the emphasis on "us" could be construed to mean "me," but he realized that hadn't bothered her when she kissed him softly on the mouth, her tongue barely touching his lips.

"You're not going anywhere tonight," she said. "You're staying here with me."

Mike wasn't about to argue. He knew if he went home it would be a rerun of last night, in and out of bed, grabbing one beer after another, trying to get just intoxicated enough to fall asleep. By the time he got up, he'd be drunk or hung over, or, worse yet, both. He didn't need that. He needed to think clearly.

"I don't want to do anything except hold you," he said. "I just want to know you're here."

"I'm glad you came to me instead of keeping this bottled up inside," Linda said. "I'll always be here for you, Mike."

Linda kissed him again and took his hand, leading him like a child into the bedroom.

An understanding silence filled the room as Linda crawled beneath the sheets and he sat on the edge of the bed, methodically removing his shoe and sock. He felt better knowing she cared, as he unbuckled his pants and struggled pulling the sliced leg of them over his cumbersome cast.

As Mike unbuttoned his shirt, he wanted to make love to Linda, to center his complete attention on the pleasure that would bring. But his feeling of inadequacy was stronger, for he felt weak knowing that he'd needed to rely on someone else to chase away his fears. For that, he felt less like a man, more like a helpless child.

By the time Mike hoisted his cast into bed beside Linda, he was exhausted. She faced him with her head on a pillow, reached out with both hands to touch his bare chest, smiled with watery eyes. He felt tears in his eyes, too.

"Thank you," Mike said, cupping Linda's hands in his. He closed his eyes in that position, thought about how he'd like to spend the rest of the week this way, the rest of his life, and somehow, he fell asleep.

15

The legal-sized pages of the crime log flew in and out of Dan Goldberg's hands as he flipped through them, searching for potential story ideas – rapes, murders, assaults and, specifically, the burglary of a certain prominent citizen's home.

Monday mornings, Dan often had a hangover, but this morning he was simply tired. He hadn't slept well after returning to his apartment Saturday night and he'd been restless all day Sunday. Maybe that was good. He hadn't felt nearly as nervous coming into the police station as he'd thought he would, probably because he was all worried out. Exhaustion helped. It gave him an I-could-careless attitude. It also helped that all the big wigs were in meetings Monday mornings to rehash weekend events and to discuss the upcoming week. He wouldn't have to talk to Assistant Chief Charles Schmidt.

Dan concentrated on the typed words in the log as he ran his finger methodically along the left column, the listing of the time each incident was reported.

There it was:

Sunday 1:07 a.m. Break-in. Stan Rankin residence.

Dan had been out of the house for more than an hour before the mayor arrived home.

"Hey, Andrea," Dan said to the woman behind the records division counter. "What's the deal with the burglary report on the mayor's house. Can you let me see it?"

Andrea stopped sorting papers at her desk and didn't say a word. She rarely did. If you didn't know her, you'd think she was a convent nun under a vow of silence.

As she stood, walked to an adjacent desk, and shuffled through report files stacked in a metal tray, Dan shook his head, once again astounded at how a woman with such a chatty, sexy voice on the phone could be so overweight, shy and homely. She squeezed through the opening between the desks and dropped a copy of the report onto the counter.

"Thanks," Dan said.

She nodded, squeezed back between the desks, and returned to her busywork.

Dan skipped the technical data – he knew where the mayor lived – and read the patrolman's report:

Entry gained by using glass cutter on back window in dining room.

Dan grinned. So far, so good.

Burglar may have been on premises when victim arrived home at 1:05 a.m. Television and VCR unplugged but left behind.

Great, Dan thought, jotting the information into his notebook. Just as he'd planned.

He scanned the list of stolen items, then looked closer:

Silverware ($3,500); silver service set ($2,000), diamond ring ($5,600), war medals ($100), 3 videotape movies ($60).

"Damn him," Dan mumbled. "What the hell is this?"

Dan hadn't taken a silver service set. He hadn't seen a diamond ring, let along stolen one. If he'd been in the bedroom, gone through the jewelry, he'd have taken more than one ring. He laughed aloud.

Andrea glanced up, a scowl on her face, as if he'd broken an unwritten rule.

"Sorry," Dan said. "I won't let it happen again."

But he couldn't conceal his smile. So what if the mayor's a crook, he thought. Aren't we all?

* * * * *

Battered and abused electric guitars, many of them with only four or five strings, hung like sleeping bats from the ceiling of Pete's Pawn Shop. Dusty, broken-down stereos lined the far wall. Cameras were stuffed into a glass display cabinet covered with fingerprints. The room smelled like a cat's litter box. It was a junkyard, not a store. Anyone over five-foot-two with hips larger than thirty inches could not walk down most aisles without knocking something over.

Dan stood inside the entrance, waiting for the tarnished silver bell to quit clinking against the glass door. He'd driven past Pete's several times but had never stopped. It wasn't normally his kind of store. But if he didn't stay out of the office on Mondays when it was slow, Margaret would give him another assignment for Sunday's paper, and he tried to avoid that whenever possible. So, after making his morning rounds, he often cruised the city before returning to *The Argus*. It wasn't yet noon.

The bell quit ringing and still nobody came to the front counter cluttered with piles of dog-eared *Playboy* and *Esquire* magazines. What type of person would buy *Esquire* in a place like this? Dan thought.

After waiting several minutes, flipping through a copy of *Esquire* with a cover of a bikini-clad woman sitting on a stack of books, he wondered how Susan Holcomb would look in a swimsuit. Not fantastic, but nice enough.

Dan opened and closed the door again. He'd have to call Susan later, he thought, as the bell rang louder than before.

"Anybody here?" he shouted toward the back.

"Back here," a muffled voice replied.

Dan followed the voice past rusting chain saws and lawnmowers. Behind an open doorway stooped a tall man with his head inside a refrigerator. He reminded Dan of an ostrich. His shoulders were almost as high as the top of the large harvest yellow appliance. The room was packed with dozens of broken-down refrigerators, freezers and stoves. Pete advertised that he had everything, and Dan believed it.

The man backed out of the refrigerator and looked down at Dan through half-frame glasses. His complexion was rough, like he'd been in at least one serious fistfight. He had to be six-six and two-fifty, a good eight inches taller and seventy-five pounds heavier than Dan, who spoke cautiously. He didn't want to rile the guy.

"You Pete?"

"Yeah." He sounded as if Dan's inquiry was an imposition. "What can I do for you?"

"Um, uh, just wondering if you've got any guns."

"You got a permit?"

"No. I've got to have one of those?"

"Yep. Get a permit, I'll show you what I got." Pete stuck his head back into the refrigerator.

"OK," Dan said. He turned to leave.

Dan had known a gun permit was required. He'd have to apply for one at the sheriff's office before he could legally possess a handgun. He'd also have to wait three days for a background check to be completed. He'd hoped to avoid that. Sheriff Bart Coleman didn't need to know Dan wanted to buy a gun. Not that it would make any difference. But it would save making up an excuse when Assistant Chief Schmidt or any of the other officers saw his name on the list. Dan had stopped at the pawnshop hoping to buy a pistol under the table, no questions asked. Now he'd have to look elsewhere.

"Hey, wait a minute," Dan said. "I was just wondering. Do you have much of a selection? Of pistols, I mean."

Pete pulled his head out of the refrigerator again. "About thirty, I'd guess, give or take a half-dozen," he said.

"Good shape?"

"Some are, some ain't." Pete stood with his right arm cocked, his clenched fist against his waist, as if waiting for Dan to leave.

"Most of them pawned by people who need the money?"

"That's all I do here. Everybody needs cash, but I don't buy from just anybody. No stolen guns."

He could have fooled Dan. With the clutter in this place, it appeared that Pete would buy anything from anybody. "How do you know?"

"You seem to be full of questions," Pete said. "Who are you, a cop?"

"I'm nobody," Dan said. "Just making conversation."

"You want to chat when you can see I'm busy?"

Dan didn't reply, but from the sound of Pistol Pete's voice, he was glad he wasn't holding a gun.

"I don't buy no stolen merchandise," Pete said. "Against the law. Cops come around every week with descriptions of guns used in robberies, stuff stolen, etc., etc., etc. I check everything. I don't need no hassles."

"Where do people buy stolen guns then?" Dan asked.

Pete looked at Dan as if he was a fool, a criminal, or both. If his eyes were chainsaws, they'd have cut Dan up and spit him out.

"Look, wise guy," Pete said. "I don't buy no stolen guns. I don't sell no stolen guns."

As Dan saw irritation grow on Pete's face, he considered explaining that he was a reporter for *The Argus*, doing a story about stolen guns. But he knew Pete wouldn't buy that, especially since he'd already tried to purchase a gun. Pete wouldn't trust Dan, just like he didn't trust cops, so Dan wouldn't get anywhere with that tact. Besides, he hadn't intended to give Pete a good reason to remember him, and he'd already gone too far for that to be the case now.

"No big deal." Dan shrugged his shoulders. "I just wanted a gun for protection and didn't want to go through the hassle of getting a permit."

Dan began to weave his way around the yard equipment again. His sixth sense told him Pete had not stuffed his head back into the refrigerator. He could feel those cold eyes knifing him in the back.

"I ain't in the habit of helping people get around the law," Pete said calmly. "There's a swap meet at the fairgrounds this week. Starts today. Maybe they got what you want."

* * * * *

At *The Argus*, Dan opened his telephone book to find the number at City Hall. He needed to talk to the mayor about the burglary. It wouldn't make more than a brief item, possibly good enough for page one since it involved the city's top dog.

The mayor's secretary answered on the second ring and put Dan right through.

"Stan Rankin. What can I do for you?"

"This is Dan Goldberg at *The Argus*. I see where your house was broken into Saturday night."

"That's right."

"Entry was gained by cutting open a window, uh, in the dining room."

"That's right."

"What was stolen?"

"Don't you have that in your report, too?" the mayor said.

"I just wanted you to confirm what it says."

"I'm sure the officer was accurate in his report."

"It says here, silverware, silver service set, a diamond ring, war medals, three videotapes. I have a total value of $11,260."

"Except for the videotapes, everything was more valuable than that to me and my wife. The silver and the ring were heirlooms from her family, the medals came from my service in the war."

"I remember seeing those medals at your summer agenda party."

"Goldberg? Now I remember you. You're new to *The Argus*," the mayor said.

"Five months is all," Dan replied. "How do you feel about the loss of this stuff?"

"You're writing a story about the burglary of my house?"

"I'm going to submit one. It's up to the editors if we run it. I figure people would want to know since you're a public official."

"I feel violated," Mayor Stan Rankin said. "Someone broke into my house while we were gone, but it could have happened while we were home. Someone could have been hurt, so we're lucky. As I said, the silver and jewelry were my wife's, given to her by her mother. They can't be replaced. I hope the police find them."

"Houses are broken into every day," Dan said. "It's not often someone picks on the mayor."

"There's plenty of crime and corruption out there," the mayor said, "but we've got a top-notch police department. As the mayor, I appoint the police chief, but I'm not in charge of the department. They do a fantastic job. But, obviously, even the best effort isn't going to nab every crook. As a taxpaying citizen of Cedar City, that concerns me. But, as the mayor, I believe the force is doing everything in its power to catch the crooks and put them in jail."

"Thank you, mayor," Dan said.

He wanted to laugh. He wanted to ask if that heirloom ring ever existed. He wanted to call the mayor one of those crooks the cops wouldn't catch. Instead, he simply said, "That's all I need for now."

* * * * *

Pete was right. Among all the antique tin boxes, polished rocks and rusted toys being set out on rows and rows of tables at the fairground's exhibition hall outside of town,

Dan found a dealer with knives, rifles, shotguns and, at the rear of one table, three pistols for sale.

The weapons man behind the table was small and old, no physical threat like Pete. His eyes were faded gray, almost colorless, and his weathered face was covered with deep wrinkles. He relaxed in a chair watching people walk by as if he didn't care if he sold anything or not. The pistols sat in open wooden display boxes directly in front of him, as if he was guarding them.

"Mind if I take a look?" Dan said, pointing to the center pistol."

"Go ahead," the man said. He didn't even stand up.

These swap-meet folks are sure trusting souls, Dan thought. More trusting than he would be.

He picked up the small gun and was surprised at its light weight. He'd chosen a Beretta 9-millimeter semiautomatic. Its sleek design was similar to that of a military issue .45, but it was smaller and not quite as powerful. Its black-plated finish was perfect. It would not shine like chrome. He removed the clip from the handle – thirteen shots in a staggered magazine. That would be more than enough. Dan closed his fingers around the grip and slammed the clip back into the handle. The more he played with it, the more he liked the way it felt.

"How much?" he asked.

"Three-fifty."

Dan laughed. "I could buy a new one, never fired, for three-seventy-five."

"Not here you couldn't," the man said. "Not today."

Dan realized the anxiousness in his voice had given him away. For some reason, he thought it would help to explain.

"A friend wants me to go to the shooting range and I don't have a gun. Don't want to use his."

The man nodded.

Dan realized how lame his explanation sounded. It was the second time in one day his story had not been believable, not even to himself. He wondered if he was losing his touch.

On the good side, though, the guy didn't seem to care. He wasn't asking any questions, wasn't insisting that Dan have a permit. He didn't seem to care if he sold a gun to John Dillinger, as long as he got his money.

"If I buy this gun from you now and I don't like it, can I bring it back?" Dan asked.

"Depends," the salesman said. He paused as if to let the word sink in. "It's Monday. I just got set up. Bring it back tomorrow, and I'll give you three hundred. It goes down fifty a day. After Sunday, I'll be gone."

Dan nodded. Everything had its price. "Gone where?" he asked, trying to sound casual.

"Illinois."

Dan was prepared to offer the man three-hundred on the spot. But he didn't want to seem too anxious again. He studied the gun some more, sliding the clip in and out of the handle, pulling the slide back as if to engage the first shell, pushing the safety button on and off. The clicking of the mechanisms made him itch to fire the Beretta, to feel its explosive power in his hand.

"I'll give you three hundred, cash," he said. "Right now."

"Three-fifty. I've got to make a profit."

"Three and a quarter," Dan offered. "I don't know what you paid for it, but that sounds like a good profit."

The man turned his left hand over and looked casually at the gold watch on his wrist, large enough that it could have doubled as a dinner plate. He glanced around the cavernous display hall, up at the open wooden rafters and bare lightbulbs that hung from single cords, down one side of the aisle and up the other. "Three and a quarter," he said, "and you can't bring it back."

Dan had no intentions of returning this beauty. It would fit his purposes perfectly. He returned the gun to its blue velveteen-lined box. "Deal."

The man stood for the first time, snapped the lid of the box shut with a pop and slid it to the middle of the table. He watched Dan count out the money on top of the box, all in twenties. From a burgundy bank deposit bag, he gave Dan a five and a ten in change but no receipt. The dealer stuffed the twenties into the bag, then flashed a huge, gold-filled grin.

Dan wasn't sure if the dealer's goofy expression was natural or if he thought it was funny Dan paid for the gun with all twenties. No matter. The deal had been transacted, so Dan tucked the box under his left arm to leave.

"It's your lucky day," the dealer said, his mouth probably more valuable than a gold mine.

* * * * *

The Beretta sang in Dan's hands as he fired off thirteen rounds at tin cans he had lined along the top board of a fence. Out in the country the explosions disappeared into the trees, swallowed up by the air. There were no echoes, just the sudden succession of the shells going off, the plinking of the tin cans, and silence.

After purchasing the gun, Dan had put it in its box under the front seat of his car and stopped at Hemsley's Gun Shop to buy ammunition.

At work, he hadn't been able to think of anything else as he wrote a few briefs, including one about the burglary at the mayor's house. Daylight was growing shorter, but it was still fall. He'd wanted to get out before sunset to try his new toy, so he hadn't hung around to chat with Mike when he showed up for the night beat.

Ten cans had hopped off the fence like scared rabbits. Holding a gun for the first time in years felt wonderful.

"This will do nicely," Dan said to no one because he was alone. "Very nicely."

* * * * *

Dan hadn't expected to buy a gun so soon. His primary plan for Monday had been to shop for a car since the lots stayed open until nine on Monday nights. He'd spent Sunday afternoon circling prospective cars in *The Argus* want ads and had called Susan several times to no avail. It was then, while daydreaming, that he'd decided to look for a gun as well as a car. He wanted to check out the black Toyota Celica first.

His red Toyota had been faithful, so why not stick with what worked? The Celica had everything he wanted – a stereo with cassette player, a sunroof, five-speed manual transmission and air conditioning – and Toyota reliability. The asking price was under seven-grand, but it had 68,000 miles on the odometer, a fact that hadn't been advertised. He wanted a car with fewer miles. He kept looking.

Five lots and nearly three hours later, he found a gray, two-year-old Mazda 626LX with only 42,000 miles Cedar City Motors. It had an excellent stereo with an equalizer, and the dealer wanted only sixty-nine-fifty. Dan figured he could talk the salesman down to sixty-five, except that he had his Corolla as a trade.

The salesman was a talker, just like Dan, but he was a good twenty years older, in his mid-fifties, Dan guessed, with a potbelly that hung over his belt and bushy gray eyebrows. He wouldn't shut up.

"Come on," Lenny said with a heavy Slovak slur as Dan backed away from committing to the Mazda. "Let me do you a favor and put you in this baby."

The test drive had told Dan this was his car. No question about it. But he wanted the trade-in difference to be less than five thousand. Lenny wouldn't drop below fifty-five.

"I told you before, I can't afford that much," Dan said. "My Toyota's a good car, plenty of years left. It'll get me where I want to go." He began to turn away. "I don't really need a new car. I just want one. No reason to go over my head in debt."

Lenny grabbed Dan's elbow firmly and pulled him closer, like he was about to tell him a secret or a dirty joke you wouldn't repeat in mixed company. He was a short man and spoke looking up at Dan's shoulder, nearly spitting in his face. "You tell me what it'll take to get you behind the wheel of this car, and I'll take it to the boss man. We'll see what he says."

Dan pondered the proposition for a moment, decided to go to his limit. He wasn't enamored with the car-buying process, had hoped to buy one by Wednesday and the dealership's nine o'clock closing time approached. Dan also had scouted the dealership, only a few blocks from *The Argus*, and liked the idea that his Toyota would sit at the back of the lot for days after the trade-in before it was sent off to auction or for reconditioning.

This was the ideal car, the ideal place, the ideal time. If Dan was to follow through with his immediate plans, he had to make the deal. But he couldn't sound too eager.

"Five thousand difference between your Mazda and my Toyota, tax and license included," he said firmly. "Lenny, that's the most I can pay. If you can swing it, great, if not, I've got to look somewhere else."

Lenny left Dan standing beside the cars and walked across the lot into the small glass-enclosed office where, beneath the fluorescent lights, he chatted with a man taller and younger than him, presumably the manager.

Dan lit a cigarette and waited. He opened the door of the Mazda and climbed behind the wheel again. He liked the firmness of the corduroy seat. He loved the throaty note of the exhaust and the smoothness of the shifter as he ran it through the gears, even as the car was sitting still. This was the car. It was the perfect setup.

Dan expected Lenny to return with a counter offer and knew the dickering could go on forever. He didn't want that. He knew if he played the cat-and-mouse game, he could probably buy the car at his price. He didn't want to wait. He didn't want to dicker. He wanted this car, to sign on the dotted line, to drive it home that night.

Dan was prepared to accept a larger difference, maybe fifty-two or fifty-three, if that's what Lenny presented. But he had a feeling that wouldn't be necessary when, less than fifteen minutes later, Lenny sauntered across the blacktop wearing a huge smile, not gold-plated like the gun dealer, but denture-white and straight.

Lenny extended his right hand toward Dan as he approached. "Son," he said, "You've got yourself a new car. This is your lucky day."

16

As Dan Goldberg sat at his kitchen table with a pen and paper to recalculate his anticipated car payments, the telephone rang on Mike Rockwell's desk at *The Argus*. It awakened him from a daydream about Linda, about the night before after spending a quiet weekend together. They'd made love for the first time since he'd been shot and she had initiated it, cast and all, which had been only a minor annoyance.

Afterward, Linda had fallen asleep in his arms and he got the most relaxing night of sleep he'd had in more than a week. He was looking forward to a repeat performance, driving over to her apartment after work and slipping into her bed.

The ring of the telephone interrupted Mike's thoughts again. He picked up the receiver. "*Argus*, Rockwell."

"You get it?"

Mike reached toward the front of his desk, near the book-like calendar, and picked up his once lost notebook. It had arrived in a plain brown envelope with his name scrawled in block letters on the front and without postage. He still hadn't told anyone except Linda that Morgan had threatened him, although he wondered about Bill Jackson.

The copy editor had leaked the story about Morgan's call all over the newsroom. A newspaper office was the last place you'd want to try to keep a secret. But Mike felt he'd done an admirable job, deflecting every question by saying that Morgan's call had come from out-of-town, that he was long gone. He had only wanted to complain about Mike's story, about how he was innocent.

Dan was the only other reporter who had any idea that Mike had lost his notebook, and he hadn't said anything about it since relaying the information to Mike that the cops would keep an eye out for it. Apparently, the missing notebook had slipped Dan's mind, and Mike was relieved. He had grown stronger the past two days and knew this was a situation he could handle himself. He wished he hadn't told Linda, but at the time it seemed imperative.

"Hey, asshole, I said, did you get it?" Morgan sounded irritated. To Mike, he always seemed impatient. No wonder he pulled the trigger so quickly and killed Collins.

"Yeah, it's right here in front of me."

"And my message?"

Mike had received that, too. It was nothing more than what Morgan told him in the previous telephone conversation. The note tucked inside the notebook instructed Mike to be prepared for a telephone call, and it included Mike's home telephone number as well as the one to his desk. Hardly impressive detective work, he'd thought, since he was listed in the telephone book.

The note had not said when Morgan would call, but Mike had expected it sooner rather than later. Thankfully, he'd been distracted by the renewed intensity of his relationship with Linda, but it had always been in the back of his mind. He wasn't prepared for the call to come so soon.

"Yeah," Mike said.

"And what about the gun? Wasn't I right?"

Mike had specifically asked Assistant Chief Charles Schmidt if the gun found in the bedroom was the murder weapon. Morgan had been correct. That gun had not been fired. Schmidt admitted to planting false information with the hope that Morgan would panic and call the cops, but that hadn't happened. Despite temptation, Mike held his tongue and, with it, the secret that Morgan had called him. He'd tell Schmidt when he thought the time was right.

"Yeah," Mike said into the phone. "Your story checked out."

"I told you," Morgan said. "I want to see you tonight."

Mike nodded. Of course, Morgan couldn't hear his head rattle. But tonight? Recollections of the long ride past the airport flashed through his mind, the gunshot to the leg, the hobbling around on the crutches that leaned against his desk. Mike wasn't ready for another confrontation with a murderer.

"You still there, Rockwell?" Morgan said.

"I'm listening." Mike considered hanging up, but he knew Morgan would call right back.

"Then listen good. I know your routine. You go out about ten thirty to make your rounds ..."

Mike wasn't surprised Morgan knew his every move. He'd probably even followed him. But hearing his schedule recited over the phone made him intensely aware that he would never be out of danger until he agreed to meet with Morgan. Not by a long shot. Mike sat upright.

"... first you stop at the fire station. Then the police station. Finally, the sheriff's department radio room."

Morgan's voice droned steady, almost as if he was reading a set of instructions written down. "You use an *Argus* car for work but park your own car on Seventh Street, near the telephone company building. It's a gold Buick." He paused.

"That's right," Mike said. He worried that Morgan knew more about him than he'd first realized. Had he followed him to Linda's apartment, too? He became worried about her safety as well as his own.

"If I was you, Rockwell, I wouldn't drive your Buick right now," Morgan added. "That could be dangerous to your health."

Mike gasped audibly and was certain Morgan heard it. The first thought that came to mind was that Morgan had planted a bomb in his car.

"When you leave work tonight, walk as if you're going to your car. But keep walking, east. If you go ten blocks and haven't heard from me, turn around, walk back. And be alone. Got it?"

"Yeah," Mike said.

"Like I said, I wouldn't drive that Buick until we've had our talk."

The line went dead.

Mike returned the receiver gently to its cradle and considered calling the police. He knew he couldn't tell Linda about his conversation with Morgan or the meeting that would take place, no matter what happened. He didn't want to alienate her again, not as long as their relationship had bounced back. He had to keep this to himself.

Had Morgan actually tampered with his car, or was he bluffing? Maybe it wasn't a bomb. Maybe Morgan planned to run Mike off the road if he tried to drive home. Mike laughed to himself, trying to believe that he'd found himself in the midst of a fictional television drama.

Yet, Morgan had promised danger. What would he do? He had sent the notebook as promised. Hadn't he told the truth about the gun?

Oh, what to do? The blue newsroom, the color that was supposed to keep everyone calm, wasn't working on Mike. He opened the once lost notebook to the illegible chicken scratches he'd written the night of the drug bust, the night of his abduction. He had to be brave. He had to go it alone. But no matter how many times Mike told himself stories like this never happen in Cedar City, his fear wouldn't disappear.

* * * * *

The evening was warm for mid-October, but the air was still cool. A slight breeze funneled between the tall downtown buildings, blowing just hard enough to remind anyone outdoors in the middle of the night that winter in Iowa approached. The breeze also carried away any smells and sounds that might have been in the air, which concerned Mike. He'd hoped to hear a sign of Morgan's presence, but the wind and the occasional swoosh of car tires on the pavement would cover any sound he made.

As Mike trudged with his crutches toward the street, he glanced skyward past the streetlights and couldn't spot any stars. He couldn't find the moon, not even a silvery outline through the clouds. A bad omen, he thought, but not as bad as a full moon.

Walking alone at night had often been Mike's escape from reality, like driving. He would take his time not going anywhere. It was an opportunity to think things through, to consider what might have been and what might be. Walking on a sidewalk in the middle of the city in the middle of the night, he had never felt alone. But, on this night, he felt as if he was all by himself, especially because it was so dark. He felt more alone than if he'd been in his apartment by himself. In the outdoors, though, there was no television to bring the images of people into the living room, no stereo to fill the air with comforting music, no familiar neighbors opening and closing their apartment doors.

Mike reached into his pocket and pulled out his car keys. He put the key ring around his index finger and held the keys in his palm. When he was in a good mood he'd flip the keys around his index finger, so they would fly through the air and return to his palm with a comforting click. He held the keys still, against the brace of his crutches, as he walked toward his car.

So many times Mike had left *The Argus* building after one in the morning and nearly sprinted to the big Buick. Then he had not been afraid of anything. He just wanted to get home and crawl into bed after a hectic night. It was never easy to leave work behind because a reporter's work was never done. There was always that story to write tomorrow, that follow-up from an event earlier in the day or that unknown story that emerged from the minds of editors or popped up on the police log.

Instructors didn't teach you about these pressures in J-school. It was not easy to do sometimes, psyching yourself down, putting everything out of your mind until the next day. It took practice to maintain your sanity, to shelve your inquisitive instincts. Every good reporter learned how to control his curiosity, but there was no way to shut it off completely.

As Mike approached his car, the Buick didn't look any different. The little dent was still in the front bumper from the time Mike lost control on a patch of ice and slid into a mailbox post. There was still a touch of rust on the center of the front bumper.

The big Buick sat next to the curb, waiting to take him home. The headlights and the chrome grill and the bumper seemed to form a face that was asking him to come along for a ride. He imagined inserting the key into the ignition, cranking the engine over, moving the column shift lever into gear and the whole thing blowing up.

Why think the worst? Mike thought. Still, he felt sure there was nothing wrong with his car. Then he remembered there'd been no obvious warning when Morgan shot him in the leg for no apparent reason other than to do it. The guy was crazy. Why didn't he get out of town, leave Mike alone? So what if he didn't kill the cop? He could go away and never get caught. Criminals did that all the time. How many murders go unsolved? Half of them at least.

But it was that touch of fear and the curiosity bred into every reporter that raised Mike's consciousness and forced him to do what he had to do. Morgan had called twice. He would continue to call or do something worse if Mike didn't help him get what he wanted. He was already making threats. What would he do next? The possibilities sifted through Mike's mind as he hobbled past the Buick along Seventh Street as Morgan had commanded.

The night grew blacker and the air became still as Mike passed a doctor's office, a car wash that was closed up, a tavern that exuded sounds of loud drunken conversations and a bakery where the smell of fresh bread made him think of morning and breakfast. He heard two men laugh behind him and turned to watch them stagger out of the bar. One man was white, the other black, and they had their arms around each other. It was impossible to tell who was the most drunk, who was helping who, but they were both bad enough off it didn't make a difference.

There seemed to be no wind as Mike reached the residential area. Old houses, some of oldest still standing in Cedar City, were crammed so close together they barely had side yards. Front porches sagged, rotted wood siding needed repairs or replacement and some paint. Maple leaves, some of them as big as a man's hand, had begun to clutter the lawns. Cracks along the sidewalk forced Mike to look down so he wouldn't catch his crutches on them. Old cars, many of them in worse shape than his Buick, lined the street because there were no driveways.

Mike heard a woman yell, and then he heard a man's voice tell her to go to hell. This was not a street Mike would pick for a middle-of-the-night stroll. He'd written numerous stories about break-ins and burglaries in the neighborhood, family disputes and unprovoked assaults, even a couple of shootings. Other than that, the area was unfamiliar, adding to his uneasiness.

Ahead, off to the right, sat MacDonald City Park. It covered nearly a full block, with sidewalks cutting it into triangle-shaped quarters as they ran diagonally from Seventh Street to railroad tracks. The iron benches were often home to drunks and derelicts who had no homes. Flower gardens, once a pride of the city fathers, had recently been turned over and replanted with grass because of vandalism. City officials claimed they didn't want to waste money in neighborhoods where the effort wasn't appreciated. When that story hit the paper a couple of years ago, Mike reconsidered his belief that everyone wanted to live in a nice neighborhood if they were only given the opportunity.

It made Mike wonder what kind of chance he had of walking past the park without being rolled by someone leaping from the darkness. The police log seemed to have one or two such incidents every week. With his crutches, Mike wouldn't be able to run, but maybe he could fight, using them as whacking sticks, as swords.

Not long ago, in the warmth of the spring, a sixty-eight-year-old man searching for a place to spend the night had been robbed of his old crumpled coat and worn out shoes. He'd found his way to the Salvation Army shelter where Mike talked to him, where he stunk of alcohol and vomit. He broke down and cried, a sixty-eight-year-old man, his tears sliding into the deep wrinkles of his leathery face. Mike would never forget the watery eyes that had seen so much and yet had missed the assailant when seeing counted the most. He had given the destitute old man five dollars only because he didn't have more than that in his pocket. Mike's story of the senseless crime, for the man with nothing but the clothes on his back, ran on the front page. It generated two weeks' worth of letters to the editor, most demanding better police protection in the park and for the elderly.

Mike wondered if he'd be writing a story about the mugging of an *Argus* reporter when the night was done. He'd had faith that, somehow, Morgan would be caught and knew he should do what he could to help law enforcement. He regretted not calling Lieutenant Sanders but, in the scheme of things, had been too afraid of Morgan's threats. Where had that led? But if a guy like that shoots you, it's difficult not to respect their actions, even if it's impossible to respect their motives. He knew Morgan had friends, and those friends could cause even more trouble. The fact that Morgan had not killed him when he had the chance seemed of little comfort. But it was the only reason Mike had to believe that Morgan didn't kill Collins.

Mike crossed the street and was hoisting his crutches over the curb when he saw movement in the darkness ahead, off to the right. A shadow emerged from behind the back of a bench, as if it was rising from a grave. Mike stopped at the edge of the streetlight's illumination and stared at the outline of a man sitting up. It did not move. It just sat there in the dark, as if a hallucination.

The shadow spoke. "Mr. Rockwell, you made it."

Morgan. His voice sounded deeper in person than over the telephone.

The breeze picked up from the direction of the park, blowing into Mike's face. It sent a slight chill along the hair of his neck. He smelled a sweetness in the air, English Leather cologne. It had been years since he'd worn it, and he swore he'd never wear it again because it reminded him of a broken high school relationship. Mike stepped closer.

"Why don't you stay right there, so I can see you," Morgan said. "You can hear me fine."

It was not a question, but Mike answered as if it had been. "Yes, I can hear you." He knew his reaction was prompted by nervousness.

"Don't get uptight," Morgan said. "I'm not here to hurt you. I want your help."

"How can I help you?"

"By listening," he said. "Reporters are good listeners, aren't they?"

Mike nodded. As long as Morgan only wanted to talk, everything would be fine. But, in the back of his head, Mike couldn't help but wonder if Morgan might want to abduct him again. That had been foremost in his mind, the main reason for his reluctance to take the walk. But leaning on his crutches, Mike realized how helpless he would be if Morgan tried something. So long as Morgan was satisfied to remain at a distance, Mike felt safe. But he thought it kind of strange that Morgan would keep him beneath the light while Morgan talked from the shadows. Anyone driving past would wonder why a man standing at the edge of the park by himself at one o'clock in the morning would be talking into the dark. Apparently, that incongruity hadn't occurred to Morgan or it wasn't a concern.

"I never shot that cop," Morgan said. "The only way I can prove it is to get a confession out of the guy who did. You need to get that confession for me."

As Morgan paused, a thousand questions exploded in Mike's brain. How could anyone but Morgan have killed Collins? Dan's story had said his fingerprints were on the gun found in the bedroom. It had not been used, but that didn't make any difference. It seemed logical that Morgan would have had another gun, maybe even an arsenal. He would have taken the murder weapon with him, tossed it. The gun that killed Collins could have been the same one he used to shoot Mike in the leg, or it could have been another one. Why did Morgan want to involve Mike, to force him to get a confession from the real shooter? Why didn't he talk to the cops? Why didn't he convince one of his other cronies to help?

Mike started to speak, but Morgan cut him off.

"Shut up and listen. I don't have all night."

"OK." The single word stuck in Mike's throat.

"I wasn't even in the damn house that night. Understand?" A breathless urgency crept into Morgan's voice. He talked rapidly and sounded desperate.

"If I was, you think I could have escaped with all them cops crawling around. Shit, no, man, we ain't dumb when it comes to dealing. I was outside watching the street. When I saw that cop car come along, I called my buddies in the house from the pay phone on the corner. I told them you was coming. I told them to say there was no crack, no deal to that undercover cop. That's what I told them to say. No deal."

That made sense. How else would Morgan have arrived at the cop car so quickly after shots were fired? But the new logic didn't put Mike at ease. He wanted to escape, to run somewhere and forget that Morgan had ever abducted him, had ever fired a gun at him. But his feet and crutches were frozen to the sidewalk.

"Sammy Rawlings or Bob Drexler did it," Morgan continued. "You've got their names. They're locked up in the joint right now. Talk to them. Tell them you talked to me."

Mike wasn't sure why he did it, just a natural reflex, he guessed, but he nodded. It wasn't meant to confirm that he'd go along with Morgan's order, but he realized Morgan took it that way.

"Tell them neither one of them will live to face a trial unless the bastard that pulled the trigger confesses. I'll make sure both of them never talk again. You tell them that."

"Yeah."

Only rapid breathing came from the shadows as a car with an odd clanking sound, probably a loose muffler, drove past. After the car turned a corner, Morgan spoke again, calmly this time.

"I'll talk to you in a couple of days to make sure you saw them. You tell me what you got."

"Just a minute," Mike said. He wasn't sure where he got his courage, but he couldn't let Morgan vanish so quickly. "I've got a question."

"You probably got a million of 'em. You reporters are worse than cops. What?"

Morgan was right. Mike's head was spinning with questions. "I need to know why you're picking on me. What's this story you want me to write? What's in it for me?"

Morgan laughed. "That's three questions. The answers are the same. Your life, kid. Ain't that enough?"

Mike swallowed hard, a lump sliding down the inside of his throat. But he spit the words out and they sounded stronger than he'd intended. "Why would you want to kill me?"

"You saw my face," Morgan said. "You can get the rap pinned on me unless one of them assholes confesses."

"I told you before I don't know what you look like."

"Think about it, Rockwell. You've heard my voice. You had plenty of time to see me. Would you trust you if you was in my shoes?"

Mike had to agree he would not. Trust did not come easy. He tried to remember what he could about Morgan's appearance, but he had been taxing his memory for more than a week and the vision had not become any clearer than the barrel of the gun and a dark stocking cap. As Mike's mind raced, a small shiny object flew out of the darkness toward his head.

Mike ducked.

The shadow laughed.

"Don't be so jumpy," Morgan said. "Show that lighter to Rawlings and Drexler. It'll prove you talked to me."

Mike clutched his crutches together under his left arm, turned around and bent over to pick up the object that had landed between the sidewalk and the street behind him. It was a gold monogrammed cigarette lighter, the initials "RMM" engraved in large cursive letters.

Mike examined the lighter carefully, running his thumb over the smooth finish and the finely etched initials. So, that was why Morgan needed to see him in person. To give him evidence that they had talked.

Mike turned back toward the dark. "This is kind of an expensive lighter to be throwing around, isn't it?"

He heard rustling where he couldn't see, the shadow of a running man disappearing into total blackness.

"Hey, where you going? Mike shouted.

No answer.

Mike stood in place, then realized he'd forgotten to ask the most pressing question. "Hey," he yelled, "what about my car? What did you do to my car?"

"Don't worry, Rockwell," Morgan shouted. The voice came from halfway across the park accompanied by a laugh. "You're my meal ticket to survival. I ain't going to hurt you yet."

17

Dan Goldberg signed the purchase papers for his car Wednesday after work. He sat in the small office in the middle of the used car lot, gazing at his Mazda through the plate glass window as a workman in gray coveralls installed the license plate he had removed from Dan's old Toyota.

For two days Dan had been waiting to pick up his car. All the paperwork, the loan approval, the tax, the title and the license, prolonged the anticipation. But the transaction all went smoothly because Dan worked for The *Argus*, one of Cedar City's most respected employers.

He had called Susan yesterday, told her the good news, then promised she'd be the first to get a ride. She had seemed less than thrilled. She told him work was keeping her busy and that she still felt drained from the painful realization that her brother was dead. Maybe by the weekend she'd feel better.

Mike hadn't showed much enthusiasm either. He had seemed preoccupied, so Dan didn't press it. What the hell was wrong with people anyway? Dan thought. Buying a new car is a big deal. He'd be happy for them.

At least Lenny was fired up. The salesman couldn't stop gushing about what a good deal Dan was getting as he shuffled registration papers around for Dan's signature. During the transaction, Lenny threw in an ice scraper, a coin holder and a key chain, all with the Cedar City Motors logo. Even though Dan wondered what Lenny's commission on the sale might be – probably good, from the way he was acting – he got a kick out of used car salesmen who tried to make you think there was no better deal in town.

Lenny left Dan alone for a minute to retrieve the loan agreement from the back office. As Dan watched a young couple examine the front of a Camaro, he reached into his pocket and pulled out two sets of keys for the Toyota. He held them up to the light and tossed the most used set on the desk. The spare set, still shiny from disuse, he slipped back into his pocket. He had never turned over both sets of keys when he traded cars and never would. Sentiment, he'd always told himself. This time it was different.

* * * * *

That evening, after test-driving his car for a couple of hours, Dan returned home to relax in front of the television. When mindless sitcoms failed to attract his attention, he shut it off and stared out the window. All he could see was a single streetlight, a yellow saucer in the dark, a UFO if you wanted to use your imagination. Sometimes life was so boring. It was time to pick up the pace.

In his bedroom, Dan stripped down to his underwear and dug around in the closet for a large grocery sack tucked behind a box of books yet unpacked from his

195

move to Cedar City. The paper sack contained all dark items – the black pants, navy sweater, marker-colored sneakers and stocking cap he'd stashed away after burglarizing the mayor's house.

He yanked the sweater over his head and tossed the sack with the rest of its contents onto the bed. In the bathroom, from beneath the sink, he pulled out another paper sack. From it he produced a light brown wig, a make-up kit, a woman's compact and false eyelashes. He applied the flesh-colored base to his cheeks. In his reflection, he saw his fingers shaking. A nervousness flowed through his veins that excited him. If someone walked in at that moment, they'd catch him in the act, wondering if he was preparing himself to look like a woman. While that wasn't the case because he had no desire to change his sex, the possibility of being caught only seemed to add to the thrill.

Dan studied his powdered face in the mirror. The makeup had lightened his skin to a sickly paleness, precisely the ghost-like effect he desired. He opened the rouge container and reddened his cheeks slightly, which made them full and round, producing a cold look, as if he had been outside in the fall wind.

Taking an eyeliner pencil, Dan drew a small dot above the left corner of his mouth and blackened it in to resemble a mole. Along the underside of his chin, where it would always be in a shadow, he drew a fine line about two inches long, blurring the dark streak with his fingertip so it appeared to be a scar. He feathered in more makeup base until the roughed-up appearance was exactly what he wanted.

Stretching the cap of the brown, shorthaired, woman's wig, he popped it over his own curly black hair. He hadn't worn the wig since he was a hippy on a Halloween night a couple of years ago and that forced him to laugh at his image in the mirror. He'd never wanted straight hair, but he had to admit it looked rather interesting.

Dan peeled the paper backing from one of the eyelashes and gently pasted it on the eyelid above his right eye. He blinked several times to make sure it was secure, that movement didn't send it across the room like a skittering spider. With the eyeliner pencil, he outlined the same eye in black.

"Perfect," Dan said to his grotesque image in the mirror. "Malcolm McDowell, eat your heart out."

Of course, Dan didn't look exactly like Alex from the movie, "A Clockwork Orange," and he didn't have the fancy red Durango 95 sports car to speed through the darkness to and from the scenes of his crimes. But God how he loved that flick, the Korova Milk Bar and the droogs with their insane "ultra-violent" mentality. The parody of "Singin' in the Rain" and the scared, pained expression on that old man's face as Alex kicked his "guttiwuts" in. Oh, the excitement Alex must have felt on the brink of being discovered.

But what Dan remembered over and over was how that, despite getting caught, Alex came out smelling like a rose in the end. All it took was to have some wits about you, and you could do anything and get away with it.

Dan returned to his bedroom and pulled on his dark pants and shoes. Opening the bottom drawer of the dresser, beneath a pile of sweaters, he spotted the now familiar wooden box. He set it on the dresser top and opened it. The sound of the Beretta banging off one round after another at the country firing range urged Dan to pick it up once again. He clutched the pistol in both hands, kissed the barrel lightly and removed the clip full of bullets. No need to carry a loaded gun until necessary.

He tucked the pistol into his pants behind his belt buckle, stuffed the clip into a pocket and picked up two sets of car keys from the dresser, one for the Mazda, which he'd be driving in a minute, and the other for his old Toyota, which he'd pick up shortly.

In the living room Dan reached behind the couch to retrieve an Iowa license plate, blue with white letters, that was registered in an adjacent county. He'd removed it from a beat-up pickup truck parked at Southdale Shopping Mall earlier in the evening while driving his new Mazda.

* * * * *

The dashboard of Dan's Mazda glowed orange and the green digital clock read 10:53. He hadn't realized he'd spent so much time with his makeup. Running his car through the gears, he felt the urge to cruise the main drag. But he had a more important task at hand, so driving for fun would have to wait for another night.

Dan circled the block around Cedar City Motors twice. The lot appeared void of human activity. On his first pass, he'd spotted his old Toyota parked in a line of trade-ins at the rear of the used car lot. He already missed the sorry old heap, but it would do him one last favor. He looked forward to hearing the familiar rapping of the worn-out tappets under the hood.

Only the streetlights along the curb illuminated the otherwise darkened used car, its display lights long ago extinguished when it had closed for the night. Traffic on the side street was nonexistent as Dan pulled into the lot and turned off his headlights. If a cop stopped him now he'd say he was visiting his old car one last time and if he was asked about his getup, he'd simply say he recently left a Halloween party. He turned the ignition off and his Mazda glided into the end spot next the Toyota. As he removed the key, he scanned the lot one last time. Still, he saw no one.

Dan shifted the Beretta behind his belt, tapped his pocket to make sure the loaded clip was still there, then grabbed two metal paper fasteners from his ashtray and the stolen license plate from the passenger seat. Slowly he opened the door, climbed out, shut it softly but didn't lock it. No one would bother the Mazda on a used car lot. Not for an hour, anyway.

He crouched low enough to keep his head below the tops of the cars as he slipped around to the rear of the Toyota. He attached the license plate with the paper fasteners and tugged at it gently to ensure that it would hold. The arrangement wasn't anything permanent, but it would serve the purpose. He didn't need a front license plate he reasoned because, at night, the headlights would hide it from view. Besides, what were the chances of being stopped anyway? Slim to none, he thought, as long as he obeyed the traffic laws.

* * * * *

Dan's plans weren't made by tossing the dice, but they might as well have been. He enjoyed craps and had played with a pair of dice Sunday while looking through the car ads, deciding on one roll that the 7-Eleven on the far southwest side would be his mark.

Cedar City had eleven 7-Eleven stores from which to choose, so Dan had assigned each a number on his die, two through twelve. He rolled the ivory cubes for a couple of hours, making up his own little game of solitaire while he watched his Chicago Bulls lose to Detroit and wondered if they were destined to be like the Cubs, congenial losers without a world championship his entire life.

In his mind, Dan had known from the start that the 7-Eleven on K Avenue would be the one. When he'd visited it soon after arriving in Cedar City, he knew it was the most isolated, the safest for a robbery. It wasn't along busy First Avenue, the city's main thoroughfare, the lighting was poor, and it was at least a couple of miles from the cop shop, the most important element of all.

Dan pulled the Toyota into the parking lot shadows, remained in his car and lit a cigarette. The glowing red tip reflected in the glass of the windshield where he blew the smoke and watched it scatter left and right, up and down, as if flying to escape. When there were no cars parked in front of the store, he rolled down his window and tossed the cigarette onto the ground. He was ready.

He had tucked the Beretta in the dark recesses of the car between the front seats, the barrel pointing down, yet had left the loaded clip lying in plain view in the passenger seat.

When Dan picked up the pistol, it felt cold in his hands. He knew it wasn't so much that the steel was cold, but that his hands were warm. His adrenalin flowed, raising his body temperature to a nervous pitch. But his mind felt sharp, and he knew he had to work fast before he lost that edge.

Dan squeezed the handle of the gun tightly and only then did it feel comfortable, like it had always belonged in the palm of his hand.

Opening the car door, Dan slid onto the parking lot and walked briskly toward the front door of the 7-Eleven. Only a single clerk, wearing his red and white smock, appeared to be around.

As Dan pushed the door open, he noticed the sign that said the clerk had only twenty dollars in change. That didn't bother Dan. He wasn't really after the money.

"Good evening," the clerk said. "May I help you find something?"

Dan raised his pistol at arm's length, sighting down the barrel as if it was an extension of his piercing eyes. He didn't say a word.

"Hey, buddy, look," stammered the clerk, no more than a kid who happened to draw the short straw for the night shift. But he waved his hands around like an old man and that thrilled Dan to no end. "I don't have any money. I can't even open the safe."

"Open the cash drawer," Dan commanded. He concentrated on keeping his voice calm and in a lower register than normal, as if he'd done this a dozen times. "Put your wallet on the counter."

The scared kid, his eyes wide with fright, did as he was told, hitting the button on the cash register to pop the drawer open and extracting a new skinny brown wallet from his back pocket.

"Put the bills from the drawer in the wallet," Dan ordered. "No change."

Again, the kid clerk obeyed, stuffing cash from the drawer into his wallet as the gun stared him in the face less than ten feet away.

"Drop it on the counter and get down," Dan said. "I'm not here to hurt you."

The kid stared, as if he'd been frozen like a deer in headlights.

"Down!"

Dan fired the gun at the cigarette rack behind the clerk, who dropped to his knees as if he'd fallen off a cliff.

Dan's second shot shattered the glass on the ceiling-to-floor beer cooler.

The third knocked a candy carousel off the counter.

Dan picked up the wallet and stuffed it into his back pocket. He turned to leave, but hesitated.

The fourth shot went through the black plastic Lotto computer as did a fifth, causing the machine to sputter and sigh as if it had been alive.

Dan laughed aloud, a screech appropriate for the Halloween season, thinking that the machine won't ever cheat anyone out of his hard-earned money ever again.

Dan learned over the counter to the clerk, huddled toward the front where he thought he'd be safe.

"Thanks," Dan said politely. "You've been very helpful. Have a good night."

Dan turned abruptly, the gun in his left hand, and skipped quickly out the door and across the parking lot to his car. He was certain drinkers at the nearby tavern had heard the gunshots, that the cops would be on their way. He picked up his pace.

With the Toyota running, as most everyone did when they pulled up to a convenience store on a cold night, his escape was rapid.

He had purposely parked across the lot, the front of the car facing toward the street, the rear perfectly visible from the store. He hoped the clerk was smart enough to memorize the license plate number, to write it down, because it wouldn't match the car. He knew the clerk would be able to describe him, that was for sure. How many men came into a convenience store wearing makeup and an eyelash? Just one eyelash?

Dan slammed the Toyota into gear and sped down K Avenue until he was out of sight, then slowed to five miles per hour over the speed limit as he always drove.

He didn't want to attract undue attention, but he did accidently cruise through one stoplight as it changed to red.

His hands felt slick on the steering wheel and the shift knob, the perspiration surprising to Dan. His eyes darted everywhere, at the cars that passed him in the opposite direction, at the cars waiting at stop signs, at the streetlights above. He imagined he heard sirens approaching, but he knew it was only his mind playing games.

Quickly, Dan jerked the steering wheel to the right and veered up a side street to follow low speed-limit residential streets as he'd mapped out earlier. The route took him back to the used car lot as directly as possible without using main streets.

The drive was only a couple of miles, but it seemed like a cross-country trek as Dan weaved in and out of older neighborhoods until he finally cruised into the alley to the Cedar City Motors lot where he cut the headlights.

Once stopped, Dan leaped out of the Toyota, ran to the back of the car, ripped off the license plate, climbed into his Mazda, tossed the stolen plate onto the floor behind the driver's seat, hid his gun between the front seats.

Dan guided the Mazda through the used car lot, waited for a passing car, turned onto First Avenue for the drive home. Only then did he realize he'd left his sentimental set of keys in the ignition of the Toyota.

"Damn," Dan shouted, slamming his open palm against the steering wheel. He'd panicked.

He quickly replayed every step of the robbery in his mind. Leaving the keys was the only mistake.

It wasn't so bad, he assured himself. In fact, it might have been the right thing to do, even if it was accidental. Any of the salesmen could have left a set of keys in a car at a used car lot. Anybody could spot the keys, steal the car for a robbery and bring it back to avoid suspicion.

So what if he didn't have a set of keys to the car. It meant there was no way to positively trace its use to him. Just because he had once owned the car didn't mean he took it on a final joy ride. He was amazed how mistakes could work out for the best.

As Dan approached his apartment, his nervousness subsided. He turned his car into the parking lot and couldn't help himself.

Dan laughed out loud and shouted, "Oh, thank heaven, 7-Eleven."

18

Assistant Chief Charles Schmidt scowled like a bulldog and leaned across his desk. "Goldberg," he said, "You sure seem to have a lot of interest in this robbery."

Dan shrugged his shoulders, trying his best to act nonchalant. In reality, his heart was beating as wildly as if he were robbing the convenience store again.

"It just seems strange to me," Dan said, "that a guy would go to that much trouble to rob a 7-Eleven when signs plastered all over the place say the clerks don't have any more than twenty bucks in the cash drawer."

Schmidt stretched like a lazy dog, extended his arms over his head, clamped his hands at the back of his neck and leaned back in his chair. He eyed Dan with expectant curiosity.

Dan knew his voice had stuck in his throat when he'd asked for details about the robbery. Had that given him away? He'd instinctively rubbed his right eye, as if to ensure that he had removed the false eyelash. He felt his concentrated effort to remain cool had been successful, so he crossed his legs and leaned back in his chair, too.

"We aren't talking about your regular stupid ass, nighttime robber," Schmidt said. He sat up, brought his hands to his stomach and intertwined his fingers. "We're talking about a nut case here. Some guy who did it for kicks. We're talking about some asshole who should be locked up in the loony bin."

Dan laughed at Schmidt's vernacular. If they hadn't already disliked each other, Dan would have been angry for the insinuation that he was crazy. But Schmidt didn't have a clue that Dan had pulled off the robbery. To Dan, he often sounded like a cop who should be locked up in the loony bin.

"You think it's funny?" Schmidt said. He placed open hands on the desk, leaned forward as if to lay all his cards on the table, raised his voice. "This is the type of jerk that's too smart for his own good. He thinks he fooled everybody by wearing that dumb disguise, from a disturbing movie that was out a few years ago, my detectives tell me. He'll try something else just as stupid. He'll botch it, and we'll nail him."

Dan nodded. "The dumb ones always do. And the cops always get him."

So far, Schmidt hadn't mentioned anything about a license plate number on the getaway car. Dan had lost sleep worrying about that. If the cops ever found out the car had come from Cedar City Motors, they'd surely discover it had once belonged to him, that he'd traded it in the day of the robbery.

But if they knew that now, that the car had been Dan's, wouldn't Schmidt mention it? Of course, he would. He'd love to make Dan squirm.

The license plate. Dan was relieved he'd taken it with him. But why hadn't he tossed it out first thing last night? Or even right away this morning? It was in his apartment, beneath the couch. He had to ditch it as soon as possible.

"This is the most dangerous criminal type out there," Schmidt continued. "He doesn't give a shit what he does as long as he gets away with it. But we'll find him. I just hope he doesn't kill somebody first."

* * * * *

The Argus newsroom woke from its usual morning slumber about eleven Thursday morning.

Reporters returned from assignments handed out the night before or first thing when they'd arrived for their day, their routine government meetings, their beats at the state and federal courthouses.

Editors stirred with caffeine-induced highs after sorting through overnight Associated Press news directories, answering mundane telephone inquiries, dozing through planning meetings and twiddling their thumbs waiting for news to happen.

Suddenly, when deadlines loomed, everyone jumped into action as if their paychecks depended on it and right there, in the center of the action, sat Margaret Myers.

As the field general instructing her troops, Margaret made snap-second decisions. Finish this story for editing before deadline, she'd command, save that story for later, eighty-six that idea because it wasn't important enough for our readers. She raised the volume of her voice a couple of notches to ensure she was heard above everyone else but remained calm and so organized in her head that she didn't miss a beat.

Dan Goldberg entered the newsroom through the back door just before noon as activity was in full swing. He'd spent more time with Assistant Chief Schmidt than planned and was running behind schedule.

He tossed his coat over the back of his chair and sat at his desk. Other reporters were busy writing stories, not only to make deadline, but also so they could take a lunch break. No one was near his desk.

Dan picked up the receiver of his telephone but didn't dial a number. He sat for a good five minutes holding the receiver to his ear, pretending to talk and listen, doodling in his notebook, glancing around the newsroom.

No one paid the slightest attention to him. Excellent.

When Dan thought enough time had passed, he raised his voice in mock anger and slammed the receiver down, pretending to hang up on somebody.

Dan stood, taking a deep breath to compose himself, and walked over to Margaret Myers' desk where she rapidly tapped the keys of her computer terminal. He waited politely until she looked up, ready to hear his litany of routine cop-shop fodder.

"What've you got for me today?" she asked.

Dan explained the robbery at the 7-Eleven, how the robber had worn a weird disguise and fired five shots inside the store. How nobody had been hurt.

"Write it up, keep it short," she said. "Is that it?"

"He just called me," Dan said.

Margaret's head swiveled from its gaze at the computer, her dark brown eyes wide, her narrow eyebrows raised. "How do you know it was him?"

"He told me about this weird disguise he wore. Chief Schmidt had already given me the information. It checked out."

"Did you call Assistant Chief Schmidt, tell him what this guy told you?"

"Not yet," Dan said. "The guy told me he didn't want the cops to know. He said he was calling to make sure I had all the facts right for the story."

"Ignore him," she said. "Write it up in a couple of paragraphs. That's all we need."

"What?" Dan said. He nearly choked on the word.

"All he wants is publicity," Margaret said. "We aren't in the business of making robbers famous, especially when they do something as crazy as shooting up a convenience store for no other reason than the thrill of it."

As Margaret turned toward her computer screen, Dan came up with a new tact.

"The guy told me he did it because he hates the lottery," Dan said. "That's why he shot the lottery machine. He took the money because he's never won anything. He felt it owed him. I think it's a good hook."

Margaret turned her head up toward Dan as if she was reconsidering.

He bit his lip.

Margaret nodded.

"Use that as your lead," she said, "the lottery angle, and that he called an *Argus* reporter and that we gave detectives everything we know. Leave out the details of anything else he told you for now. We don't want everybody who loses at the lottery to go around shooting up convenience store terminals.

"After you're done writing, make sure you call Schmidt, tell him what this guy told you. It's the right thing to do. Then, if we help apprehend this nut, that can become part of a follow-up story."

Dan couldn't come up with any more arguments in his quest to include information from his manufactured telephone call.

For an instant Dan was so angry at Margaret he wanted to scream. But if he started yelling, he knew he might say something he'd regret later, something that would give himself away.

"OK," Dan said. "Whatever you say."

"Anything else?" she asked, her focus on her computer as she tapped the keys.

"Just routine stuff."

19

Mike's stomach lurched into his throat, as if to heave the partially digested ham sandwich he'd had for lunch. He sat in his car with a distressed father, blue lights from an ambulance flashing across their faces. It was almost nine Thursday night, plenty of time for Mike to write his story. But he wasn't sure he'd make deadline as they stared at the gray, aluminum-sided, two-story house. The ambulance had arrived too late. So had Dennis Young.

Young had found his wife, Kathy, and their two-year-old son, Brian, dead in the front seat of the car parked in his driveway. It had been shut in the garage, its motor running, when someone had called the police. The victims' skin was all white, their lips pale and nearly blue. Kathy had fallen on top of Brian as if she had tried to protect him. Or smother him. No one knew for sure. They had stopped breathing.

When Mike had shielded his eyes to look through the passenger-side window of the car to see mother and son peacefully dead in the front seat, he was reminded of angels he'd drawn as a youth in Sunday school, white like the blouse Kathy Young wore, halos like the pale blue cap on the little boy's head. He couldn't get the connection out of his mind.

Dennis Young admitted to police that he and his wife had argued and that he'd walked to the corner bar for a couple of drinks to calm down. Kathy had threatened suicide, but she'd done that before. He didn't think she'd do it. He had no idea she'd take their son with her.

Mike could smell alcohol on Dennis Young's breath, but he didn't believe the young man was drunk. His reflexes and speech seemed normal, as normal as they could be under the circumstances. After the police had questioned him, after they wouldn't let him into his own house until they'd had the opportunity to look around, he had agreed to talk to Mike in *The Argus'* car. It was a secure sanctuary from the television cameras and crews that had shown up, from curious neighbors and passers-by who gathered along the curb behind the yellow tape strung around a pair of large oak trees that had lost most of their leaves. The conversation centered around Dennis Young's wife.

If Mike relied on intuition rather than his reporter's instincts, he would have let Dennis talk about anything he wanted to talk about. But, no matter how difficult it was, his job was to get the story. He recalled how Dan criticized him for not putting enough personal detail into his stories. Since Dennis had given Mike an opening, he had to take it. He had to ask every necessary question. That's what Dan would have said.

Mike kept his voice to a gentle whisper to convey the sympathy that he felt.

"What was the argument about?"

"It was nothing," Dennis said. He wore a baseball cap the same pale blue as his dead son's, a blue-black flannel shirt with the top three buttons open to the thick black hair on his chest, blue jeans and dark heavy boots, probably with metal-reinforced toes like construction workers wore to protect their feet. He shook his head and turned away from the house. "Nothing," he said. "Nothing."

Mike hesitated for a moment before deciding to embrace a more aggressive Dan Goldberg approach.

"Apparently," Mike said, louder than intended, "it wasn't nothing, or your wife wouldn't have done this." His voice had remained calm, not overbearing or demanding, as he tried to uncover the facts, but he knew immediately that his statement had hit Young like a punch in the gut.

Dennis Young glared at Mike, his eyes on fire like those of a jack-o-lantern on Halloween night.

"I was having an affair," he shouted. He didn't take his eyes off Mike. "OK, is that what you want to hear?" He raised his arms abruptly, not as a threat to Mike, but his knuckles pounded into the ceiling of the car. He moved his face within inches of Mike's. "Is that going to make your damn story better? Huh? Huh?"

Mike retreated as much as he could in the confines of the little Ford Escort wagon.

Dennis backed up, too, his unshaved face red from anger, his squinting eyes glistening with the beginning of tears. His voice calmed to a conversational volume. "You can tell the world I killed her because I had an affair, and it broke her heart. She didn't want me to have our kid either, so she took him with her. Is that fair?" He choked on the words. "You tell me, is that fair? Is that fair?"

Tears filled Dennis Young's eyes, flooded down his cheeks as he buried his face into his hands, his elbows on his knees.

Mike felt tears in his eyes, too, but he didn't lift his head. He concentrated on the reporter's notebook in his lap, writing down as much as he could as fast as he could. He blinked his eyes rapidly to maintain focus and thought about how this was the worst part of his job, about how he wasn't invading anyone's privacy because Dennis Young had agreed to talk, about how he was simply doing what a reporter is paid to do.

Young remained silent until a police officer rapped on the car window and motioned for him to get out. Mike felt anger and sorrow simultaneously for Dennis Young as he watched the adulterer, the suddenly childless father, climb into the back seat of a police car. But the real victim was the little boy, two years old and trusting the love of his parents, and that they would take care of him. The boy hadn't had a choice. His mother made that for him.

The thought churned Mike's gut again, stirred it up as if there was a blender inside, as if a mixture of non-compatible chemicals was about to explode. He was so angry he couldn't see straight.

* * * * *

Some newspaper stories write themselves, especially when a reporter is on a strict deadline. Mike returned to the office by ten with less than two hours to put his murder-suicide story together. It was scheduled for page one in all editions.

The words flowed faster than beer on a Friday night as he began, rarely glancing at his notes. He felt he knew the agony Dennis Young was going through, what Kathy Young had endured.

Mike began having second thoughts about his job as he described Dennis Young's temper tantrum, his feeling of helplessness as he endured the pain of loss. He wondered if the situation would have been so bad if the media hadn't been there. He wondered if Dennis would have hit him if the cops hadn't been there. He allowed thoughts of the cigarette lighter in his pocket, the failure of the cops to prevent his own kidnapping, to intrude, and tried to push them out of his mind. Maybe Linda was right. Maybe reporting was dangerous.

He took a gulp of coffee and knew his stomach couldn't take much more of this. His mind raced. Suicide really affected the people who were close to the victims. But who was the victim? In this case, there really were three.

It had not been easy convincing Dennis Young to reveal the reason behind the suicide. Now that Mike knew about the affair, every reader of *The Argus* would know about it, too.

Was that fair to Dennis? But had he been fair to his wife? To his son? Could that justify telling his story, like giving an eye for an eye or a tooth for a tooth?

As Mike honed his copy, checked and rechecked his notes for accuracy, the thoughts and the reasons and the guilt wouldn't go away. He included all of the details, the story as he saw it, but he wondered, under the circumstances, if he was being as objective as possible.

* * * * *

When Mike's telephone rang, he was so deep in thought he didn't hear it even though it was the loudest in the newsroom. He was too wrapped up in the murder-suicide story.

"Hey, Rockwell, answer your phone," Bill Jackson yelled.

"What?" Mike said.

"Grab your phone. It's ringing off the hook."

"Oh, yeah, sorry." Mike picked up the receiver. "Rockwell."

"Well, hotshot, did you talk to my buddies?"

Morgan.

"I can't talk now," Mike said. "I'm working on a story, and it's deadline," Mike lied. He had finished the story and reread it three times. It was ready to go. Deadline was a half hour away. But he didn't want to talk to anyone, especially Morgan. He wanted to read his story one last time, to make sure it was perfect.

"If you don't talk to me now, I'll just get back to you later."

"I know," Mike said. At the moment he didn't care what Morgan planned to do.

"I mean it," Morgan said. "I ain't giving up. You talk to Rawlings and Drexler. You find out which one them bastards pulled the trigger."

"Fine," Mike said. He hung up the phone. He didn't want to talk to anyone.

When Mike's telephone rang a couple of minutes later, he wasn't going to answer it, but he knew Jackson would be on his case. He knew it was Morgan calling back and prepared to defend himself from the gun-toting pest again. He picked up the receiver, planning to leave it off the hook.

"Hi, honey." It was Linda. "Are you about done for the night?"

"Yeah," he said abruptly.

"What's wrong with you?" Her voice went from sweet to hurt.

"Nothing. I'm sorry I snapped."

"It doesn't sound like nothing. I just called to see if you're going to visit me tonight."

"I'm not sure."

"So, what's the matter? What's wrong?"

"Deadline," Mike said. He told her quickly about the murder-suicide, how the story was slated for the front page, how he felt the pressure to make it perfect.

"I think you should come over," she said, her voice sympathetic. "You sound like you need company to relieve that stress."

"I'll be all right."

"Please, Mike. Let me be with you."

"Let me think about it, and I'll see," he said. "I'm not sure I'd be good company. If I'm not there by one, don't expect me."

"Mike, I'd like to see you."

"What's wrong with you?" he said. Linda's pleading tone was unusual, considering the way she'd been treating him lately, and it irritated him. "You sound strange."

"I just want to be with you."

"Sometimes I need to be alone," he said. "You know that."

"You know I worry about you."

Mike inhaled deeply, using the long pause to compose his thoughts. He had to be gentle if he was going to convince Linda to leave him alone. "Honey," he said. "I'll be all right. Just knowing you're thinking about me helps. I'll talk to you in the morning."

Linda sighed. "Mike. I love you."

"I know you do," he said. "Love you, too."

Mike hung up the phone, glanced at the clock, turned back to his computer, filed his story.

He picked up his crutches from the floor by his desk, poured another cup of coffee at the newsroom relief station, hobbled back to his desk to wait for Bill Jackson to edit his story and ask questions to clarify details. He tried to clear his mind, as if hitting the delete button on a computer terminal, but it didn't work.

"Hey, Mike, this is a great story," Bill said, punching keys on his terminal to roll the green text off the screen to save it into the central storage bank before calling it back for a headline and formatting. "Super job."

"Thanks," Mike said. A Jackson compliment was rare, so he wasn't sure what to say. "It wrote itself."

"I mean it. Great stuff. It's not like this happens every day."

Jackson paused for a couple of moments as Mike stood over him, both examining the story on the screen as Jackson played with headlines. Finally, he glanced up at Mike. "No questions. Not one. Good night."

Mike hobbled away, grabbed his coat from his desk chair, stuffed his notebook into a pocket and eased down the empty back stairway of *The Argus* building into the darkness of the alley.

He didn't even worry about the possibility that Morgan might be there as the autumn breeze swirled around his bare head. Once Mike climbed into his gold Buick, he drove straight home.

Crawling into bed, Mike tossed and turned all night. It could have been too much coffee. It could have been the reality of the murder-suicide. More likely than not, though, his restlessness became horrid when he thought about how abruptly he had treated Linda on the phone.

20

Two weeks had passed since Mike was shot in the leg, and he felt absolutely overwhelmed, trying to cope with too many challenges. The murder-suicide that appeared on the front page of that morning's *Argus*. Morgan's incessant telephone calls and threats of violence if Mike didn't help clear him. Linda's elusive, yet protective, behavior. It was all too much.

Mike wanted to run away from it all, a thought that brought him a moment of levity. How far could he get on crutches?

When he called just before noon to check in with Margaret Myers about the murder-suicide story, to make sure Dan Goldberg would check with the cops for a follow-up during the day, the always perceptive editor apparently sensed the exhaustion, the depression in his voice.

"It's been two crazy weeks for you," Margaret said. "Take tonight off and enjoy a long, relaxing weekend."

Mike was flabbergasted. That had never happened. A free vacation day. On a Friday night. At least something was going right.

He called Dan at *The Argus*, who gave him a surprising pat on the back for the murder-suicide story and said he'd buy the first round, if Mike and Linda wanted to join him and Susan at the Fox and Hounds after his shift ended. Mike was surprised that Dan was seeing Susan, but he said he'd call Linda, that they'd be there unless he told Dan otherwise.

When Mike called Linda to apologize for his behavior, to give her the good news that he'd been granted a surprise day off, she suggested they get together for drinks and see where it led.

Mike told her Dan offered to buy the first round if they stopped at the Fox first, which prompted hesitation from her until Mike said that Susan Holcomb, the dead cop's sister, would be there, too. Earlier, Linda had expressed interest in meeting any woman who would date Dan Goldberg, so she agreed, only if Mike promised they'd leave after two rounds of drinks.

At the Fox and Hounds Lounge, the *Argus* regulars drank and smoked and talked over each other at the regular tables pushed together in the back near the free appetizers as Mike and Linda joined Dan and Susan at a corner table near the front.

As Mike sat down, he realized the last time he'd seen Susan was that cold day at the cemetery when she had buried her brother. He knew Dan had seen her once since then but wasn't aware that their relationship had gone any further. He wanted the scoop from Dan but couldn't ask with Susan and Linda present. He was surprised that Susan appeared to enjoy Dan's company and, as usual, the early conversation centered around the news.

"I'll never understand what drives some people to do the things they do," Susan said. "I mean, this guy has got to be a real psycho, chaining women up in a basement and killing them one by one. Chopping them up. Cooking their body parts on his stove." She shuddered. "It's just not right. It's gross."

Dan had steered the conversation to the gory front page, the banner headlined story in that morning's *Argus*, the story that had taken precedence over Mike's local murder-suicide piece.

A Baltimore man had been arrested for kidnapping young women, raping them, chopping them up into human steaks, stuffing them into huge freezers when he was finished with them. To dispose of the evidence, he'd allegedly prepared the human meat as anyone else would prepare beef – ground, roasted, fried, barbecued and boiled.

The worst part, at least to Susan, was that the story said he fed his early victims to his later victims without telling them what they were eating.

Mike kept a careful eye on Susan since Dan first mentioned the story. He thought about how insensitive he'd been, bringing up such a gruesome story about death so soon after the shooting of her brother. She didn't seem to mind, though. In fact, she dove right into the conversation and kept the topic alive.

"It makes you wonder what other sick things are going on out there that we don't know about, doesn't it?" Susan said.

"If I ran this paper I'd blanket the front page with stories like that, like the one I wrote about that kid and the train," Dan said, fixating again on his first sensational story at *The Argus*, the one about the young boy whose head was decapitated by the huge steel wheels of a train and the grieving reaction of his mother.

"Give 'em what they want," Dan continued. "Readers don't give a damn about a fancy, state-fair quilt some little old lady's been patching together for twenty years."

"There, you're wrong," Mike said. "We need all kinds of stories, good to balance out the bad. Iowans enjoy reading about the accomplishments of people they know. They like to see familiar names doing good. They like to think we're all neighbors. Good neighbors. They talk about that stuff, too."

"Community journalism," Dan said, exhaling a cloud of smoke from his Kool cigarette. "I'd like to burn the moron who came up with that oxymoron. You don't think readers talked about that kid getting his head sliced off? It's like the movies. People say they like love stories, but it's blood and guts that sells tickets."

Mike cupped his right hand over his forehead and ran it back through his sandy-colored hair, leaving a rooster tail behind. In five years on the night beat, he'd visited at least a dozen murder scenes, countless fatal crashes, even interviewed a couple of rape victims as long as he promised not to use their real names. Each time he'd left the most sensitive details in his notebook.

As Mike recalled one of the worst stories he'd ever covered, a murder-suicide on the west side, where a man had shot his wife in the head five times before turning the revolver on himself, he twisted a napkin around his index finger in anguish. He thought of other episodes, too.

"You look pensive, my friend," Dan said. "Be careful or you'll drown in your beer."

"My first day on the job ..."

Dan stifled a yawn with a closed fist. Susan and Linda listened politely.

"... I'd started eating lunch at my desk when the scanner crackled, with everybody talking at once – the cops, the sheriff's department, the fire department. They were called to the Brown Derby Tap on Twelfth Avenue, in The Flats. The bar's not there anymore, they tore it down.

But I'd never been down in that area, never been around black people much, living in small-town Iowa all my life. Down there, I realized what it was like being a minority."

"Like being a Jew," Dan said. "I don't think so. You were there for an hour, maybe two. I live with it every day. There must be a reason you're telling this story."

"Yeah, man, listen. It was my first day working in a city bigger than ten thousand people. It was a shooting in broad daylight. Supposedly at least one guy was dead. I'd never covered anything like it. And here I'm ordered to get out there as fast as I can and to take a photographer with me. That was a relief. I wasn't going alone."

" 'Cause you didn't want your honky ass sticking out like a sore thumb."

" 'Cause I didn't want to get shot."

Dan laughed. "By the time you got there, the shooter was long gone. Or he was dead."

"I didn't know that. It was my first live shooting, and Jimmy was going with me."

"Jimmy?" Dan roared. "Jimmy Wilson? I've been here what, four, five months, and it didn't take me a day to see the guy's a joke. One of the first stories he told me was when he forgot to put film in his camera and stood there snapping pictures as the courthouse dome burned. He came back to *The Argus* with nothing."

"I didn't know about Jimmy, yet, either. First day, remember? So, I follow Jimmy who's got cameras dangling from his neck, ready for any situation. He runs past the TV cameras in front of the Brown Derby and around to the back door, figuring he can sneak inside.

"Well, a cop's there, guarding the door, and Jimmy knows him. They're talking like old friends when some hyperactive guy who says he's friends with the victim causes a ruckus. As the cop calms him down, Jimmy grabs my arm and drags me into the dark bar.

"Before anyone can stop him, Jimmy takes a couple of flash pictures of this white guy who had been sitting at the bar, his head with his brains blown away laying on a grilled cheese sandwich. You couldn't tell the difference between blood and ketchup. His brains were strung out down the bar.

"It was the grossest thing I'd ever seen, and it was just as gross when Jimmy showed me the black and white photo later."

Dan threw his head back in a laugh. "And *The Argus* never used the picture."

"Of course not."

"Yet you told everyone in the newsroom what you'd seen. Jimmy probably flashed copies of his pictures all over the place. And you never even described the scene to readers, right?"

Mike shook his head. "I wrote that he was shot in the head while sitting at the bar. I can't believe you'd even consider writing more than that. Hell, I couldn't eat for two days, and I used to like grilled cheese sandwiches."

Dan smirked. "Jimmy told me that story, one of his favorites, but he didn't say you were with him. He said he put a print of the mangled head on the newsroom bulletin board for a caption contest. Somebody wrote beneath it, 'Grilled cheese sandwich devours man.' Jimmy keeps that one in his files."

"You're as sick as he is," Mike said.

"At least I didn't blow it. The grilled cheese would have been a nice touch. You ever read stories about the shootings in Chicago in the '20s and '30s, how reporters described the gangland shootings, the blood and guts everywhere? If I want to get back there, I've got to write like those boys did. Great stuff."

"Yellow journalism," Mike said. "Half of it was made up, fake news, hearsay, fiction. Reporters in those days embellished everything they wrote."

"My God, Rockwell, you sound like one of our readers, not a reporter," Dan said. "The truth too much for you?"

"There's the truth, and there's what people need to know," Mike said. "They are separate, distinct matters."

"You're an '80s cliché," Dan said. "You should be drinking scotch instead of beer. Then you could become a real journalist."

"Oh, stop it," Susan said, hitting Dan playfully on the shoulder. "Just because Halloween is coming up, you guys don't need to gross us out. Enough about the news." She smiled, but there was a serious tone in her voice. "You guys aren't going to solve anything talking like that."

Mike felt Linda's knee brush against his leg as if to say you've been ignoring me. She nodded, as if to agree with Susan, then rested her chin on her open palm, her eyes half open, looking bored.

"Yeah," Mike said, "I think this is enough trying to gross people out. Let's change the subject."

Susan nodded, the gleam in her brown eyes welcoming an ally.

Mike had immediately liked her, but he had withheld a final assessment until then because he wasn't the type to make snap judgments. She was attractive, but not beautiful. Her dark hair was too full, for one thing, poofed up as if she was a movie star in a low-budget flick.

Yet, the smallness of her nose, turned up slightly, and her razor thin lips accentuating full, round cheeks, presented the refined look of a model. She also appeared intelligent enough, except for the fact that she was with a person like Dan Goldberg.

Dan wore a huge grin as if he was choking on a secret. This was the first time since Dan had been in Cedar City that Mike had seen him out with a woman. It wasn't necessarily surprising, considering Dan occasionally talked about old girlfriends in Chicago, just weird.

Being with this woman affected Dan in an adverse way. He was more obnoxious than ever, pining to be the center of attention, chugging his beer, interrupting conversation by talking loudly and wearing the top three buttons of his shirt unbuttoned to show the thick, dark hair on his chest.

Mike wasn't surprised at the change either, but he didn't like it. And in that lull, as the conversation waited for someone to pick it up, Mike noticed that the silver chain around Dan's neck had a new ornament on it, several times larger than the swastika Mike had remembered.

"I see you're wearing a cross," Mike said. "Where'd you get that?"

Dan inhaled deeply so his chest filled his shirt, then reached inside and retrieved his new medallion so that everyone at the table, especially Susan, could see it.

"I picked it up at a flea market," Dan said. "It's an Iron Cross, like the Germans gave their war heroes."

"Is it real?" Susan asked, her inquisitive nose inches from the cross as she examined it, which caused Dan to smile broadly.

"No, I doubt it," he said. "The Germans gave them out like candy, and the soldiers who won them tossed them away like gum wrappers. There aren't a whole lot of real ones around."

"It's probably a replica from the '60s," Linda said. "I've heard hippies had a thing for them."

Mike smiled. "Dan still does."

"It's part of my heritage," Dan said, defensively. "Some kraut probably got a cross like this for gassing a hundred Jews. Making his quota. It was a lot of damned senseless killing."

Dan's bitterness about the Holocaust was understandable but confusing to Mike who didn't understand why he'd wear a symbol of German oppression. Dan also didn't need to be so outward about an event that happened more than forty years ago, a tragedy he could do nothing about. Apparently, Susan felt the same way. She abruptly backed away from the medal.

"I agree the Holocaust was horrible," Mike said, "but I don't understand why you'd wear something that represents the other side."

"I'd think you'd know me by now," Dan replied. "Controversy is my middle name. If I can screw with your mind, I'm all in."

An elongated silence enveloped the table as each person took a casual sip of beer.

Mike tried to come up with a new topic, but when you're a newspaper reporter, you tend to talk about the news, whether it's local or national, yesterday or in the ancient past. He thought about the shooting of Susan's brother and the fact he had been outside the house when it happened, and the sound of Morgan's demanding voice filled his head again.

That was what bothered him about Susan being there. That and Morgan's insistence that Mike talk to his jailed accomplices. Mike couldn't clear his mind enough to think of anything constructive to say. He should have known Dan would come around.

"Hey," Dan said, looking directly at Mike. "Did I tell you this nut case who robbed the 7-Eleven called me yesterday?" Dan smiled again. "He said he wanted to make sure that I got everything right in the story and that he blew away the lottery machine because he never won."

Linda started, glanced at Mike as if to say that sounded similar to Morgan's threatening call.

It seemed a strange coincidence to Mike, too, that a 7-Eleven holdup man would call Dan shortly after an alleged murderer had called him. There was no reason not to believe Dan. He was a reporter, and reporters were honest. They had to keep everything above board.

What bothered Mike was that a trigger-happy Morgan could be shooting up convenience stores for the hell of it.

"So, what did this guy sound like?" Mike asked.

"Oh, uh, just like any man on the telephone who sounds desperate," Dan said. "It's hard to describe voices. You just know them when you hear them again."

"Did he sound nervous?"

"I really don't remember." Dan seemed to shrug it off almost as quickly as he'd brought it up, as if he wanted to forget it. "The guy wanted publicity. That's what Margaret said."

Mike felt he knew Morgan well enough to know that he wouldn't have called Dan for publicity. At least not about a shoot-'em-up convenience store holdup. And if Morgan was innocent of killing a cop, he wouldn't do something that asinine to get himself into more trouble than he already faced.

Mike remembered that he'd told Dan about Morgan's first call. But he hadn't told anyone, not Dan or Linda, about the follow-up calls, or the meeting in the park, or the engraved cigarette lighter in his pocket. He chalked it up to coincidence that they'd both received calls from criminals after the act.

Dan didn't seem to want to discuss his call any more so Mike quit asking questions. But he couldn't erase Morgan's voice from his mind, his insistence that Mike talk to the two men in jail associated with the drug bust gone bad. Mike hadn't even made an attempt yet, but he had considered buying a gun for his own protection and for Linda's, too, but he hadn't mentioned that to anyone either. He hated guns, but this was one time when owning one might not be such a bad idea. He looked at Dan.

"Do you know anything about guns?" From the corner of his eye, Mike saw the surprise on Linda's face. She hated guns, too.

"Oh, not a whole lot," Dan said. "I'm not much for guns. Why, you thinking about getting one?"

"Maybe," Mike said. "But I don't know the first thing about them. Where would you go to buy a used one?"

"I suppose it depends on what you want. If you wanted a new one, you'd go to a sporting goods store, so they might have used ones, too, trade-ins. You could try pawn shops. They get junk like that all the time."

"You are not buying a gun," Linda said. "I won't allow you to have one."

"Whoa," Dan said. "If the man wants a gun, he gets a gun. It's not your decision. It can't hurt to have one if you feel the need for protection. I can understand Rockwell's concern. After all, he did get shot, and you never know when something like that might happen again."

Linda's green eyes did a slow burn on Dan.

Mike knew she didn't like Goldberg, especially his way of instigating controversy for the pleasure of it. She had accused Mike of changing since Dan arrived at *The Argus*, that he'd become more reckless, more confrontational, more aggressive. She had complained that Dan was the type of person who influenced others the wrong way and that she didn't want Mike falling under his evil spell.

"You know, of course, you've got to get a permit at the sheriff's office," Dan said. He ignored Linda, who turned away. "They make you wait three days, so you don't do anything rash, so you cool down if you're thinking about buying one for revenge.

"You can always apply for the permit and think about it," Dan said. "That doesn't mean you have to buy a gun."

21

After Mike Rockwell and his girlfriend Linda excused themselves from the Fox and Hounds for needed time alone, Dan Goldberg talked Susan Holcomb into sharing a pizza and another pitcher of beer before leaving. Then he convinced her to join him at his apartment for a nightcap.

Susan said she was tired, but Dan felt he knew her well enough that he could coax her into staying out. She finally gave in, but only agreed to go to his place as long as she could follow Dan in her car rather than ride with him.

A bad sign, Dan thought, but not the end of the world. He was pleased she finally seemed to be loosening up after her brother's death.

When Dan had called Susan on Thursday evening, she seemed in a better mood than Wednesday. When she hedged on going out with him, he'd told her she still hadn't gone for a ride in his new car. She laughed and said, "OK." In fact, she agreed that it might do her some good to get away from her usual crowd. Her friends were all sympathetic about her brother, but they were uncomfortable talking about it, too. Her coworkers had become distant. A new environment, new people, might be what she needed.

"I had a good time tonight," Susan said as Dan unlocked his apartment door. "Linda and Mike are a pleasant couple."

"Rockwell gets too uptight," Dan said. "He wants to get married, and she keeps putting him off."

Dan opened the door, reached inside to flip on the light and guided Susan into his living room.

"Well, she is younger than he is," Susan said. "It takes a while for some people to make a commitment, especially when they know it's for a lifetime."

Dan motioned for Susan to sit on the dark chocolate-colored velour couch that faced an entertainment center, an older color television on top and separate stereo receiver and turntable components below, all flanked by a pair of rather large loudspeakers.

"Beer fine?" Dan asked, walking toward the kitchen.

"Sure," Susan said, draping her coat over a chair and making herself comfortable on the couch. She glanced around the apartment as Dan opened the refrigerator and retrieved a pair of glasses from a kitchen cabinet.

The morning newspaper was assembled neatly on one end of the blond coffee table and a silver dish on the other end held clear-wrapped caramels.

A VCR in the entertainment center flashed midnight or noon, depending on your interpretation of the time it would take to properly set the clock.

The apartment-beige carpet, apartment-beige walls, and popcorn ceiling reflected the same generic appearance as the front of the square brick building when they'd approached.

But photographs in black and white and color, in a variety of sizes, in simple black frames so as not to distract from the pictures themselves, prompted Susan to stand again, to take a closer look.

The still-life of a juicy cluster of freshly peeled and dissected oranges arranged on a dark reflective surface made her mouth water. The smaller black and white portrait of a woman in her late 30s, an older photograph with a sepia tone, accented the anguish in the woman's large eyes. A third photograph, the largest in the room, appeared to have been taken at dawn or dusk, a shiny reddish-orange cluster of adjacent railroad tracks and switches, gradually melding into one set of tracks that curved around a dilapidated white building as they became narrower and narrower in the distance until disappearing into the glare of the sun on the horizon.

Dan handed Susan a glass of beer, clicked his glass against hers, and said, "Cheers."

"This apartment's nicer than I thought it would be," she said.

Dan grinned. "And what's that supposed to mean?"

He kept his tone amicable because he'd spent Thursday evening picking up and dusting in anticipation that he'd bring her to his apartment before tonight was over.

"Young single guys usually don't care that much about where they live. Or what conditions they live in," she said, taking a sip of beer. "This is a refreshing change."

"Thanks," he said. "I hate clutter."

She smiled. "I suppose you never throw your clothes on the floor either?"

"Well, I wouldn't go that far," he said. "My mother raised me right, though. If I don't have time to pick them up, I throw them in the closet and close the door."

Susan laughed.

"What's so funny about that?"

"I was laughing because I'm not that way at all. I either throw stuff all over the place, or I pick everything up. It's never in-between for me."

"So, which is it most often, neat or messy?"

"I'm usually neat. But this last week, I've let the place go. I'd be embarrassed to let anybody see it. I've let everything go."

Dan knew what she meant. When he severed ties with his father right before he began college, Dan let everything go, too, especially his life. They'd grown apart by then, but the fact that Dan planned to never see his father again, even to argue, had presented him with a weird loss of identity. He'd never prayed for prayer's sake, and he didn't pray for his father either. But after Dan came out of a weeklong drunk, he studied bits and pieces of the Torah and the Talmud.

That was the first time Dan had broken the tomes open since he studied Judaism in elementary Hebrew class but he hadn't paid much attention to them since that time. Rereading the laws helped him discover a little more about his passive-aggressive father, a lot more about his people, but very little about himself.

Dan studied about the persecution of the Jews, how even three thousand years ago they had preached about peace and brotherhood. He had always seen his father as a timid and shy man outside of his clothing store who wouldn't stand up for his own beliefs, except to his kid and employees, when all along he'd been doing exactly what Jewish tradition instructed.

It aggravated Dan that such a belief in peace and brotherhood could destroy a man's sense of self-worth to the extent that it could make him seem, at least to others, to be ashamed of what he was.

After learning of John Wayne Gacy's arrest, Dan began reading stories about World War II, which reinforced his belief that too many Jews were passive like his father, letting the world push them around. He wanted to be different. He wanted people to know that he was not afraid of who he was.

Dan hadn't thought about that for a long time, not until he'd read in September that John Wayne Gacy's appeal of his murder convictions on the grounds of ineffective counsel had been dismissed. For a long time Dan had known that he and Gacy had one thing in common – their fathers belittled them into feeling worthless.

The story last month reiterated the finding that Gacy had been diagnosed with an anti-social personality, that he was capable of committing crimes without remorse. He was biding his time on death row painting pictures of clowns because he was infatuated with them, for he had often dressed as Pogo the Clown to feign friendliness.

"Hey," Dan finally said, "you want to watch a movie? I've got about forty. I like them all, so you can choose any one you want."

"I couldn't stay awake for an entire movie," she said, glancing at her watch. "It's almost midnight now. I'd turn into a pumpkin before it was over."

"If you fell asleep, it wouldn't bother me," he said. "I'd just put you to bed."

"That's what I'd be afraid of." She looked at him from the corner of her eye, but she did smile. "I suppose you'd crawl in under the sheets right after me."

Dan tried to appear timid, as if he hadn't meant to insinuate anything, even though getting her into bed had been his intent all along. "I could sleep on the couch."

"You could," she said. "But would you?"

"Of course," he said, leaning over to put his arm around her. "If that's what you'd want." He squeezed her waist gently, letting her know that if she was joking about sleeping together, he was, too. But he also gave her an ever so slight push toward the bedroom if she wasn't.

Susan swayed in the opposite direction, breaking the touch his arm off her hip as she moved to the middle of the room.

"I like your photographs on the wall," she said, stepping toward the landscape of the railroad tracks. "What's this one supposed to symbolize? That your life can be screwed up until you find the right set of tracks and then, if you follow them, they'll lead you around the rotten parts into the golden years of your life?"

She turned and faced him, a hint of a smile on her face.

"If you want to look at it that way, I suppose you can," he said. "Or you could look at it the other way, that it's a sunrise not a sunset, that life begins somewhere in the distance and as it gets closer and closer to the end, it gets so complicated that you don't know which set of tracks you're on."

"That's too pessimistic," she said, turning back toward the photograph. "I'd rather look at it my way. That somewhere out there, everything gets better. Maybe you don't know what to expect, but it's got to be an improvement."

As Susan stood in front of the picture, Dan stepped back to study her figure, the way her shoulders sagged and her arms hung limp by her side in dejection. Her hips curved widely beneath her gray tweed skirt so that her calves seemed too thin beneath its hem.

Susan was far from perfect, but the way she stood with her hips cocked slightly made Dan desire her.

She slid over to the picture of the grieving woman.

"What's the story behind this one?" she asked. "Something bad must have happened to someone close to her."

Dan slipped behind Susan, so he could look at the picture over her shoulder. He wished he'd taken it down because now he had to explain its history.

The woman's face was filled with sorrow because the photograph had been snapped at the moment she learned her daughter had been found dead beneath a bridge on the Chicago River. Dan had been at the scene with the photographer and the picture had run with his story.

The photograph had won an award; the story had not.

"She just found out that her fourteen-year-old daughter had been raped and murdered," he said. "The girl's body was found along the Chicago River. The photographer and I were with the cop when he told her what happened."

"Who took it?"

"Roger Nicholson. He was a photographer at *The Weekly Enterprise* when I worked there. He was the best."

"It's so sad," Susan said. "Invasive, too. A woman shouldn't be put in front of the public like that. That's got to be one of the toughest jobs a cop has, to tell a mother her daughter has been murdered."

Dan remembered how the woman, he couldn't recall her name, had broken down and cried after receiving the news.

He'd had difficulty talking to her, trying to get her to tell him how she felt. He resorted to describing only what he saw for the sake of accuracy and never forgave her for holding back, for not at least giving a quote he could use. He'd just been doing his job, but she didn't seem to care.

"Why do you have it on your wall?" Susan asked. Her dark eyes appeared sad and distant. Dan knew she was thinking about her brother.

"It reminds me that life isn't always all it's cracked up to be." His words were slow and deliberate. "You can be going along and everything is fine and then, in an instant, something or somebody comes along to screw it all up."

Dan paused.

"It reminds me," he said, "that I can always do better in my job because I did a lousy job on that story."

"You seem so negative," she said. "Would you have run a picture of me like that after my brother was shot, if you'd have been there with a photographer and he took my picture?"

Susan stared into Dan's face.

"Would you have used that in the paper?" she asked.

"It depends," he said, swallowing hard to give himself an extra moment to compose his answer. "I've got to be honest. It wouldn't be my decision. But if the picture told the story, like this one did, then I'd think an editor would use it."

"You don't have to be so honest," Susan said, turning her head back over her shoulder to look away. Her voice was cracking.

"Sometimes," she said, "it's better not to say anything than tell the truth."

Dan knew she was right. He could be as deceptive as anyone. But when it came to reporting a story, talking about it, he tended to be more honest than necessary to explore every detail and justify its existence.

He couldn't tell if Susan was angry or if she was just sad, but in the instant she turned away, he saw the blank expression on her face and tears forming in her eyes.

Dan put his hands on her shoulders and turned her gently toward him. He placed one hand on the back of her head, pulling it into the soft nook between his shoulder and chest.

Susan was shaking ever so slightly, as she had done when he'd hugged her at the cemetery, and he felt the moisture of tears soak through his shirt.

"Dan," she said, her voice muffled between stifled sobs. "I loved my brother so much. I miss him."

"I know," he said. "You will for a long time."

They remained embraced in the center of the room for several minutes.

Dan remembered how strong she had been at the cemetery, how she barely cried when he hugged her there, but now it seemed like she wouldn't stop. Her tears soaked the front of his shirt.

He remembered how he'd cried after he decided never to see his father again, how it had not happened for several days, not until he'd sobered up. He realized Susan was experiencing the same turmoil, but enough was enough.

Once again, a night hadn't turned out as planned. Now he had no prayer of getting her into bed. He felt relief when she finally broke their embrace, so he didn't have to push her away.

Susan's eyes were bloodshot, smeared black with mascara, but she managed a weak smile.

"Dan," she said. "I'm not ready to get close to anyone. I think it's time for me to go."

"I can tell." He nodded. "You need to be alone."

"Do you understand?"

"Of course," he said.

Dan retrieved her coat from the back of the chair and helped her put it on as she stretched her arms out to accept the sleeves.

He should have known this wouldn't work out. All he'd wanted was a meaningless relationship, a little more than a one-night stand, but not much more than that.

Damn. Why did he pick women like this? Why had he wanted to see Susan again, knowing she was still recovering from the death of her brother?

He was angry with her, but he was more angry at himself. He wanted to talk some sense into her, to convince her that life goes on, but he didn't want to waste weeks doing it, only to get her into the sack, then go through the anguish of breaking if off and dealing with her broken heart.

Why the hell, Dan thought, didn't his plans work out like they were supposed to?

As Susan buttoned her coat, he turned her around and kissed her on the forehead.

"Is that all I get?" she said.

As Dan kissed her on the lips, she forcefully kissed him back, mashing his lips against his teeth as if to prove that she could be aggressive, too.

It was more than he'd expected, but not what he wanted, a reward kiss for being a good guy.

"Thank you," she said. "I appreciate your kindness, but I just can't forget about my brother ... and my husband. Not yet."

Oh, God, Dan had forgotten about her husband, the former cop who had been killed in the road construction accident. How could he be so stupid? She probably hadn't spent a night with anyone since he'd died. Her crying session made more sense.

"I know," was all Dan could say, as he walked her to his door and she stopped him there. "Drive carefully," he added.

"I will."

He helped her descend the stairs to the sidewalk, her head bowed to watch each footstep. He stood outside the front door as she climbed into her car and started the engine. He didn't close the door until she had driven away.

Inside his apartment, Dan grabbed another beer and began to pace.

"Damn, damn, damn," he said. "Damn, damn, damn."

He hadn't wanted to get involved with anybody, not now, not here, in a long-term relationship, not a complicated relationship, anyway, just for sex. And suddenly, now that Susan was gone, he felt the walls closing in around him.

He had pursued her, she had turned him down, but that last kiss indicated that she expected to see him again and again.

Dan stopped in front of the black and white portrait of the sad-eyed woman, the mother of the murdered girl, and knew it had been the cause for him going to bed alone.

He cursed himself for leaving the portrait up, cursed the woman for her story, cursed his passive-aggressive father, cursed the German concentration camps that had murdered so many Jews and turned the generations to come into such submissive wimps.

He ripped the picture off the wall and threw it across the room. The glass shattered into six million pieces.

* * * * *

Mike Rockwell and Linda Reynolds tossed and turned in her bed, unable to fall asleep. First, he'd hold her and couldn't get comfortable, so he'd roll away. Then she'd wrap her arm around him, snuggle up against his back and be unable to fall asleep, so she'd roll away.

"What the hell is wrong with us?" Mike said, sitting up.

"Don't ask me," Linda said. "I'm so tired, you'd think I could sleep standing up."

"Me, too. But I can't shut my damn brain off."

"Count sheep."

"I've counted so many sheep I should be a shepherd."

Linda laughed. "Sometimes you're so funny. You'd make a great shepherd."

"I tell you one thing. I bet a shepherd doesn't have any problems that keep him awake."

"No? He just has to watch out for wolves in sheep's clothing," she said. "You think that'd be stress-free?"

"A hell of a lot easier than trying to figure out what's going on with my life right now," he snapped.

"Oh, honey," Linda said. She rolled over and wrapped her arm around his waist, tucked her head into his chest. "You've just got to leave work behind."

"It's more than work I'm worried about," he said.

As Mike's mind pounded, her head on his chest rose and fell with each breath. It was heavy, yet comforting, as he ran his fingers through the length of her hair.

Mike knew he couldn't discuss Morgan, not anything beyond the first call, anyway, because he hadn't told Linda anything about the second call, the meeting in the park, the investigative work Morgan wanted him to do. As far as she knew, Morgan had disappeared, and the worst of that situation was behind them.

He couldn't bring up his lingering doubts about their relationship, not as she stroked his chest with her warm, smooth hand. She'd already heard enough from him about that, and they'd agreed the next step was up to her. If he brought it up, she'd probably toss him, naked, out into the street.

But he could talk about Dan.

"I don't know what's going on with Dan," he said. "One minute I think I've got him figured out, and the next minute I don't have a clue.

"He was his cocky self around Susan tonight, maybe even more than usual. But, at work, he's been super nice to me lately, like he wants something, like he's trying to hide something. I don't get it."

"You don't get it because you've only known him for a few months. That's hardly enough time to judge somebody. And, besides, we all change."

"But he's getting weird. That Iron Cross on his necklace makes no sense at all. Why would a Jewish person, one who despises the Holocaust as much as Dan says he does, wear something like that, a symbol of German supremacy? He said he likes to be controversial, but I still don't get it."

"It doesn't matter what religion Dan is, or that he's from a big city, or even that he's a reporter," Linda said. "He's the type of guy who likes to be the center of attention. Sometimes he'll do whatever it takes to make sure that happens."

"I know one thing," Mike said. "I wouldn't trust him to pay back a five-dollar loan."

Linda ran her fingertips gently up the side of Mike's neck, up on his chin, up to place her index finger across his lips as if to shush him.

"I bet there are a hundred things you can't explain about everyone you know, and you know at least a hundred people. That means there are thousands of things you can't explain about people."

Linda laughed.

"Quit trying," she said. "Dan was his usual, cocky self. I didn't see any difference. You're the one I should be worried about."

"Maybe I am just imagining it, but he seems preoccupied with weird stuff, aggressive and violent stuff. The Iron Cross, the guy in Baltimore who cut up women, his stories about tragedy, especially the one about the kid hit by a train that I've heard a million times."

"I'll admit I was wondering how Susan was taking all that," Linda said.

"It makes me wonder what's wrong with her. I don't know why any normal person would put up with his crap. I was ready to slug him."

"My sweet, wouldn't-hurt-a-fly Mike Rockwell, slug somebody? Come on. Now you are sounding like Dan."

"I know. That's what bothers me. I really felt like hitting him, and I don't ever remember feeling that way about anybody."

"Relax," Linda said. "Dan's acting like a sixth-grade boy, and so are you. If he was younger, I'd say he'd grow out of it, but that's doubtful now."

"Spoken with the wisdom of a teacher who's dealt with these situations before."

"It's not as if you and Dan are best buddies," she said. "You're coworkers who are friendly with each other. If you'd met Dan outside of work, I doubt that you'd be friends. He's not your type. It's as simple as that."

"So, what is my type?" Mike asked.

He knew he was baiting Linda, but it was worth a shot. "Any ideas?"

In an instant, Linda crawled on top of Mike, her naked body hot against his, her tongue licking the underside of his neck, the side of his jaw.

"Mmmm," she mumbled, "let me take your mind off everything but me."

Mike wrapped his arms around Linda's waist, ran a hand into the small of her back and over the curves below, her warm flesh melting into his.

When she became the instigator, when having sex was her idea, Mike knew she was aware that she could command one-hundred percent of his attention. And she was right. He didn't think about anything else.

22

Time inched forward for Dan Goldberg, and he couldn't understand why. Usually when he was busy, he'd look at a calendar and be amazed that it had been so long since the first of the month or the first of the week or the last time he had a day off.

It was Saturday, only three days since he'd shot up the 7-Eleven. It seemed like years ago; it seemed like yesterday.

Dan could still picture the clerk's frightened face as he pointed the gun at him. The memory made Dan laugh. It was the first time he'd realized that a gun was more powerful than money. He'd taken less than twenty dollars from the 7-Eleven, not even enough to buy the Walkman he'd stolen from Target. If he'd really wanted to, he could have taken a lot more. He could get anything he wanted with a gun.

Dan recalled, when he was seven or eight years old, how his uncle had taught him to shoot in the woods behind his rural Rockford barn.

Uncle George had warned him that guns were to be used only for target practice or protection. He went through a litany of rules, all of which Dan had forgotten, except that guns were dangerous, and they could go off at any time, sometimes when you least expected it. His uncle always kept the guns, a .45 revolver, a couple of .22 rifles and a .410 shotgun, locked up.

Uncle George once caught Dan trying to break into his gun cabinet and yelled at him as if the world had come to an end. Putting on his innocent face, Dan had said he just wanted to practice. Uncle George bought it, said, "OK," and they took a .22 rifle out behind the barn.

Uncle George promptly shot a jackrabbit as it skittered across the yard. He was making a point, although Dan didn't know it at the time. Dan had never been hunting, never seen an animal shot to death.

The soft and fluffy gray animal, bloody and lifeless on the ground, scared Dan enough that it made him cry. He had remembered his first picture books about Peter Cottontail, a young innocent rabbit who was simply mischievous, who got into trouble but was able to return home to his mother.

Only as Dan grew older did he realize that the lesson Uncle George taught was that real guns weren't like those on television, that death in real life wasn't acting, it was permanent. Dan had cried again as they picked up the dead rabbit with a shovel and buried it behind the barn.

Still, Dan's fascination with guns lived on and thrived from the moment his peace-loving father forbade him to own a gun. He bought his first pistol soon after he began covering the police beat for the Chicago weekly, a .38 Special like those worn in a concealed holster beneath a suitcoat by the detectives he admired.

Dan fired the gun weekly at the outdoor police range with the officers, who taught him to concentrate on his target, to squeeze the trigger gently in one smooth motion.

Once, he hit the bull's-eye six straight shots from ten yards, an accomplishment that would have earned a cop special accolades. After Dan became that good, he sold the .38. He didn't need to practice anymore; he was as good as he'd ever need to be.

But Saturday afternoon, the sun warming the cold autumn air out in the country with a new pistol in his hands, Dan felt rusty as he plinked cans off the same wooden fence he'd used Wednesday.

Shooting a gun wasn't like riding a bicycle. It took practice. He'd owned the Beretta only a week, and this was only his third shooting session, if you counted the shots he'd fired inside the 7-Eleven convenience store.

Yet, as he continued to practice, as he filled and refilled the clip, set up and shot down the cans, he felt his shooting eye return.

After he knocked off all thirteen cans with a full clip, he was set. It didn't matter that he stood but a half-dozen paces away. That's all the better he'd need to be if he were to use the gun again.

* * * * *

The sun had nearly set, but Dan wasn't ready to head home. Sleep had been elusive the past week, his brain working overtime, so he'd relied on a few drinks every night to doze off. As far as he was concerned, that was the only way to ensure sleep.

Pot would do the same thing, but he didn't have any. In fact, he hadn't smoked any marijuana since moving to Cedar City.

Instead, Dan lit a cigarette and slipped the Beretta into his glovebox. He nestled a spare clip beside it and slammed the door shut. He knew carrying a loaded gun in the glovebox was illegal, but who was going to care, here?

Dan had a craving for a drink, so he needed to find a bar.

If he was stopped, the cop would ask to see his driver's license and, if he didn't already know the cop, he'd say he was a reporter for *The Argus* and that would be that. Cops in Cedar City, in any city for that matter, were easy on people they knew, people in the media. It was good public relations.

As Dan ran his Mazda through the gears along the curvy blacktop roads in the country outside Cedar City, he smiled at the recent commercial he'd seen on television with "Rockford Files" star James Garner touting Mazda performance.

"It'll spoil you for anything else," Dan said out loud, gunning the engine around a curve as the rear tires squealed to maintain their grip.

* * * * *

"Give me a light and not one of those stupid butt lights," Dan told the bartender at The Silver Nugget. "I want a Miller Lite."

The bartender chuckled, as if he hadn't heard that lame joke before, retrieved a bottle of beer from the cooler and set it and a glass on the bar. Dan had put a dollar down.

"It's a dollar and a quarter," the bartender said.

"In this dive?" Dan said, reaching into his pocket for a quarter.

"Nobody's forcing you to drink here."

"I was just shittin' ya," Dan replied, flipping a quarter on the bar. "Here you go, partner."

"The last of the big-time spenders," the bartender said, picking up the coin and plinking it into the cash register drawer.

The Silver Nugget was a country bar, not a country-western bar per se, although it catered to rural folks who rode in on horseback for a drink or two or three. It was the closest watering hole to Dan's shooting range, along a highway on the east edge of Cedar City.

Dan thought about James Garner again, only this time his "Maverick" days, when in the Old West it was impossible to get picked up for drunken horseback riding. He wondered if that was the case now. Hell, the horse knew the way home.

From conversations with police officers, and from scanning the logs, Dan also knew The Silver Nugget had a sleezy reputation. It catered to locals who wanted to get away from prying eyes in town, but not too far out, for a secret rendezvous or to pick up a loose stranger. Rooms at The Silver Spur, a run-down but convenient motel next door, rented by the hour.

As Dan glanced around the room, he decided that his first visit to The Silver Nugget would be his last. While the exterior was quaint with natural, wind-ravaged wood, and black metal horse-head hitching posts lining an un-painted wooden sidewalk that emitted a hollow sound when patrons wearing cowboy boots clicked their heels, the floor inside was bare concrete. It could be hosed down after the rough and ready cowpokes got sloshed and spilled their beer, or their guts, on rowdy weekends.

A small elevated stage sat in the far corner, a rack of colored spotlights suspended above it to shine on the bands as they cranked up foot-stompin' music. The inside walls, rough and unpainted, too, were covered with elec-tric beer signs and glossy posters, including a handful of older ones that depicted John Travolta as the "Urban Cowboy."

Across one wall hung a loose white banner with blue script, "Friday's are Silver Bullet Night at The Silver Nugget."

Dan chuckled at the advertisement for Coors Light because it reminded him of his early drinking days, when Coors was a special beer that required a trip to Colorado or having connections with bootlegging friends who brought it back to the Midwest. Not so, anymore, Dan knew, now that it was exported to the Midwest.

The centerpiece of The Silver Nugget was the huge bar shaped like a horseshoe to promote eye contact, so you could sit on one side and ogle the customers on the other. Dan imagined horny and spurious Iowa cowboys circling the bar to lasso their lassies.

Only two other men sat in the bar, and they eyed Dan suspiciously from the other side of the horseshoe as if he was a cattle rustler who'd ridden in from south of the Pecos on a stolen horse. The lassies, he was sure, would show up later and receive much friendlier scrutiny.

Dan lit a cigarette and thought about calling Susan, to ask if she'd like to join him somewhere for a drink. Maybe he could get her drunk, and the evening would work out better than last night.

There was something about the karma in this place that made him want to see her. Maybe these country bars had something to them after all, he thought, pouring the rest of his beer into the glass. Maybe there was something in the air.

Dan drained his beer as an old man sidled up next to him at the bar.

"Howdy, partner," the man said. "Looks like you need another beer."

"You buyin'?" Dan asked.

"Sure am, partner," the stranger said. "What'll you have?"

"Another one of these," Dan said, holding up his empty bottle. What the hell, he thought, why turn down a free beer?

Dan tried to get a better look at his new companion without seeming too obvious. The guy's hair was white, not gray, sparse and unkempt. His large nose had red veins visible even in the dim light. He wore a red-checked flannel shirt and new blue jeans appropriate for The Silver Nugget, but out of place on this old geezer.

Something else about him didn't seem right, either, but Dan wasn't going to worry about it.

The bartender brought a round and then another and another. Whatever had bothered Dan about his new friend didn't bother him anymore, not when there was free beer involved.

Dan was getting drunk and having a good time. Chuck Lawton was buying the beer and keeping Dan in stitches, not because Dan was laughing with him, but because he was laughing at him.

The old geezer was so ridiculous, he was funny. And the drunker they both got, the funnier Chuck became.

"I parked my pony out front," Chuck said. "She wanted to come in, but I told her they'd just make horse dovers out of her." And he started laughing uncontrollably.

Chuck Lawton said he was sixty-seven, a retired Cedar City businessman out for a good time. His wife died before they were able to enjoy retirement together, but he couldn't let that hold him down.

Chuck was feeling his oats, looking for a new wife, a filly, maybe just for one night or maybe for the rest of his life. He'd never been to The Silver Nugget either, but he'd heard about its reputation. Every time the front door opened, his beady little eyes turned hopefully toward it.

Dan introduced himself as Dan Garner, an accountant with a small firm in Cedar City. It was the first thing that came to mind. He said tax season after the first of the year would keep him hopping, so he was taking advantage of the down time to explore new watering holes.

Chuck liked that idea.

By the time Dan and Chuck got to know each other, The Silver Nugget had filled up. Dan's eyes roved around the place, too.

As the band warmed up in the corner, he'd polished off at least half a dozen beers. It was too late to call Susan, but he wished he could. Most of the women here were at least forty, over the hill and looking to restore their youth with a fling or two. Most of the men fit the same worn-out mold.

"The women around here sure are ugly," Dan shouted over the music into Chuck's ear.

"Not to a dirty old man like me," Chuck yelled back. "I'm ready for a roll in the hay with any one of 'em. One of these fillies must be desperate enough to latch onto a horny old geezer like me."

His words were slurred.

"I just got to figure out which one I want."

Chuck laughed again and coughed violently.

"You OK?" Dan asked, patting Chuck on the back.

"You bet." Chuck cleared his throat with a deep cough. "All the smoke."

Dan knew Chuck was in no shape to satisfy a woman, age-wise and otherwise. He was plastered. And Dan hadn't seen anything that remotely caught his interest.

"It's time to head 'em up and move 'em out to more promising pastures," Dan told his companion.

"Hell, no," Chuck said. "I'm just winding up."

He put his hand in the air, twirled it around as if he had a rope and yelled in his slurred manner.

"Hey beer-tender, a round for the house."

"No," Dan said. "You can't do that. There's got to be a hundred people in this place."

"What the hell, it's only money," Chuck said. "I got more where that came from."

He leaned toward Dan and lowered his voice. "Maybe this'll get me that woman I want."

Dan didn't doubt that Chuck had probably bought a woman or two with a few drinks, but he wasn't sure it had ever been done with this much bravado.

"There isn't anything in this place for you," Dan said. "They probably all got syphilis or AIDS or who knows what."

"At my age, who gives a damn? I'm ready for boot hill sooner than later."

Chuck laughed as he extracted a thick wallet from his back pocket and fumbled it open.

When he flipped two one-hundred-dollar bills onto the bar, Dan saw several more bills in the wallet. He was loaded in more ways than one.

"Hey beer-tender," Chuck shouted again, waving the money in the air. "I said a round for the house."

The bartender had ignored the first call, but the waving of bills caught his attention. He slid in front of Chuck, took the bills, examined them.

"He doesn't really mean that," Dan said. "He's just drunk."

"Of course, I'm drunk," Chuck shouted. "That's why I'm doin' it. I ain't no stingy Jew-boy accountant."

He laughed again as the bartender began popping open a half-dozen bottles of beer at a time, distributing them to the customers of The Silver Nugget, telling them it was on the older gentleman at the bar.

"Hey, asshole," Dan said, shoving his bottle of beer toward the back of the bar, as if he wasn't going to drink it. "What the hell's wrong with being Jewish?"

"You?" Chuck asked. "I never would have guessed."

Dan clenched a fist beneath the bar, felt himself sobering up real fast. "I'm proud of it," he said, "Jews are ..."

"Aw, shut up and drink your beer," Chuck interrupted. "You don't talk politics or religion in a bar."

Then Chuck smiled, an exaggerated grin, and put his arm over Dan's shoulder.

"Don't worry about it, partner," he said. "You're still my friend."

At that moment Dan didn't care if he was Chuck Lawton's friend, if he was his best friend. Maybe the guy was drunk, but that was no excuse to spout off at the mouth.

Alcohol enhanced the truth in some people, and Dan was sure he hadn't mentioned his Jewish heritage in their conversation. Maybe Chuck was referring to the fact Dan hadn't bought a round in the three hours they'd been drinking. But every time Dan had tried, Chuck insisted he put his money away.

Even if that was the case, Chuck didn't have to resort to name-calling. With a Jimmy Durante nose like his, Dan thought, he had no room to talk. The bigoted son-of-a-bitch would pay for this.

As Dan continued to fume, the bartender returned and gave Chuck a stack of bills.

"What's your name?" the bartender asked. "I'd like the band to announce you just bought a round for the house so my customers can thank you."

"Howard Hughes," Chuck laughed. "I don't want publicity. I'm just a Good Samaritan."

He winked at Dan, as if they shared a secret.

That only incensed Dan more. Chuck's little jokes weren't funny anymore. Dan was pissed. But he managed to maintain his control.

"I think it's about time we got you home, so you can sleep this thing off," Dan said. He put his arm around Chuck and squeezed his shoulder firmly.

"I've been drinkin' all my life. I know my limit."

Sure, Dan thought, you know your limit when it comes to beer, but you still need a muzzle on that mouth of yours.

And at that instant Dan realized why he'd been able to remain calm enough to refrain from violence. All of those bills stuffed in Chuck's wallet.

The plan was simple, and it was perfect. All he had to do was lure Chuck outside.

How?

Dan drew a blank. The beer was having an adverse effect on his brain, too.

Then it came to him. A woman. That was it. Chuck would do anything for a woman.

"Hey, Chuck," Dan said, leaning over to whisper in his ear. "There isn't much action here. Let's go find us some real women."

Chuck's head bobbed as if his neck was a spring, and he smiled as if his face had been painted on an inflatable clown, one of those full-size punching bag clowns that rocked back and forth with each blow. He wouldn't last much longer.

"Come on," Dan said. "It's Saturday night. The bar at the Singleton Motel will be packed with women on the make. We can find us some decent broads there."

Apparently, as Chuck swayed on his bar stool, the fact not one woman had approached him after he bought the house a round registered in his mind. He glanced at his wristwatch and then at Dan.

"Hell's bells, partner, it's not even ten. We got a lot of time," he said, drunkenly sliding off the bar stool and snapping his fingers, as if he wanted to dance.

Chuck swiveled his hips, although not quite in time to the music. He put on his jacket.

"Danny Boy," he said, "let's go find us some hot women."

Dan chuckled as he stood up. His head spun slightly with the sudden movement, but he knew his mind was clear enough for a little harmless heist. Chuck was so drunk that taking his wallet would be a piece of cake.

In addition, Dan thought, it would make a great story to write. The Silver Nugget wouldn't like it, but what the hell? Dan didn't like the Silver Nugget. It'd be a double shot.

As Dan followed Chuck through the front door he realized everyone in the place would remember Chuck, and many of them would see the two of them leaving together. The bartender, for sure, would remember.

Dan had to take care of that somehow. For a moment he considering going into the bathroom, telling Chuck to meet him outside, but he didn't know if he could trust the old guy to get to his car on his own. He put his arm around Chuck, guiding him out the door.

"You're really a great joker, Chuckie," Dan said. "I'm so glad I met you tonight."

"Me, too," Chuck said. "I like a guy who can take a joke. We're gonna have a hell of a time with these women you got us lined up with."

"We sure are," Dan said. "Why don't we take my car?"

"You bring me back here?"

"Chuckie, I won't have to. You'll be staying with a hot filly tonight, you sly devil. And when you've slept it off, you can bring a cab out here to get your car."

"Yeah," Chuck said. "A filly. Ride 'em cowboy."

Dan unlocked the passenger door of his Mazda, took Chuck by the elbow and helped him plop into the seat.

The night air seemed to revive him. For an old guy with a six-pack or more under his belt, he was sure excited about his prospects. He was rarin' to go, Dan thought, in the vernacular of The Silver Nugget.

As Dan drove out of the parking lot, ideas churned through his mind. Where could he get this over with quickly?

Somewhere secluded. It had to be out of the way, but someplace Chuck might go on his own.

Dan glanced at Chuck, who had his eyes closed and his head tilted back between the seatback and the doorjamb.

He had to think fast. Chuck would wake up and be suspicious if they didn't arrive at the Singleton soon.

They cruised past the entrance to the shooting range Dan had left earlier, adjacent to the five-hundred-acre Indian Creek Park, a golf course, riding trails and hills for tobogganing.

Dan glanced at Chuck who still had his eyes closed. The comfort of the bucket seat and the little bit of exercise walking to the car must have knocked him out. He wouldn't know where he was going, a break for Dan, as he turned onto a gravel road and drove slowly, so the rough road wouldn't wake Chuck.

Dan checked the rearview mirror to make sure the highway wasn't visible behind him, pulled over to the side of the road and cut the lights. He stared into the darkness to detect the presence of other cars and didn't see any.

Perfect, Dan thought, reaching into the back seat for the black stocking cap with holes for his eyes and mouth. He stretched the cap over his head, adjusted it so he could see, then reached across the sleeping Chuck to open the glovebox.

Dan removed the Beretta but left the loaded spare clip alone. He knew the clip in the gun was empty; he'd counted each shot of his last practice session at the range.

Chuck wouldn't know the gun was empty, though. The sight of it would scare him enough to hand over the cash.

Dan pulled the clip out of the gun, then slammed it back into the handle so it clicked loudly.

At the sound, Chuck stirred, opening his eyes to the darkness around them.

"Where are we?" he said.

"OK, buddy," Dan said, disguising his voice by raising it an octave. He figured Chuck was so drunk, he wouldn't know exactly what happened or who had robbed him, only that he'd been in a car and the robber had shoved him out into the park before driving away.

"Time to wake up and smell the roses, old man," Dan said. "This is the end of the line. Hand over all your money."

"My God," Chuck screamed, as if waking from a nightmare.

He stared at the barrel of the Beretta at pointblank range. His face was a mess, twisted out of shape from age and drunkenness and fear, as if he was the "Singing in the Rain" victim in Dan's favorite flick, "A Clockwork Orange."

"You're trying to rob me."

Without warning, Chuck shoved his forearm into the pistol, temporarily knocking it out of the way. He threw open the passenger door and ran into the darkness.

Stupid, Dan thought. But he couldn't just sit there, let Chuck escape.

He leaped out of the car, tucked the pistol into his belt and chased the old man through the wet grass, slick beneath his feet on the semi-frozen ground.

Dan's shoes slipped with each step, but he was gaining on Chuck. He didn't want to hurt the old guy, he just wanted to scare him a little and grab the money. He could use a few extra hundred bucks.

As Dan nearly fell, he grabbed a tree for support and stopped momentarily to catch his breath. Old Chuck was surprisingly spry.

After composing himself, Dan resumed the chase with a vicious smile on his face. Hunting was fun.

Up ahead, Chuck fell to his knees as he tried to scramble up a small hill among a cluster of trees. Dan caught him by the collar and pulled him upright, surprised at how much he weighed.

"OK, buddy," Dan said. "I don't want to hurt you. Just give me your money."

"You lousy bum," Chuck said. "I'm not giving you a dime."

Dan threw Chuck to the ground and, as he stumbled, his head cracked solidly against the trunk of a tree.

"I've had enough of your name-calling," Dan said. "Get your ass up, and give me your money."

Chuck's body lay slumped at the base of the tree. He was not moving.

Dan laughed.

"You're in for more than just a hangover in the morning, old man," he said.

Dan leaned over to remove Chuck's wallet. His hand was on the leather when, suddenly, Chuck swung his arm and struck Dan across the side of the head. The blow nearly knocked him off his feet, but it also freed the wallet from Chuck's pocket.

"You bastard," Dan shouted.

He picked up the wallet, stuffed it into his back pocket, pulled the gun out of his belt.

"You want me to blow you away?"

Chuck didn't respond. He had rolled over on his back, facing Dan and the barrel of the Beretta.

Dan stepped back and laughed again.

"You shouldn't flash all that money to strangers in bars," he said. "You never know who might want it."

Dan pulled the trigger on his gun to scare Chuck. He expected to hear the empty click of the hammer.

Instead, the Beretta kicked under the power of an exploding shell. The bullet slammed into Chuck's chest.

For an instant, Dan stood absolutely still.

What had he done? He'd never fired a gun at another man, not even an empty one.

It wasn't supposed to be loaded. How could he have counted wrong? A shell must have been in the chamber. It was the only possible explanation. It was an accident.

Dan crouched beside Chuck, picked up his limp wrist, felt for a pulse. There wasn't one.

Dan wasn't sure if he'd have been able to tell anyhow, the way the blood pumped though his own veins and throbbed in his fingertips. He wasn't a doctor, it was just what he'd seen them do on television.

He dropped Chuck's hand and looked around the park. Now what?

Dan had to get the hell out of there. As he ran down the hill, another idea came to him. He'd definitely sobered up.

He returned to Chuck's body and searched through the pockets until he found a set of keys. He stuffed them into his coat pocket and sprinted back to his car. Tossing the pistol into the glove compartment, Dan drove straight ahead without turning on the headlights.

In the darkness, Dan could barely make out the road ahead as he inched forward despite the urge to speed away. If anybody had been in the park, close enough to hear the shot, he had to escape as quickly and quietly as possible without being seen.

The park had another entrance, on the other side, and he'd have to get closer to it before he could chance turning on the lights.

Dan's heart beat so rapidly he had to concentrate doubly hard on driving. He squinted into the darkness, worried that he'd smash into a tree, destroy the front of his new Mazda, leave himself stranded near the scene of his crime.

He drove even slower. A baby could crawl faster than this, he thought, wiping sweat off his forehead with his forearm.

What the hell was he going to do?

* * * * *

The flow of adrenalin and the idea that he could get nailed for murder cleared Dan's head as he sat in the Mazda smoking a cigarette in the parking lot of The Silver Nugget. He didn't feel the least bit drunk as he watched inebriated patrons come and go in small groups. He had to wait until no one was in the lot to make his move.

Dan held Chuck's keys up in the light, the GM symbol engraved on them. He speculated that Chuck owned the shiny big black late-model Cadillac. A guy with his money would obviously drive a luxury boat, one that didn't fit in

with the dirty, battered, rusty heaps that made up the ma-
jority of the vehicles parked at The Silver Nugget.

Dan opened his door a couple of times, only to retreat
back into his car when a vehicle pulled into the lot.

Finally, he yanked the sleeve down on his jacket and
rubbed the cuff over the keys. He had to remove his fingerprints. He'd seen enough "Columbo" episodes to
know that he'd removed Chuck's fingerprints, too, but he
had to be safe.

When the coast was clear, Dan climbed out of his
Mazda and locked it. He tried to appear nonchalant as he
strolled across the parking lot to the big Caddy, inserted
the key in the passenger side lock and turned it.

Dan was mildly surprised that it worked, even though
he had expected it to.

Carefully, with his hand retracted inside his jacket
sleeve, he opened the Cadillac's door and climbed in, the
dome light fading to dark in the gray interior.

His fingers were numb. He wished he'd remembered
to bring a pair of gloves. Not only would they have kept
his hands warm, they'd have made the job of not leaving
fingerprints behind much easier.

Dan slid across the Cadillac's bench seat and settled
behind the wheel. He inserted the key into the ignition
and the engine turned over on the first try.

With the lights automatically on, he put the big car into
gear and wheeled it out of the parking lot, onto the highway, back into the park where he'd taken Chuck a half-
hour earlier.

Once he crested the hill, Dan pulled to the side of the
road and cut the lights. He locked all the doors with the
power lock button on the armrest, then manually unlocked the driver's door and opened it, leaving the keys in
the ignition.

After climbing out, Dan pushed against the door panel to shut it, careful not to smear Chuck's prints on the outside handle.

The urge to escape as quickly as possible overcame Dan's inclination to walk back into the woods to make sure Chuck was dead. He couldn't risk being seen.

He wished he'd worn his burglar black clothes, but that was stupid. This hadn't been planned. It was all spontaneous.

Dan convinced himself that what he wore, his jeans and navy jacket, were dark enough. He had no choice.

He sprinted along the gravel road toward the blacktop highway a little more than a mile away, then walked back to The Silver Nugget and his Mazda.

This plan had to work he told himself. It had to work.

As Dan followed the highway, he kept his head down so no one would think he was hitching a ride. He considered walking in the ditch, but that would appear suspicious.

If someone offered him a ride, he'd say he was out for a breath of fresh air to sober up after too many beers at The Silver Nugget.

He jammed his hands into his jean pockets to keep them warm, then remembered he had Chuck's wallet in his back pocket.

Dan opened the wallet, extracted the wad of hundred-dollar bills and stuffed them into his jeans, then heaved the wallet as far as he could into the darkness, into the woods adjacent to the ditch.

Finally, Dan arrived at the parking lot, unlocked his car, started it up and smoked a cigarette.

Second thoughts surrounded him inside the Mazda like the smoke. He had planned to drive away, but a fresh idea popped into his mind. More elaborate, yes, he thought, but it would throw suspicion off him.

First, Dan took Chuck's money out of his pocket, folded it neatly and placed it into his car's glovebox beneath the Beretta.

Then, Dan re-entered The Silver Nugget, the loud music of the country band and drunks shouting above the noise, the smell of spilled beer and perspiration, the lights flashing on the stage and the dimmer lights of the horseshoe bar.

A queasiness in Dan's gut made him feel as if he'd never left. He spotted an empty stool, slipped onto it and the bartender recognized him immediately.

"You again?" he said. "I thought you and your rich buddy left."

"We did," Dan said. "But he must have gotten lost."

Dan felt he was choking on his words and hoped the bartender didn't notice.

"I was supposed to meet him at the Singleton bar, and he never showed up. I thought maybe he came back here."

"Nope," the bartender said. "Haven't seen him since the two of you left together."

"Well," Dan said, "he was pretty wasted. He probably decided to go home."

"Maybe," the bartender said. "I can't worry about every customer who comes in here, but I liked that guy. Nobody's ever bought a round that big, and he left me twenty bucks for a tip. You want something to drink or not?"

"Sure," Dan said, smiling. "Give me a light beer."

"I know," the bartender said. "A Miller Lite."

"Right," Dan said.

As the bartender reached into the cooler, Dan glanced around as if nothing had happened.

Dan sipped his beer out of the bottle, breathed a sigh of relief, lit another cigarette.

He spotted two women dancing together, liked the shorter one in tight blue jeans and a light blue blouse with blonde hair down to her shoulders. Maybe she'd be all right for a night, he thought. He could use the diversion.

23

Dan Goldberg gazed around the second-floor lobby of the police station as he sat in a chair waiting for his standing Monday morning appointment to see Assistant Chief Charles Schmidt. A glass cabinet that could have been a high school trophy case displayed, instead, drug paraphernalia – bongs, roach clips, bent spoons, mirrors and syringes. Dan had seen it all before and not behind glass.

The humming of the fluorescent light fixture above irritated Dan to no end. One of the tubes was flickering on and off. If he had his gun, he could blow it away. The vacuum tube would implode on impact.

That was exactly how he'd felt the past two days. He stayed home all day Sunday wondering when the telephone would ring. He had wondered when police would find Chuck Lawton's body.

He hadn't gotten word until a few minutes earlier, as he checked the police log, when a secretary let it slip that a body had been found early that morning in the park. Dan had summoned extreme willpower not to show any emotion.

So, waiting for Schmidt, he twiddled his thumbs and crossed and recrossed his legs. He always hated waiting, but even more so now. He was anxious to get on with it, to find out just how much the cops knew.

Dan stared at the floor, counting the number of black tiles and then the number of white ones. He was tired and hung over. He'd drunk a lot Saturday and hadn't slept much since leaving The Silver Nugget early Sunday morning.

No matter what he tried to think about, he couldn't get the fact that he had killed a man out of his mind, so he had drunk more Sunday. No doubt he'd been stupid. It shouldn't have happened. But he felt confident he had covered his tracks.

No matter how much Dan thought about every detail of the events leading up to his robbery of Chuck Lawton and Lawton's death, he had his doubts. He knew he could never be sure of anything. But as many times as he'd rehashed it all, the drinking and befriending of Lawton which he could not deny, and the mugging and shooting in the park, which he was supposed to know nothing about, Dan felt prepared for the test that was to come.

Nobody knew as much about Saturday night's murder as Dan, and that was exciting. Knowledge was king. It would be thrilling to watch the investigation unfold, to see just how much the cops figured out, to see how close they came to the real scenario.

Obviously, Dan thought, if the cops went to The Silver Nugget, they'd learn he had talked to the victim before he died. The bartender would certainly identify Dan.

Yep. When Dan would interview the bartender for *The Argus* story, he'd be recognized. That was covered. He had returned to The Silver Nugget searching for Lawton. No one in their right mind, he reasoned, would go back to the scene of the crime – the scene before the crime – if they were guilty. Not unless they were stupid beyond comprehension or they were the most calm, cool, and clever criminal ever.

In the former case, the cops would catch the murderer immediately. In the latter, they'd never even suspect Dan.

At last Schmidt's office door swung open. Sally Weber from Channel 10 news emerged, a cameraman on her tail.

Every time Dan saw her, he heard Don Henley's lyrics, the "bubble-headed bleached-blonde," the "I coulda been an actor, but I wound up here," the "hit 'em when they're down" of his "Dirty Laundry" single. Sally fit the stereotype perfectly, a gorgeous blonde so narcissic and ignorant of real news that she couldn't get out of her own way. Her on-air presence was as flat as Mr. Rogers in his neighborhood but at least she looked good. That was all that counted to be a news star in small-market television.

"Hi, Dan," Sally said in her sweet, slightly nasal, over-the-top voice. She strutted up to him with her perfect posture and her nose cocked ever so slightly in the air. "You might as well go in. Chief Schmidt said that if anyone was waiting, I should send them in."

"Sure, Sally," Dan said.

He knew the antagonism in his voice went right over her head, yet he couldn't help but hesitate and watch her strut in her tight skirt toward the steps. More than once he'd thought that a night with Sally could be sweet, so long as she kept her mouth shut.

Schmidt was shuffling papers on his desk as Dan entered.

"Busy day, huh?" Dan said.

"I suppose you've heard about the body found in the park this morning?"

"You might say that," Dan said.

He started to sit in the chair.

"Don't sit down until you close the door," Schmidt said, a serious tone in his voice and a stern look on his face. "I would have called you earlier, but I knew you'd be in this morning, so I waited. I need to talk to you."

"Oh, yeah?" Dan closed the door. He knew what was coming, even though he had to fake it. "What about?"

"Sit down."

"Close the door. Sit down. Do this, do that." Dan sat in the chair. "I'm not one of your lackey detectives."

"You ever see this guy?"

Schmidt tossed a black and white photograph onto the front edge of his desk to face Dan.

Dan picked up the picture.

"Sure, Saturday night at The Silver Nugget. It's Chuckie."

"Chuckie?" Schmidt acted surprised. "You called him Chuckie?"

"Sure," Dan said. He was amazed he didn't feel the least bit nervous.

"I met him at The Silver Nugget on Saturday night. We hit it off, and he bought me a few beers. Bought the bar a round, in fact. Nice old guy, a little crazy, and he was sure getting smashed. What'd he do?"

"You ever see him anywhere else?"

Dan shook his head. He forced a quizzical expression because he had a triple role to play now – reporter, innocent bar patron and deceptive killer.

"No, why?"

Dan paused for a long moment, staring at the professional portrait of the old man in a suit and tie, his hair darker and trimmed shorter than it had been Saturday night, his nose not so large and the veins in them not visible in black and white.

"This isn't recent."

Schmidt kept his eyes on Dan as he leaned back in his chair, planted his right elbow on an armrest and propped his body up with it. But he didn't say a word.

Dan looked back at the picture, gazed at Schmidt, returned his eyes to the picture.

"Wait a minute," he nearly shouted. "Indian Creek Park's pretty close to The Silver Nugget. Is this the guy you found in the park?"

"You got it, bright boy," Schmidt said. "And from what we've been able to figure out, you were the last person to see him alive."

"Me?" Dan wriggled in the chair, shifted the picture of Lawton from one hand to the other. He had no trouble acting uncomfortable because he was.

He had to give Schmidt credit for his approach, springing that information on him at the outset.

"So?"

"So," Schmidt said. "You know how it is with us cops, when we put one and one together."

"Wait a minute. Are you accusing me of killing him?"

"Until we find a better suspect."

"Oh, come on!"

Dan stood up and threw the picture on the desk.

"Shit, man, are you off your rocker?"

He paced the room, acting frantic and scared. He turned away from the assistant chief, then back toward him.

"What the hell's the motive? Why would anybody kill a nice old guy like that? For God's sake, he was buying me beer all night."

"From what we understand, from the description the bartender gave us, a guy who looked like you left The Silver Nugget with Lawton. Want to tell me about it?"

Dan stared into Schmidt's eyes, trying to burn a hole through them, two elementary-school kids in a stare-down to see who blinks first. He'd read psychology books. He knew liars look away when they're confronted.

"Here you're accusing me of killing a guy I had a few drinks with because I was the last person you know who saw him alive," Dan said. "Ludicrous!"

Dan felt his heart race but forced himself to sit back down in the chair, to calm his manner.

"I don't think I have to answer any of your questions unless I get an attorney first. Isn't that the way it works?"

"With criminals, yeah," Schmidt said. "If you've got nothing to hide, you can trust me. We'll work together on this."

Dan rubbed his chin and allowed his gaze to float around the room. Work together? He thought. Since when did the cops want to work with the media?

Schmidt didn't know anything more about Dan's in-volvement in Lawton's death than he'd already said, oth-erwise Dan would have been arrested.

Now was the time to play it cool, to act like he didn't have anything to hide, to take the offensive in a non-threatening way.

"This sounds kind of like an exclusive to me," Dan said. "I tell you what I know, and you don't give it to an-ybody else until it's published in the paper. You tell me what you know, too, so I can stay ahead of TV on this all the way." He breathed a sigh of relief, feeling he'd ex-pressed himself very clearly. "Deal?"

"I don't make deals with reporters or witnesses or kill-ers," Schmidt said. "I could throw your sorry ass in jail for obstructing the investigation if you don't tell me what you know. Then you would need an attorney."

"I told you," Dan said. "We were together at The Silver Nugget. We left in our own cars."

"So, you admit you were the last person to see Lawton alive," Schmidt said. "Help me out here, Goldberg. We need to solve this case as soon as possible. Cooperate."

Dan detected the desperation in Schmidt's voice, but he still wondered how much he should reveal. If a mystery witness existed, he might have seen Lawton climb into his Mazda in the parking lot. But if Schmidt knew that, he would have said so. Everybody at The Silver Nugget was getting wasted. Even if someone had seen Dan and Lawton in the same car, that person wouldn't remember it the next day.

In that moment of silence, as Dan reviewed his story in his mind one last time, he bowed his head and let an uneasy grin escape, a grin he tried to hide with a frown. He thought about Rockwell's murder-suicide story on Page one, Rockwell's kidnapping story, Rockwell's follow-up piece on what it had been like to be shot.

No more all-of-the-glory-for-Rockwell. Even if Dan couldn't get an exclusive, this was his story. He'd scoop Rockwell and Sally Weber and all the other news media.

Dan looked Assistant Chief Schmidt in the eye.

"I didn't kill him," Dan said. He lowered his elbows to his thighs, leaned over to look at the floor, intertwine his fingers between his knees. "I can't believe that nice old guy is dead."

Dan glanced up at Schmidt. "He shouldn't be dead."

In the next fifteen minutes Dan told his story. He recounted Chuck's introduction, the first round of beers, the next ones, Chuck's insistence on buying the bar a round, his flashing of hundred-dollar bills, his sorrow at the death of his wife, his desperate search for companionship at all costs.

"Chuck was a horny old man," Dan said. "I suggested we go to the bar at the Singleton Motel because a lot of hot women hang out there. We walked into the parking lot together and, at first, he got into my car. Then he had a change of heart, said he'd rather drive. He wasn't in any condition to do that, but I wasn't going to argue. That was the last I saw of him."

Dan hesitated as Schmidt scrawled on his legal pad, letting him catch up before he continued.

"I drove to the Singleton and figured Chuck was behind me. But he never showed. I waited for half an hour and drove back to The Silver Nugget, figuring he might have passed out in his car or decided to go back inside. The bartender said he hadn't seen Chuck, so I thought he must have driven home. I had a beer, then came home myself."

Even though Dan was done with his story, Schmidt continued writing. For a moment that made Dan uneasy, until Schmidt looked up again.

"Anybody see you at the Singleton?"

Dan removed his glasses, rubbed the bridge of his nose with thumb and forefinger. He was thinking, and he wanted Schmidt to know that.

Why hadn't he at least made an appearance at the Singleton? Even if it had been a half-hour later, bartenders would have had no reason to be that accurate about the time they saw a stranger who had one beer.

In hindsight, that might have been a better alibi than returning to The Silver Nugget.

"I doubt it." Dan shook his head. "I didn't get out of my car, and I didn't see anyone I knew in the parking lot. I've only been in town a few months."

"So, what you're saying is that you don't have an alibi for the hour or so from when you left The Silver Nugget until you returned?"

Once again Dan stared at the assistant chief. Games. He was tired of them. But he knew looking away would only make Schmidt suspicious.

"When you're single, hitting one bar after another by yourself, you never know if somebody will remember you. I never knew this Lawton guy until Saturday night. I had no idea he'd turn up dead. That's the truth."

Schmidt nodded. "No alibi." He wrote on his pad. "Sorry, Goldberg, but that's the way I see it. We've got to consider you as a suspect, at least until we can come up with a better one."

At the spur of the moment, Dan decided it was time to become visibly shaken. For one thing, his insides had churned with each lie. For another, it was pretty natural for someone wrongly accused of murder to act a little crazy while denying it.

"This is ridiculous," he said.

Dan stood, with hands on his hips.

"A guy's in the wrong place at the wrong time so you accuse him of homicide simply because you don't like his attitude. I can't believe it."

"It happens all the time," Schmidt said. The nasty smile on his face told Dan he was enjoying this moment. "Don't you watch TV?"

"You're just doing this because you hate my guts. If that's the case, I could sue you for harassment, for false accusations."

"I don't think so," Schmidt said. "For one thing, we aren't going to arrest you."

He tossed his pen on the legal pad and leaned back in his chair.

"But Goldberg, if I were you, I wouldn't go anywhere for a while."

Dan knew it was his turn to smile.

"I'm not planning to go anywhere. I've got a murder story to write. An exclusive. Now it's my turn to ask the questions."

"Go right ahead," Schmidt said. "I'll tell you what I told the others."

"Which is?" Dan poised his pen, ready to write.

"We found Charles "Chuck" Lawton after someone reported an abandoned car on the gravel road about a quarter-mile into Indian Creek Park. The keys were in the ignition of his Cadillac, so we searched the area. His body was found close by in the woods. His head had been smashed against a tree. We're not sure, but the coroner thinks he died from a concussion. We'll know more after the autopsy."

Schmidt paused to sip his coffee.

Died from the concussion? Dan thought. My God. He looked up from his notebook, caught himself just in time before he asked about a bullet wound.

Schmidt hadn't said anything about Lawton being shot. He wondered if this was a ploy by the assistant chief to withhold information, to see if Dan would slip up. He stared at Schmidt, waiting for him to continue.

"Also, he was shot. Once in the chest."

Dan breathed a sigh of relief, a sigh he hoped wasn't apparent to Schmidt. Keeping that information to himself would have been murder.

"It's unlikely the bullet killed him," Schmidt continued. "It pierced his lungs, but it was too far away from his heart to cause immediate death. That's why we think he died from the concussion, from being slammed into the tree. At his age, the brain is easily damaged. And from what you and the bartender say, alcohol was most likely a contributing factor. We're waiting for the blood-alcohol level test results, too. You can get that later."

Dan nodded.

"That's about it," Schmidt continued. "You know as much about how he got there as we do. He must have decided to drive through the park for some reason instead of meeting you at the Singleton."

"Why would he do that?"

"Your guess is as good as ours. Maybe he got lost," the assistant chief said. "Maybe he changed his mind. If he hadn't been shot, we'd probably assume he got out of his car to take a leak, slipped and fell, hit his head and died. But the gunshot wound changes all that. His wallet was missing, too, so we assume he was mugged."

Dan nodded again, his heart and mind racing to see which would explode first. If only he hadn't pulled the trigger. But he'd thought the gun was empty. It was supposed to be a joke.

"I didn't know the guy," Schmidt continued, "except to say 'hi' on the street, but from what I understand you could never guess what he might do next. He was eccentric. I'm sure you've heard about that."

"No," Dan said. "I just met him Saturday."

"Oh, yeah, you're new in town. You don't know about Charles James Lawton III."

"The Third?"

"Check your files. His grandfather founded Lawton's, the dress shop for women that's all over the Midwest. They must have fifty, sixty stores. When Lawton the third retired a few years ago, he sold out because he didn't have a son to inherit the business. His wife died a couple of ago at their place in Florida, but apparently, he didn't want to go back there. He'd been hanging around Cedar

City, giving thousands and thousands of dollars to a lot of causes in the city. He was loaded. He gave half a million for the new library."

"Wow," Dan said. "Looking at him, you'd never know."

"Every once-in-a-while," Schmidt continued, "we'd hear about him going into a bar and buying people drinks to spread good cheer. He had a heart of gold, but a pickled liver. You could ask him for the shirt off his back and, if he thought you needed it through no fault of your own, he'd take you downtown and buy you a new wardrobe.

"If he thought you were a beggar, a man who preferred to stand on a corner with a tin can instead of looking for work, he didn't have the time of day for you. That became Lawton's legacy, to help those too proud to ask, but to ignore, and sometimes chastise, anyone who thought they had a right to a hand-out."

Assistant Chief Charles Schmidt turned his bulldog eyes on Dan, sipped at his coffee, coughed to clear his throat.

"The only thing he and I had in common was our first name," Schmidt said. "But, like everyone else in town, I thought of him as a friend. This whole community is going to be pretty upset when they find out old Charles James Lawton III was murdered. Word's already spreading like wildfire."

Schmidt leaned forward, pounding a clenched fist on his notepad, a squint to his eyes as he stared at Dan.

"That's why we're going to solve this one as quickly as possible. People want to know. We're going to get the fucker who did this."

24

City Editor Margaret Myers exhibited more excitement than Dan had ever seen from her when he told her he'd been drinking with Charles James Lawton III the night he was killed.

First, she hadn't heard that it was Lawton's body found in the park.

Second, she hadn't known Dan was acquainted with Lawton.

But the main reason for her overzealous reaction was that in their conversation, Dan referred to Lawton as a common drunk.

Margaret rose from her chair, a rare occasion, and regained her composure. She was tall enough to look Dan straight in the eye.

"We will not depict Mr. Lawton as a drunk," she said calmly. "He's done too much good for Cedar City to be known that way after he's dead."

"The guy was smashed out of his mind when I left him at The Silver Nugget," Dan insisted. "Assistant Chief Schmidt told me he's been seen buying people drinks in some of the sleaziest bars in town."

Dan couldn't help himself and became more argumentative.

"I didn't know Lawton before Saturday night. I didn't know it was his body found murdered in the park. I didn't know anything about the guy until I went to the cop shop. I never said I'd make him look like a common drunk, but I think it's important to the story for readers to know he was plastered."

By the time Dan finished his spiel, he was shouting.

Everyone in the newsroom stopped what they were doing to witness this rare confrontation with the most powerful person in the newsroom.

"Come on," Margaret said coolly. "We're not talking about this out here. Into the conference room."

It was an order.

Dan watched Margaret march toward an open door at the back of the newsroom and followed her into the small conference room that had no pictures on the walls, no coffee pot, no slide screen or projector to cause distractions. It was furnished with only a large, imitation walnut table and eight semi-comfortable chairs on casters.

Editors planned each day's newspaper in this room. Job evaluations and raises were handed out here. So were pink slips.

As Dan closed the door, he felt as if every eye in the newsroom had been on him. Raising your voice in *The Argus* newsroom was a cardinal sin. Raising your voice to Margaret was like committing hara-kiri. She was like God.

When Dan was seated, he tried his best to suppress a grin. He knew everyone in the newsroom would sacrifice a choice assignment for the ability to become invisible, to sit in on this conversation. His expression didn't escape Margaret.

"Do you think this is funny?" she asked, standing at the opposite end of the table.

Dan allowed the smile to blanket his face.

"I thought this was a professional organization. You know, open doors, open conversations. And here you are, dragging me behind a closed door, so people out there can't hear what we're talking about."

"You were shouting, not talking," Margaret said.

She maintained her serious tone, her stern, teacher-like expression.

"Dan, I pulled you in here for your sake, not mine. There are a few things we need to get straight."

"That's what I figured."

Dan calmly removed the cap from his pen, put it back on again. He repeated the procedure over and over, purposely not looking at his boss.

He felt like a child shoved into a corner with a dunce's cap, not a professional reporter. He felt as if his father was yelling at him. He listened but didn't pay close attention.

"First, we do not yell in the newsroom," she said, taking a step toward him. "The public has access to that area, and we don't need people outside the organization seeing staff members at each other's throats."

Dan nodded. He was thinking cover-up. The public should know that news people are human, too.

"Second, I don't give a damn if you yell at me."

Margaret punched an index finger into her own chest.

"I've been in this business more than twenty-five years, and that's long enough to know when raising your voice is justified and when it's not. When you yell, at least be smart enough to know what you're yelling about."

"I know what ... "

"Shut up," she said. "You can speak when I'm done."

Dan had never heard Margaret be so aggressive, not even in previous closed-door meetings they'd had. Usually it was a conversation, not a beat-down. She'd at least listen before taking a stand.

Dan nodded, playing with his pen and the cap. She was pretty feisty when she wanted to be, and he respected that. She was confident of herself and her decisions. But he also had realized long ago why some people called her M&M, not only because those were her initials, but because she had a sweet candy coating that, when you bit into it, would melt in your mouth.

"Third," Margaret said, "I don't know how they did it in Chicago, but here reporters don't run the newsroom. Your job is to gather the information, write the stories. My job is to edit your stories, decide where and how they'll be used. Understood?"

Dan nodded.

"Good. Now, if you would have checked the files on Charles James Lawton III, you would have found out that he has donated money for a new hospital wing for cancer research, for a good share of the cost of a new library, for remodeling the art museum and community theater, for a city park that will be named after him.

"Most importantly, as far as this story goes, he's donated thousands of dollars for a detoxification center at the hospital because he knew he had an on-again, off-again, drinking problem. He wanted to help other alcoholics overcome theirs. He has – I mean, had – admitted his drinking problem publicly. Everybody already knows that.

"You also would know," she continued, "that he was on the Chamber of Commerce board, is a former Cedar City school board member and was still a minor stockholder of *The Argus*.

"Those, my friend, are enough reasons why we will not paint a picture of this man as a common drunk."

Dan laid his pen on the table.

"You're saying he was a sacred cow."

"That's your wording, not mine. He was a pillar of this community, and his name will be remembered long after you and I are gone."

"Uh-huh," Dan said. "Then I suppose you don't even want me to mention that he was drinking."

Margaret inhaled deeply, as if to gather her thoughts.

To Dan, it seemed a stalling tactic.

If Dan hadn't been so angry when they'd come into the conference room, these additional revelations about Lawton would have made him a nervous wreck.

As it was, the anger kept his nerves at bay even as he realized he'd become wrapped up in a story more significant than he could have anticipated. Not only had he killed a man, he had killed one of the most prominent men in the city's history.

On top of that, because he had stood up for what he believed regarding news coverage, Dan might be in jeopardy of losing another job.

For the first time since she had sequestered them in the conference room, Margaret took a chair. She sat right next to Dan.

"I didn't say we'd hold back information that's pertinent to the story, that he was at The Silver Nugget," she said. "It's a fact of the story that he was there. Everyone will report that.

"If the blood-alcohol test shows he was impaired, we'll use that, too. You can even say he bought you a drink or two. It'll give us a more personal angle than what anybody else will have.

"But we will not make a big deal about it. We will simply use that to paint the big picture. We will not call him a drunkard or imply it beyond what the public already has known from his past."

"I got you," Dan said. "It's not lying if we don't tell the whole truth."

"It's not your place, or the newspaper's, to be judge and jury about a man who is dead," she said. "We present the facts and let them stand on their own for the readers to decide. People who knew him will make their own judgments. People who didn't will rely on reports from the media."

"What you're saying is, we will depict him as a great guy because he gave all of this money away. But we won't say anything bad about him because he didn't know what he was doing when it came to alcohol."

"We could discuss our opinions about this matter until we're both blue in the face," Margaret said. "I've told you how we'll handle this story. And I'm telling you that, as long as you're employed by *The Argus*, you will follow my directions. If you don't like it, you can find another job."

"Fine," Dan said. "You're saying this is the end of our discussion."

Margaret Myers stood up.

"On that, you are correct."

She opened the door and walked out of the conference room, leaving Dan alone with his opinions, his thoughts, his fear that the accidental death of Charles James Lawton III had become a story too big for even him to handle.

* * * * *

By the time Dan dragged himself out of the conference room chair, Margaret had returned to her desk where she pecked away at the computer keyboard as if nothing had happened. It was her way of showing she had control.

Margaret had been the first to enter the conference room and the first to leave. Definitely a cool customer, Dan thought.

Even though he had a better understanding of what made his boss tick than he'd had a few minutes earlier, he still thought her policy stunk.

As Dan wrote about the death of Charles James Lawton III, the newsroom telephones rang off the hook, and he overheard half-conversations. Most callers, it seemed, learned about the murder on the radio or by word-of-mouth and wanted to know if the story was true.

Credibility.

Even if radio was the most immediate news source, a few listeners still regarded it as a step above rumor. By evening, they'd see the television reports and believe the to be true.

Yet a handful of people wouldn't be completely convinced until they read about it in the morning newspaper. They could count on *The Argus* for the details, for the truth.

Reading was believing and for Dan, when it came right down to it, that's why he'd become a newspaper reporter. That's why writing this story gave him a sense of the power he craved.

In one way, nothing was working out as Dan had imagined. In another way, everything was.

Dan was on his biggest story since joining *The Argus*, the biggest story of his young career, because it involved him. It demanded a banner headline on the front page. His byline would be at the top of the story, and he would tell his audience that Charles James Lawton III had bought him a drink, more than one drink, at The Silver Nugget, before someone gunned him down.

Despite the confrontation with Margaret, Dan couldn't help but smile. Finally, a dream had come true. He was the news, the day's major news.

In the back of his mind, though, Dan continued to have an inkling that this story would grow increasingly troublesome for him. The cops, incompetent as they sometimes seemed, would be on this case like flies on a horse's ass. They might stumble onto something he couldn't foresee.

As Dan wrapped up his story, read it and re-read it, he considered each word carefully. But his mind continued to wander, always to the same questions. Would he slip up? Would he get caught?

By the time Mike Rockwell entered the newsroom for the night beat, Dan Goldberg was so engrossed in his own thoughts, he didn't notice his desk-mate approach.

"I understand you fell into a hell of a story," Mike said.

"Yeah."

Mike acted puzzled that Dan didn't want to brag it up.

"What's up with you?" Mike asked

"This murder is getting to me," Dan admitted. "The more I learn about it, the more I've got to cram into my story. It's a huge pain in the ass."

"It is," Mike said. "Any big story is a big pain. Lawton did a lot for this town and now he's dead. Murdered."

"Yeah," Dan said. "But everything's getting blown out of proportion."

"Are you sick or something? I thought this was the type of story you thrived on. The big one splashed all over the front page. The fame. The glory. And hell, you were even with him before he was killed. At least you didn't get shot like I did."

"Doesn't that seem strange?" Dan said. He stopped typing, looked up from the computer screen. He couldn't believe his luck. Here he'd worried about how he'd explain the similarities in their big stories and Rockwell dropped it right into his lap.

"You get shot by a drug dealer," Dan said, "and I'm with a guy, a prominent guy in town, who gets murdered right after I spend an evening drinking with him. Doesn't that seem too coincidental to you?"

"I thought about that," Mike said. "But, hey, coincidence happens. Nobody knows that better than a reporter."

Mike placed a hand on Dan's shoulder.

"You've just got to chill."

Dan's stomach turned over as he returned his concentration to the computer. One minute he'd been ready to confess everything. Now it was all falling into place. Sometimes it seemed too easy.

25

After staying a couple of hours later than usual Monday night at *The Argus* to answer a few minor questions from Margaret about the murder story he'd submitted, Dan needed to find a bar to drink in and get drunk, or bar hop and get drunk, or stay home and get drunk

He needed to get drunk.

Even though Dan was physically and mentally drained by the time he left work, there was zero chance he'd fall asleep without some help. It would be worse than finals week in college.

Sometimes the only solution to overcome stress was to get so rip-roaring drunk he passed out.

So what if alcohol shrunk his blood vessels and destroyed millions of brain cells. Dan wasn't a fitness nut.

What did a few million brain cells matter when he had billions?

On his way home, Dan picked up a case of Miller Lite and popped open the first one without eating supper. By the time he finished his third beer in less than half-an-hour he was feeling light-headed.

Dan had considered hiding his pistol somewhere or even getting rid of it, in a ditch or the river. But then he figured there had to be hundreds of Berettas in Cedar City. Unless the cops got hold of his gun and ballistics tested it against the one that killed Lawton, he had nothing to worry about.

The cops weren't going to get Dan's gun, so he left it in the glove box of his Mazda.

After finishing his fourth beer, Dan thought about his weak alibi. Not good. Not good at all.

No one could put him close to the Singleton Motel bar or even inside The Silver Nugget at the time of Lawton's murder, although the cops couldn't be specific about the time of death without autopsy results.

Dan felt some reassurance knowing that thousands of other people had been in their cars at the time of the murder, and none of them could account for their whereabouts. Then again, those people hadn't been seen with a murdered man an hour before his death.

The afternoon in the Target store, when he'd ripped off the Walkman, everything seemed so simple. It hurt no one. If he'd been caught, no one would have thought much about it. Shoplifting wouldn't send him to jail without bail, nail him with a fine he couldn't pay, or end up on his resume.

A murder conviction?

What had Dan been thinking? He hadn't intended to kill Lawton. He hadn't intended to kill anybody. It was supposed to be a routine holdup. Take the money and run.

The evening Lawton climbed into his car, Dan relished the feeling of power holding a gun in his hand. He'd slammed the clip into the handle strictly for Lawton's benefit. His only mistake was not counting the number of shots he'd fired at the shooting range.

One lousy bullet left in the chamber. One lousy bullet.

Now look where he was. In a hell of a lot of trouble.

Another beer gone, Dan thought maybe this was all Uncle George's fault. If he hadn't locked up his gun cabinet, prompting Dan to break into it, he wouldn't have had such a fascination for guns.

It's always what you want and can't have that causes problems.

Dan could claim insanity, blame it on his uncle.

You keep things away from kids, you tell them no, they're only going to try to get it, to challenge you.

If Dan had been allowed to shoot, this wouldn't have happened. He wouldn't have even purchased the .38 years ago in Chicago.

Oh, but the power of that Beretta. Never had Dan been able to control other people like he'd done with that gun. He closed his eyes and saw fear in the 7-Eleven clerk's face. He saw the surprise in Lawton's eyes.

How many beers was this now? Dan thought, turning another empty can over in his sink because, after all, it was worth a nickel deposit. He counted six empties before opening the refrigerator for a seventh.

It was Lawton's fault, all Lawton's fault, because he fought back.

Idiot.

If he hadn't done that, if he'd just handed over his wallet to the thief in the stocking cap mask, he'd be alive.

It was Lawton's fault. Stupid old man. He forced Dan to use the gun.

No, he hadn't.

Assistant Chief Schmidt said Lawton died from the blow to his head, the impact of his soft old melon against the tree as he fell.

Dan examined his hands, the lines that turned and intersected in his palms like railroad tracks, the soft pink flesh that had never seen hard labor, the fingerprints that swirled elliptically in concentric circles.

These were the murder weapons, he thought.

He hadn't needed a gun to kill a man. His bare hands had been enough.

Historical black and white photographs popped into Dan's mind, German soldiers and rail-thin starvation victims, crude concrete gas chambers and metal flesh-fueled incinerators.

Dan thought about the six million Jews murdered in concentration camps during World War II. Some were shot down by rifles, by machines guns. Most were marched to their deaths. It had all been intentional. No accidents in concentration camps.

Did Iowa have the death penalty for murderers?

Dan had no idea. Probably not. It was an antiquated law, as old as the Tanakh, as old as an eye for an eye.

But he wasn't going to get caught. No way.

But, what if he did?

He'd probably rot in jail. Like dying of disease or starvation. Could anything be worse than that?

Dan left an empty can beside the full sink and popped open another beer. He lost track of how many it had been.

Maybe he could overdose on alcohol. Probably not.

How about adding sleeping pills? No.

He could just blow his brains out.

He had a gun.

Suicide would prove his guilt, Dan reasoned. He remembered telling Rockwell at the cemetery that suicide was a permanent solution to a temporary problem. He couldn't give in that easily.

Dan simply wasn't going to get caught.

This whole experiment had begun as a challenge, and now it was out of control. He'd fight through it.

Dan had committed the ultimate crime, murder, and now he had to prove that he could get away with it.

Just once.

He'd never kill again.

Like that incessant roller coaster, up and down, over and under, thoughts raced through Dan's mind as if they would never stop.

He wanted to vomit.

He wanted to pick up the phone and call Susan.

He wanted to bring "Chuckie" Lawton back to life, find him a woman, send him on his way with his wallet and life intact.

Susan. The old guy had been right about one thing. Women could take your mind off what bothered you.

Dan dialed her number.

"Hey," he said as soon as she answered. "Dan Goldberg here. How's everything?"

"Fine," she said flatly.

"How 'bout going out for a drink?"

"It's late," she said. "I've had a busy day."

"Well, a drink can be good for that. Take your mind off your troubles. How you doing?"

"It sounds like you've already had a few drinks," she said.

"Couple of beers is all. Sorry I started without you."

"That's OK. Maybe it's a good reason for me to stay home tonight."

"How about tomorrow? Drinks and dinner?"

"That's still the middle of the week," she said.

"We'll go early. I'll pick you up at six."

"I don't think so, but maybe some other time."

"I'll call you, you don't need to call me," Dan said. "You pick a place to go. I'll call you."

"Bye, Dan."

The line went dead as Susan hung up.

Dan stared at the telephone receiver, replaced it into its cradle.

Alexander Graham Bell sure invented a fantastic piece of equipment, Dan thought. Everyone knew his name. That's how you became famous.

Dan popped open another beer and paced around his apartment.

He dropped the needle of his turntable onto George Thorogood's track, "I Drink Alone."

He turned up the volume so the driving beat filled his apartment.

He flopped onto the sofa, on his back, closed his eyes.

Susan was right.

Dan's mind continued to race, and he was in a crazy mood. No telling what he'd do if he went out in public.

* * * * *

The throbbing pain of a hangover surged through Dan's head as he woke up in a cold sweat on his sofa Tuesday morning. A buzz came from the short in the left speaker of his stereo, so he turned it off, checked the sink for empty beer cans and found beside them, on the counter, an over-cooked frozen pizza minus one slice.

The oven light was still on, so he turned it off. He didn't recall turning it on, but he wasn't surprised.

When problems drifted in and out of Dan's mind, he was liable to do anything. Any time he'd ever been in trouble it had been the same, as if a certain segment of his life was about to end. Not quite like death, but certainly a reasonable facsimile.

That's when Dan remembered his nightmare. He'd been in jail, the decrepit little county lockup on the island in the middle of the Cedar River. A miniature Alcatraz surrounded by water. He'd screamed his innocence from behind cold metal bars in his hands, the cell behind him painted turquoise with a stainless-steel toilet and a thin bare mattress on a springless metal frame attached to the wall. He recalled handcuffs on his wrists, the ride in the back seat of a cop car smelling of vomit, the fingerprinting at the check-in desk, the rough shove by a larger-than-life police officer as if he was a sack of potatoes.

Dan didn't remember an arrest or a confession, but the dream had been vivid enough that he checked his fingers for ink and found none.

He tossed the pizza onto an empty shelf in the refrigerator, washed his hands, poured himself a glass of tomato juice and used it to chase a couple of aspirin.

He didn't have time for breakfast, so he woke himself up with a semi-cold shower, dressed quickly and arrived for duty at *The Argus* a few minutes late, which was no big deal, even to Margaret Myers.

As expected, Tuesday became a long day. Assistant Chief Schmidt allayed any fears that Dan's dream had been real when he said there were no new suspects in the Lawton murder. Dan was the only suspect, but there wasn't enough evidence to arrest him.

"Yet, anyway," Schmidt added with his usual dog-eat-dog grin.

The rest of the media knew of Dan's connection to Lawton from his newspaper story, but Schmidt hadn't told anyone Dan was a suspect. There was no need. The last guy to see a murder victim alive was always a suspect.

Lawton's murder became the topic of conversation all around Cedar City. It had to be, since everyone at *The Argus* was talking about it.

The one question that constantly floated around the newsroom was the same one everybody in Cedar City was asking: "Why would someone kill nice old Charlie Lawton?"

By the time four o'clock rolled around, Dan had had enough. He needed to escape early. He needed a drink. A stiff one.

Dan beat the crowd to the Fox. As he started on his first beer at the bar, early customers were talking about the murder, too. It seemed Charlie Lawton occasionally stopped in to buy the place a round.

"The son-of-a-bitch who killed him should be hung," one white-haired old man said, tilting a cocktail glass up to his mouth.

"That's too good for him," a companion at the bar replied. "They should hook him up to one of those old torture machines and stretch him out like a rubber band. Make him suffer."

"It sure is something," the middle-age woman bartender said, dunking her hands into the soapy water in the sink behind the bar. "We get us a cop shot and now Charlie's dead. I thought this was a safe place to live."

"They say these things come in threes," the first man said. "Or is that just celebrities?"

"Don't worry, Donna," the second man said. "Nobody will come after you unless you put too big a head on my next beer."

The group of regulars chuckled, and in his mind, Dan could hear Charlie Lawton laugh, too. He knew the joking was an uneasy relief valve, but that didn't make him feel any better. In Chicago, a death like this would have been a neighborhood thing, a brief story in the rest of the city. Most people in Chicago wouldn't have known a thing about it or cared.

Despite his better judgement, Dan ordered a second beer at the bar but moved to the newsroom's regular table in back. He already felt a slight buzz, no doubt from the alcohol still in his system from last night's drinking binge

As Dan expected, a couple of other news people from *The Argus* trickled in and joined him. He actually didn't want them there, but he also didn't want to drink alone. He wished Susan had agreed to meet him, but that wasn't going to happen.

One of his colleagues, now numbering half-a-dozen, talked about how big Lawton's funeral would be on Friday.

"You going?" John Morrison asked Dan. John covered the education beat and his horn-rimmed glasses fit the role perfectly. "You knew him better than the rest of us. He never bought me a drink."

John lifted his glass as if to toast the dead man.

"That's a jerk-ass thing to say," Dan said. "He only bought me a drink because I happened to be there that night. I didn't know him from Adam. He's caused me more grief than I care to think about."

"Right," John said. "Just because you were with him doesn't mean the cops should suspect you. What did Margaret say about that?"

"Nothing," Dan said. "We never talked about that possibility."

He drank from his mug of beer, stuck a cigarette in his mouth. As long as he had something between his lips, it was a good excuse not to speak. He took his time opening a book of matches, tearing one out, closing the cover, striking the match and touching the flame to the end of his cigarette. Dan knew he'd been more quiet than usual, and it didn't surprise him too much when John picked up on it.

"They can't nail you for this," John said. "Schmidt's just being Schmidt. They know you didn't do it."

"They know it, and I know it," Dan said.

Even if other people believed his innocence, he still had to convince himself of the lie.

"I was just thinking," Dan said. "What if this guy who killed Lawton is the same guy who killed the cop and shot Rockwell?"

"Oh, God," Laura Minor said, putting the green sweater sleeve that covered her hand over her mouth. "I never thought of that."

Dan didn't have time for the mousey-eared, freckle-faced kid who rewrote press releases for the lifestyle section, handled phone calls, and helped lay out pages for the Sunday paper.

"It doesn't make sense," John said. "The guy who shot Collins was a drug dealer. He was saving his own skin. It's not like that would turn him into a serial killer."

"Don't drug users need money?" Dan asked. "If he knew Lawton had a lot of dough on him, wouldn't it make sense that he'd roll the helpless old guy for extra cash? That Silver Nugget is a pretty sleazy place. Anybody could have been there that night."

"If he was a petty drug dealer, sure, I could see it," John said. "If he wanted a quick couple-hundred bucks and was stupid. Or high. But from what Rockwell wrote about Morgan, he was a professional. Big money. And he was smart enough to change cars and to shoot Mike in the leg, so he could escape." John paused to glance around the table. "I think he'd be more likely to extort money from Lawton, not kill him."

"Maybe that's what he was doing, and Lawton changed his mind," Dan said. "Maybe the death was an accident. Maybe whoever killed him didn't mean to kill him at all."

"Even if it was an accident, the murderer shot Lawton in the chest. For some reason he wanted to make sure he was dead. That hardly sounds like an accident."

"Yeah," Dan said. He hadn't thought about it that way, that maybe he had pulled the trigger because he wanted the old man dead. "The killer probably shot him because he didn't know the blow to the head already could have killed him."

"Come on you guys," Laura said. "You'd think you were playing 'Miami Vice' or something. This isn't Miami."

"If only it was," Dan said with a feeble laugh. "Looks like we've got a cold winter ahead."

That did it. Everybody started talking about the weather, the most popular topic in the Midwest, in Iowa, in Cedar City, because it could change with the blink of an eye, from sunshine to rain, from warm to cold, even from uncomfortable to tolerable.

Dan smiled at his success, changing his colleagues' conversation to the mundane. He stubbed out a cigarette, drained his beer, excused himself by saying that he had to meet a friend for dinner.

The late October wind whipped dry leaves and dust from the parking ramp across Third Avenue into Dan's face as he walked the two blocks back to his car parked in the ramp next to *The Argus* building where the digital clock on the roof displayed 7:37, a reminder to Dan that it wasn't very late. But it also was a number that made him think of a jet plane, of taking off for somewhere warm and safe, never to return to Cedar City.

26

As Mike Rockwell hobbled to the desk he shared with Dan Goldberg in *The Argus* newsroom a little before five on Tuesday, he thought it strange that Dan was nowhere to be seen. It seemed particularly unusual, since the Lawton murder was hot. But then, as he propped his crutches against the desk, Mike saw the note Dan had scrawled on a page ripped from his reporter's notebook. It read, simply, "Talk to you tomorrow. Dan"

After scanning the news directory to read Dan's follow-up story that stated no suspects had been arrested regarding the murder, Mike checked in with Margaret Myers to learn he wasn't expected to do anything with the story. She seemed slightly preoccupied as she told him to go about his regular rounds.

Back at his desk, Mike reached into his pocket and extracted the gold Zippo cigarette lighter. He ran his thumb over its engraved initials and inhaled deeply. Morgan was like an itch inside his cast that wouldn't go away.

For days Mike had put off talking to Sammy Rawlings and Bob Drexler. He checked the jail log each evening to see if they were still there. Neither had posted bail.

Mike hadn't gone further because he had no desire to get mixed up with Morgan's cronies. But it was now at the point he didn't have a choice.

The telephone calls he expected to get from Morgan, the calls he worried about every minute he sat in the office, every time his phone rang, were driving him crazy.

As he prepared to make his Tuesday night rounds, the phone rang. It was Morgan. Mike kept the conversation short, especially after Morgan threatened to come down to *The Argus* to personally escort Mike to the jailhouse.

Mike had no choice but promise that he'd talk to Morgan's friends that night.

He opened the lighter and spun the wheel with his thumb. A flame shot almost a foot high before it died down to a normal height. It was the first time he'd lit it. He stared at the blue base of the flame, the hottest part, a good place for Morgan.

Mike snapped the lighter shut and returned it to his pocket. Despite his apprehension at going undercover for Morgan, at gathering information without talking to the cops first, he had to stop at the jail. Maybe he could get that confession Morgan wanted, clear himself from this mess, even receive credit for solving a murder.

But, on his way to the jail, Mike still had huge doubts about Morgan's story. And now there was Lawton's death. Did Morgan have anything to do with that? Who knows? Maybe Linda was right. Telling everything he knew to the police was probably the best solution. But until Morgan was caught, wouldn't that only put him in more danger if Morgan somehow learned that he'd squealed to the cops?

For more than five years Mike had been stopping at the jail twice a day, many times in the middle of the night while cops hauled in criminals, and he'd never felt as uneasy as he did this time, walking up the cold gray steps on his crutches. He pressed the buzzer to alert a deputy that he wanted to enter. A loud, lower pitched buzz responded, tripping the security door's magnetic lock. Mike pulled the door open and hobbled into the sparsely furnished lobby with a small end-table and two straight-back chairs for visitors forced to wait.

"Hi, Mike," the deputy said from behind a glass security window with a built-in speaker that made his voice sound as if he was taking an order at a fast-food joint. The first time Mike had entered this room, the arrangement reminded him of a Dairy Queen and, many times since, he'd joked with officers about ordering a butterscotch Dilly Bar. He didn't feel like jesting now.

"Hey, Tommy," Mike said. "I need to find out what you know about a couple of your inmates."

"Sure thing. Come on around, and I'll tell you whatever I can," the deputy said, standing to activate another buzzer.

The deputy was tall and lanky, maybe six and a half feet, with a bushy brown mustache and the brim of his deputy's hat pulled down over his eyes as if he was a cowboy squinting into the sun.

Mike dragged open the second heavy security door, entered the office and sat in a chair facing the half-dozen black and white surveillance monitors above the desk. The pictures were fuzzy, sent by cameras oscillating from their perches high in the corner of each jail cell, but he could see one inmate sleeping on his back on a bare mattress with his head propped on a pillow, another one playing solitaire with a deck of cards on the bed, another smoking a cigarette and flicking the ashes into the stainless-steel toilet.

"I didn't think you allowed smoking in the cells," Mike said.

"We don't," Tommy replied, glancing up at the monitors before he swiveled his chair around to face Mike. "But when a guy's got a three-pack-a-day habit, what can you do? He's at the end so he doesn't bother anybody but the guy next to him, and they're longtime buddies. Came in together."

"Sammy Rawlings and Bob Drexler?"

"How'd you know? Oh, right, you were there when the dope heads were arrested."

"I was there earlier, but by the time they were caught, I was on my little joy ride in the country, getting my leg shot up," Mike said, holding up one of his crutches.

"Sucks, doesn't it?" Tommy said. "But at least you weren't killed like Collins."

"I'm sorry about that. Did you know him?"

"I didn't know Collins, not even to see him. He worked undercover all the time I've been here, never came to the jail as far as I know. Uniformed officers always brought in his prey."

"Prey?"

"Collins was a hunter. Everybody knew that about him. I heard he thrived on playing his role as a drug buyer, wearing his deadbeat camouflage, talking like he had no education, acting stoned even when he didn't have to. If the Cedar City PD had anybody who could have been a TV cop, it was Collins."

"Now he's dead."

"And the police department is worse off for it."

"Who killed him?"

"Ronald Morgan. I can't believe we haven't caught him yet. Every cop wants to be the one to drag his ass in, if not shoot him on the spot. He's probably three states away by now, maybe even in Canada or Mexico."

Mike knew otherwise, that Morgan wasn't far away at all, but he couldn't say anything, at least not to Tommy who would blab the information to everyone he knew.

"Are you sure Morgan's the killer?" Mike asked. "What about Rawlings? Drexler?"

"Those dope fiends? They wouldn't know which end of the gun to hold, shit from Shinola, you know what I mean?"

"I've been assigned to talk to them."

"Sure," Tommy said, his mustache twitching as he tilted his hat back. "They'd probably enjoy the company. I'll bring one of them in the visitor's pen. Go ahead and wait for me there."

Keys jingled against handcuffs hanging from Tommy's belt as he disappeared into the hallway, down past the visitation room, the interrogation room, the door to the janitor's closet and the metal lockers where deputies stored their guns before entering the cells.

Mike picked up his crutches and made his way into the familiar visitor's area accessible by a door to the hall. It was a small room with two straight-back chairs exactly as those in the lobby. They faced a built-in stainless-steel desk that spanned the eight-foot width of the room topped by a yellowed, well-scratched Plexiglas divider with telephone receivers on either side that separated him from the inmate area.

As Mike opened his notebook, he watched Tommy lead a small, skinny, undernourished man in an orange jumpsuit with his hands cuffed in front of him to the single metal chair on the other side of the divider.

Tommy left the room, closed the door behind him, emerged in the entryway where Mike sat.

"Here's Drexler," he said. "Let me know when you're done, and I'll take him back and bring you Rawlings."

"Thanks," Mike said. "This probably won't take more than a couple of minutes."

Mike pulled the Zippo lighter from his pocket, held the monogrammed side against the Plexiglass and picked up the telephone receiver. He had to wait for Bob Drexler to slide close enough to the desk to pick up his phone.

"You recognize this?" Mike said.

"Nope," Drexler said.

His shoulder-length greasy hair appeared as if it hadn't been washed in a week, his pock-marked complexion was unshaven for at least that long and his eyes, a cool gray with a redness around them, twitched from side to side. He acted as if he'd rather be somewhere else.

"Look at the initials."

"Don't mean nothing to me."

"Ronald Morgan."

"So."

"I met him once in MacDonald Park." Mike said. "He gave me this. Said it would convince you I had actually talked to him."

"A lot of guys know Ronnie."

"He said you killed that cop the night of the drug bust."

"Not me. I don't have no gun."

"Who did kill him?"

"Search me."

"What were you doing there that night?"

"Getting high, man. That's all I was doing."

"Did you see the shooting?"

"I didn't see nothing. Just heard the shots and then these cops came running in. Here I am."

"You're innocent?"

Bob Drexler nodded. "We done?"

Mike called out to Tommy, who hauled Drexler away and replaced him with Sammy Rawlings who, in contrast to his cohort, sat upright in the metal chair, almost as if at attention.

Sammy Rawlings' eyes were a vibrant Paul Newman blue, yet they seared an image of criminal defiance into Mike's brain. His blond hair was cropped short, like that of a soldier, and his shoulders were wide with large arms and muscular biceps that strained at the short sleeves of his orange jumpsuit. His chest also filled the prison garb, and his neck, thicker than the width of his jaw, had a tattoo that covered one side, although Mike couldn't tell what it was supposed to be.

Again, Mike held the monogrammed face of the Zippo against the Plexiglas, but he didn't have to wait for Rawlings to pick up the phone.

"That's Ronnie Morgan's." Rawlings' voice was low and authoritative, not squirrely like Drexler's. "How'd you get it?"

"He gave it to me."

Mike realized that Rawlings was the man he'd seen on the monitor smoking in his cell, so of course he'd recognize a cigarette lighter that he'd probably borrowed at one time or another.

"Morgan said you shot the cop that night a couple of weeks ago."

"No, sir. Ronnie's a liar. I no more killed that cop than I killed that runt in the barracks. He wouldn't leave well enough alone."

Mike didn't know what Rawlings was talking about, but he'd ask Tommy about it.

"Then who did kill him?"

"The cop?"

"The cop."

"Ronnie and Bobbie and me and the cop were the only ones in the house. You figure it out."

"You didn't do it?"

"No, sir."

Mike stared back at Rawlings. They were at a silent stalemate, and he didn't know where to go from there. All he knew was that he would make a lousy police interrogator because he didn't know who to believe. That, and that he wouldn't want to run into Rawlings in a dark alley.

"I'll talk to Mr. Morgan again," Mike finally said.

"Yes, sir. Please do that."

After Tommy took Sammy Rawlings back to his cell, Mike asked about the death of a man in barracks.

"Oh, that," Tommy said. "About a dozen years ago Rawlings was acquitted of murder, of manslaughter, when he was in the Army. Our records showed a handful of witnesses claimed Rawlings was only defending himself in some kind of petty argument. He only hit the other guy once, on the side of the head. That's all it took."

As Mike Rockwell left the jail, his mind trying to sort out the truth from lies, only one thing became perfectly clear. He understood why Tommy bent the rules, why he allowed Rawlings to smoke in his cell.

* * * * *

For nearly twenty hours, Mike kept his interrogations of Bob Drexler and Sammy Rawlings a secret. But Wednesday night, when he showed up for work at *The Argus* where Dan sat at their desk figuratively twiddling his thumbs, Mike couldn't help himself. He had to tell someone.

"Come on," Mike said, balancing on his crutches and motioning with his head toward the small interview room in the far corner of the newsroom. "We need to talk."

Dan smiled as he rose from his chair. "Oh, good, secrets. Lead the way."

After Mike and Dan settled into chairs on opposite sides of a small table, after Mike had set his crutches aside and Dan had closed the door, Mike spoke first.

"So, you see us as friends, right?"

"Yeah," Dan said. "But that doesn't mean I'd take a bullet for you."

"I wouldn't expect that. But we can trust each other, right?"

"As coworkers, yes. As friends."

"Good," Mike said. "I told you Ronald Morgan, the guy who shot me in the leg, was calling me here, at work, wanting to meet with me."

"You did."

"And that he said he didn't kill Collins, the cop."

"Yes."

"That he knew who did."

Dan nodded.

"But I didn't tell you I met with him."

"No, you didn't." Dan raised his eyebrows and squirmed in his chair.

"But I did."

Mike placed the gold cigarette lighter on the table.

"He gave me this. Every time he called, he'd swear he didn't shoot Collins. He said it was one of the other guys, Sammy Rawlings or Bob Drexler, the two men arrested that night. He told me this lighter would prove that I'd talked to him and help me get a confession out of one of them. He said if I'd do that, it'd be worth my time." Mike hesitated. "He said it would be worth my life."

"Nice," Dan said, turning the lighter over and over in his hands, opening and closing the top, flicking it to light. "I've never had a Zippo. But these aren't my initials."

"It's Morgan's."

Dan laughed. "I know that. But you're telling me you had all these conversations with a guy like Morgan and you didn't tell anyone, not even the cops. Are you crazy?"

"Now I am."

"Why? All you do is take this to the guys in jail and get one of them to confess. Then you're off the hook."

"I did."

Mike folded his hands together on the desk, raised his index fingers as if making a church steeple.

"Drexler said he didn't do it. He's such a squirrely punk, I believe him. If he did it, he probably wouldn't remember." Mike took a deep breath. "Rawlings already killed one man, long time ago when he was in the Army. Some fight with a little guy. One smack to the head killed him, but Rawlings was acquitted, allowed to leave the Army with an honorable discharge. The way he didn't want to talk about that, I don't think he's dumb enough to kill somebody else and have to go through it all again. I believe him."

"So, there you go," Dan said, handing the lighter back to Mike. "He's your guy. Morgan shot you and threatened to do it again. He was the damn cop killer."

"Why would he say he wasn't and send me on this wild goose chase?"

"He's a criminal He lies all time. He probably thought one of his buddies wouldn't remember who shot Collins and blurt out something like, 'Maybe I did it, and don't remember.' That could get Morgan off the hook."

"Maybe is hardly a confession. I was stupid to go along with Morgan's proposal, but his threat, if I went to the cops, scared me. Now I'm back where I started. There were three guys in the house. One of them had to have killed the cop, but all three say they didn't do it. Nobody will say who did."

"Sounds like a job for Assistant Chief Schmidt," Dan said. "Turn it over to him."

"But if he knows I've been sitting on this for more than a week, he'll be pissed."

"Come clean," Dan said, shrugging his shoulders. "The earlier the better. Then you won't have to worry about it."

"Sure. He'll probably charge me with obstruction for withholding evidence."

"No, you're buddies with Schmidt. He'll probably get you round-the-clock protection if he thinks Morgan's a threat to your life. He's already got two killings on his hands. You think he wants a third?"

"Oh, thanks," Mike said. "You sound like you want me dead, so you can write about it."

"I want Schmidt to worry about you and forget about me and this whole Lawton deal. Who knows, maybe Morgan did kill Lawton. We've speculated about that before. Maybe arresting him for killing the cop will prompt his confession on that, too."

"That doesn't make sense to me. Morgan's hiding out, not drinking in public. Life sure would be a hell of a lot easier if people just confessed."

"I'd agree with that," Dan said.

He sat back in his chair with his arms across his chest, his eyes closed, and his head bowed.

"You praying for me?" Mike asked.

Dan raised his head, opened his eyes. "No, for me."

"What do you need prayers for?"

"My confession. As long as you trust me, I trust you. I'm going to tell you something I haven't told anyone else."

"OK, I'm listening."

"Remember that Walkman I gave you?"

"Sure. When I got out of the hospital."

"It's hot. I shoplifted it when I was doing that shoplifting story. I wanted to see how difficult it would be."

"Stolen? You gave me a stolen Walkman?"

"Hey, it just walked out of the store." Dan laughed. "I couldn't take it back. Target doesn't even know it's missing."

"But I do."

"So, you take it back."

"I can't. I gave it to Linda, and she uses it all the time."

"What she doesn't know won't hurt her. It's no big deal."

Mike didn't know what to say. He remained silent.

"I'll tell you who's a crook," Dan said, leaning across the desk toward Mike. "Our honorable mayor."

"Stan Rankin? What makes you say that?"

Dan sat up, tugged at the chain around his neck and pulled the Iron Cross up into plain view. "See this? It was the mayor's. I stole it from his house."

"When did you do that?"

"When I burglarized the place."

Mike shifted his gaze from Dan to the lighter on the table back to Dan. He'd been so preoccupied with his own predicament, he hadn't even paid that close attention to other stories in the paper, but he remembered Dan's account of the burglary at the mayor's house.

"It was a stupid challenge," Dan continued. "Like the shoplifting. To see if I could do it. But do you remember when the mayor reported the burglary? He claimed all sorts of other stuff was taken. A diamond ring, for instance. I didn't take that. I didn't even see one in the house."

"Why would he do that?"

Mike was preoccupied with his fellow reporter sitting across the table, a petty thief, a nighttime burglar. He should have listened to Linda when she'd said Dan was acting stranger than usual, that she had suspicions about his new medal.

"Insurance," Dan said. "He'll probably collect thousands of dollars in a settlement with his insurance company. The crook."

"Why would you even try something like that? Do you know what would happen if you got caught?"

"That's all I did, Mike. I swear. My heart was beating out of my chest for twenty-four hours after that. I was sweating bullets when I talked to Schmidt about it. Enough. End of story. No more following through on crazy ideas for me."

Mike wanted to believe Dan, but he wanted to ask more questions, too, especially about his night with Lawton. But a knock on the door of the interview room, the sudden entrance of Anthony A. Aaronson who excused himself for interrupting, put an end to their conversation. Anthony wanted to interview a young woman with him, and Dan was more than willing to let him have the room.

"Time for me to go home," Dan said. "I've got a dinner date with Susan, and I don't want to be late."

Mike grabbed his crutches and strode behind Dan into what, at first glance, appeared to be an empty newsroom.

Only after he'd made his way to their desk did Mike realize most everyone was huddled around Margaret Myers' desk and that, in the center of the huddle stood Jennifer Drake holding a pink bundle in her arms.

"How about that," Mike said. "Jennifer's here with her baby. Come over and meet her."

"Why would I want to do that?"

"She's the reporter you replaced. You should at least say hello."

"Can't," Dan said. "I'm running late to see Susan. I'll meet her some other time."

Mike watched Dan stuff his papers and notebook into his drawer on the desk they shared, slip his arms into his coat, scramble out the side door toward the alley as if he was allergic to his predecessor.

Turning on his crutches, Mike approached the mob of well-wishers to join them in welcoming the woman who had been the most popular person in the newsroom.

Mike smiled, knowing that Jennifer had her baby girl, that she had escaped the blue room for a pink blanket and probably a child's bedroom painted pink.

But, as Mike dragged himself across the blue carpet, between the blue desks and surrounded by the blue walls, he felt anything but calm. Dan had confessed to crimes, petty crimes at that, but still crimes. Mike couldn't help but wonder if there wasn't more to Dan's story about being with Lawton the night he was killed.

27

Dan Goldberg met Susan Holcomb at the Fox and Hounds Lounge for one drink after work Wednesday, then walked with her two doors down to Zimmerman's, a longtime Cedar City restaurant known for its seafood.

When Dan had joked about stopping at McDonald's for a Big Mac and fries, Susan playfully hit him on the shoulder. But that was the last time she showed any spunk as they consumed a meal of tossed salads, homemade biscuits, fried clams and shrimp, in relative silence.

Susan didn't say much either when Dan ordered a round of after-dinner drinks.

"We don't seem to be having such a fantastic time," Dan said, setting his half-empty whiskey and Coke on the table.

"I guess I'm not good company tonight."

As Susan looked at Dan with a non-descript expression, a flatness to her mouth and dullness in her eyes, he was reminded again of the day they had met at the cemetery. That not only had her brother died, but so had her husband.

For some reason the image of Lawton's last minutes in the park flashed through Dan's mind, too, and he became annoyed. All this death wasn't good for anyone, which is why he didn't bring up the story he'd written about Lawton although he was itching to know what Susan thought about it.

As if reading his mind, she mentioned that she'd read the morning paper. She said his account of Lawton's life, his contributions to the community and all, was an excellent tribute to a great man. But she seemed perturbed at Dan, that he'd been hanging out at a place for "undesirables," at The Silver Nugget.

Before Dan had the opportunity to respond, Susan expressed sympathy for Lawton and his family, not knowing them personally, but sad that the virtuous life of someone who had done so much for her hometown had met such a tragic and senseless end.

Dan agreed, but then their conversation dried up again.

Discouraged by Susan's lack of communication, Dan didn't ask if she wanted another drink. He figured the relationship wasn't going anywhere and thought, with his wild mood swings of late, it would be best if he was alone. At least she didn't know what he knew about Lawton's death, a secret he'd have to take to his grave.

Dan paid the dinner tab, helped Susan with her coat, held her arm lightly as he led her from Zimmerman's into the air outside, warmer than it had been for a couple of days.

A train whistle blew loudly behind them, and the sweet aroma of Cap 'n' Crunch Crunchberries from the cereal factory was in the air. In the shadows of the streetlights, only a slight breeze whipping down Third Avenue. Susan tucked her arm inside Dan's open coat and wrapped it around his waist. She snuggled her head against his shoulder.

Dan appreciated the gesture of kindness, that a certain amount of loneliness and desperation could be chased away by the simple touch of a woman's hand, even if her heart didn't seem to be in it.

"Dan," she said, "maybe when life settles down a little for both of us, conversations will be more entertaining."

He placed his hand on hers and said, "I hope so," even though he wasn't sure he meant it. "Would you like me to walk you home?"

"That would be nice," she said. "But I know my way."

"I know you do, but a little company couldn't hurt."

"It's only a few blocks."

"If that's what you want."

"For now, yes."

Susan released her arm from Dan's waist and smiled. Then she pecked him quickly on the cheek, a friendship kiss.

"Call me whenever," she said.

"Sure," he said.

"Bye, Dan."

At the intersection where Susan had turned left, where Dan would continue along Third Avenue, he hesitated to light a cigarette.

He watched Susan's figure fade into the semi-darkness of the streetlight illuminated sidewalk along the row of closed businesses. He was certain she had meant the kiss as a final goodbye. He doubted that he would see her again.

* * * * *

Dan tossed his cigarette onto the sidewalk, stepped on it with the toe of his shoe and ground it into the concrete to make sure it was out. He was in no hurry and didn't feel like stopping somewhere else for a drink, so he turned into a small greenspace, one cater-corner from *The Argus.*

He strolled along the diagonal sidewalk past a miniature State of Liberty toward the golden lights of a four-story public parking ramp.

He wandered past a bench where a homeless man, he presumed, slept beneath a couple of heavy plaid blankets. He looked up into the trees where a murder of crows blackened the sky as they had bedded down for the night.

Dan was feeling alone again, surrounded by the stillness of night, his mind drifting from pitying himself to contemplating a visit to a new bar where he could have another whiskey, where he could meet some new people.

After Dan smoked a couple more cigarettes and took a couple of laps around the park, he turned toward *The Argus* building. He was surprised to see that the illuminated time-temperature on top said it was forty-five degrees and a quarter after ten.

As Dan cut into the alley, a wind tunnel that produced a breeze even on still nights like this, he felt a slight shiver up his spine as he came upon a stocky man in dark clothing leaning against *The Argus* building smoking a cigarette.

At first Dan thought the man might be someone he knew from the newspaper out on a break. But, as he neared the smoker, a man he'd guess slightly older than himself wearing an open dark green, waist-length jacket, a red plaid flannel shirt and blue jeans, Dan didn't recognize him.

While it seemed strange, maybe even suspicious, that anyone other than an *Argus* employee would be smoking in that alley, Dan didn't give it a second thought. He veered to the opposite side of the alley, to give the smoker his space, and nodded a greeting toward the stranger.

"Hello," the man said, as if he'd been startled by Dan's streetlight shadow slipping silently down the alley.

"Nice night," Dan said as he made brief eye contact, but kept walking. "A little cold here in the alley, though."

"Cold as hell," the smoker said, his raspy voice catching on the words as he exhaled.

"Stay warm," Dan laughed, shouting over his shoulder as he strolled into the parking lot and made his way to his Mazda at the far corner.

As Dan inserted his key into the Mazda's lock, he glanced down the alley once more.

The stranger had moved to the recessed doorway of the side entrance of *The Argus*, his giant shadow cast by the overhead light extending across the alley.

The heavy metal door of the employee entrance swung open and, from behind it, Mike Rockwell emerged on his crutches.

His curiosity piqued, Dan climbed into his car but didn't start it, shivering silently inside as he stared through the windshield into the alley trying to figure out what was going on.

He rolled down the car window and lit a cigarette, blowing the smoke outside as he tried to listen.

From the intonation of the voices, it seemed that Rockwell knew the stranger as they stood about six feet apart. Their voices grew louder, but Dan couldn't understand the words.

An argument. Why?

Suddenly, in his mind, Dan heard the voice of serial killer John Wayne Gacy from a decade earlier demand that he come inside the house, that he drink some lemonade, that he be a good young man and listen to his elders.

In that moment, Dan put two and two together. The stranger had to be Rockwell's abductor, Morgan.

Why hadn't he thought about that when he first saw the guy in the alley?

Sensing impending danger, Dan thought his presence might be helpful to Rockwell. But, to be on the safe side, he opened his Mazda's glove box, withdrawing his Beretta and the loaded clip. It wouldn't hurt to have protection, he thought, slamming the clip into the gun.

Dan hesitated inside his car, the gun resting on his right thigh, as he flicked his cigarette outside and concentrated on the scene down the dark alley.

When the voices grew even louder, Dan decided it was time to move.

Dan climbed out of his car as Rockwell took a swing at the stranger with one of his crutches.

Dan hustled down the alley as the confrontation continued to escalate between his best friend at *The Argus* and a drug dealer accused of killing a cop.

28

Even though Wednesday was "Hump Day" for most people, the half-way mark of their workweek, it was like Thursday to Mike Rockwell. After his night shift ended, he had only one more day until his weekend.

What a welcome relief, Mike thought, as he arrived for work and began the tedious chore of letting himself into *The Argus* building with his security ID card, waiting until the lock clicked to fling open the door, then wedging a crutch against the door to squeeze into the small landing at the foot of bare concrete stairs.

As Mike plopped one rubber foot of his crutches in front of the other slowly up the stairs, dragging his shoed foot and cast after them, he was happy to have spent the entire day at home sleeping late, taking a long shower, washing a couple of loads of laundry, scrubbing his sinks and toilet, even dusting the lightbulbs in the ceiling fixture of his kitchen. But, no matter how much he tried to occupy his time with busy work, Mike couldn't forget his failure the night before when neither Rawlings nor Drexler would confess to being the trigger man in the death of undercover police officer William Collins.

Once inside the newsroom, as soon as Mike saw Dan Goldberg seated at their desk, he knew he had to tell Dan all the details about his meetings with Morgan and his cronies. He and Dan had conferenced in the interview room a dozen times before, but never had they confessed so much to each other as they had Tuesday.

The relief Mike had felt after spilling his guts was replaced by trepidation, concern and even a twinge of fear after Dan admitted to criminal activities, his shoplifting at Target and his burglary of the mayor's home. As they'd left the tiny interview room, a cramped space that always made Mike uncomfortably warm, he had an inkling that Dan hadn't told him everything.

But Mike let those worries slip to the back of his mind the moment he spotted Jennifer Drake, his cherished desk-mate before Goldberg's arrival. If anybody could make him feel better, it was Jennifer with her wit and wisdom, her sarcasm and sanity, her honesty and honor. They had been able to trust each other with everything before she'd left to have her baby.

Mike's irritation with Dan for leaving without at least meeting Jennifer also disappeared as he approached the newsroom gathering around his longtime friend, as the huddle parted to let him hobble closer to the new mother with child. Dan didn't know what he was missing.

"Mike Rockwell," Jennifer exclaimed, as if they hadn't seen each other for years. "I heard about you getting shot, about you being on crutches. I'm so sorry."

"It wasn't your fault," he said. "I want to see your baby girl."

Jennifer hadn't changed a bit since she'd left, but then again it had been only six months. She still looked so young, younger than her thirty-one years, with light creamy skin and a nose slightly too wide for her face and a full head of hair, brunette, brushed back over her ears with slightly side-swept bangs that covered her eyebrows. Her crystal blue eyes continued to shine with the brightness of her early pregnancy, the wonderment of motherhood that she had said would change her future forever.

"Amanda," Jennifer said, brushing the pink blanket aside from her baby's face, "meet Mike Rockwell."

"She looks just like you," Mike said as the fuzzy-haired, porcelain-skinned baby turned her head toward him. "The same hair, the same face, the same blue eyes."

"You don't have a clue," Jennifer laughed. "All babies are born with blue eyes. We just hope that doesn't change."

"If they stay blue," Mike said, "she'll always remind you of this place."

"Ha, ha," Jennifer said. "I don't need my daughter to remind me of *The Argus*. How could anyone who's worked here ever forget it?"

"We miss you, Jennifer," said Elizabeth Anne Dawson. "When are you coming back?"

"Not as long as I've got this angel to look after," Jennifer said, nudging her nose against Amanda's rosy cheek. "Not as long as I plan to have a couple more just like her."

Margaret Myers placed a hand on Jennifer's shoulder to get her attention and spoke in her usual loud manner even as a glistening in her otherwise stoic eyes gave away her emotions.

"We don't want you back, Jennifer," said the matriarch of the newsroom with an unusual smile. "You've got your most important assignment right there in your arms."

"Why, thank you, Margaret," Jennifer said. "Not every woman wants to be a mother, but if you decide that's what you want, you've got to give it your full attention."

Jennifer tickled her daughter's stomach.

"Amanda's my priority now."

As Amanda stretched a hand into the air, Mike held out his index finger for her to grab. He was intrigued by the size of the baby's tiny pink fist, all wrapped around just one adult finger.

Mike wondered what it would be like to bring another life into the world. To have the responsibility for another human being. To know that your little child could grow into a wonderful woman like Jennifer.

* * * * *

When the telephone call came from Morgan, after Mike had made his early rounds, he wasn't surprised. Still, he wished there was some way to identify the caller before he answered so he could either ignore it or be more prepared.

"So, Rockwell, did you talk to my boys?" Morgan asked.

"They both said they didn't do it," Mike said.

"Bullshit," Morgan said. "They're both liars. One of them shot the cop, and the other knows who did."

"I'm just telling you they both denied it."

"I want my lighter back."

"What?"

Mike heard what Morgan said, but he didn't want to believe it. He didn't want to see the guy who put him on crutches again.

"My lighter. My mother gave it to me. I want it back."

"OK."

Mike wondered if he was joking.

"You go on your last rounds of the night at ten-thirty, after you've watched the news. I'll be waiting for you in the alley outside *The Argus*. You can give it to me then."

The line went dead.

* * * * *

Time stood still one minute and raced the next as Mike Rockwell rewrote a couple of press releases, compiled a list of drunken drivers, filled his coffee cup even when it wasn't empty and contemplated calling Linda even though he couldn't talk to her about anything that was on his mind.

At his desk, Mike held the gold lighter in his hands again, turning it over to the monogram and back to the smooth side. He wished he'd never seen the damn thing, never agreed to meet Morgan in the first place, never gone on that drug bust.

He watched the clock and knew he couldn't turn the hands back. Finally, it was time to monitor the ten o'clock TV news. He just wanted to get it over with.

By the time Mike turned the television off in the conference room, he realized he hadn't written down even one news tip from the broadcast. Either there hadn't been anything worth noting, or he'd spaced it off completely.

"All they did was read the morning paper," Mike reported to Bill Jackson as he grabbed his jacket from the back of his chair. "I'm off on my midnight ride," Mike joked, as usual, even though he had nothing to laugh about.

Mike struggled on his crutches to the stairway entrance, opened the door and slid past it to stand at the top of the stairway. He counted the concrete steps, and there were exactly fourteen, even though he already knew that after running up and down them at least half-a-dozen times a day for more than five years.

On crutches it was more difficult walking down the stairs than dragging himself up, but Mike had developed a method. Tucking both crutches into his left armpit and holding onto the handrail with his right hand, he semi-slid his hip down as he hopped from one step to the next with his good right foot.

Mike hadn't worried about falling since the first couple of days with crutches but, for an instant, he thought taking a tumble might not be so bad if it meant he didn't have to face Morgan.

At the bottom of the steps, Mike realized he had no choice but to open the door to see if Morgan had showed up. He turned the knob, pushed the door open and shuffled to the concrete landing in the alcove.

Mike stuck his head into the alley, first turning right, then left. The glow of a cigarette caught his eye as a dark figure approached.

"Rockwell, I see you decided not to stand me up tonight," Morgan said.

"I've got your lighter. Let me get it out of my pocket and then you can go," Mike said, holding the door open with his body braced against it.

From the elevated landing, Mike seemed a good foot taller than Morgan even though he knew that wasn't the case.

"Like hell," Morgan said. "We've got something to settle first."

"I told you all I know."

"I think you're lying. You never talked to Rawlings or Drexler."

"I did so. They said they didn't shoot any gun."

"They said I did it."

"No, that's not what either one of them said."

"But it's what you believe."

Mike couldn't deny that.

As head of a drug-buying operation, Morgan had to exert some authority and wielding a gun wouldn't be beyond the realm of possibility to carry that out. And now that Mike got his first good look at him beneath the light of *The Argus'* employee entrance, he saw that Morgan's face had been through the wars.

He had a large nose bent to the left as if it had been broken more than once. A deep scar on his right cheek appeared to have been caused by a slashing knife. Cold dark eyes said "I could kill you in an instant if that's what I need to do."

"Rockwell," he said, "that's what you believe."

"Here's your lighter. Take it and go."

Morgan stuffed the lighter into his jeans pocket.

"I'm not going anywhere until you promise to do everything you can to get me off the hook for killing that cop."

"I'm going back upstairs," Mike said, still standing above Morgan. He knew he had to be aggressive, even as his heart beat a million times a minute, even as his head felt light and his good leg shivered with nervous tension.

"Like hell you are," Morgan said.

He jammed his right hand into his jacket pocket, swung it away from his body as if he hid a pistol.

"If I let you go," Morgan said, "you'll call the cops. Tell them I'm out here."

"No, I won't," Mike protested.

He turned on his crutches, shoved his shoulder against the open door to make room for re-entry into *The Argus*.

"I'm going back inside."

"I said you ain't going anywhere."

Mike braced his shoulder against the door and lifted his crutch with his right hand. He swung it around with all his might and caught Morgan on the side of the head. He watched Morgan stagger away, then scrambled inside the building.

Mike tried to pull the slow-closing heavy door shut behind him, knowing that if it latched, Morgan couldn't follow him inside without a security card.

Somehow, though, Morgan recovered in time to grab the outside doorknob to prevent Mike from latching the door.

Not knowing what else to do, Mike abruptly let go of the door and spun to begin his ascent on the stairs inadequately illuminated by the bare lightbulbs. He heard Morgan groan and tumble to the ground outside.

Mike climbed the stairs, one crutch after the other, hoping that Morgan would change his mind about chasing him into the building. If he could reach the top of the stairs beside the newsroom entrance, he'd be home free.

Despite concentrating on his mad dash, Mike thought he heard a voice outside shout, "Stop!" He couldn't be certain.

As Mike reached the top steps, the heavy entrance door at the bottom landing slammed shut behind him. At the top landing, he turned around to see Morgan with his left foot on the lowest step, his right hand still jammed into his jacket pocket.

"Rockwell, I told you to stop," Morgan shouted.

In the hollow stairwell, bare poured concrete and concrete block, his voice reverberated as if he were God speaking from the sky in "The Ten Commandments."

Mike reached for the knob of the door to the newsroom as Morgan came up the first six steps.

"Stop!" Morgan yelled.

As Mike looked down, afraid Morgan would shoot at any minute, the entrance door behind Morgan swung open.

"Stop!" shouted Dan Goldberg, who trained a pistol at Morgan's head. "I said, stop!"

Morgan spun around to face Goldberg and a gun went off.

Then there was another shot and another and another ricocheting everywhere. They echoed in the sound chamber of the stairwell, each one as loud as an exploding firecracker, together as deafening as an entire string of them.

At the top of the stairway, Mike Rockwell collapsed.

In the eerie silence that followed, his crutches slipped from his grasp and clattered down the stairway like wooden toboggans on a rough downhill run.

The crutches came to rest at the bottom of the stairs, near the lifeless forms of Ronald Morgan and Dan Goldberg.

29

On Thursday morning, the sun rose in the East over Cedar City as it always did, but as the darkness of the night gave way to the light, the world seemed off-kilter.

The morning anchors on the three local television stations and the news readers on the city's half-dozen radio stations reported the shooting at *The Argus* with trepidation, as if they each knew that, but for the grace of God, they were spared such mayhem and chaos in their own newsrooms.

Through the bedroom window of an apartment on the city's east side, the sunlight slipped between drawn curtains as the orange digits on the nightstand alarm clock flipped to 6:25 and the child-like voice of Cyndi Lauper sang about "True Colors."

Laying on her side facing the alarm clock, the sun now streaming on her face, Linda Reynolds opened her eyes.

With a lime green bedspread pulled up to her chin, her red hair tousled on the pillow, Linda rubbed caked sleep from her eyes, red from crying. She sighed, a shiver even though she was plenty warm, and when the six-thirty news came on, she reached out to turn off the radio.

In the silence of her bedroom, Linda rolled over toward the other side of the bed and wrapped her arm over the chest of a snoring Mike Rockwell. She nestled her face against his shoulder, kissed his warm skin, listened to him breathe heavily. She smiled even though he couldn't see it.

Mike opened his eyes.

"Good morning," Linda said, almost in a whisper.

Her sleepy green eyes shone like emeralds in the morning light as she shifted her naked body tightly against his.

"Good morning," Mike said, taking her hand in his, squeezing it gently.

Linda's presence, the softness of her skin against his, the scent of sleep in her bed so early in the morning, the sound of her steady breathing as he remained on his back, enveloped Mike in a sense of calm.

Mike hadn't slept well, but somehow, he had drifted off. The exhaustion from the night before had been overwhelming. It hadn't helped that Linda was overly sympathetic when she picked him up at *The Argus*, then furious with him after he admitted keeping his ongoing hassle with Morgan a secret from her.

Only after Linda settled down did she admit that knowing the details as they occurred would have turned her into a worrywart, would have driven her crazy. Now that Morgan was dead, they could both relax.

"My ears are still ringing," Mike said. "Every time I go into that stairwell, it'll probably all start again."

"I bet."

"I still can't believe Dan was there. He probably saved my life. And now he's dead."

"He's your hero," Linda said. "Whoever would have thought those words and Dan Goldberg's name would be used in the same sentence."

Mike suppressed the urge to pull Linda's head off his chest, to kiss her. Instead, he stroked her auburn hair and closed his eyes. She seemed so comfortable with her head on his shoulder, her mussed hair tickling his cheek.

Mike felt fortunate to have her by his side. These moments were always the best, he thought, the closeness of two people intertwined in each other's lives when words only got in the way.

Suddenly, Mike was jostled from his sleep as Linda leaped up out of bed, shouting, "Oh, my God, I'm going to be late for school."

Mike watched her trot naked, as if in a dream, into the bathroom, then closed his eyes because he didn't have to go anywhere all morning.

The next thing Mike knew, Linda was kissing him awake again, standing over him, all dressed, her hair brushed straight, a smile in her eyes.

"You can stay here as long as you want," she said.

"Thank you," Mike said.

"You know," she said, "we've got that charity Halloween party at the school tomorrow night."

"Under the circumstances, I don't feel much like going," he said. "Besides, what would I dress as, a zombie on crutches?"

"Actually, that would be kind of cute."

"I don't want to be cute. I want to be scary."

"Mike Rockwell, you're plenty scary enough to me."

As soon as the words had come out of his mouth, Mike knew it was the wrong thing to say. But Linda leaned over and kissed him again.

"I love you," she said.

"I love you, too, Linda. Maybe I'll change my mind about that party, but I've got to get through today."

"You'll do fine," she said. "You always do."

Linda picked up her purse from the bedroom dresser, exited to her living room, and, as she left, locked the apartment door behind her.

Restless now that he was alone, Mike rolled over in bed to turn the radio back on. The first song was by Boston, the band's new ballad, "Amanda."

Mike smiled, thinking about Jennifer Drake and her baby girl and wondering if she had chosen the name before the song came out.

But diversion from the truth lasted only so long. For the hundredth time, in his mind, Mike replayed the events of the night before.

The shots came as he stood at the top of the stairs. Dan's sudden appearance not only surprised Morgan, it shocked Mike, too.

Dan stood there unwavering with a gun, a black pistol aimed at Morgan, and Morgan twirled around, and the shots went off, and the noise became unbearable as the stairwell became a shooting gallery.

The next thing Mike remembered, Bill Jackson helped him stand at the top of the stairs and led him to his chair in the newsroom.

There were the distant sounds of ambulance and police car sirens growing louder. The questions he asked that nobody could answer.

Only later, as a uniformed police officer questioned Mike, did he learn that Morgan was dead at the bottom of the stairs. That Dan Goldberg had been hauled away in an ambulance. That it didn't look good for him either.

Somebody had retrieved Mike's crutches from the stairwell, and he called Linda to please come get him.

When Linda was in the newsroom, hysterical but supportive, it was Bill Jackson who came over, put a hand on

Mike's shoulder, told him Dan died on the way to the hospital.

Even then, Mike couldn't forget the questions he had for Dan Goldberg.

How was it you happened to be in the alley when Morgan came to see me?

What were you doing with a gun?

Did you shoot first or did Morgan?

Why?

Now, Mike would never get those questions answered.

He had thought he'd read Dan Goldberg in the short time they'd worked together but now, more than ever, he realized he hadn't known him at all.

Except for the few minutes their shifts overlapped at *The Argus*, except for the half-dozen evenings they drank beer at the Fox and Hounds Lounge, they were strangers.

Mike couldn't get over how fortunate he'd been that Dan happened to be walking down the alley when he needed him the most. It seemed like such a farfetched coincidence, yet there was no other way to explain it.

Linda was right. Mike had feared for his life. Dan Goldberg was his hero.

30

Shortly after noon Thursday, well ahead of the start of his shift, Mike Rockwell slipped his identification card into *The Argus'* electronic reader at the employee entrance off the alley. He felt eerily calm as he opened the door, adjusted his crutches beneath his armpits and entered the stairwell that had been the scene of the shooting.

With a single bare lightbulb hanging from above, he studied the concrete for signs of blood and didn't see any.

At the top of the stairs, where Mike had passed out, he opened the door into the newsroom and became an instant celebrity, albeit a reluctant one. As he reached his desk, a half-dozen people gathered around to heap praise on his bravery, to pelt him with questions, until Margaret Myers came to his rescue.

"Mike," she said, "I didn't except to see you so soon. Let's go into my office."

Margaret didn't have an official office, but she occasionally referred to the conference room as such, so Mike followed her there and sat down as she closed the door.

"Wow," she said.

The expression on Margaret's face halted Mike from saying anything, as if he were a deer frozen in a car's headlights. With that one word, she stopped the world.

"Are you OK?"

Mike nodded.

"You don't have to be here. Somebody else will write the story."

"I need to be here," Mike said. "It's my story. And Dan's."

"I understand," Margaret said. "But you're too close to this story to write it. Later, though, I think a follow-up would be more than appropriate. It would be welcome."

"But I ..." Mike protested, before she cut him off.

"You should go home now, Mike. You need a few days off to recover."

"I'll be fine."

"We will see you Monday," Margaret said, standing, as usual, to signify the meeting was over.

"I want you to know," she added on her way out the door, "that the daytime police beat is open if you want it. That decision is yours."

* * * * *

In the days that followed, the shooting at *The Argus* became national news and Mike Rockwell found himself in the middle of it. Beginning Friday, Halloween day, he fielded telephone calls at home from reporters at *The New York Times* and *The San Francisco Chronicle*, from *The Miami Herald* and *The Chicago Tribune*. He told them only sketchy details about his involvement, saving his true feelings for his own personal account in *The Argus*.

The local ABC television station asked Mike to conduct an on-air interview to send to affiliates, but he flatly refused. He didn't want to be on television.

When Mike came to work on Monday, he thanked Margaret for the time off. He praised reporter Anthony A. Aaronson for his succinct and factual accounts of the shooting and for leaving him out of the stories as much as possible. And he read the reports of the shooting in area newspapers, ripping the pages from those papers to save as tear sheets for his personal file.

Most every story centered on the shootout at *The Argus*, the fact that two newspapers reporters were involved and that one of them had died. The other dead person, Ronald Morgan, was often described as a drug kingpin in Cedar City who had hounded Mike Rockwell for weeks because Morgan had been accused of killing an undercover police officer during a drug bust gone bad that Rockwell had witnessed. The death of William Collins was mentioned in all of accounts, because he was the reason for Morgan's presence. But less than half of them even mentioned the murder of Charles James Lawton III because the reporters outside the Cedar City coverage area were largely unaware of any possible connection.

As Mike went on his rounds, he deflected questions about his feelings from his contacts as much as possible. He asked Assistant Chief Schmidt for any new details, in particular the ballistics reports from the guns used in the shooting, and was told he'd be the first to know.

Walking around with crutches only served to remind Mike of his ordeal as he sat at his computer to begin writing his first-person account. Margaret had told him the story would run Sunday, on the front page, so he had until Friday noon to finish it. He rejected dozens of false starts, probably because he wasn't under strict deadline. He had too much time to overthink everything.

While the aftermath of the shooting remained foremost in Mike's mind, he also was weighed down by the decision he had to make, whether he would leave the night beat or stay on it. Linda had made her opinion clear and, like Margaret, said she would stay out of it, that it was a decision only Mike could make.

* * * * *

A week after the shooting, Mike Rockwell hobbled into the newsroom a little after nine in the morning to fine-tune his first-person account before turning it over to Margaret for editing and comments. He wanted to call Dan Goldberg a hero for saving his life but came up short on making a declaration that strong. He had an inkling Margaret wouldn't see it that way with Dan's possible involvement in Lawton's death.

Rather, Mike downplayed sensationalism for the truth. He rehashed his kidnapping and shooting injury at the hands of Morgan and expanded it with his innate fear of reprisal for being a possible witness to the shooting of a police officer. He admitted that he was afraid of Morgan the night of the shooting at *The Argus*, but didn't think Morgan would actually kill him because Morgan was still claiming his innocence in the cop killing and wanted Mike's help to clear him. As far as Dan coming to his rescue, Mike called Dan a valued co-worker and a loyal friend who did what he thought was right.

Dan Goldberg, the reporter, wouldn't like the story one bit. Dan Goldberg, the friend, would understand.

At his desk, Mike couldn't help but think again that if he would have taken Margaret up on her offer six months earlier, none of this would have happened. Dan Goldberg wouldn't have come to *The Argus*. They wouldn't have become competitive adversaries for page one bylines. He wouldn't be on crutches. Dan Goldberg wouldn't be dead.

Mentally drained, yet with emotions roiling around in his gut, Mike called Assistant Chief Schmidt to see if there was anything new. Schmidt was in a morning staff meeting, but his secretary promised Mike she'd have him call as soon as it was over.

When Mike's phone rang almost immediately after hanging up, he knew it couldn't be Schmidt. For a split second he was haunted by Morgan's voice, then realized the threatening calls were history. He was pleasantly surprised it was Linda, calling during her open morning class period.

"So how are you feeling?" Linda asked.

"Better now. For a minute there, when the phone rang, I thought it was Morgan."

"You don't have to worry about that now, thanks to Dan."

"I know," Mike said. "But I'm still trying to wrap it all up."

"Good luck."

"Thanks. I'll need it."

As Mike hung up the receiver, he stared at it for a long time. Why hadn't he told Linda that, just that minute, he had decided to take the day job? Maybe because he wasn't one-hundred-percent sure that's what he wanted. Maybe because he wanted to tell her in person, to see the look of happiness on her face.

Why? Mike thought.

Of all the questions he'd asked in his career, the "Who?" "What?" "Where?" and "When?" questions, he knew the most important question was always "Why?"

It was the most probing question, the most difficult to answer, the one that every reader would ask.

"Why, why, why?"

As Mike contemplated the end of his story, he wished he could ask those questions of Dan. Why was he in the alley? Why did he have a gun? Why did he give up his life to save Mike?

Overwhelmed by his lack of answers, Mike was relieved when Assistant Chief Schmidt called back with ballistics reports on the guns Morgan and Dan had used.

"Rockwell," Schmidt said, "I'm giving you exclusive information here because I like you, and because the shooting happened at your place, at *The Argus*. I think you'll appreciate that when you hear it."

"Thank you," Mike said.

"So, how are you doing?" Schmidt asked.

Mike was surprised. Never had the assistant chief asked him a personal question, let alone one like that.

"Fine," Mike said. "Still a little shaken, but fine."

"Good," Schmidt said. "So, I've got some good news and some bad news for you. What do you want first?"

"The good news."

"Morgan's .38 was the same gun that killed Collins during the drug bust. It was the same one that wounded you."

"That means you've solved the killing of your police officer. Too bad you can't prosecute him for it."

"Not so fast," Schmidt said. "We found a second set of fingerprints on the gun, the best one on the underside of the barrel. They belonged to one, Robert Drexler. Since he's still in custody, we confronted him about Collins' killing. He confessed."

"What?" Mike said. "Bob Drexler told me he didn't have a gun, that he didn't fire one that night."

"He'd told us that, too, at first. But now that Morgan's dead, now that we've got the prints on the gun, we pressed Drexler. We told him we knew he did it, that he'd never sleep another day in his life because Morgan's ghost would haunt him forever. And he bought it."

"What?"

"Unbelievable, right? But we'd heard Drexler is very superstitious, believes in ghosts and all that. Probably all the drugs he's taken. But he told us he fired the gun, that after it went off he tossed it to Morgan who ran out of the house to get rid of it."

"That's when Morgan tried to escape in the cop car and saw me."

"Right," Schmidt said. "It's probably why he didn't kill you. Why he just shot you in the leg."

"Wow," Mike said. He sighed. "Morgan wasn't a killer. He was telling the truth all the time he was calling me. He had the evidence with him all time."

"I didn't say either one of these guys was a genius," Schmidt said. "But we've solved the murder of Collins and we'll put this Drexler away for the rest of his life."

Mike digested the news methodically but quickly. He jotted down that last quote from Schmidt. He couldn't believe Morgan had involved him but, as he thought more about it, the scenario made sense if Morgan wanted to avoid time in jail. If Morgan had approached the cops, they would have assumed he was lying because he possessed the evidence, the gun with his prints on it. Drexler never would have confessed.

"So," Mike said, "the bad news?"

"Goldberg's gun was the same one that killed Charles Lawton. A 9-millimeter Beretta."

Mike was stunned into silence. He didn't know what to say. He wasn't exactly surprised because he'd had his suspicions after Dan confessed to shoplifting at Target and burglarizing the mayor's house. It's just that Schmidt's words seemed so final.

"You know I didn't care much for your buddy," Schmidt continued. "Off the record, I wish he was still alive. There's no reason Lawton should be dead. Goldberg should be rotting the rest of his life away in prison."

"I understand," Mike said.

He'd heard about the animosity between the two from both sides, from Dan after a few beers, from Schmidt the few times he called him for information on other matters.

"So you think Goldberg killed Lawton?" Mike asked.

"I do," Schmidt said. "We're still trying to piece everything together, but your fellow reporter wasn't what I'd call an upstanding citizen of Cedar City. Once the ballistics reports came in, we checked his apartment to see if we could track down his connection to the gun."

"And?"

"Nothing there about that," Schmidt said. "But we found the chest of silverware from the mayor's house and the stolen box of war medals, with one of them missing. Your Goldberg was wearing that one, the Iron Cross, when he died."

Mike wanted to tell the assistant chief to check into the mayor, to ask if the cops had found the other items listed on his burglary report in Dan's apartment. But he knew that was useless, that it was Dan's word against the mayor's, and Dan was dead.

"The day before he died," Mike said, "Dan told me about breaking into the mayor's house just for the challenge of it. He confessed to shoplifting, too. But he vehemently denied killing Lawton. He said he didn't do it."

"How many criminals do you know who always tell the truth? Goldberg might have been OK at one time, but it sounds to me like he went off the deep end."

"Yeah," Mike said. "I don't know why. We worked together and we were friends, but it's not like we shared deep secrets with each other. The only thing I know is that he hated his father, hadn't spoken to him in years. He was from Chicago and worked for a weekly newspaper there before he came here."

"We knew the Chicago connection," Schmidt said. "We tracked down his parents, had the body sent there. His mother told us the same thing about his relationship with his father, but she didn't think that would have triggered this type of behavior."

"I wouldn't know," Mike said. He suddenly felt guilty for not trying to contact Dan's parents, too. For not asking about the funeral. For not attending. For not paying his last respects to a colleague who most likely had saved his life.

"Sometimes we never know why people do the things they do," Schmidt said.

"We don't," Mike said. "But I do have other questions. Here at *The Argus*, do you know who shot first?"

"You're the only witness, and you don't know," Schmidt said. "They were at point-blank range. Morgan was hit three times in the chest and died at the scene. Goldberg was hit once in the chest and once in the head. I don't see how he lived long enough to not die until after they loaded him in the ambulance."

"What now?"

"We can't charge Goldberg with murder because he's dead. We've got evidence with the gun, but unless there's a trial with a guilty verdict, we can't be certain he did it.

"We can put the gun at the scene, but without witnesses or confessions, who's to say somebody else didn't pull the trigger?" Schmidt continued. "Who's to say that, under some unexplainable coincidence, Goldberg just happened to end up with a hot gun?"

"But you're closing that case, too?"

"We're closing it unless some other evidence surfaces. I'd say there's less likelihood of that happening than a snowball's chance in hell."

"Here, I wanted to believe that Dan Goldberg was a hero for saving my life," Mike said. "He was a murderer."

"You've got to call it like you see it," Schmidt said. "I can only give you the information. You've got to write your own story."

When Mike hung up, he put his elbows on his desk, cradled his face in his hands, took a deep breath.

Dan had preached the importance of finding the truth, of including all the crucial details in a news story. He'd been a friend, but a liar. A reporter, but a criminal. A hero, but a murderer.

Dan Goldberg had been the biggest hypocrite of all

Mike sighed.

With time, the details would fade. But he'd never erase the horror of nearly being shot to death twice, then discovering that the friend who saved his life could have been more terrifying than the man who abducted him.

* * * * *

For fifteen minutes that Friday morning, Mike stared at the words on his computer screen, confused now about how he almost labeled Dan Goldberg a hero when he was a murderer. Unable to rectify the problem in his story, Mike bounced on his right foot to the coffee machine, filled his cup and realized that Margaret would want a separate story for Saturday's paper, a story that one of her reporters, a dead one at that, most likely killed Lawton.

Mike set his coffee cup on his desk, grabbed his crutches and hobbled over to Margaret. When she looked up from her keyboard, anger welled up in his gut.

"Yes," Margaret said.

"I just talked to Assistant Chief Schmidt," Mike said. "The ballistics reports are in. Dan Goldberg's gun was the same one that killed Charles Lawton."

Margaret pursed her lips, bit the bottom one with the top row of her teeth, closed her eyes and opened them.

"We knew that might be the case," Margaret said. "We'll need a news story on that, but I'll assign it to someone else."

"I thought you might," Mike said. "There's another story, too. Morgan didn't kill Collins. Bob Drexler confessed to it this morning. It's kind of complicated, but they found his fingerprints on the gun Morgan had in his possession. Drexler has been charged with murder."

Margaret crossed her arms over her chest, glanced down at her keyboard, then up at Mike.

"It's been a month since Collins was shot," she said. "You've talked to Drexler so you know what he's like. You've got the details. Is this a story you could write?"

Mike's jaw dropped. He couldn't believe that Margaret would let him have this one. But she was right, he had the details, and this was about the drug bust he'd been covering in the first place, not the shooting later inside *The Argus* building. This had nothing to do with Dan.

"You damn right," Mike said. "I'll get right on it."

"We need that for tomorrow," Margaret said. "Finish up your Sunday piece first. We've decided to move that to the front page of the second section and we'll label it a commentary."

"That's fine," Mike said. After all, Margaret was the boss. And he felt a weird sense of relief that his first-person story wouldn't have top billing, that more than a week after it happened his account would appear more as a column, as a piece of reflection rather than news.

As Mike wrapped up his stories, he thought about Jennifer Drake and the bucolic life she had planned for her daughter. He thought about his love for Linda Reynolds and Margaret's offer to switch to dayside reporting, which could make everybody happy.

It had become mid-afternoon in the newsroom, a peaceful and calm time, as Mike gave his words one last inspection. He was leaving early on a Friday, a weekend to himself, a weekend with Linda. He knew it was time to give up the chaotic lifestyle of the night beat. He would give his acceptance to Margaret before he left for home.

Mike Rockwell smiled, more settled and sure of himself than he had been in a long while, as he finished his story about Drexler's confession.

As always, Mike typed a dash, a three, a zero, and another dash. It was the symbol, "-30-," that since his days in journalism school, signified the end of a story.

* * * * *

Two weeks after Dan Goldberg had died in the stairwell shootout at *The Argus*, Mike Rockwell sat on the cold stainless-steel table of his doctor's office and watched the metal saw slice through his cast. He absentmindedly listened to the doctor's instructions, that he'd still have to be careful walking up and down stairs, but that the tibia bone had healed properly and was as good as new.

Mike's mind was on the recent conversation he'd had with Linda after he told her he was leaving the night beat.

"To hell with our deal," he had said, getting down on one knee and opening the little box with a diamond ring inside. "I'm not waiting for you to ask me, I'm asking you. Linda Reynolds, will you marry me?"

"You know I will," Linda said. "Yes, yes, yes." And she wrapped her arms around his neck, kissed him all over his face, then pulled back to look him in the eyes. "Welcome back, Mike Rockwell."

With the cast gone, Mike was overjoyed. Linda would be ecstatic. No more inadvertent bumps in the night. For the first time in forever, he felt whole again.

On his way into work, Mike scaled the back stairs carefully, keeping a hand on the rail as he took one step at a time, as he cherished the silence in the echo chamber – no crutches banging on the handrail, no voices shouting from below, no gunshots ringing in his ears.

As he neared his desk, Margaret approached with a smile on her face. "You'll be glad to know, Mike, we've set up two interviews for the nightside job. We should have you on days in two or three weeks."

"Thank you," Mike said. "You don't know how good that makes me feel."

As Mike Rockwell sat at the desk he had shared with Dan Goldberg, as he planned his routine for the night, he decided to straighten it out for a new reporter.

For the first time since Dan Goldberg had joined *The Argus* more than six months earlier, Mike opened the drawer that had been Dan's. He hadn't done so in all that time because he respected Dan's privacy.

Mike laughed as he found the usual items – the half-used reporter's notebooks, stick ballpoint pens without caps, bent paper clips, a No. 2 pencil with the eraser chewed off and a ceramic coffee mug missing its handle.

Mike laughed even more when he found the bottle of Whiteout, the sticky jar of rubber cement and the two red grease pencils with strings hanging from their tips, all items from the old days that he had left in the drawer the last time he cleaned it out.

But, beneath that junk, beneath a couple of red matchbooks from the Fox and Hounds, Mike found a well-worn manila folder, pen scratches on the outside from testing old pens, the initials "JWG" written on the tab.

When Mike opened the folder, his heart skipped a beat.

Inside was a clipping from the Sept. 12, 1986, *Argus* with a Chicago dateline about the denial of an appeal filed by John Wayne Gacy on the grounds that he had inferior representation at his 1979 murder trial. The mug shot of Gacy was circled several times in red ink.

Shuffling through the file, Mike found newspaper clippings dating back to December, 1978, with black and white photographs of men excavating the graves of victims from around Gacy's suburban Chicago house.

Below the newspaper clippings, Mike found a Sept. 14 receipt from a Kentucky Fried Chicken in Waterloo, Iowa, just fifty miles from Cedar City, with a notation in Dan's handwriting that Gacy once managed the store.

That receipt was on top of a paycheck stub for $163.56 to Dan Goldberg dated July 9, 1976. It had come from PDM Contractors, 8213 West Summerdale, Norwood Park. Proprietor: John W. Gacy.

Mike turned to the latest article, read that Gacy had been convicted of killing thirty-three young men, ages fourteen to their early twenties. That he had been diagnosed with an antisocial personality. That he was capable of committing crimes without remorse.

With pay stub in hand, Mike calculated that Dan had been eighteen when he worked for the mass murderer.

Mike again looked at the mug shot of Gacy and wondered if Dan had circled it out of hatred or adulation.

Wow, Mike Rockwell thought, Dan Goldberg was also a victim. It's not where we're going that makes us who we are, it's where we've been.

ABOUT NIGHT BEAT

Dave Rasdal wrote the first draft of *Night Beat* early in 1987 as a contemporary novel, which is why it centers around the newsroom of a Midwestern daily newspaper in 1986. He completed re-writes in 1989 and 2006, but the manuscript remained on the shelf due to obligations with work and family.

The *Night Beat* manuscript was dusted off in mid-2018 as the national press faced more intense scrutiny and criticism due to the proliferation of social media and accusations by the current national administration that it produced "fake news"

Except for rearranging some of the chapters, polishing the prose and revising the ending, Night Beat remains true to the original manuscript.

Even though that means the story takes place more than 30 years ago, *Night Beat*'s intent is the same – to show that no matter the size of the city, people have always had a certain distrust of the media, reporting news can be a tough job fraught with tough decisions, and news gatherers are only human, sometimes corrupted by their own egos.

Dave Rasdal thanks everyone who helped him develop and finetune *Night Beat*, but wants to give special mention to those who have provided valuable feedback – the late Ed Gorman in 1987, Deb Wiley in 1989, Suzanne Rasdal in 2006 and Mary Sharp in 2018.

27555441R00216

Made in the USA
Lexington, KY
05 January 2019